THE MAN BY THE CREEK

A JOE COURT NOVEL

BY
CHRIS CULVER
ST. LOUIS, MO

Contents

Chapter 1

J ulie hated every part of this. Her back ached, and her gut felt fluttery. She almost felt pregnant, but she couldn't have been pregnant unless she had somehow missed the end of her self-enforced celibacy. This was all nerves. It almost made her sick. Elijah giggled and laughed as he rolled on the carpet.

"You're going to wrinkle your shirt," she said. "Don't you want to look nice for your daddy?"

Elijah's father, Ryan, wouldn't care about wrinkles, but Elijah's grandma would notice. She'd probably take pictures of those wrinkles, the abrasions on his knees, and the scrapes on his forearms and send them to her lawyer. She'd been angling for full custody since the day Elijah was born and wouldn't hesitate to twist a few facts to her purpose.

Elijah was three and all boy. Dirt, noise, and lovable energy combined to form the one person in the world Julie loved above all others. He got the abrasions on his knees falling at the playground, he got the scrapes on his forearms after chasing a ball into a rosebush, and he got the bruises on his sides after rolling down a hill at preschool and wrestling with his friends. Elijah was her lovable goober. Seeing him laugh and roll around usually would have made her smile. Today, her throat felt tight, and a heavy knot had formed in her belly—just as it did every two weeks.

Elijah rolled onto his back and giggled again. Then he put his hands and feet in the air, expecting her to tickle his belly. She forced herself to smile at him and was grateful that he couldn't tell the difference between a pained grimace and a grin. His lips curled upward.

"Sweetie, Mommy's got to pack," she said. "Go ask Grandma for some juice."

He kicked his feet and wriggled his fingers. It was a new game for them. The neighbors had adopted a Labrador Retriever puppy who loved getting his belly scratched. When Elijah saw how much attention the puppy got, he mimicked the dog. It was cute.

"Sorry, baby," she said. "Momma's got to work."

He kicked his feet again, still grinning. Julie didn't use to worry about Elijah when he went to visit his father. She had missed her son, she had wished he were with her, and she had thought about him all the time, but she hadn't worried about him. Then, six months ago, Elijah broke his arm, allegedly after falling from a tree in Ryan's backyard. Boys climbed trees. It was part of childhood. Why Ryan let Elijah climb that high, he wouldn't say.

Ryan and his mom took Elijah to a fancy doctor only rich people could see—a concierge physician, he had called him.

That doctor had swooped in and taken care of everything. He X-rayed the arm, made sure the break aligned so the bones would grow correctly, and put him in a cast. Then Ryan drove him home on Sunday afternoon. He didn't even call her to tell her Elijah had hurt himself. When confronted, Ryan claimed it was his weekend, and he didn't need to call her for a minor emergency.

"I love you, Mommy," said Elijah, his feet on the ground but his hands still held in front of him. At one time, hearing Elijah say he loved her would have melted her heart and guaranteed that she'd play with him for at least a few minutes. The manipulative little poop knew that, too. Still, it made her smile.

"I love you too, sweetheart, but I'm working," she said, focusing on the clothes and bags on the bed in front of her.

At first, when Julie had learned Elijah broke his arm, she had been so angry she couldn't even think straight. Bumps and bruises were a part of life, especially for active little boys, but she didn't appreciate Ryan's handling of the incident. He pushed her aside like she didn't even matter, like she wouldn't care.

Elijah's pediatrician had different concerns. He had requested the concierge physician send over the X-rays, but Ryan's doctor stalled and fought the request. First, he had claimed that their offices' document storage systems were incompatible. Then he asked for a hundred-dollar fee to send

3

the X-rays over. When Julie paid, he said his assistant had accidentally destroyed the X-rays.

Dr. Singh was concerned about child abuse. At Elijah's age, bones could flex, and it took a big fall to break them. According to Elijah's chart, he had a spiral fracture of his forearm, a rotational injury. It could have happened if Elijah fell out of a tree and landed funny, but Dr. Singh didn't think the story made sense. He argued with the other doctor, but it didn't go anywhere. Then he suggested she take him to the children's hospital in St. Louis for an orthopedic surgeon's opinion.

Surgeons and X-rays cost money, though, thousands of dollars in this case. Julie's family didn't have thousands of dollars lying around. Dr. Singh didn't care about affordability. He argued that if she cared about her son, she'd get it done. Then he accused her of allowing her son to be abused and dropped them from his practice.

It had been an ugly situation, and it had been Ryan's fault. He had a bad temper. He had never hit her but had, allegedly, pushed his ex-girlfriend. Some days, Julie wished she had never met him. Andrea and Frank, Ryan's parents, loved Elijah, but Ryan was a jerk. Unfortunately, the court said Ryan got Elijah for two weekends every month. If she didn't cooperate, Ryan's family would sue her. They might even take away her son. It all came down to money and power, and Ryan's family had both.

Julie had spent almost an hour packing Elijah's bags. Everything was just right. The irony of it was that Andrea would never use anything Julie provided. She'd have her own set of expensive, stain-free clothes that Elijah only wore while visiting her, and special toys for him to play with.

Julie had bought Elijah a few clothes, but most everything they owned had been given to them by other moms whose kids had grown up. Julie didn't care that Elijah's clothes were hand-me-downs. Ryan's mom, though, worried about status. Maybe one day, Julie'd have enough money to care about other people's feelings, but for now, she focused on survival.

As she folded a T-shirt in midair, Julie noticed the bags sliding to the right as Elijah pulled on the bedspread. She grabbed the suitcase before it could topple over the side.

"That's a bad idea, honey," she said. "You're about to learn a hard lesson about gravity."

He tugged a couple more times, pulling more of the blanket toward him.

"It's a tent!"

"It sure is," she said. "You know what? I bet Grandma would love some company in the kitchen."

Elijah pulled the bedspread taut over his face.

"I can see you," he said.

"That's a fifteen-year-old blanket, so that tracks."

"What's tracks?"

She looked at Elijah and shook her head.

"I don't know, buddy," she said. "Go ask Grandma for an Oreo. Tell her I said you can have one."

He rolled onto his belly, pushed up, and sprinted out of the room. She watched him go, and somehow, the lump in her throat grew even larger. She forced herself to breathe. Everything would be just fine. Ryan was Elijah's daddy. More than that, Ryan's parents loved their grandson and wouldn't let anything happen to him. The broken arm was an accident. Surely Elijah would have told her if Ryan had hurt him. She was his mom, after all. It was her job to protect him. He knew that.

She wiped her watery eyes and sucked in a breath. She'd miss Elijah, but her baby would come back to her. He wouldn't have any new bruises or broken bones, and he'd have stories to tell her of adventures with his grandparents and daddy.

"You're fine, Julie. Everything will work out."

This was a familiar pep talk, one she gave herself every time Ryan had a weekend. It rarely helped. After checking everything for the fourth or fifth time, she lugged the bags to the front hall of her parents' four-bedroom 70s ranch. Julie had loved growing up in that house, but she never expected to raise her own kid there. Her parents hadn't either. Life was funny sometimes. It didn't give a damn about your plans, but sometimes it gave you wonderful things you never knew you wanted.

While Elijah ate a snack, Julie packed her old Toyota Rav4 and made sure Elijah's car seat was secure. Then she plodded back inside to get her boy, who was sitting at the small breakfast table off the kitchen beside his grandma, Julie's mom. He seemed so small. She blew out a slow breath and forced a smile onto her face.

"Okay, sweetheart," she said. "Are you ready to see your daddy?"

He nodded and slipped off his chair. Lisa reached for her and squeezed her hand but said nothing. Julie tried to smile but couldn't. Julie's mom squeezed her hand again.

"Drive safely," she said. They were just going across town, but Julie nodded and picked up her toddler and carried him to the car. The drive took ten minutes. Julie left her lower-middle-class world and entered the world of doctors, lawyers, and businesspeople. Ryan lived in his parents' five-thousand-square-foot brick home on a big lot on Pinehurst. It was beautiful. As a child, Julie had dreamt of living in a big house, but the dream had lost its allure since then.

Ryan came out of the front door as soon as she parked.

"You're late," he said. Ryan was tall and well-built, and he walked with a confident gait. In another year, he'd go to college. For now, he worked odd jobs, most recently with a residential construction firm. Julie didn't know why he bothered working when his parents bought him anything he wanted, but, as he reminded her, it wasn't her business, anyway. "Drop off is at nine."

Julie opened the rear passenger door to get Elijah.

"It's ten after. It's fine," said Julie. "Elijah's got three bags in the back. Is your mom around? I wanted to tell her about Elijah's napping schedule. He's been a little off today."

Ryan opened the small SUV's rear door.

"Mom and Dad are in Florida," he said. "They're fishing and playing golf."

Julie drew in a breath and stiffened. Ryan scowled.

"It's fine, Julie," he said. "I can take care of my son for a weekend."

She blinked, her heart racing.

"Have you ever taken care of him by yourself? It's not the same. It's a lot harder, especially with him cranky," she said. "He was up late last night. There was this owl outside, and it kept hooting all night. Maybe I should just take him home. We can postpone until your parents are back."

"No."

Elijah was still in his car seat. Julie thought about driving off. Surely Ryan wouldn't stop her. He didn't even want a kid. These weekends were for his mom.

Julie almost pleaded, "You sure? It's no problem. Maybe you can have him during the week."

"I've got plans, Julie. Now come on. The judge says this is my weekend. Hand Elijah over, or I'll call the police. Again."

Julie shook her head.

"Why do you..." She paused and licked her lips. "What are you guys going to do?"

"That's none of your business."

Somehow, that cut through her nervousness and slowed her racing heart.

"It is my business. Elijah is my son. Last time you watched him, he came home with a bruise on his back. Before that, he broke his arm here. What happens if he hits his head? Are you ready for that?" she asked. Elijah started to fuss and try to get out of his seat, so she put a hand on his chest, holding him still. "Unless you tell me what you plan on doing with my son, we're leaving right now."

"He's my son, too," said Ryan. Julie squeezed her jaw tight and raised an eyebrow. Ryan scowled again. "We're going for a nature walk, okay? I found a list of activities online. Kids like nature walks."

Julie breathed a little easier and started helping Elijah out of his seat.

"That sounds fun. There's a dad's group at the Methodist church on Saturday mornings, too. It's nine to eleven. My dad takes Elijah sometimes. Henry from Elijah's preschool goes, and they run around and have fun for a few hours. Then, he comes home and takes a long nap. It's a good break."

"Scott isn't Elijah's dad. He doesn't get to take him to dad's groups. It's not fair."

"We didn't know that you'd care."

"I do," he said. "Elijah's my son. I get to say how he's raised."

She softened her voice and nodded.

"You're right. We can sit down and talk about it."

"Later," said Ryan, looking at Elijah and holding out his hand. "Come on, big man. I've got chocolate pudding inside. You want some?"

Elijah nodded and smiled. Julie drew in a breath and swallowed hard before setting her son on the ground. Elijah took his dad's hand, and the two started toward the house, the bags slung across Ryan's back.

"He's going to need a nap soon," said Julie. Ryan held up a hand, showing he had heard her, but neither turned. Julie watched them go inside then shut the door behind them.

Although it was still early in the morning, Julie drove home and went straight to her room to lie down, knowing she had just left her heart behind her and wishing she had any other choice.

Chapter 2

My bug spray was supposed to last eight hours, but apparently the makers hadn't tested their product in St. Augustine County in the spring. When I swatted a mosquito, another took its spot. Sweat beaded on my forehead, chest, and upper back. My black polyester St. Augustine County Sheriff's Department polo—our new spring-and-summer uniform—clung to me when I didn't fan the collar. Roy, my Chesapeake Bay retriever, snapped his jaws as a bug flew near. Then he licked his nose and panted, his tongue sticking out.

"I'll get you some water in a minute, dude," I said. "We shouldn't be out here long."

He looked at me and licked his nose, which I took as a sign that he understood. I had taken to bringing Roy to work lately, mostly because I enjoyed having him around. He was trained as a cadaver dog, but his trainers had never used him in the field. Their vets ran every test on him they could, and his trainer worked with him for months, but Roy just didn't like work. He flunked out of the cadaver dog program and came to live with me. Since then, he had become a little more spirited. He still loved lying on the couch, but he ran and played some, too.

I reached for my radio inside the marked SUV I had signed out from the motor pool.

"Trisha, I'm at the coordinates. The caller's SUV is in front of me, but there's nobody around. You still got them on the phone?"

In bigger departments, there would have been specific procedures to use when speaking on the radio to keep communications succinct and clear. I'd clear the line, I'd give my radio call sign, and then I'd give a ten-code that corresponded to the sort of call I was making. Without those procedures, the dispatchers couldn't route resources to the correct places effectively. My department, now with twenty-seven sworn officers after a recent round of forced retirements, had no such problems.

"They're in a cave," said Trisha. "You have Roy with you?"

"I do," I said.

"Maybe he can find them. If he can't, they said they followed a trail. The cave has a small opening beneath a limestone ledge. You'll see some legs sticking out."

I paused and nodded as I processed that.

"Are the legs connected to anything, or are we talking about body parts?"

Trisha chuckled.

"They're connected to a heavyset man who is alive and well."

"That's unfortunate," I said. "Roy's good at finding dead people. He's iffy on the living."

"At least it's a nice day for a walk."

I grunted.

"Yeah. At least we've got that going for us," I said, fanning my collar. "Thanks, Trisha. I'll see what I can find."

I had parked on the side of a two-lane road halfway between the towns of St. Augustine and Dyer in St. Augustine County. The nearest grocery store was fifteen minutes away in St. Augustine. Dyer had a small gas station, but its owner rarely worked and otherwise kept the pumps in front of his station off. There were no other businesses.

Our wayward spelunkers had arrived in a Honda Pilot SUV with Illinois plates. If we had to call the fire department for help, this would become an expensive afternoon for non-residents. Previously, I rarely considered the county's expenses, but now in the midst of our financial crisis, thoughts of expenses rarely left my mind.

I returned my radio to the car. Then Roy and I walked down the road about a quarter mile before finding an old Ford pickup beside a trail that cut through the woods. I wrapped his leash around my hand and started walking. Roy was a good dog and kept his shoulder at my hip even as he sniffed the air. As a cadaver dog, he could smell human remains some distance off, but he didn't seem interested in anything here except the squirrels. Hopefully, that meant I wouldn't be finding a body.

I walked another quarter mile before coming across a stone ledge, a small hole in the ground near tree roots, and the lower part of a torso protruding from a larger hole in the ground underneath the ledge. Roy went to the small hole, sniffed, and then barked.

"Hey!"

The voice belonged to a woman. The legs sticking from the entrance hole kicked. I tugged Roy back and shone my flashlight into the hole.

"Hey, yourself," I said. "I'm Detective Joe Court with the St. Augustine County Sheriff's Department. You guys hurt down there?"

Three people started talking at once. I heard a few tidbits about a hike, but then everyone started shouting. It sounded like they were okay. Rain had left the ground spongy, so the cave's interior would be damp. Hopefully, we wouldn't have to worry about a flood. With at least one good-sized hole, they'd have plenty of air, too.

I pulled back and assessed the torso while the people inside the cave argued. The torso's owner looked pretty well wedged into the cave's narrow opening. We couldn't enlarge the opening, but maybe we could grease the guy's belly and pull him out. I stuck my face back in the hole. They were still arguing, so I whistled to get their attention.

"Okay, folks, I'm assuming there are no other exits," I said.

"The cave goes on, but it's flooded," said the female voice again. "We're stuck."

"And to be clear, nobody's bleeding, having chest pain, breathing problems, or anything like that?"

The cave went quiet. Then a man answered.

"I think we're okay."

"Can I get your names?" I asked. The woman was Deborah, and her male companion was Jackson. Tony was wedged tight in the entrance.

"Tony's not with us," said Jackson. "He just followed us in. This is all his fault."

"I don't care who's with who," I said. "My job is to assess the situation and get you out. The good news is that nobody's in immediate danger. The bad news is that I don't know how to help."

They started yelling at each other again. I closed my eyes and scratched my cheek before whistling again for their attention.

"We're not sharing the treasure," said Deborah before I could say anything. "No matter what Tony says, we did the legwork. He shouldn't get a share just because he followed us in."

I gritted my teeth before speaking. Treasure hunters. I hated these people.

"To be clear, did you find Darren Rogers's secret stash inside the cave?"

Nobody spoke for a moment.

"They didn't find shit," said Tony.

"And they never will," I said. "Darren Rogers, our former County Executive, was a horrible human being who lied, schemed, and hurt people his entire career. He didn't give a damn about St. Augustine or its residents. He was only interested in himself. He was a murderer and a thief."

They paused.

"What'd he do with his money?" asked Jackson. "If he embezzled millions, where'd he put it?"

I sighed. St. Augustine was a county with a history—little of it good. In the seventies, the wealthiest man to ever live in St. Augustine, Stanley Pennington, raped and murdered a young girl at a local summer camp. Rather than prosecute Pennington, the county sheriff covered it up. Pennington's wife murdered him. The county covered that up, too, but as penance, a young man named Darren Rogers made Pennington's widow sign away the family fortune.

Years later, Susanne Pennington, the best friend I've ever had, told me she planted a poison tree that day. Her money had paid for the county's first Spring Fair, it allowed Ross Kelly to buy several hundred acres and create Ross Kelly Farms, it created Reid Pharmaceuticals, it created a truck stop and hotel; it changed the town in hundreds of ways. Without money, St. Augustine would be a rural county full of farms and little else. With that money, it became a tourist destination with thriving bars and restaurants and even a very expensive private college.

Beneath its bucolic exterior, though, a cancer had festered. St. Augustine had been sick. Its murder rate had been three times the national average, our opioid usage had been astronomical, and underage prostitutes had flaunted their wares in a truck stop's parking lot. Behind it all had been Darren Rogers. He had spent years pushing his vision for the community on us, all the while embezzling from the county and borrowing from low-life money lenders to fund property acquisitions for his personal portfolio. With Rogers's death, our community had a chance to heal, but first it had to survive the turbulent period ahead.

"If I knew where he put his money, I'd tell the US Attorney," I said. "Now I'm going to call the Department of Natural Resources and ask for guidance. In the future, don't believe the shit you see on TV about hidden treasure."

They grumbled, but I ignored them and pulled out my phone. I had one bar, so I walked back toward the road for a better connection. The treasure hunt nonsense had started when a big YouTube influencer stumbled across newspaper stories about our difficulties and paid us a visit. His assistant tried to interview me on camera, but I told her I couldn't comment. Somehow, they deduced that the official story as told through publicly available reports and newspaper articles made little sense, and the correct story must have involved a vast conspiracy to conceal a secret buried treasure. The video received millions of views, and idiots had inundated us ever since.

I spent the next half hour on the phone before a ranger at Castlewood State Park took me seriously and told me what he'd do in my situation. I thanked him and walked back to the cave. The spelunkers were quiet, so I knelt beside the hole.

"Okay, guys," I said. "I'm back."

Before I could tell them the plan, Jackson started speaking.

"Deborah and I have been talking."

"Whispering like rats, you mean," said Tony, quickly. "If you were talking, I'd be included."

They started yelling at each other about whether Tony would be included in the proceeds of any treasure buried inside the cave. I gritted my teeth and counted to ten before yelling.

"If you guys don't shut up, I'm leaving."

They went quiet. I gave them a moment and then started to speak, but Deborah cut me off.

"Dynamite," she said. "It'll clear the entrance."

I rubbed my eyes.

"Jesus, Mary, and Joseph," I said, straightening. "I'm not paid enough to deal with this."

"Don't leave," said Jackson. "That was just a preliminary plan. We'll come up with something else."

"I should hope so," I said. Roy must have sensed my annoyance because he started whining. I scratched his ears to let him know everything was fine. Then I knelt down again.

"I'm going to take off Tony's shoes and tickle his feet until he pees himself. The pee will provide lubrication and shrink his bladder—and hopefully—his midsection. Then I'm going to pull him out."

"That's the best plan you've got?" asked Tony, his voice almost panicky.

"That's the only plan," I said. "And I'll be honest, this may not work. In that case, we'll go with the dynamite. Sound good to you guys?"

Nobody seemed enthusiastic, which usually meant the plan was okay. I started undoing the laces on Tony's hiking boots when my phone rang. It was my station. I released the foot, stepped toward the cars—to the shrieks of the spelunkers—and answered.

"Please tell me we've got a dead body somewhere," I said. "Otherwise, I'm about to take off a tourist's shoes to tickle his feet and make him pee."

Trisha paused.

"I don't know how to respond."

I sighed. "Sorry. What can I do for you, Trisha?"

She paused again.

"We've got a body, but I can send Marcus," she said. "Since you're busy."

"Please God, no," I said. "Can you track my GPS?"

She paused.

"Yeah. I've got your coordinates on my screen."

"Send some uniforms out here," I said. "I'll take the murder."

"I'll send Bob and Katie to your coordinates. Anything they should know about your foot guy?"

"Oh, no," I said. "I'd hate to ruin the surprise. Once they get here, they'll understand the situation. Meanwhile, text me the address of the body."

"Will do," she said. I thanked her, hung up, and walked back to the cave. Tony was kicking his feet, but still stuck.

"You guys doing okay?" I asked.

"We're pushing on him, but we can't budge him," said Deborah. "He pulled my hair."

"Then stop pushing him," I said. "Listen, you guys hang out here for a while. I just got a call about a potential homicide."

Tony kicked his feet even harder. It looked as if he had wriggled backward.

"You can't leave us," said Jackson. "We're stuck here."

"Don't worry," I said. "I've called in our cave rescue team. They're on the way."

"Are you serious?" asked Deborah. "If you had a cave rescue team, why didn't you call them right away?"

"That is a good question. Rather than answer, what do you say we try to dislodge Tony?" I asked. "You guys push his shoulders, and I'll pull his leg. And Tony, if you pull Deborah's hair, I'll arrest you for misdemeanor assault."

They paused.

"Okay," said Tony. "I'll try to pee if I can. It's hard with people around."

"I'm sure it is," I said. "I'll give you a minute."

He agreed, and I backed off. Then, a few minutes later, I grabbed his foot and told Deborah and Jackson to push while I pulled. For a moment, nothing happened, but then Tony shifted, and he popped out. The sudden movement made me lose my footing. I tried to step back, but I tripped over Roy and fell on my butt. The dog yelped and licked my face until I pushed him away. The bottom of Tony's shirt and top of his pants were wet, and his face was red. He flopped onto his back and exhaled.

"You breathing okay, Tony?"

He held up a hand and gave me a thumbs-up, panting. Then I looked toward the cave.

"Deborah and Jackson, are you guys okay in there?" I called.

"I fell and scraped my knee," said Jackson.

Before I spoke, I squeezed my jaw tight.

"Sorry to hear that, buddy."

"It's all right," he said. "We'll wait to come out until the pee dries."

"Good idea," I said. "If you guys are okay, I'm going to head out now. Two of my colleagues are on their way to provide additional help if needed."

Tony sat up, nodded, and ran a hand across his scalp.

"Thank you."

"Sure thing," I said. "All three of you, remember what I said earlier: Darren Rogers didn't hide treasure anywhere in

St. Augustine. Before he died, he transferred his holdings to an offshore slush fund beyond the purview of the US government. That's why we can't find his money. It's probably in a South American bank by now, not buried in a cave in the middle of nowhere. He was a lot of things, but he wasn't stupid."

"Oh," said Jackson. "That makes sense."

"Terrific. Enjoy your time in St. Augustine," I said. "Sergeant Bob Reitz and Officer Katie Martelle are on the way. They'll help you if you need it. And no more spelunking. This is private property. If it happens again, I'll arrest you for trespassing."

They grumbled but seemed to agree. Roy and I left them there, and I checked my text messages. Instead of sending me an address, Trisha had sent me a set of coordinates. That likely meant I'd be trudging through the woods or a field again. Hopefully, I wouldn't have to make someone pee themselves again.

Chapter 3

I drove across the county on a rough highway for about twenty minutes. Then I pulled off onto an even rougher road and drove for another ten minutes into a deep pine forest. Thirty or forty years ago, thick virgin forest likely covered this area, and I would have seen black walnuts, poplar, and gum trees on an undulating landscape. Scrub brush would have covered the ground near the road where the sun hit, but the forest canopy would have been thick enough to prevent most plants from growing near the forest interior.

Now, we had an engineered forest, one carefully managed to produce the maximal amount of timber in the shortest period. Periodically, the timber company would clear-cut sections and then plant new southern yellow pine trees in place of the old. In theory, the planting and harvesting method produced high-quality, sustainable quantities of wood for the construction industry. In practice, I couldn't help but feel it turned a once verdant, unspoiled area of natural beauty into an impoverished landscape of boring homogeneity.

Nobody had asked me, though.

As I drove deeper into the woods, the gravel roadway gave way to hard-packed earth crisscrossed by tree roots that made my SUV shudder as it passed over them. I was glad I hadn't brought my old Volvo station wagon; it would have fallen apart. Every few moments, I glanced back at Roy in the back seat. He peered out the window, his mouth open and his tongue hanging out. He seemed to be enjoying himself.

Eventually, the road widened, and I found a pair of St. Augustine cruisers parked under the shade of some very tall southern yellow pines. I parked near them, got Roy from the back of the car, and listened. Birds chirped and small animals scurried over the pine needles and around the trees. I couldn't see my team, but Roy stuck his nose in the air and sniffed. Then he started pulling on the lead.

Trisha hadn't lied; my cadaver dog had smelled a body.

"Okay, buddy," I said, patting his side. "Let's find it."

Normally, I kept Roy's lead tight around my hand, but here, I gave him some room to move and hurried after him through the woods. The ground felt spongy, but I didn't worry too much about my footing on the pine needles. The air was crisp and clean, but as we walked, a fetid odor began overtaking everything else. It wasn't a decomposing body; the smell was more earthy than that. A creek ran through the woods by my old house, and every spring, I smelled a similar sewage-like odor after rainstorms and floods. It meant we had water nearby, which meant we'd have mosquitoes, too.

I should have sprayed on more bug repellent when I had the chance.

After a few minutes of walking, a uniformed figure spotted Roy and me and waved.

"Joe?"

I waved back.

"Doug?"

"Yeah. Body's over here," he said. "Step carefully. There's a lot of mud."

Officer Doug Patricia was in his mid-forties. He had been our night dispatcher, but St. Augustine County no longer had a full shift at night. Now, when someone in St. Augustine called 911 after eight at night, the call was routed to a Highway Patrol dispatcher. Our officers were on standby for emergencies, but the Highway Patrol's troopers handled most calls for service. It was far from ideal, but we had to deal with reality.

Doug was right about the mud. It slurped with every footstep I made and soon caked Roy's legs. The dog didn't seem to mind, but it nearly took off my shoe at one point. If I had known it was this thick, I would have worn rain galoshes instead of tennis shoes.

I stopped and stood beside Doug and Officer DeAndre Simpson. Our victim looked like a Hispanic man in his mid-thirties. He had neatly styled black hair, and he wore a suit. Blood spattered his white shirt and radiated from a point in his chest where his heart had once been. Now, it was just a bloody hole the size of my fist.

"That's a big entry wound," I said, my hands on my hips. "This guy get hit by a cannon?"

Doug and DeAndre smiled but still looked grim.

"Whatever hit him, it was big," said DeAndre. "The coroner might know more."

"We'll ask him what he thinks," I said. "You guys arrive together?"

DeAndre shook his head.

"I was here first, ma'am," he said.

"Great," I said, reaching for a notepad in my purse. "Tell me what we've got, but before you do, let me congratulate you. I heard on the grapevine that your wife is pregnant."

DeAndre drew in a breath through his nose and closed his eyes. Doug shook his head. I mouthed *what?*

"I'll express your congratulations to my wife's boyfriend," said DeAndre. "As far as I know, their baby's healthy, so that's something."

"I'm sorry," I said. "I didn't know."

"It's alright," he said, taking a notepad from his utility belt. DeAndre and Doug wore uniforms very similar to mine, but where I wore jeans and a black polo shirt, they wore khaki pants, a utility belt, and a gray polo shirt. "The call came at 4:09 PM from a hiker. He gave us latitude and longitude from his cell phone. I drove out and parked by the road. The caller was waiting for me and led me to the body. I checked the victim's neck for a pulse but found nothing. There's a creek nearby, but the water's low, and I didn't think we'd have to worry about it rising and washing away evidence."

I wrote down the details and then glanced up.

"Mud's thick. You notice any footprints near the body?"

He closed his eyes, drew in a slow breath, and nodded.

"Yeah. A lot of them. The caller walked around the body to see if he was dead. I checked the area out, too. Sorry."

"That's fine," I said. "Have you seen the forecast?"

"Weatherman said more rain, but he also said it'd be fifty degrees this week. Who knows?"

I nodded. A little rain wouldn't be a big deal. Footprints were tough. A good footprint could break a case, but they were rare. A lot could go wrong. Thick, sticky mud didn't allow a footprint to imprint with much detail, while hard, dry mud didn't allow a foot to implant enough to form a recognizable print. You had to get lucky. That didn't happen often.

"I need a formal statement from the 911 caller. One of you mind taking him back and babysitting him for a while?"

"He's in my car," said DeAndre. "I'll take care of him."

"I appreciate that. Doug, get out a notebook and pencil. You're going to be my second on this," I said. DeAndre asked if we needed anything else. I said no, so he headed out, and I focused on Doug. "First, we need lights and the generator. With rain forecast, we need to process the scene quickly and thoroughly before it hits. Second, call the coroner. Tell him he'll need to bring a back brace and be ready to carry the body out. It's too muddy for a gurney. Third, I need you to call Kevius. I need a crime scene tech here."

Doug scribbled notes and then glanced at me.

"You want me to call Darlene, too?"

I shook my head.

"Darlene's great, and I wish we could bring her in, but the county will have to pay overtime. I don't think we can afford her, especially when we've got Kevius. He'll get the job done."

Doug nodded and wrote it down, then glanced at me.

"Will she be okay with you calling in her subordinate without talking to her first?"

I nodded.

"She'll be fine," I said. "We've talked about the possibility. She's been around long enough to understand local government. Cash is tight right now all over St. Augustine. We've got to do our part to preserve what we've got."

He looked over my shoulder toward the body, then nodded.

"Sounds like you've got this, boss," he said. "We need anything else?"

"No, but I'm going to walk with you to the cars," I said. "I need my digital camera and some crime scene tape."

We started walking. It had been a while since I last took official crime scene photos, but I could document a scene. Doug would witness everything I did, too, which helped.

As Doug called in extra help, I grabbed crime scene tape, a flashlight, a digital camera, and rain boots from my trunk. I changed my footwear, trudged back, and established a perimeter thirty feet around the body. We were deep enough in the woods that we didn't need to worry about unexpected visitors, but the tape would prevent my team from stepping where they shouldn't. I crossed under it and turned on my department's Nikon D850 camera. Each picture I shot would contain metadata with the time and date I had taken it.

Once I returned to my office, I'd append the metadata file with additional information so everyone would understand when and where I had taken the picture and with what equipment. I'd also add a unique identifier to each picture so I could then append notes in a written report explaining what I was hoping to capture and why I thought that was important.

Our victim was as dead now as he'd ever be. Nothing I did would bring him back. Today, though, I became his voice. I'd use every resource I had to find his murderer, and if I couldn't, I'd save my reports, photos, and findings in the hope that someone else could. Because that, too, was at the heart of my work: hope that the world could be better than it was. Most days, I wished reasons for that hope were easier to find.

Chapter 4

B efore taking my first picture, I sketched the area in my
notepad and then broke my sketch down into grids
for reference. In years past, our crime scene techs would
have documented the scene and collected evidence while I
interviewed witnesses, but for now, that was my job, and I
hoped to do it well. I didn't have surveying equipment, but
my search area was a square twelve paces wide. A creek ran to
the south. Woods surrounded us to the east, west, and north.

I snapped pictures and used a voice-to-text app on my
phone to dictate what each picture was intended to capture
and which quadrant of my grid I was looking at. It was slow
going, but thorough. Doug returned a few minutes after I
started working and took over the dictation while I took
pictures.

Eventually, I made my way to the body. Aside from the
massive wound on his chest, he looked like a healthy, Hispanic man in his mid to late thirties. His skin was still intact,
and I couldn't smell decomposition yet. According to my
phone, it was seventy-seven degrees with seventy-five percent

humidity. With weather like that, his soft tissues would have broken down quickly. He hadn't been dead for long.

I knelt beside him and stared at his face. He was handsome and well dressed. His brown eyes were wide open. They stared at the forest. Some early forensic scientists postulated the eye was like a camera. They believed it captured and stored images and that if investigators could somehow peer through the eyes of the dead, they'd find their murderer. I wondered what my victim's eyes had seen before he died. He didn't look scared, but bodies rarely did upon death. If anything, he looked peaceful.

"Why are you here?" I asked, my voice low.

"You talking to me, Joe?" asked Doug. I glanced up at him. He stood beyond the crime scene tape near the creek.

"Just talking to myself," I said. "You're in pretty good shape. You think you could lug a two-hundred-pound body over this terrain?"

Doug shifted and then looked in the direction we had parked.

"Doubtful. That's a long walk to the road with a heavy weight. If I were twenty, I might have been able to do it. Now, no way."

I slipped my phone into my pocket and snapped a pair of polypropylene gloves onto my hands so I could feel the mud. It was squishy, wet, and very dark, and it smelled like shit. It was mostly clay, which meant it didn't drain well. Animals used the creek as a water source, and they likely left feces all around us, but this stink was so pervasive it made me think it came from bacterial growth in the soil. More important than any of that, it didn't leave a red stain on my gloves.

I straightened.

"If our victim was shot here, he would have bled out into the soil. I'm not finding blood, though. This was a dump sight. You see any tracks from a wheelbarrow or cart?"

"No. We've got footprints galore, but no other tracks."

I hadn't seen any, either. I clicked my tongue a few times, thinking. Then I walked to the body and started counting my paces as I walked toward the road again. Doug followed and did likewise. He was almost six inches taller than me, so his steps carried him further than mine. Despite that, we came to similar estimates once we reached the car. Three hundred yards.

"Did you see our 911 caller?" I asked, standing beside my SUV.

Doug nodded.

"He was older than me and thin. He looked like a marathon runner."

"You think he could have carried a body through the woods?"

He considered before shaking his head.

"It'd be hard alone, but I bet he could do it with a helper."

I nodded and shielded my eyes from the setting sun as a minivan came bouncing down the trail toward us. The driver flashed his lights, and I waved. It was Kevius, our forensic technician. Behind his minivan came a black SUV driven by Detective Marcus Washington. Hopefully, the coroner was close by. The two men parked and exited their vehicles. Marcus had brought lights, a generator, and a big party tent to cover the scene in case it rained.

Roy and I walked through the woods as my team put up the tent. My dog had a good nose and could differentiate a lot of different smells. Where I found the mud smell overpowering, Roy could tune everything out but the unique smell of a decomposing human. For half an hour, we looked for blood, body parts, or other victims. We found nothing. We didn't even find footprints or ruts from a cart.

The sun was getting low as we got back to the body. Our temporary volunteer coroner—Dr. John Gardner, a retired ophthalmologist with an interest in forensics—was hovering over the body. Marcus stood beside him. He nodded to me and smiled at Roy.

"Hey, buddy," he said, kneeling near the dog. Roy licked his hands as Marcus petted his cheeks and neck and scratched his ears.

"You guys find anything interesting?" I asked.

"I checked the victim's pockets, but he didn't have a wallet," said Dr. Gardner, flipping open the victim's suit jacket to expose the interior. "I found something interesting, though. Maybe you can use it."

Marcus and I both stood on either side of the coroner. The jacket had a patch sewn onto the interior pocket.

*Designed Exclusively for Frederick Knowles, Bespoke Tai-
lors, Miami, Florida. Cut, tailored, and fitted by Elliot
Knowles. Northeast 71st Street.*

"So it's a bespoke suit," I said. "Tells us something about
our victim. Guy had money."

"It'll give you an ID," said Gardner. "A suit like this will
cost you six or seven thousand dollars. The tailor spent time
with your victim and likely got to know him well. He'll know
your victim's name, he'll know what he does for a living...if
he made the suit for a special occasion, he might even know
about your victim's love life."

I considered the doctor and felt my lips curl upward.

"Good eye, Doc," I said. "Anything else you can tell me?"

"Rigor has set on his face and extremities but not his torso,
and his liver temperature was ninety-five degrees. Given the
ambient temperature and the degree of rigor, I'd estimate he
died somewhere between three and six hours ago. I might
narrow that down once I autopsy him."

"That's terrific. Thank you," I said, standing and glancing
at Marcus. "You mind supervising the scene out here?"

Marcus smiled.

"I think I can handle that. Kevius has a metal detector, and
he's off looking for shell casings, but I'm thinking this is just
the dump site."

"And why do you think that?" I asked.

He looked toward the body.

"Not enough blood on the ground. He bled out elsewhere."

"Then we are of one mind, my friend," I said. "Roy and I walked around earlier, but I couldn't find drag marks or tracks from a wheelbarrow or other cart. Our shooter carried him in. Given the weight, he probably had help. I'm going back to the office to interview our 911 caller. He's been stewing for a while. I'll call the tailor, too. If anybody needs anything, call me."

They agreed, and I drove back to my station. My department worked out of an enormous former Freemason's temple that the county had purchased years ago when the Masons left town. For years, it had been a beautiful dump with a roof that leaked, plumbing that banged around, poorly sealed windows, and heat that worked only periodically. In the recent past, though, the county had spent millions renovating the facility. Now, we had a state-of-the-art station big enough for a department five to ten times our size. Most of it sat empty and unused. It was a shameful waste of money the county didn't have.

I checked on DeAndre and our 911 caller to make sure they were okay. They were bored, but fine. I'd get to them as soon as I could. In the meantime, I called the Miami tailor's shop from my office. A woman answered but said the shop was closed.

"I appreciate that," I said, "but I'm calling about something important. I'm a detective in Missouri, and I've got a murder victim who died wearing one of your suits. I was hoping you might help me identify my victim."

"Couldn't you just check his driver's license?"

I forced myself to smile.

"If he had a driver's license, I would get his name from that. Unfortunately, his murderer didn't see fit to make things convenient for us. If you could get me a name, I would appreciate it. It'd allow me to call his family."

"Okay," she said, breathing deeply. "What can I do?"

"Is Elliot Knowles around? The patch on the jacket says he tailored the suit."

"He is here. Please hold."

I gritted my teeth and waited. My conversation with Mr. Knowles was quicker. I sent him a photograph of the victim's face. As Dr. Gardner had suggested, Knowles knew his clients well and identified my victim as Mannie Gutierrez. Knowles had tailored him a new suit every year on his birthday and described him as gregarious, kind, and generous. Nobody ever spoke ill of him.

"He have a spouse or significant other?" I asked.

Knowles drew in a breath.

"Mannie loved women, and women loved Mannie."

"So he played the field," I said. Knowles clucked his tongue.

"No, no, no," he said. "Mannie was a gentleman. He respected his partners. All of them."

I jotted a few notes and nodded.

"How about his work? You know anything about that?"

"He was an attorney for a boutique firm in town."

Again, I nodded and jotted notes. With our adversarial legal system, lawyers had more opportunities to make enemies than most professions. It was possible a client murdered him, but it was equally possible a former lover, legal adversary, or random drug addict killed him. This conversation, unfortunately, opened a lot of doors. Knowles gave me the law firm's name, and I called them next.

For about fifteen minutes, I talked to the firm's managing partner. She seemed genuinely upset that Mannie had died. Mannie had no spouse or children but had been close to his parents. He had brought his mom to the firm's last holiday party, apparently, as his date. Most of his colleagues found it endearing. Since she knew the family, she and Mannie's direct supervisor offered to do the next-of-kin notification. I'd have to call the family later for background information, but I didn't see a problem with that.

"Do you have any clients in Missouri?" I asked.

She hesitated.

"No, sorry. Our firm specializes in admiralty law. Most of our clients work in international shipping."

I leaned back in my chair.

"So Mannie wasn't here for work."

"No. Sorry."

We talked for another couple of minutes, but I didn't learn anything helpful. I thanked her for her time, hung up, and read through my notes. So Mannie, a wealthy lawyer without apparent ties to the community, traveled over a thousand miles to an impoverished former tourist town in eastern Missouri. There, someone shot him in the chest, dumped his body in the woods, and disappeared.

Human beings were both complicated and simple. We acted on our desires. The reasons for those desires were complex, but if you understood someone's wants and needs, you could predict how they'd act. I didn't yet know why somebody wanted Mannie dead, but I would eventually. Then, the story would make sense. Until that moment, I had a mystery.

I hated mysteries.

Chapter 5

Julie wore a pink V-neck T-shirt and jeans. Had she been in high school, she could have worn the outfit to class. Stacy wore a red midi dress with a neckline cut so low that every man in the building had followed her boobs with their eyes. Madison wore black pants with a white top. Julie's friends were cute and dressed to go out. This was supposed to be a fun, carefree evening, but Julie couldn't stop thinking about Elijah and Ryan. Why did Ryan want Elijah if his parents weren't there? What were they doing? Did Elijah have enough to eat? Did Ryan get frustrated and yell at him?

Julie felt paranoid, but she had reason to be paranoid. Ryan was Elijah's legal father, but he wasn't a dad. He had never taken an interest in his son. The judge had even noted that in their last custody hearing. Why did he want him now? He should have been overjoyed to party with his friends. Julie would have taken Elijah for the weekend and canceled her plans with her friends. Ryan's sudden interest felt wrong, but she couldn't change the situation. Instead, she focused on her friends and told herself everything would be fine. She hoped she was right.

"Your classes still going okay, Stacy?" she asked. Stacy was a freshman at Mizzou and had driven home for the weekend, while Madison was a freshman at the University of Missouri-St. Louis. She lived at home still and commuted to the city for class. Julie was the hostess at an expensive French restaurant in town. They all lived different lives, but Julie loved them all the same. Stacy and Madison were her best friends. She had missed them.

"Classes are fine," said Stacy. "My roommate's still dumb. She's lucky she doesn't have gonorrhea, the way she hooks up with people. I stay with friends across the hall more often than I sleep in my bed. It almost feels like an anthropological experiment, like I'm an observer watching an unfamiliar culture with practices and mores different from my own."

"Yeah, because you were so chaste in high school," said Madison, smirking and tilting her margarita glass and watching the liquid cover the salt on the rim. They had a table at The Barking Spider, a crappy dive bar in St. Augustine County. Neither Julie, Stacy, nor Madison was over twenty-one, but each had a passable fake ID, and the bouncer at The Barking Spider didn't hassle the locals.

Stacy laughed.

"Maybe I do have a passing familiarity with my roommate's culture."

Julie snorted and picked up her half-empty beer glass. She rarely drank beer, but she had to drive home to her parents' house after this. Madison and Stacy had different expectations at home. If they stumbled in drunk, their moms and dads might lecture them, but the girls went to college. Taking an Uber home because they were too drunk to drive made them seem responsible. If Julie stumbled in drunk, it'd be a problem. Julie loved her friends, but they lived in different worlds now. She appreciated that they still let her visit, though.

For an hour, they talked and ignored the men who visited the table and offered to buy them drinks—none of which they accepted. The girls were cute and young, which, apparently, made them fair game. Thankfully, most men left when asked. Others, the bouncer had to kick out. It was a Friday night, but few tables held customers. Business across the county had slowed when the former government fell apart. A lot of restaurants and bars had closed permanently.

Elijah always stayed in Julie's mind, but she pretended this was a typical night out with friends. It felt good to relax.

"Your mom and dad have Elijah tonight?" asked Madison. She was on her second or third drink and seemed more relaxed than she had been earlier. "It must be great having parents to help."

"They're a big help," Julie said, looking down at her water bottle—she had switched from beer after a single drink. "When I was growing up, they were good parents, I guess, but now that they're grandparents, they're on a whole other level. I couldn't do it without them."

"My mom would help if I had a kid," said Stacy. "My dad, though? He'd disappear with a fishing pole before I could even introduce him."

Julie smiled.

"When Dad learned I was having a boy, he bought a camo onesie, like he was going to take an infant hunting. It was cute. I bet your daddy would surprise you. And if you're interested in babies, there are men galore in this very bar who'd help you with conception."

Madison and Stacy laughed. They focused on their drinks for a moment.

"You okay with Ryan moving?" asked Madison.

Julie looked up from her drink.

"Excuse me?"

"Ryan," she said. "He's moving. My sister's got a crush on Ethan Pettrica. She's been hanging out with him some. He was going to help Ryan move this weekend. Packed up his car and everything this morning."

Ethan and Ryan were best friends and had been since grade school. Julie's heart started beating harder.

"Where's he moving?"

"Somewhere in St. Louis," she said. "Lexi didn't give me any details."

"And he's moving this weekend?"

Madison nodded. Julie pushed her bottle to the side and leaned forward.

"Call Lexi and get some details," she said.

Madison held up her hands, almost defensively, before reaching down to her purse for her phone.

"I'm sorry," she said. "I thought you'd be happy. It's not like Ryan's much of a father. If he's moving, he might leave you alone more."

"He's not a good father," said Julie, her voice harder than she expected, "but this is his weekend. He's got Elijah right now. I knew something was wrong this morning when I dropped Elijah off. Ryan was nervous about something. If he's moving, I want to know where my son is."

Stacy drew in a sharp breath, and Madison started dialing. She couldn't hit the right buttons, though. She was too drunk. Stacy reached for Julie's arm.

"This is just a misunderstanding," she said. "Ryan's not a..." She paused. "He wouldn't just, you know..."

"Run away with my kid?" asked Julie, finishing the thought. She squeezed her jaw tight and breathed through her nose, trying to stave off a panic attack. "He doesn't want a kid. He takes Elijah once a month because his mom wants to see him. This is wrong. He can't just up and leave with my son. I'm going to call him."

She reached into her purse for her phone while Madison struggled to contact her sister. Ryan's phone rang four times before going to voicemail. Rather than leave a message, she called back. It rang four times again before going to voicemail. Then she tried a third time. The phone went to voicemail right away. She called again. This call, too, went to voicemail. He was ignoring her, so she texted him.

Pick up.

She called again. As expected, the call went to voicemail. This time, she left a message.

"Ryan, we need to talk. I heard you were moving, and now you're not taking my calls. Call me back."

She hung up and waited. Madison put her phone down.

"Lexi said she'd call Ethan and ask for details," she said. "She didn't know anything more."

"That's okay," said Julie, drawing in a breath. "Ryan's going to call me. I wouldn't have left Elijah with him except that he said he'd call the police if I didn't. Something's wrong here. I don't like this."

The table was quiet. People laughed at tables nearby. Julie counted to sixty before sweeping her phone off the table and into her purse.

"Can you girls get an Uber tonight? I'm going to Ryan's house."

"Sure," said Madison. "Do you need help?"

"No. This is between me and him," said Julie, shaking her head. "I'm going to straighten this out."

"It's going to be okay," said Stacy. "And I'm sorry."

"Nothing to be sorry for," she said. "Everything's fine."

Some guys at a nearby table called out to her, but Julie ignored them and hurried out of the bar. Once she got in her car, she squeezed the steering wheel hard and took a couple of deep breaths to calm herself down before twisting the key and heading out. Her chest felt heavy. No matter what she did or how she held herself, she couldn't seem to get enough oxygen.

"Breathe, Julie," she said. "Just breathe. You're fine, Elijah's fine, everything's fine."

Despite her self-assurances, Julie stepped on the gas hard and felt the car accelerate down a dark country road toward Ryan's house. His neighborhood looked just as it had earlier. The houses were large, and their exterior lights overpowered the darkness, forming pools of iridescence in the desolate night. Once she reached Ryan's house, she slammed on the brakes, threw the car into park, and ran out. Ryan opened his front door before she could knock. He wore mesh shorts and a T-shirt. The evening had cooled, and he rubbed his arms for warmth.

"What do you want?"

"I want to see my baby," she said. "Where is he?"

"Sleeping. It's night."

Julie shook her head and tried to push past him.

"Let me in. I need to see him."

Ryan caught her and pushed her back onto the porch.

"You stay right there, or I'll call the police. This is my weekend, and Elijah's asleep. You wake him up now, he's going to be cranky tomorrow. Is that what this is about? You trying to ruin my weekend?"

"This isn't about you," she said. "This is about him. I want to make sure he's okay."

"He's fine. We had a real good day. We went to the playground. I put him down at 7:30 and watched a movie. Where have you been?"

She started to say she was out with her friends, but then she caught herself.

"That's none of your business."

"My life's none of your business, either," he said. "Now, if you could move along, I'd appreciate it. I'm going to go back to my movie."

He stepped back to go inside. Julie drew in a breath.

"Ethan told Lexi you were moving."

Ryan scowled and shook his head.

"Ethan and Lexi need to keep their mouths shut."

"So you are moving?" asked Julie. "Ethan said he was helping you move this weekend."

Ryan put his hands on his hips.

"Ethan needs a calendar," he said. "It's not this weekend. It's soon, okay? I'm getting an apartment in St. Louis. You think I'm some kind of loser who needs his mommy and daddy, but I don't. I've got a job, I make my own money, I buy my own food... I'm moving into my own place finally."

She drew in a breath and softened her voice, feeling her shoulders relax.

"That's good," she said. "Good... good for you. That's real good. What will we do about Elijah?"

"I don't know, and it's too late to argue." He paused. His eyes flicked up and down her. "You're drunk, aren't you?"

She scowled.

"No. I went out with Madison and Stacy. We had a drink. That's it."

He rolled his eyes.

"Figures they'd put you up to this. They're more screwed up than you are."

"Excuse me?"

He crossed his arms.

"You heard me," he said. "My mom was right about you. You're just poor white trash who doesn't know any better."

"You slept with me without a condom. If I'm poor white trash, what does that make you?"

He considered her.

"It means I made a mistake. One day, I'll put that mistake behind me, but you'll be poor white trash your whole life."

"You're an asshole," she said, trying to step past him once more to get inside. He stepped in front of her again. "I'm getting my son. Get out of my way."

"Elijah's asleep in his room. Get off my property, or I'll call the police. I'll tell them a drunk girl is harassing me and my son. Then I'll take you to court. After my lawyers are done with you, you'll be lucky to see a picture of Elijah once a year."

She brought a hand to her face, her skin flushed, and her lips quivering.

"Fuck you."

"You already did," said Ryan. "Honestly, it wasn't even that good. Stick to blow jobs. You were better at those."

She wanted to slap him. Instead, she balled her fists and held her breath. As she turned to walk to her car, he called out again.

"See you Sunday. I'll tell Elijah you came by."

It took everything she had not to turn around and attack him. Instead, she walked to her car, muscles all over her body tight. Her hands trembled as she sat and put the car in gear. She left Ryan's neighborhood and drove to an office building. It was the first place to stop. The parking lot was dark. She parked beside the FOR LEASE sign out front. There, she closed her eyes and squeezed her jaw tight. She didn't cry, but she was close.

Julie didn't care about what Ryan thought of her. He was a jerk. She had seen that years ago when they were dating. She worried about her son.

Ryan was right. Her family didn't have money. If he wanted Elijah, his family had the resources to get him. It'd only take one slip. If her friends got caught with a fake ID, they'd pay a fine and do some community service, but they'd go right back to college and continue on with their lives. If she got arrested, Ryan and his parents could hold it over her head to extract whatever they wanted from her. They'd take her to court and cost her money she didn't have. Julie's family had barely paid off the legal bills from their last custody fight.

Another fight in court would bankrupt them. Ryan's family probably had a lawyer on permanent retainer.

Until Elijah could decide things for himself, Ryan would have power over them both. She had always known that, but he hadn't flaunted that power before. Now she felt sick, but she couldn't change the situation.

At least as long as Ryan lived.

Chapter 6

A fter identifying my victim, I was ready to talk to our 911 caller. He and DeAndre were sitting in the second-floor conference room and using the AV equipment to watch a movie on Netflix. DeAndre nodded to me, and I pulled out a black leather chair from the table.

"I didn't know the projector was good enough to play movies," I said, watching as Jennifer Aniston and Adam Sandler sipped champagne on a boat. DeAndre reached for a remote to turn everything off. Then he stretched. "Sorry to keep you guys waiting. It's a homicide investigation. Everything takes time."

DeAndre waved away my concern, but our witness, a heavyset man in his mid-fifties, narrowed his eyes at me.

"You should apologize. I've been here for hours. I don't mean to speak ill of the company, but I would have much rather been at my cabin watching TV."

"Like I said, I apologize," I said, reaching into my purse for my phone. "When I work a homicide, I'm working a case that could send somebody to prison for the rest of his or her life. If I rush, I might miss something that could keep an innocent person from prison. I don't want to do that."

"It's been hours. Had I known you'd waste my time, I would have kept hiking and ignored the body."

I nodded, considered him, and drummed my fingers on the table.

"I understand your annoyance. Let me buy you dinner and make it up to you. Have you eaten, DeAndre?"

"No, ma'am," he said.

"You guys want a pizza?"

The witness leaned forward.

"Honestly, I'd rather just go home."

I glanced at him.

"You found a body in the middle of nowhere within hours of the victim's death," I said. "The area's so remote I had to drive for ten minutes off-road just to reach the location. Your presence there is an amazing coincidence, or it's not a coincidence at all. My job is to determine which is the case. That answer will determine whether you go home tonight at all. So, you want pizza, or you want a sub? I'll get either, but you're not going anywhere until I eat."

He raised bushy gray eyebrows.

"I'm a suspect?"

"Yep," I said. "Pizza or sub? Which do you want?"

He shook his head.

"I wish I had never come here."

"That's a common lament of late," I said. "I'm going to order a pizza. What do you want on yours, buddy?"

The two men gave me their orders, and I called The Pizza Palace from my office. Their food was greasy and tasteless, but they were open, and they promised to send a delivery driver within half an hour. While I waited, I called Marcus for an update. He and Kevius were still at the crime scene, but they were packing up their cars as we spoke. Dr. Gardner had our victim at the morgue already and planned to autopsy him at seven AM. I made a mental note to attend if possible. Marcus and Kevius had searched the area, but they hadn't found footprints, drag marks, or other tracks to explain how the victim arrived, nor had they found the round that killed him. It wasn't a waste of time, but it was pretty close to one.

I suggested they both go home and rest. After the call, Roy and I waited in the lobby for the pizza guy. The building felt eerie and quiet.

Eventually, dinner arrived. I brought it upstairs and got to work. We ate, and I interviewed. Our witness was Todd Murphy, and he came to St. Augustine from Paducah, Kentucky, to seek Darren Rogers's supposed treasure. Unlike most of our visitors who searched the county at random, Mr. Murphy had gone to the library before arriving in town. He had learned that Darren Rogers's family had once owned the swath of property on which we had found Mannie, our victim.

I wrote notes and glanced at the man.

"So you're a treasure hunter," I said. "What made that spot special? Why'd you search it?"

He shrugged.

"Five million cash in hundred-dollar bills weighs over a hundred pounds. If Darren had five million dollars cash—which is what they're saying he hid—there aren't many places he could have taken it."

"I see," I said, nodding. "And you think he put his money there?"

"It was a good spot," said Murphy. "That land had everything you could want. Darren owned it, so he knew what the area was like. It was remote, but accessible if you followed the creek. You could have even taken a wheelbarrow to carry the cash.

"To find Darren's money, you've got to think like Darren. These people climbing cliffs and diving into caves are nuts. Darren wouldn't have hidden his money in a cave at the bottom of a cliff. The man wasn't a mountain climber. He was like me. He was smart."

I jotted down notes but didn't think he had said anything profound. Then I thought better of it.

"You think you could have pushed a wheelbarrow along the creek?" I asked.

"Easily," he said. "The ground got a lot of sunlight, so it was dry and hard. You stepped five feet away into the woods, you'd have mud up to your ankles, but right on the edge where the sun hit, you were golden. It was a nice walk on a sunny day."

My team and I had assumed our killer had parked alongside the same road we had. I hadn't checked near the stream. I doubted Marcus had either.

"Tell me about your hike," I said. "Where'd you start?"

He cleared his throat.

"I don't want to say. It's my home base. I've still got other places to search."

I smiled at him and thought through my response.

"Your strategy makes sense," I said. "You're using your brain. That's impressive. I'm not a treasure hunter. I'm just a lady doing her job. If I found the treasure, I'd have to turn it in. I've got no reason to go out looking for Darren's money. You do, and I encourage you to keep looking. If anybody's going to find it, it'll be someone like you. I need to find out who killed my victim. For all I know, his shooter's targeting treasure hunters like you. If you help me find him, I'll be able to keep you safe. If you refuse because you don't want to compromise your search zone, I get it, but you'll be taking a risk. It's your choice, but think it through."

Mr. Murphy went quiet and then leaned back and crossed his arms. He looked at DeAndre.

"That right?" he asked. "If she finds the treasure, she's got to turn it in?"

DeAndre sighed and nodded.

"Yeah," he said, drawing the syllable out. "It's a county government thing. Since Darren Rogers stole from the county, we've got an obligation to return it to the county. Then, it'd get lost again, and a county councilor would start driving a Porsche to his new vacation home."

Murphy snorted and shook his head.

"Isn't that the truth?" he said. "Bureaucrats are only good for screwing up your day and robbing you blind."

DeAndre nodded.

"You got that right," he said, glancing at me. "Some days, though, you get lucky, and your bosses approve you for overtime for staying at work far past your regular stop time."

"Those of us in county government aren't all bad," I said. "And yeah, Officer Simpson and I are lucky because we're both going to be pulling overtime for staying late at work."

Murphy considered us both.

"All right," he said, nodding. "If you're not in the game, I believe you. I'm staying in a cabin I rented. It's by the college. It's a good location. I don't even have to move the car to start the search."

I didn't know the cabin, but if he had parked near Waterford College, I knew the area.

"If you started near the college, you had a pretty good hike," I said. He agreed.

"Started at six in the morning and brought lunch and a canteen," he said. "Like I said, it was an easy walk near the creek."

I nodded and looked at DeAndre.

"Just to settle my curiosity, did you check Mr. Murphy's hands and clothes for GSR?"

"I did," he said. "Came back clear."

Then he wasn't our killer, but he might have walked the same path our shooter had. As soon as we had some light, Roy and I would take a walk. I grabbed a napkin and wiped my mouth.

"I appreciate you calling us when you found the body, and I hope you enjoy the rest of your time in St. Augustine," I said. "Once you're done with dinner, I'll drive you back to your cabin and car."

He closed his pizza box.

"I'm ready to leave now." He paused. "I've been cooperative, haven't I?"

"You have," I said, nodding. "Thank you."

"In the spirit of cooperation, could you take care of a speeding ticket? The missus likes to speed."

I glanced at DeAndre. He closed his eyes but raised his eyebrows.

"Did it happen in Missouri or elsewhere?" he asked.

"Missouri," said Murphy. "Near Perryville. Trooper clocked Janet at ninety-three in a sixty-five-mile-an-hour zone. It's a pricey ticket, but I've been here for, like, four or five hours."

DeAndre drew in a breath and sighed.

"I'll see if I can call in a favor."

Murphy stood up.

"You guys are all right," he said. "I appreciate it."

DeAndre grunted and stood as well.

"I'll drive you back," he said before glancing at me. "You need anything else, Detective?"

"No," I said, already digging through my purse for my keys. I unclipped one from my keyring and slid it down the table toward him. "Take the SUV I signed out this morning. It's got a full tank, and it's comfortable. I've got my personal car in the lot when I leave. Meantime, I'm going to research our victim. Maybe I'll get lucky and find he had a murderous girlfriend."

"You think that's likely?"

"Nope," I said. "It'll be a waste of time, but at least I'll get free pizza out of it."

He looked back to the table.

"I'm not sure if The Pizza Palace is worth it."

"Me, either," I said. "See you tomorrow. Roy and I will do some paperwork and hope we don't die of boredom before dawn."

Chapter 7

DeAndre and Mr. Murphy left after our interview. For a few minutes afterward, I wrote notes in my office and ate cold pizza. Detective Marcus Washington and Kevius Reed arrived after that. Mud caked both of their trousers up to their waists, and they looked tired. Kevius said hello, but then went to his own office to catalog evidence. Marcus leaned against my doorframe and crossed his arms.

"You order enough pizza for everybody?"

"I ordered three mediums," I said. "Todd Murphy—the guy who called in the body— took one. DeAndre took the other. I've got half a medium with tomatoes, green peppers, and Italian sausage left. It's yours if you get cleaned up. You smell like you've been rolling around in manure."

He raised an eyebrow.

"You're hardly flowers and sunshine yourself, Joe," he said, winking. "You traipsed through the same mud I did."

I looked down at myself. I guess I did have mud on my jeans.

"Your honesty and tact are refreshing," I said. "At least go wash your hands."

"Sure thing, Mom," he said, straightening. He left to get cleaned up, and I smiled and finished my interview notes. Marcus didn't stay long afterward, but we walked through our case so far, and he ate the rest of the pizza. We were lucky we still had petty cash for food during long shifts. Last I checked, the budget still had a few thousand dollars in it. It was a lot of money, but with twenty-seven officers, we could blow through it in a month. For now, the department had what it needed, but difficulties loomed. Hopefully, the county would pass a new charter and issue bonds once more. We couldn't keep going like this.

Marcus left my office a little before midnight. Kevius clocked out after that. I took Roy out for a late walk, and then he curled up beside my desk on his bed and slept. I should have gone home, but my apartment was even emptier than my station. At least here I had the chance—however slim—of running into somebody. At home, I was well and truly alone.

I didn't want to contemplate my life, so I focused on the case. Mannie Gutierrez lived in Miami and came here for a reason. His suit told me he had money. With Uber and other ride-sharing apps, he didn't need a car, but I doubted he was sleeping under the stars. He likely had a phone as well. It'd be nice if I could find that.

I started by pulling his credit—which, unsurprisingly, was excellent. He had three credit cards, a two-million-dollar mortgage on a condo, and half a dozen other mortgages on smaller properties. They were rentals. Mannie had millions in liabilities, but minimal credit card debt. Moreover, he was current on all loans and had a retirement fund worth well over a million dollars. I wasn't a forensic accountant, but he looked to be good with money.

Next, I called his credit card issuer's law enforcement helpline. This late, I got through to a representative and explained the situation. After faxing them an official request on department letterhead that confirmed that Mannie Gutierrez was dead under suspicious circumstances and that access to his credit card information would allow me to investigate his death, they emailed me a list of his hundred most recent charges, including one at a hotel near Busch Stadium in St. Louis.

I pushed my chair back and grabbed Roy's leash from the coat hook near my door.

"Hey, dude," I said. "We've got to go."

Roy lifted his head but lowered it again. I lowered my voice.

"Buddy, we've got to go."

He lifted his paw as if to wave me away, so I knelt and scratched his side. Then I hooked the leash to his collar.

"Up and at 'em," I said. "Time to go."

He made a grunting sound and rolled onto his belly and lumbered to his feet. I locked my office and headed out. The night had become chilly. Somewhere up the road, a resident's wind chimes rang in the breeze. I had given DeAndre the keys to my department-issued SUV for the night, so I walked to my old Volvo station wagon and sighed. Someone had written CUNT on the hood with shaving cream.

CUNT was a new one. A couple of weeks ago, somebody had scribbled BITCH on the windows with permanent marker. Nail polish remover erased the marker, but it hadn't felt good to see. Before that, somebody had drawn penises all over my driveway in sidewalk chalk.

As a police officer, people rarely liked me. I tried to treat people well, but I couldn't always be Officer Friendly. Some days, I had to be the bad guy.

Not six months ago, I sent most of our county council to prison for corruption, money laundering, embezzlement, and dozens of other lesser felonies. They were criminals, but they had turned St. Augustine into a thriving tourist town with a vibrant arts scene, excellent restaurants, and amenities that would have made many big cities jealous. We had a Michelin-starred French restaurant in town. Based on our population, it never should have survived. Instead, it thrived with tourist dollars.

Unfortunately, after Darren Rogers died and his co-conspirators went to prison, the bill collectors started showing up. Our former county council had made promises they couldn't keep, and the county had bond payments we couldn't meet. It didn't help that our former county executive had hired a professional shooter to murder his political enemies or that our former sheriff had murdered our former county executive.

Life had become bleak. The tourist trade was down at least fifty percent; restaurants, hotels, and businesses were closing; and our once-excellent school system had gone to a four-day week to save money. The school board was even talking about closing the high school and shipping students to nearby districts. We had gone from one of the best-funded county governments in the state to one of the most impoverished. People looked for someone to blame, and a lot of them found me.

I tried not to care what people thought of me, but it still hurt. Those who didn't blame me still knew what I had done. Until recently, my friend Cheryl ran a coffee shop and bakery called Rise and Grind. When the tourists stopped coming, her shop stopped turning a profit. Then it started eating into her savings. She had to shut down. Cheryl was my friend, and even she told me it was hard not to resent the person who had inadvertently stomped on her dreams.

I put Roy in the hammock slung over my rear seats. He put his head between his paws and went to sleep. Then I grabbed a towel from my trunk, wiped away the shaving cream from my hood, and headed out.

I hit the outskirts of St. Louis in about an hour and parked under the awning of the hotel fifteen minutes later. A bellhop waved and walked toward me as I opened the rear door for Roy. He got out, yawned, and then dove into a play bow. I scratched his ears and hooked a lead to his collar.

"I'm sorry, ma'am," said the bellhop, "but we don't allow animals in the hotel."

"That's fine," I said, unhooking the badge from my belt. "He's my partner, and we're not staying. You got a night manager?"

He nodded and led me inside. It was a gorgeous old building. White marble floors stretched from the front to the rear. Balconies on the second floor allowed guests ample places to sit and overlook the lounge and enjoy the light from the crystal chandeliers. The bar and restaurant were closed and dark. A rack by the front door held day-old copies of *USA Today* and the *St. Louis Post-Dispatch*.

The bellhop led Roy and me to the front desk. A middle-aged man emerged from a small office. His white Oxford shirt looked crisp and clean, as did his navy blazer and trousers. He looked at Roy.

"I'm sorry, ma'am, but we can't allow animals into the building unless they're service animals."

"Roy's a cadaver dog, and I'm Detective Joe Court with the St. Augustine County Sheriff's Department. How are you today?"

He hesitated and straightened.

"I'm well," he said. "Do we have a problem?"

I tilted my head to the left.

"I wouldn't call it a problem," I said. "It's more like a situation. A guest at your hotel was found deceased in St. Augustine County this afternoon. I need access to his room. I'd also like to see any security camera footage you might have of Mr. Gutierrez entering or exiting the hotel. It'd be nice to see if he was alone or with guests."

The manager brought a hand to his forehead before typing on a computer.

"We do have an Emmanuel Gutierrez registered," he said, nodding. "Do you have a warrant to search his room?"

"The dead don't have privacy rights. I don't need a warrant."

He drew in a breath.

"I understand your position, but company policy requires me to see a search warrant before I allow anyone into the room."

I leaned forward and put my elbows on the counter.

"That's a reasonable position," I said, nodding, "but I don't know where Mr. Gutierrez died. For all I know, the crime scene's just upstairs in his hotel room. It's been a long day. I don't want to fight."

"Our rooms have locks. Your scene is safe."

I folded my hands together and sighed.

"Okay. Fine," I said. "We'll play hardball. You heard any sounds like gunfire lately?"

The manager's lips formed a tight, thin line.

"This is a large city. We're close to the interstate and a major train yard. It's a noisy neighborhood, unfortunately. Thankfully, our building is well soundproofed."

"I'm glad for your guests. Reading between the lines, is it fair to say you've heard noises that sound like gunfire in the recent past, but you can't be sure?"

The manager closed his eyes.

"When train cars link up, they can bang together; when cars have accidents on the interstate, you can hear the thump for miles; and when electrical transformers explode, you can feel it in your chest. Cities are noisy. Our guests accept it because they know they are safe within these walls."

"My victim died between one and four this afternoon. Did you hear anything then?"

The manager said nothing. I glanced at the bellhop.

"You hear anything, dude?"

He held up his hands and stepped back.

"I'm staying out of this, ma'am."

I nodded to both men.

"Guys, I'm not here to jam you up. I'm here to do my job. Let me in Mannie's room. He's dead, so he won't complain. That's the easy choice. If you want the hard choice, I'll call the city police department and get a couple of uniformed officers down here. Then, we'll start knocking on doors, asking if anybody heard gunfire between one and four this afternoon. It'll piss off your guests, which I'd rather not do. So what's your preference? Easy or hard?"

The bellhop looked at his boss, his eyes wide. I nodded toward him.

"He works for tips. Come on. Cranky people tip poorly, and your guests will be royally cranky if I wake them up now."

The manager rubbed his eyes and then reached beneath his desk for a keycard.

"Fine," he said. "I'll escort you up. Please don't knock on any doors, and if your dog barks, I'll have to ask you to leave."

I looked at Roy.

"You heard him. No barking," I said. Roy yawned, showing his confusion. I scratched his ears and then looked at the manager. "Thank you for your cooperation. Let's go."

Chapter 8

The manager led Roy and me to a modern, comfortable guest room with a terrific view of Busch Stadium. It had a king-sized bed, low-slung dresser, and a matching chest of drawers. A flat-screen television hung from the wall. In the bathroom, off-white tiles laid in a herringbone pattern covered the floor. The same tiles in a horizontal pattern surrounded the bathtub. A long marble counter and sink held a travel toiletries bag containing a comb, deodorant, and everything else Mannie needed to groom himself. A pill container held a month's supply of Lexapro, an anti-depressant. I found no condoms, birth control pills, or other signs that he had a partner.

The bedroom was more interesting. Two suits hung in the closet. He had planned to stay a few days and meet people, possibly clients. A rolling overnight bag on the dresser held undershirts, pajamas, boxer shorts and some more casual clothing. None of that interested me or told me much about him. The box on the table by the window, though, spoke volumes. It held five prepaid cell phones, still in their packages.

Prepaid phones always captured my interest. Maybe he bought prepaid phones and gave them out to vulnerable people so they could call emergency services, maybe he was paranoid and worried that people were listening to his conversations, or maybe he bought them for clients who worried their competitors were conducting corporate espionage against them. All those things were possible, but nine times out of ten, people purchased prepaid phones in bulk to hide illegal activities.

Beside the box, I found a tan leather messenger bag. I opened it and sighed.

"Well, shit," I said. Roy stopped snoring and popped his head up. "Cash. I've got to call the locals."

Roy lowered his head. I pulled out the cash. We'd have to count the money, but if I believed the markings on the straps, he had twenty-five thousand dollars. I sighed again, pulled out my phone, and called the St. Louis Metro Police Department's liaison office. Nobody answered after four rings, so I hung up and searched my address book for the number of their central dispatcher. She connected me to the watch commander at the downtown police station.

The moment I introduced myself and told him what I had found, he cut me off and said he was sending a pair of detectives. While I appreciated the quick response, this had nothing to do with collegiality or professionalism. This was about money. Even if they had nothing to do with the case, a portion of any cash confiscated at a crime scene in St. Louis would go to the local police department. They wanted their share.

I closed the door, made sure it locked behind me, and headed downstairs to the lobby where I waited for the better part of an hour for two detectives to arrive. St. Louis had a big enough department that its investigators specialized. These guys were general assignment detectives, which meant they worked major theft cases, check and credit card fraud cases, and identity theft.

We talked for about fifteen minutes in the lobby, and then the manager and I led them upstairs where we counted the money. As expected, it came out to exactly twenty-five thousand dollars. The two detectives stared at the piles of cash. Then one looked at me.

"So who in your station knows you're here?"

I forced myself to smile.

"You thinking of robbing me?"

"No, ma'am," he said, shaking his head, his lips flat. "I'm wondering why you came up here alone in the middle of the night. Did you expect to find money?"

I crossed my arms.

"No. I came here hoping to find a hotel room. We're a small department. Detective Washington, my partner, is home with his family. He needs the time with them. We're all overworked."

The other detective nodded and looked around.

"We're not exactly flush with free time here, either," he said before focusing on me. "Aside from the money, what else did you find?"

"Prepaid cell phones," I said. "Feel free to search the room yourselves."

"We will," said the first detective. "So who knows you're here?"

"I don't think it matters, nor am I comfortable with how this conversation is going," I said. "If we want to keep talking, why don't we close up this room and go to your station? I'd be more comfortable where there are witnesses."

The two male detectives looked at one another. Then they looked at me. One kept a neutral expression, but the other twitched, like he was trying to smile but couldn't.

"There's no need for that," he said. "We'll bag the cash, take it to our vault, and go from there. Thanks for the call, Detective."

The second detective started reaching for the money. I cleared my throat.

"I'm going to need a receipt," I said, reaching into my purse for my phone. "While I'm here, I'm going to take some pictures, too."

I lifted my phone to shoulder-height and snapped their pictures. Neither looked amused, but I didn't care. Next, I snapped a picture of the money, including the papers on which we had written our figures while counting it. Finally, I zoomed out and took pictures of the messenger bag and table to orient myself to the scene. I had already taken pictures of the room and furnishings, but these I took for the detectives' sake.

"You have what you needed?" one asked. I nodded.

"Yep, we're good," I said, putting my phone back in my purse and pulling out my wallet. I removed two business cards, which I then handed to the detectives. "That has my cell number and email address on it. Be sure to have your crime lab email me the receipt once you turn in the cash."

"You think this is drug money, honey?" asked the second detective. I shrugged.

"I'd give it at least fifty-fifty odds," I said. "If it's not for drugs, it's for something else illegal. You don't carry around twenty-five grand to buy ice-cream cones. And I'm not honey. I'm Detective Court. It's on the business card I gave you."

The first detective looked at my card and nodded.

"All right, Detective," he said. "We'll be in touch."

I nodded, and the two left. If we could prove Mannie had used the money in furtherance of a criminal enterprise, St. Augustine County would eventually get part of the seizure. The rest would go to St. Louis, the lawyers, and the federal government. It'd take months—if not years—to work its way through the court system, but we could certainly use the boost. That was a concern for the future, though. It'd be daylight in a few hours. I wanted to attend Mannie's autopsy, I needed to find his car, I needed to interview his parents...I had a lot of things I needed to do. To do any of that, though, I needed some sleep.

Roy and I left the hotel, got in my car, and I headed south to St. Augustine. The dog and I lived in a two-bedroom apartment above an old garage beside a beautiful old mansion. That apartment was home for now, but it wasn't a permanent home. We'd find a new place eventually, but for the moment, it was good enough. We went up. I flopped onto the bed. Roy jumped beside me and curled up at my feet. I don't know which of us fell asleep first.

If it were up to me, I would have slept until ten or eleven the next morning. Unfortunately, Roy loved mornings and children. A couple of months back, I used other people's money to create a women's shelter. It helped a lot of people, so many that I had purchased a second building down that road that had once been a bed-and-breakfast. The shelter annex, as we now called it, held five families. The main building held eight. At any given time, there were eight or nine kids living in the building, and Roy loved them all. Mostly, they loved him, too.

At eight, he hopped off the bed and started whining because the kids were outside playing. Then he started pushing my arm with his nose. On most days, his interest in the local kids wasn't a problem because we were already getting ready for the day by the time they got on the bus. Today, I groaned and pushed him away.

"Can't I just sleep, buddy?"

He whined and dove into a play bow, which usually meant he needed to go outside. I closed my eyes and sighed.

"Okay. Fine. We've got work to do, anyway."

I put on jeans and a sweatshirt and stepped into a pair of nice leather slippers my mother had given me the previous Christmas before grabbing his lead. Four kids were playing some kind of game, but they stopped and bounded to us as soon as they saw Roy. Most of the kids petted him, but one bent down and hugged him. If my dog could make those kids' lives better for just a little while, it was worth getting up in the morning.

Once the kids resumed their game, two of their moms came to me to say good morning. Women came to that shelter because they didn't have a safe home elsewhere. I didn't know all their stories, but I had interviewed a few upon entry. I had even arrested the boyfriend of one resident for rape in the first degree. With a little luck, most of the residents would use their time in the shelter to heal and restructure their lives.

I talked to the ladies for a few minutes, but everybody had work to do, and Roy wanted a walk. I liked hearing about their kids, though. Maybe one day, I'd have my own. First, I'd have to meet somebody worth having kids with, so that would be challenge one. I had time. A little, at least.

Roy and I walked around the block, and I finished getting dressed. By the time he and I made it to the office, Sergeant Bob Reitz had long since finished the morning briefing, and

Dr. Gardner had finished his autopsy on Mannie Gutierrez. As expected, Mannie had died of the gunshot wound, and our time of death was approximately one to four in the afternoon yesterday. From the report, it looked as if Dr. Gardner had done a fine job, but I hadn't learned anything new.

In my office, I wrote a report outlining what I had done the previous night. The St. Louis crime lab's evidence vault had also emailed me a receipt for the cash the two detectives had checked in. There were a lot of procedures in place to safeguard that money, but first I had more pressing issues to deal with than proper ownership.

Mannie was an attorney who specialized in maritime law. He would have understood the conditions under which the US Coast Guard could board a vessel at sea, the laws that governed international ports, and the laws that governed salvage operations, possibly even immigration laws. If I were a smuggler looking to move illicit goods into the US through Miami, I'd look for an attorney just like him. That he died with a pile of cash and a box of prepaid cell phones added to the intrigue.

After saving my report, I checked through Mannie's most recent credit card charges again. In addition to the hotel, he had spent almost three hundred dollars at a car rental facility in St. Louis. Most rental car companies kept pretty close tabs on their vehicles, so I called them and asked to speak to the manager. I told her who I was, why I was calling, and requested that she locate Gutierrez's car for me. It took a little work, but she eventually pinged the car's GPS and told me its location. I thanked her and hung up. Then I looked at the dog, who lay on his bed beside my desk.

"My victim's car is half a mile away. You up for a walk, dude?"

He was on his feet before I finished speaking.

Chapter 9

Mannie had parked on a residential road in a historic district a few blocks from downtown St. Augustine. In big cities, the area would have been primed for rapid gentrification, but in St. Augustine, things moved slowly. Older homeowners hung on as long as they could, while younger homeowners rarely had the money required for whole-house renovations. Improvements came in chunks. One house had clearly replaced parts of the front porch, another had new windows, and a third had a new roof. It was already a beautiful street. In five or ten years, it'd be an expensive one, too.

Roy and I walked until we found Mannie's red four-door sedan. The windows were intact, and the doors looked locked. There were two cell phones on the front seat. This was a good break. I pulled out my own phone and called Kevius to let him know I needed him to fingerprint a car. While I waited for him, I started knocking on doors in the hopes that somebody would have seen him park. Unfortunately, no one I spoke to had seen him.

So that was a waste. When I got back to the car, I found Darlene McEvoy kneeling beside it. Darlene was in her mid-fifties and had an advanced degree in chemistry. She could have landed a job with any police department in the country, but she worked in St. Augustine because her husband taught at Waterford College. Without her, a lot of bad people would be walking the streets. That she was agreeable and easygoing, too, added to the package. She stood and smiled at me.

"Hey, Joe," she said. "My tech says you've been keeping him busy lately."

"I have. Kevius has done well, too," I said. "We're lucky to have him."

"We'll be lucky to keep him," she said, turning back to the car. "He's looking at other jobs. His girlfriend's worried that he'll be downsized."

I brought a hand to my neck and tilted my head.

"The worry is well founded," I said. "Hopefully, the Charter Commission will sort things through soon. With a new charter, the county can issue bonds or borrow from the state. Without it, we're in trouble."

"You're making sure they're covering us, right?"

Darlene wasn't my only colleague to ask me questions like that. Officially, I was the commission's non-voting law enforcement adviser. Unofficially, I sat in meetings, took notes, and made suggestions nobody seriously considered. Everybody on the commission was doing his or her best, but at the negotiating table, I couldn't do shit. Nobody considered my voice because I couldn't offer anybody anything. The committee's rules required me to be present for all voting, so, theoretically, I could shut the entire thing down by staying away. I hadn't wanted to exercise that power, but maybe I should.

"I'm doing the best I can. The commission picked me, but they didn't give me any power to do anything."

She nodded and drew in a breath.

"I appreciate that you're doing your best," she said. "It's a shitty situation."

"Yep," I said. "So what have we got?"

"Nothing," she said. "Door handles have been wiped."

I scowled.

"The victim was a lawyer who specialized in maritime law, and I found a ton of cash and several cell phones in his hotel room this morning. He owned a multi-million-dollar condo in Miami and half a dozen rental houses. All told, this guy's worth well over four million dollars, and it's all clean. We might be into something here."

"So you're thinking some kind of organized crime?"

"It's looking like a possibility," I said. "I'm thinking he's moving drugs, guns...some kind of contraband. His shooter dumped him so deep in the woods we never should have found him. It looks like his car is clean, too. Our shooter knew what he was doing."

Darlene nodded and bit her lower lip.

"Why here?"

"That's the million-dollar question," I said. "Mannie could buy drugs, guns, women, chemicals, boats, cars...anything he wanted in Miami. It's weird he'd come here."

Darlene considered and then looked at a tree nearby.

"MDMA?"

I tilted my head to the side.

"It's possible, I guess. I busted a small ecstasy ring a few months ago. They made about a hundred thousand pills a year. A big lab in China or Mexico could produce tens of millions cheaply and efficiently. Mannie would have known how to protect drugs from customs searches, too. I can't see him wasting his time here for ecstasy."

Darlene smiled.

"You think he came here to pay homage to Darren Rogers? The money could be an offering. He could be our own version of Jesús Malverde."

"I don't know who that is."

Darlene lowered her chin and raised her eyebrows.

"Patron saint of narco traffickers, thieves, outlaws, and poor people. You've never seen Breaking Bad? It was a good show."

I snickered.

"If the church starts canonizing people like Darren Rogers, a dead guy in the woods will be the least of our concerns. I'm pretty sure that's a sign of the end of the world. And I don't watch much TV. It's too depressing."

"That, I understand," she said before nodding to the car. "You want me to break in, or do you have the keys?"

"The rental company's supposed to unlock it remotely," I said, pulling out my phone. Darlene nodded, and I called the rental company's manager. She unlocked the doors. Ten minutes later, we learned our shooter had wiped the interior, too. Mannie had left a pair of cell phones on the front seat, but they, too, were wiped clean. Darlene bagged them both and handed them to me. A passcode locked each phone.

Breaking into a phone was hard. Some even wiped themselves clean if you input the password incorrectly too many times. The state crime lab had pretty good technical support techs, and they might be able to break into the phones, but it'd take weeks if not months. By then, our shooter would probably be in Cuba or Brazil. We'd figure something else out.

"Thanks for your work on this," I said, locking the car. "I think we've gotten everything we could out of this."

Darlene agreed and started gathering her gear. Within five minutes, she was gone. Roy and I walked down the street again, and I made a note to myself to try talking to the neighbors again later that evening when people would be home from work. Even if our shooter had wiped down 90 percent of the car elsewhere, he would have spent a few minutes at least wiping down the steering wheel, gear selector, and door handles here. If he had parked in front of my house, I would have wondered what he was doing. Maybe I'd get lucky and find out the people who lived here were as nosy as I was.

As Roy and I walked back to our station, I called the rental car company and told them they could pick up the car at their leisure. They seemed appreciative. After that, I sat and wrote reports, turned the phones over to the evidence locker, and nearly fell asleep at my desk. I rubbed my eyes and looked at the dog.

"Hey, man, do you want to go home?"

Roy panted and licked his nose. That seemed like a yes to me, so I signed out of my computer, locked up the office, and headed to the car. Twenty minutes later, I was asleep on my bed at two in the afternoon. It was glorious…until my phone rang.

Roy lifted his head but put it back down again. Given the chance, he'd probably sleep sixteen to eighteen hours a day. I wish I had that kind of flexibility in my schedule. I rolled over and grabbed my phone from the end table. It was my little sister, Audrey. She didn't usually call this time of day, so I answered without hesitating.

"Hey, Audrey," I said, squinting in the late afternoon light. I pulled my phone away from my ear so I could see the time. It was a little after three.

"You sound tired. Did I wake you up?"

"I caught a murder, so I haven't had a lot of sleep recently. What's up?"

"Oh," she said, her voice soft. "That's good, I guess. You're working, I mean. I was kind of hoping you were sleeping in after a night of drunken debauchery."

I laughed and blinked. My eyes were still misty with sleep, but I sat up anyway.

"I don't even have time to get drunk anymore."

"You have time to have dinner with your sister?"

I swung my legs off the bed.

"It's a little early for dinner, but I've always got time for you. I can get my laptop, and we can chat on video."

"I'm at Mom and Dad's house. PJ's with me. We're making dinner. I was hoping you could join us."

PJ was Audrey's on-again, off-again boyfriend of the past year. They had moved to Chicago together after graduating from college. Audrey and I had talked about PJ, but I had never met him. I hadn't expected to, either. She liked him, and he liked her, but they hadn't been serious about each other. Had his job been in St. Louis or Nashville, they would have probably met other people and drifted apart. Something must have happened if they were making the family dinner. Maybe she realized he was more than a booty call. Good for her. And him. I smiled.

"I'll be there," I said. "Is there room for a plus one, or is this a dog-free event?"

"Dad would never forgive you if you left Roy at home. I'm pretty sure your dog is his best friend."

I looked at the dog and nodded.

"Male friendships are weird, aren't they?"

"Yeah. When PJ's friends come over, they all sit around in our living room, play video games, and say horrible things to each other. Then they laugh."

I tilted my head to the side.

"So are you living with PJ now?"

Audrey went quiet.

"It's complicated. We'll talk tonight."

"Okay," I said, nodding and sitting straighter. "Roy and I'll be there."

She thanked me and hung up. I looked at Roy.

"I hope Audrey isn't homeless."

Roy tilted his head to the side but then licked his nose. Reading into his body language, it meant he was confused but didn't care too much. I slid off the bed. He stood, stretched, and then jumped down beside me.

"Okay, dude," I said. "We're going to go for a walk. Then we'll get dressed and head to Mom and Dad's house."

As soon as I said walk, he dove into a play bow and then stood expectantly, shifting his weight from one side to the other. It seemed like he was up for the plan. As I went to grab his leash, I couldn't help but think of Audrey. I hoped she was okay.

Chapter 10

My parents lived in Kirkwood, Missouri. It had been a great place to spend my late teenage years. Doug and Julia Green gave me my first home. They weren't my birth parents, but they were my mom and dad. Some people were lucky and met their families when they were infants. I had to wait sixteen years to meet my family.

Life was never perfect between us. We argued and carried things too far. Eventually, though, we came back together because we were family. I had a biological brother, too. I hadn't seen a lot of Ian lately, but he was a good kid. I loved him, too. Growing up in the foster care system, I had dreamt of having a big family, of being part of something. After years of spending birthdays and holidays with strangers, I had never imagined I'd one day walk into a room full of people who loved, respected, and accepted me. If I lived to a hundred, I hoped that I'd never forget how special that feeling was.

Roy and I parked in front of Mom and Dad's ranch-style home. My adoptive brother Dylan's Jeep was in the driveway beside Dad's truck, and Audrey's Toyota Camry was parked on the street. My Dad had been a great fireman for many years. Unfortunately, he was a lousy retired person. He couldn't relax. His garden was beautiful, but it didn't require a full-time gardener. He tried golf, but he didn't like it. Two years ago, he had started woodworking. He filled the garage with tools and called it a shop. His bookshelves, end tables, and outdoor furniture filled the house now. He liked it, and Mom encouraged him—mostly so he wouldn't sit around and bug her all day.

The moment I stepped foot on the grass, Dad came out of the front door and knelt down, his arms open. The dog pulled and whimpered. I sighed and let go of his leash. Roy bounded to Dad, jumped on him, and the two tumbled to the lawn. It was like a YouTube video of a toddler seeing his mom after a prolonged absence. Roy jumped around and licked Dad's face, and Dad reached into his pocket for a tennis ball. Instantly, Roy's body went stiff, and he stared at the ball as if nothing else in the world existed.

If I had thrown a tennis ball, Roy would have retrieved it once or twice, but then he would have ignored it. He and Dad would play all day if I let them. They had a special relationship. I wasn't jealous, but I did kind of wish Dad would say hello to me before wrestling with the dog on the front lawn.

"Hey, old man," I said, walking toward them. Roy hurried to my side, nuzzled my hand, and then sat beside Dad on the ground. "You build anything cool lately?"

"Working on a bed," he said, nodding. "Your mom saw it in a store and loved it, but it was a little expensive. I'm going to build it."

"Okay," I said, nodding and smiling. "What does Mom say about that?"

"She's excited."

I nodded again.

"Is she excited for real, or is that just what she tells you?"

He looked at Roy and spoke in a silly, cartoonish voice.

"Your mom is kind of mean, isn't she? Yes, she is. Yes, she is."

Roy yawned, expressing his confusion. Then he stuck out his tongue and started panting. I squeezed Dad's shoulder as I walked toward the house. Before opening the door, I paused.

"Roy would love a walk," I said. "He's been cooped up in the car for an hour."

"I've been waiting for it all day," said Dad, already pushing up from the grass to stand. I left Roy and Dad outside. My parents never had buckets of money, but they got lucky when they bought their house. Today, a doctor would have struggled to buy a home in their neighborhood, but when Mom and Dad went house hunting last, they had stretched and bought it as a fireman and detective. I walked through the entryway to the kitchen at the rear of the home.

The air smelled like garlic and basil. A tall man wearing an apron stood at the stove. He had shaggy brown hair, bushy eyebrows, and a day's worth of stubble on his chin. When he smiled, the corners of his eyes wrinkled. I had met a few of my sister's high school boyfriends. They had been handsome athletes, preoccupied with themselves. This guy looked different.

"You must be PJ. I'm Joe. I'm Audrey's sister."

He crossed the room to shake my hand.

"It's nice to meet you. Yeah, I'm PJ. Audrey and Julia went to the store to get wine. I'm making dinner. Your dad's been hanging out by the front door. I don't know why. Dylan's in the basement playing a video game."

I nodded and considered him.

"If they're out buying wine, that answers one question," I said. "Audrey's not pregnant."

PJ swallowed but said nothing. Then he hesitated and half turned toward the stove.

"I'm making spaghetti and meatballs," he said. "I should get to that."

I blinked a few times.

"That was a joke," I said. PJ sort of laughed, but he had his back to me, so I couldn't see his face. Then I heard footsteps behind me as Dylan hurried up the basement steps. My brother was a student at the University of Missouri-St. Louis and usually lived in a dorm. He was smart, but he let his penis control the wheel too often. It had taught him more than a few lessons lately. He nodded hello to me but focused on PJ.

"Did I hear right? You knocked up my sister?"

He held up his hands.

"I love your sister."

"She's pregnant, isn't she?" asked Dylan, covering his mouth. "That's why you guys came down. She didn't drink last night. Now it makes sense. She's pregnant."

PJ said nothing. Cornering him wasn't fair, but I hadn't planned it, either.

"You guys are adults," I said. "It's okay if she is. Have you told our parents yet?"

"Shit. You'll have to tell them," said Dylan. "Dad's cool, but Mom..." His voice trailed off. "She'll kill you. You've got to run. Mom was a cop. She wouldn't even get in trouble for it."

I stepped in front of my brother.

"It's okay. Mom's got a temper, but you're adults. She'll be excited."

PJ swallowed and drew in a breath.

"Audrey told her a few weeks ago," he said. "We waited to tell you guys in case she miscarried. This wasn't planned. We were just... you know..."

"I get it," said Dylan, nodding. "You have a few drinks, and uglies get bumped. Next thing you know, you're in your girlfriend's kitchen making spaghetti because she's got your bun in her oven. Does Dad know, too?"

PJ nodded. Dylan drew in a breath.

"In that case, I'm going to go back and play Elden War. It's a pretty cool game."

PJ's eyes widened.

"It is good. I just got a PS5, and—"

"Dude," said Dylan, interrupting him and holding out a hand in a stop motion. "You don't have time for games anymore. Have you met my sister? She's a lot. Even when she's not pregnant, she yells all the time. And she's so mean. Instead of buying a PS5, you should have bought a helmet."

PJ straightened. I glanced at him and then looked at my brother.

"Go downstairs and play your game," I said. "You're scaring him, and you're speaking ill of someone he loves. Now he's probably wondering whether he should defend Audrey and piss you off or keep his mouth shut. It's a tough place to be, so let's just wish him well and leave him alone."

Dylan considered and then nodded.

"Yeah, sorry. Good luck, man. And Godspeed."

He went downstairs, and PJ drew in a slow breath.

"Thank you. That was awkward. Audrey said you were the nice one in the family."

"Dad's the nice one," I said, going to the fridge for a beer. I twisted the top off. "I'm going to go out back. Stay here and keep making dinner."

He turned to the stove again. My throat felt tight, my legs felt heavy, and my stomach felt as if someone had just punched me. I forced myself to smile and slipped through the French doors in the kitchen to the backyard. Then I sat down and put my beer on the table.

CHRIS CULVER

I wanted to be thrilled. My sister was starting a new and exciting part of her life. She had a job, an apartment, and someone who loved her. She deserved those things. I wanted to be happy for her. Instead, I felt a weird heaviness in my gut.

Audrey and Mom came back a few minutes later. I congratulated Audrey and hugged my mom. Then I went to the front porch and sat on the steps until my dad and Roy returned. Dad sat beside me. Roy sat at my feet.

"You look sad. You okay?" asked Dad.

"PJ told me about Audrey," I said. "Dylan and I forced it out of him. We didn't mean to."

Dad put his arm on my shoulder, and I leaned against him.

"I'm happy for her," I said, my voice soft. "PJ seems nice."

"He is, I think. Audrey loves him, and he loves her. Plus, he knows that if he's ever mean to her, your mom would kill him."

I swallowed hard but said nothing. Dad was kind and good. I trusted and loved him. I had almost trusted another man once. He was a detective, and I had cared for him. That didn't work out, though.

"I'm tired of being alone."

"You're not alone," said my dad. He let me stay beside him. Then he squeezed my shoulder. "You want me to drive you home? We'll say you got sick."

I considered it, but then shook my head.

"This is her day," I said. "I want to be here for it."

Dad nodded and then lowered his voice.

"They're engaged," he said, his voice a whisper. "PJ came by the house two weeks ago and asked me first. He thought that was important. Afterward, he took Audrey out and proposed. I think they were going to announce it tonight. Mom doesn't know."

I closed my eyes and drew in a breath through my nose.

"That's wonderful."

It was wonderful, too. She deserved to be with someone who loved her—especially now. Neither of us spoke for a few minutes. I drew from that silence. Then I drew in a breath.

"I assumed Dylan would have kids first."

Dad grunted and petted Roy.

"Your mom thought it'd be him, too. I had hoped it'd be you. Audrey was a bit of a shock."

I laughed.

"You and Mom have a little betting pool going?"

Dad smiled and shook his head.

"It wasn't like that. We're parents. We worry about our kids. One day, if you want it, you'll find out what it's like. You'll be a good mom. Everybody lives life on different time-lines. It's unfair to compare yours to someone else's."

I blinked hard and felt my eyes grow glassy.

"I wish my life would get going."

"It will, if that's what you want."

I almost contradicted him, but the door opened, and Audrey stepped out. She didn't need to see me upset on such a happy occasion, so I turned and pretended I was grabbing something from Roy's mouth. Then I rubbed my eyes and looked at her.

"There you guys are," she said. "Dinner will be ready in ten or fifteen minutes."

Dad started to say something, but I cleared my throat and spoke over him.

"Roy ate something he shouldn't have," I said. "I'm going to walk him around the block, so he pukes on a random stranger's lawn instead of Mom and Dad's."

"I appreciate your thoughtfulness," said Dad. "We'll see you inside when Roy's feeling better."

"I hope he feels better," said Audrey. I smiled at her. It was easy because I loved her and was happy for her.

"He will."

She nodded before she and Dad walked inside. Roy didn't follow. He just looked at me, his mouth open and his tongue sticking out as he panted. I petted him.

"Thanks for being here, dude," I said. "Let's walk. We'll come back."

Chapter 11

I stayed at Mom and Dad's house until about nine. It was hard and wonderful. Audrey and PJ were both happy. Mom and Dad gushed over their future grandkid. Even Dylan seemed excited. I was happy, too. Before leaving, I hugged Audrey and told her I loved her, and I shook PJ's hand. I didn't know when I'd see them next, but maybe Roy and I could drive to Chicago to visit in the next couple of months. It'd be fun.

The drive home was easy. When I arrived, I walked Roy around the block, opened a bottle of vodka, put on a Thelonious Monk album, and got drunk.

I had a funny relationship with alcohol. Some days, I hated it. Other days, I loved it. When my workload was heavy, I didn't even think about it. I would come home so exhausted that I'd flop on the bed, fall asleep, and wake up refreshed the next morning. On the slow days, when I had time to think, booze became more appealing.

For most of my life, I had pushed away everybody around me. My biological mother had lost me to the foster care system when I was a child, and I had bounced around from

CHRIS CULVER

house to house. I had almost found a home once. Heather and Todd Cohen had wanted to adopt me. I was in elementary school, and I had lived in their house for a few months. I loved them, and I think they loved me. With every hug and kind, encouraging word, I trusted them more. Once I realized that, I knew I had to leave.

You had to let people hurt you. Erin Court, my biological mother, had taught me that. Before she lost me, Erin had broken my heart every day of my young life. She was a drug-addicted prostitute who left me in the car when she visited clients in cheap motels and who forced me to beg for food from the managers of restaurants at closing time. I didn't know people lived differently.

I loved Erin, despite what she had done to me. She had yelled at me; she had asked me to buy her drugs when she was in rehab—I was a teenager at the time—and she had abandoned me when I needed her most. When I was a sixteen, my foster father drugged and raped me on the couch in his living room. He had done it to other girls, too. I had needed Erin, but she didn't come. My biological mother, through her actions and inactions, taught me I could never trust anyone. My real mother and father—Doug and Julia—had taught me how wrong she was.

I wanted somebody who would love me despite my hang-ups, somebody worth trusting, somebody patient, forgiving, and kind. Unfortunately, I had never met anybody like that. Maybe I never would. So I drank until I passed out. It was easier than dealing with feelings I didn't want to have.

Roy, as was his custom, woke me up the next morning by standing on the bed, shaking his body, and licking my face. My head pounded, my belly ached, and my eyes stung in the early morning light. I pushed Roy's face away from my own, and he jumped off the bed and barked, his tail wagging as if this were the greatest day of his life.

Some days, I wished I had been born a dog.

After making coffee, I changed into leggings and a sweatshirt and took Roy for a run. My head felt as if a maniacal fairy were hammering the inside of my skull, and my belly ached. It was my penance for being an idiot and getting drunk. By the time I finished running half an hour later, I felt better than I had upon waking. Afterward, I fed Roy and drank coffee and thought through my day.

The county's Charter Advisory Committee met at noon, but I had the morning to myself, and I dove into my work. I grabbed my laptop and my case notepad and flipped to a clean page before checking my email. The coroner had already emailed me his preliminary findings, but he had submitted his official report late yesterday. Mannie Gutierrez had died of a penetrating injury to his thoracic cavity consistent with a gunshot. Likely, he had died instantly.

Aside from the chest wound, Dr. Gardner had found no other major injuries to his person, no burns, no visible injection points, little damage to his liver, and an intact septum. If he had smoked crack, his fingertips would have had distinct calluses; if he had injected intravenous drugs, he would have track marks; and if he had snorted cocaine, the doctor would have noticed damage to his septum. His liver would have likely been shot to hell, too. By all appearances, Mannie had been healthy when he died.

The round that killed Mannie had passed clear through him. Gardner noted that both the entry and exit wounds were sizable, but he didn't speculate on the round itself. He noted a few things, though. First, the victim had no defensive wounds anywhere. He didn't fight back. Second, the victim's skin was clear. If he had been shot with a .45-caliber pistol at close range, there'd be stippling on the victim's skin where burned gunpowder hit the exposed flesh. There'd also be powder all over his clothes. The doctor had found none, though. Gardner's note emphasized that the round passed through the victim's sternum, heart, and back without deviating from its course. Whatever he was shot with, it was big.

That was an important detail. The entry wounds from a large-caliber pistol like a .45 were usually small—nickel-sized or less. The wound on Mannie's chest was a gaping hole. Someone had shot him with a long gun—maybe a shotgun with a lead slug or a large-bore rifle.

It was a little after nine. Trisha, our dispatcher, was a churchgoer, so I figured she'd be awake. I called her cell phone and waited through two rings for her to answer.

"Trisha, hey, it's Joe Court. You got a minute?"

"Maybe just a minute," she said. "I'm teaching Sunday school today."

"I won't waste your time," I said. "I'm looking over the autopsy file for the Mannie Gutierrez murder. He died on Friday afternoon. Did we get any calls about gunshots or loud noises on Friday?"

She paused.

"I'd have to check the call sheet, but I don't think so," she said. "We had traffic accidents, petty theft at the grocery store, and a domestic dispute; I remember those." She paused. "I don't think we had any reports of shots fired."

"That's what I thought. Thanks."

She wished me well and hung up. I jotted down my thoughts. St. Augustine County was rural, and a significant portion of our population enjoyed outdoor activities. They hunted, fished, camped, canoed, kayaked—pretty much everything one does in Boy or Girl Scouts. In town, people owned guns, but they didn't shoot them in the streets. If they did, the neighbors called the police.

The evidence led me to believe Mannie had died deep in the county after being shot by a long gun. It sounded like a hunting accident that the hunters tried to cover up. Those didn't happen often, but occasionally hikers would veer off established trails and end up in areas with game. Accidents happened, especially with drunk hunters.

But Mannie hadn't put on a five-thousand-dollar suit to hike through the woods. And even if he had, he wouldn't have parked in a residential area. We had plenty of public parks with trails and expansive parking lots.

Putting it all together, I realized that I barely knew more today than I had on Friday when we found Mannie's body. We didn't know where he died, we didn't know what caliber of weapon was used to kill him, we didn't know why someone would want him dead, we didn't know who he intended to give his prepaid cell phones to, we didn't know what he planned to do with his cash, and we didn't know why he was in St. Augustine.

Still, we knew a few things. Human beings had the same basic needs: food, clothing, and shelter. We had seen his clothing, and I had visited his hotel room, but I had seen no food yet.

Until recently, St. Augustine had almost fifty restaurants. Mannie had to have eaten somewhere. I called up my reports and searched my laptop until I found an email from Mannie's credit card company that listed his last hundred charges. He had eaten in St. Louis a few times, and he had gone to the grocery in St. Augustine once. He had also eaten at a Chinese restaurant in St. Augustine and spent twenty-nine dollars. I ate at the same restaurant often and rarely spent over fifteen bucks. Maybe he just had a huge appetite, but I doubted it. He had company.

I made sure I had a clean picture of his face and then headed out. The restaurant occupied the bottom floor of a two-story, brick row house. It had a vacant storefront to its left. The storefront to its right held a custom card and print shop. By their display window out front, they were particularly proud of their graduation and wedding announcements.

The Mystic Garden—our Chinese place—needed a makeover, but the food was good. I went to the glass front door and peered inside. It was locked, and the dining room was empty. I knocked a few times, but nobody answered. They weren't expecting visitors, so I walked around the block until I found the alleyway that ran behind the businesses. Then I followed the sounds of banging pots until I found the rear door. A middle-aged man in black trousers and a white shirt stood outside the restaurant's open doorway.

I flashed my badge at him, and he tossed the butt of a cigarette to the ground.

"Can I help you?" he asked, smashing his cigarette with his foot.

"I hope so," I said. "I'm looking for information about a customer who ate at your restaurant on Thursday. His name is Mannie Gutierrez. I'm trying to figure out if he was alone or with a guest."

"We have a lot of customers, miss," he said. "And we know little about most. I don't know what you expect us to have."

"I was hoping you might have a surveillance camera in your dining room," I said. "Mr. Gutierrez is dead. He may have eaten with his murderer."

He sighed and reached into his pocket for his pack of cigarettes.

"You mind?" he asked. I shook my head, and he lit up. "We keep a camera behind the register, but it's for the staff. We put it in after a guest complained that one of my employees made a copy of his credit card. Ling's a good kid, though. She wouldn't have stolen from anyone in a million years."

"Would your staff remember?"

He took a drag on his cigarette and shrugged.

"Doubtful," he said. "What time did he come?"

"A little after eleven on Thursday."

"I'll ask my servers. You want to stick around?"

"If they're available, just bring them out here. I'd rather talk to them in person."

He hesitated, but then nodded and went inside. Five minutes later, he came out with two young women. One wore black pants and a sweatshirt from UCLA. The other wore a black dress and leggings. I introduced myself and explained why I was there. Both women looked uneasy.

"The lunch rush is pretty busy," said the UCLA fan. "We had five or six tables each. We don't have time to chat with customers."

"I understand it's a long shot," I said, "but it's important. Anything you tell me is helpful."

They didn't seem enthusiastic, but they looked at Mannie's picture. The UCLA fan shrugged and stepped back. The young woman in the dress studied him and nodded.

"He came in. He was with a doctor," she said. "They tipped well."

"You sure?" I asked. She nodded. "How do you know he was with a doctor?"

"She wore scrubs from St. John's. I've seen her, but I wouldn't say she's a regular. She's pretty. She has brunette hair down to her shoulders."

I took out my notepad and jotted down the details.

"You know her name?"

Both women shook their heads.

"She older than me, you think?" I asked. The young woman in the dress squinted before nodding.

"She was, but not by a lot."

So she was Mannie's age. We talked for another few minutes, but they couldn't remember any additional details. That was okay. I had what I needed.

Before leaving, I gave them my business card and asked them to call me if the woman came in again. Then Roy and I hurried to my station. I had reports to write, but I had a young medical professional to find. I had an actual lead. It felt pretty damn good.

Chapter 12

I had about an hour before my meeting with the county's Charter Commission, but already our station had come alive. On most Sunday mornings, we'd have a dozen officers on call but nobody in the building. The Charter Commission meetings, though, seemed to bring out the best and worst of our local population. We held them in the largest courtroom in the courthouse. The room had excellent acoustics, and the building had metal detectors at each entrance. Surveillance cameras captured every proceeding.

The Charter Commission's first meeting had lasted fifteen minutes before a man named Paul Schweitzer called in a bomb threat. Schweitzer called it in from his neighbor's home phone, so we arrested him for making terroristic threats and swept the building with bomb-sniffing dogs. We didn't find anything, and upon interrogation, Schweitzer admitted to making a false threat. He claimed the threat was a political protest against a totalitarian regime bent on...doing something to him. He never specified which rights of his we threatened.

Marcus Washington and I questioned him for almost two hours. He was scared. Schweitzer's world was changing, and he wasn't prepared for that change. He was older than me—probably in his mid-fifties—and he had lived in St. Augustine County his entire life. For his entire life, he had understood how the rules worked. If he left people alone, they'd leave him alone. He lived on twelve acres that had been in his family since the Civil War. His property lacked running water or electricity, but he didn't care.

Mr. Schweitzer was a homesteader, and he had lived off the grid. He had hunted deer, rabbits, and squirrels, and he had grown and canned his own vegetables. During the Spring Fair, he had rented a table in the arts space and sold handcrafted canes, cutting boards, picture frames, and other small woodworking projects. The little money he earned had bought him everything he couldn't make himself. To hear him tell it, he had lived like a king.

All that changed when Darren Rogers died. Prior to Rogers's death, the county surveyor hadn't visited the Schweitzer homestead in years. After the accountants discovered the financial hole we were in, though, they tasked the Assessor's Office with finding additional revenue. Schweitzer hadn't paid taxes in almost twenty years, so he was an obvious enforcement target. He ignored the county's letters and chased off the assessor with a shotgun.

We would have sent uniformed officers to the place to talk to him, but he didn't give us the chance. He called in a threat, and we arrested him. He wanted to go to jail. Prison was easier than facing a world he didn't understand.

I hung my badge on a lanyard around my neck and checked my holster to ensure my pistol was snapped in place before locking my office door. Bob Reitz and several officers were already in the lobby, getting ready to head out. Each officer wore a tactical vest and a pistol, but none carried rifles. I nodded to the sergeant and Officer Alisa Maycock, who was standing close to him.

"What's shaking, Bob?"

He smiled.

"Just enjoying my Sunday morning."

I looked at Alisa.

"Any news?"

"The racists are out," said Alisa. "They set up early before the counter-protesters could arrive. The reverend plans to make an address."

That explained the glum faces, at least. Like most places, St. Augustine had people of all beliefs, faiths, creeds, and orientations. Usually, we got along pretty well—if more by accident than purpose — but the Church of the White Steeple, our local racist stronghold, liked to stir shit up.

"They leave the kids at home, or did they bring them?" I asked.

"They brought them," said Bob. "Whether they'll stay is another story."

The presence of their children was a good sign. Many White Steeple members would say horrible, racist things in front of their children, but they wouldn't endanger them. If they did, we'd have Children's Services pay a visit to their compound.

"Do your best," I said. "I don't know what help I can give, but I'll be inside."

Bob smiled.

"Given the state of St. Augustine right now, I'd take the racists over your job any day."

"Me, too," I said. "See you guys later."

They wished me well, and Roy and I started walking. The courthouse wasn't far. As Alisa had said, the racists held signs, flags, and kids on the sidewalk. They shouted at cars that drove past, but they weren't hurting anybody. Counter-protesters shouted from another location. They, too, held signs and carried flags, and also shouted at passing cars. Neither side openly carried firearms.

I kept my head down, walked past them, and headed toward the building. The courthouse's security team kept the place shut tight. They waved me through the security checkpoint and suggested I meet the commission in the second-floor conference room.

For half an hour, I sat and waited while the commission members chatted. Then we filed into the courtroom. I had testified in a lot of courtrooms over the years, including this one. Most had a judge's bench, a witness stand, and tables for the prosecutor and defense. This was an appellate court-room, though, so it had seating for seven judges. Its wood paneling, decorative molding, and chandelier made me feel small in comparison.

Right at noon, we opened the doors, and the crowds started pouring in. Today, the commission had scheduled a listening session, allowing community members to line up and tell us what they wanted from their government. Each speaker had two minutes, so theoretically, we'd get through twenty-five to thirty residents. In actual experience, few speakers limited themselves to two minutes. We tried turning off the microphones, but that just led to people shouting. Hopefully, today would be more orderly than past meetings.

The first speaker was a middle-aged woman who used her time to speak about the importance of education, partic-ularly special education. She wanted the charter to reflect the county's commitment to a five-day school week and eq-uitable education for all children. That seemed reasonable. The second speaker wanted the charter to declare St. Au-gustine a special district for marijuana cultivation, sale, use, and research. We thanked him for his time. The third speaker glared at the second speaker and spoke about the evils of marijuana and demanded that the county charter make the cultivation of marijuana illegal. We thanked her, too.

Then came Reverend Michael Clarke, the official leader and spokesperson of the Church of the White Steeple. He wore a suit, and he nodded to us all.

"Afternoon, folks," he began. "You all know me, and I know you. You're good folks, all, and you've been put in a difficult situation. I'm here to make your lives easier. I know what this county wants and needs."

Clarke reached behind him to a member of the gallery. The gallery member handed him a thick stack of paperwork. Clarke thanked him and turned to us.

"I have in my hand the signatures of five hundred of my fellow St. Augustine residents, and they know what they want St. Augustine to be: a home and community solely for our white brothers and sisters. It's time we stood up for what's ours."

Most of the gallery started booing, but a depressingly large—and very vocal—group started cheering. I slumped in my chair and swore under my breath. The booing and cheering continued for another minute. Jerry Baker, a high school math teacher and assistant football coach who sat on the commission, stood, cupped his hands around his mouth, and yelled for people to settle down. I thought he'd succeed, but then, as if sensing we would end the meeting, people began pushing toward the microphone for their turn.

I stood up and shook my head.

"Calm down," I said, scanning the room. We had five officers inside for crowd control and maybe two hundred civilians. This could spin out of control. "Everybody's going to get their turn. Calm down. Don't worry. Your voices matter."

And then it happened. A loud, almost metallic crack echoed through the chamber. It hadn't come from inside. The walls muffled the noise, but it was clearly a gunshot.

The room went quiet. For one split second, nobody moved. My eyes focused on the bailiff at the main exit. He wasn't moving.

"Everybody stay seated," I shouted. "You're safer here than outside. Nobody needs to panic."

The crowd looked uneasy, but nobody moved. The bailiff had locked the rear doors but hadn't touched the side doors. Anybody could come in. I slowly pulled my phone out, turned so the crowd couldn't see me, and called Bob Reitz's cell phone. He answered immediately.

"Joe, hey," he said. "We've got a situation out here. Idiot shot himself in the leg reaching for his pistol. I've got my belt on his thigh now as a tourniquet, but he's lost a lot of blood. Anybody in there a paramedic? We're doing what we can out here, but we're out of our depth. People are getting angry. The white supremacists think the anti-racists shot him. The anti-racists think he was shooting at them. Nobody's reaching for firearms, but they're not backing down, either."

I swore under my breath and looked toward the gallery.

"Hold tight," I said. "I've got a guy who can help. I'll bring him out in a minute."

Bob agreed, and I hung up. I tied Roy's leash to my chair and closed my eyes tight before stepping down from the judge's platform to join the gallery. The man beside Michael Clarke stood as I approached, but Clarke put a hand on his side, telling him to sit back. Then Clarke stood and nodded to me.

"Detective," he said. "It's always nice to see you."

"You, too," I said. "We need to talk."

He looked to his followers.

"I keep no secrets from my friends."

I looked to the racists. Some gave me hostile looks. Others merely looked disinterested. I squeezed my jaw tight, loath to give a racist showman an even bigger stage than he already had.

"There's a situation outside. I need you to de-escalate it before people get hurt."

"Blessed are the peacemakers, for they shall be called children of God," he said, smiling. "I'll help you, of course, but I'll need a favor in return."

"What favor?" I asked, crossing my arms and trying not to look too angry.

"When the time's right, we'll talk."

"Fine, Don Corleone, let's go," I said, motioning him forward. Clarke took a step and then turned toward his followers.

"I have to bring peace outside," he said, looking toward the commission members. "This only proves the necessity of my proposal. Think about it. War or peace. Civilization or barbarism. That's the choice—"

I grabbed his elbow. If he had been older, I would have been gentler.

"We've got to go, folks," I said, interrupting him. "The longer we dawdle, the more likely people outside will be hurt."

I led Clarke through the exits and outside the building. Immediately, one group of protesters started cheering, while the other started booing. Bob put up his hand and furrowed his brow. I held a hand toward him and leaned closer to Clarke.

"De-escalate this and send your people home before they start pulling guns. If this turns into a shootout, I'll arrest you for inciting a riot and felony murder."

Clarke nodded and turned to the racists.

"My friends," he shouted. Instantly, the racists went quiet. The anti-racists started shouting louder, but Bob and I waved them down. They, too, quieted. "Our struggle is real and obvious, but now isn't the time for bloodshed. Go home and regroup. Our brother is injured because he was provoked by barbarous thugs. We won't allow them to take more of us. As Jesus said to Peter, I say to you: Put your sword back in its sheath."

The anti-racists booed again—rightfully so considering the racist had shot himself in the leg while trying to reach for a gun. As Clarke had requested, though, his group dispersed.

With the racists gone, the anti-racists had no one to scream at. They departed as well, leaving the sidewalks mostly empty. A siren shrieked in the distance. Bob looked at me and exhaled.

"I don't know if I should thank you or lecture you about the risks of enabling a shithead racist who's going to use us and claim the police are on his side."

I sighed and shook my head.

"You use the tools you've got," I said. "Even the shitty ones. How's our shooter?"

"Alive."

"Everybody else is alive, too. Let's call that a win and move on."

Chapter 13

It took us almost two hours to sort out the mess in the courthouse. Nobody inside was hurt, so they shuffled out, some looking shell-shocked. Outside, Bob arrested the gunshot victim for making terroristic threats, reckless endangerment, and a host of other crimes. We got lucky. If he had pulled that pistol and shot somebody, we could have dozens of body bags instead of one idiot with a wound.

While Bob worked at the courthouse, I returned to the station and wrote a detailed report for the prosecutor. Dozens of protesters had witnessed the shooting, but each statement provided only a small view of a larger event. We needed a cohesive narrative to put the shooting into context. Without that narrative, the prosecutor might undercharge the shooter, believing he had suffered enough. A superficial gunshot wound wasn't enough, though. He could have killed people.

At about three, I saved my document to our department's cloud server and returned to my regular duties. Mannie Gutierrez had died after eating with a St. John's hospital employee. I needed to find her, so I walked Roy to my car and drove to the hospital. In a world where fewer and fewer small towns had any sort of emergency medical care, St. Augustine was lucky to have a hospital with seventy-five beds, an ER open twenty-four hours a day, and specialists who could tackle an awful lot of injuries and illnesses. If I needed an organ transplant, or if I had cancer or another serious disease, I'd go to St. Louis, but for most things, I could stay local. I appreciated that.

I parked and asked to speak to an administrator at the receptionist's desk. It took a little while, but eventually the hospital's Assistant Operations Manager came to meet me. She was probably fifty, and she wore brown slacks and a white shirt that hung off her thin torso and billowed when she walked. Instead of answering my questions in the lobby, we walked to the security office's conference room, outside the view of any patients.

"Afternoon, and thanks for meeting me," I said, reaching into my purse for my wallet. I pulled out a business card and slid it across the conference table toward her. "As I told the receptionist, I'm Detective Joe Court with the St. Augustine County Sheriff's Department. The business card has my cell phone, email address, and work phone. I'm rarely at my desk, so my cell is the easiest way to get in touch with me if needed."

She looked at the card and nodded but didn't pick it up. Her smile was stiff.

"I'm Janelle Rivas. What can I do for you, Detective Court?"

"I'm investigating the death of a man named Mannie Gutierrez. Is that name familiar?"

She blinked and raised her eyebrows before shaking her head.

"It isn't, but we have almost three hundred full-time staff members and over a hundred part-time workers. I don't know everybody." She paused and lowered her voice. "Is he one of ours?"

"I don't think so," I said. "He's an attorney, and we found his body in the county on Friday afternoon. We believe he died earlier that day. The day prior to his death, we believe he ate lunch with someone affiliated with this hospital. She was approximately thirty to thirty-five, had brunette hair, and she wore hospital scrubs. She's one of the last persons to have seen my victim alive."

She drew in a breath.

"That describes dozens of employees," she said. "What color were her scrubs?"

I flipped through my notes before glancing up.

"I do not know. I didn't think to ask."

Ms. Rivas pushed back from the table and reached into her pocket for a big cell phone. She flicked a finger across the screen and typed.

"When did this lunch take place?"

"Thursday at eleven."

She focused on her phone again and then glanced up.

"If I assist you today, will I be consigning one of my employees to prison?"

I considered my answer. Ms. Rivas's title was Operations Manager, but she could have been a lawyer. I liked lawyers. They understood the legal system, and they understood that they shouldn't take my questions personally. Unfortunately, their legal training sometimes left them inflexible.

"She's a person of interest," I said. "I have no reason to believe she hurt Mr. Gutierrez, but I need to speak to her all the same."

"If you don't believe my employee hurt Mr. Gutierrez, why do you need to speak with her?"

I forced myself to smile.

"Unfortunately, this is an active investigation. I'm limited in what I can say."

Ms. Rivas leaned forward.

"As an administrator at this hospital, I'm duty-bound to protect the people inside it—patients and employees. You've given me very little reason to help you out. Presumably, I'm not interfering with your investigation by refusing to cooperate. Correct?"

I squeezed my jaw tight before answering.

"You're not engendering good will with the local police, either."

She seemed to consider but then shrugged.

"I think I can live with that," she said, standing. "I'll escort you to the front door. In the future, please leave your dog at home."

I pushed back from the table and stood.

"He's a certified cadaver dog," I said. "He's my partner. Where I go, he goes."

She smiled.

"Then I'll escort you both to the front door. Have a nice day, Detective. In the future, if you need medical assistance, we're more than happy to help. For any other inquiries, I'll have you contact our general counsel."

"Sure," I said, wrapping Roy's leash around my hand to keep him close. The dog, Ms. Rivas, and I left the conference room and crossed the lobby. At the front door, she wished me well and watched as I put Roy in my car. I was frustrated, but I didn't dwell on it. Instead, I jotted down notes about the conversation. Then I stopped. Ms. Rivas had asked me what color scrubs the woman wore to lunch.

I considered that before grabbing my phone and navigating to the hospital's website. It took about ten minutes before I found the HR department's page and another five minutes before I found the employee handbook. I browsed until I found a section on employee uniforms. Each department, apparently, had different colored scrubs. Those who worked in pediatrics wore purple, those in radiology wore gray, pharmacists wore black, paramedics wore polo-style shirts...the list went on for about a page.

My phone said it was a little before four. It was very late for lunch or early for dinner, but I didn't care. I drove toward The Mystic Garden and parked out front. The dining room was empty. The smoker emerged from the kitchen. He smiled at first, but then he recognized me, and the smile became pained.

"Can I help you, Detective?"

"I hope so," I said. "Is it too late to order takeout?"

His face went serious.

"It's never too late to order takeout."

I didn't anticipate having a lot of time to cook dinner in the next few days, so I ordered enough food for four people, figuring I could eat the leftovers for dinner. Before the smoker could take my order to the kitchen, I cleared my throat.

"Are your servers still around?"

He paused.

"My daughters are. You talked to them earlier."

"Can I talk to them again? I've got one question."

He nodded and said he'd send them out. Roy and I sat and waited on a bench near the front door. The two young women emerged from the kitchen about five minutes later. They both smiled at me.

"Dad's making your dinner," said the UCLA fan. "What can we do for you?"

I looked at the young woman in the black dress.

"You mentioned my murder victim ate lunch with a doctor. What color were her scrubs?"

She blinked and frowned for a moment.

"Blue, I think. A light blue. Like a sky blue."

"Awesome," I said. "Thank you."

They smiled and went back to the kitchen, and I pulled out my phone. According to the hospital's HR manual, my doctor was a surgeon. I browsed the surgery department's page until I found a directory. The hospital employed three general surgeons, a surgical oncologist, an orthopedic surgeon, and a colorectal surgeon. Four were men, but two were women. Unless I got really unlucky, my mystery doctor was Cassandra Rice. She was beautiful. Lucky Mannie.

Fifteen minutes after I placed my order, the smoker came out of the kitchen with my food. I took it home, put it in my fridge, and fired up my laptop. According to the license bureau's database, Cassandra lived just outside town. I recognized the road, but I couldn't remember the particular house. She was thirty-six, five foot five, and weighed a hundred and thirty pounds. She didn't live alone, either. Matthew Rice, presumably her husband, also listed the address as his primary residence. He was fourteen years older than Cassandra. It was quite an age gap.

Love, lust, loathing, and loot. They were the four L's, the four most common motives I found in murder cases. Cassandra was a beautiful surgeon. Mannie was a handsome, successful attorney Cassandra's age. Everybody I had spoken with loved Mannie. He was good with women, he loved his mom, and he knew how to take care of money. He was a good match for a surgeon. They ran in similar social classes, they were both well educated, and they might have had some overlapping interests.

From the start, I had been missing a piece of the puzzle. This might have been it. I closed my eyes and let my mind wander.

Mannie and Cassandra met somehow, and they fell in love—or at least in lust. He flew to St. Louis, checked into a hotel, and bought prepaid cell phones, which he and Cassandra could use to hide their relationship. They had lunch together at The Mystic Garden. Unfortunately, Matthew somehow learned about his wife's relationship. He became jealous and shot Mannie. Then he dumped the body in the woods.

Todd Murphy, the man who found Mannie's body, said the ground near the creek was firm. Matthew could have put Mannie's corpse in a cart or wheelbarrow and carried the body himself. The timber company wouldn't have found him before animals scattered the bones. We would have been lucky to ID him, let alone find a suspect. Instead, because of a stupid YouTube video about a treasure hunt, we found him within hours.

It was a skeleton of a theory, but I liked it. It gave me a framework through which I could understand the case. Now, I needed to fill it out and see if it held up.

Chapter 14

M atthew and Cassandra lived about five miles outside the town of St. Augustine. I knew the area pretty well, so the drive was easy. The Rices lived on an undulating, hilly plot big enough that I could barely see the home from the main road. I turned down the driveway. The home's front lawn had room for horses, cattle, or crops, but no animals grazed, and no food grew. Instead, grass stretched from the horizon to a line of woods beyond the house. Silver maple trees lined the driveway and swayed in the evening breeze. I opened my windows. The air was crisp and sweet.

At one time, I had owned a similar property—five acres that I had purchased and over a hundred that I had inherited from my neighbor, Susanne. I missed my old country house, but even more, I missed my friend. Everyone deserved a friend like Susanne. I wished I hadn't lost her as I had.

As I drove, the white siding of the Rice's two-story farmhouse came into clearer view. A pair of rocking chairs sat on the covered front porch, while big picture windows would have allowed ample morning sun into the front rooms. A matching detached garage had room for four cars. I parked on a paved parking pad beside the garage and got Roy out. A man opened the door before I knocked. His white polo shirt draped off his shoulder and tapered down to a narrow waist. He was handsome and fit.

"Matthew Rice?" I asked. His eyes flicked to Roy before he nodded. I unhooked my badge from my belt. "I'm Detective Joe Court with the St. Augustine County Sheriff's Department. Everything's fine. I'm not here to deliver bad news, so don't worry about that. How are you this afternoon?"

He looked quizzical, but then he shrugged.

"Fine, I guess," he said. "But if you're looking for donations to a charity, skip the chat, and tell me how much you want."

I smiled.

"Unfortunately, I'm here about a case. Are you married to Dr. Cassandra Rice?"

He straightened and nodded.

"I am. Why?"

"Is she around?"

He crossed his arms.

"No."

"Will she be around later?"

"If you tell me why you need to speak to my wife, perhaps I can help you."

I tilted my head to the idea and considered him.

"You work in the ER at St. John's."

He shifted.

"I do."

"You patched me up once. You're a good doctor."

His smile was tight.

"I do my best."

"I try my best, too. Just like you, I make decisions based on imperfect information. Sometimes that imperfect information leads me astray, but other times, it leads me correctly. Today, my incomplete information led me to your house. I need to talk to Mrs. Rice. Will she be around later?"

He looked down and sighed, his arms still tight.

"What information led you to Cassandra?"

"This is an ongoing investigation. I can't get into it. Sorry."

He drew in a slow breath.

"Does Cassandra need a lawyer?"

"That's a personal decision. If she'd like a lawyer for questioning, she can have one."

"It's a personal decision, but you won't give me any information that I can use to make it. That's not helpful."

I considered what to tell him. Cassandra's meeting with Mannie could have been innocent. The servers from The Mystic Garden had said the lunch rush was busy, so maybe Cassandra and Mannie shared a table to avoid a wait. Or maybe they had a business meeting. Or they could have been having an affair. I didn't know enough to make a judgment, and I certainly didn't know enough to inject doubt and jealousy into a stranger's marriage. A white lie seemed justified.

"The sheriff's department has received reports of break-ins in the area. Callers have said they've seen figures walking around at night, but they weren't able to give descriptions because it was dark. We've had some vehicle break-ins, too. Anything like that happen around here?"

"We have a garage. Nobody's breaking into our cars."

"Have you seen strangers around the neighborhood?"

He narrowed his eyes.

"What does this have to do with my wife?"

"Do you or your spouse own any firearms?" I asked.

He snorted and threw up his hands.

"Why does that matter?"

"Because we suspect the thieves might have been looking for guns or drugs. You and your spouse are both physicians, so you both have access to prescription drugs. You wouldn't keep drugs in your car, I know, but patients might not realize that. My station has received reports of unknown individuals in your area. It's possible a patient has followed you or your spouse home from work because they think you are more likely than the average person to have guns and drugs. Do you own any firearms?"

"We do," he said, his voice sharp. "We keep them in a gun safe. In addition, I have a pistol in our bedroom for personal protection. Is that a problem?"

"Not at all," I said, shaking my head. "Do you own a shotgun?"

He sighed.

"Yes. A Remington 870."

"Do you know where that gun is right now?"

He paused. I waited for him to speak. Finally, he sighed again.

"It's in my gun safe. Did a patient threaten my wife? Is that why you're here?"

"I have no reason to believe you or your wife are in danger," I said.

He threw up his hands again.

"Then why are you here?"

I smiled.

"Just looking for information. Were you around the house on Friday afternoon?"

He drew in a breath and shrugged.

"I don't remember," he said.

"That was two days ago," I said, smiling. "It'd be really helpful to know whether you were here."

He closed his eyes and clenched his mouth shut.

"I was off. Last week, I worked Monday through Thursday and had a long weekend. I go back to work on Tuesday."

"That is a long weekend," I said, nodding and raising my eyebrows. "Four days off. Was your spouse off at the same time, or were you alone?"

He shut his mouth.

"It's time for you to go."

"Okay," I said, reaching into my purse for my business card. "Thanks for your time, and sorry if it was frustrating.

This is my business card. When Mrs. Rice comes in, please tell her to call me. It can be day or night. I'm on call twenty-four hours a day and always keep my phone with me."

He took my card and stepped back.

"Please get off my property. Neither my wife nor I are interested in helping you."

"I understand," I said, stepping back. "Have a good day, sir."

He went inside, and Roy and I walked to the car. Ideally, Dr. Rice and I would have had a cordial conversation in which he had answered my questions honestly without engendering any suspicion, but murder investigations rarely ran smoothly. The more information I could withhold and the more imbalanced I could make him, the better. He couldn't plan a response if he didn't understand what I was doing.

Matthew was a suspect. If his wife was sleeping with Mannie, he had an obvious motive, he owned a shotgun powerful enough to blow a hole through Mannie's chest, and he was away from work. Aside from that, he looked fit enough to wheel Mannie through the woods on a cart and dump him. I had a lot of work remaining, but I suspected Matthew Rice had a tough future ahead of him.

I took notes and then backed out of the driveway. Then I headed to the house next door. A young woman—probably high school age—answered. She and I spoke for a few minutes, but she didn't know a lot about the Rices. Her mom and dad, when they came out, knew even less. None recognized Mannie or had heard his name.

The neighbor on the other side focused on my phone for almost thirty seconds before nodding and saying he had, in fact, seen him. Unfortunately, he thought Mannie had fixed his air conditioning six months back. I doubted that, but I thanked him for his time anyway. The neighbor across the street didn't recognize Mannie but said he had seen a red, four-door sedan parked in the Rice's driveway. Mannie had rented a red Chevy Malibu, but I hadn't mentioned it.

"Why'd you bring up the car?" I asked. The neighbor, an elderly man named Michael Wall, shrugged. We were on his expansive front porch. He sat on a two-person swing, while I stood. Dirt clung to the wiry gray hair of his beard and coated his hands. A shovel leaned against the exterior of the porch.

"I just thought it might be important," he said. "I try to spend as much time outside as I can this time of year. The garden needs it."

My heartbeat increased, but I tried to keep my excitement contained.

"Tell me about this car."

He raised his eyebrows.

"Isn't much to say, really," he said. "I saw the same car drive past three times. It kept slowing down. I thought it was somebody casing the place, like he was going to rob it."

I nodded.

"Did you see the driver?"

"Not well," he said. "I was up here, and he was down there by the road."

I looked toward the street. It was a good two hundred feet away, so I nodded and returned my focus to Mr. Wall.

"So the car just drove by?"

"No," he said, shaking his head. Then he nodded. "It did at first. Then it pulled off on the side of the road, right in front of the house. I almost went out there, but then a man stepped out. He was on the phone, and he looked around. Then he got back in the car, drove about a hundred feet down the road, and turned into the Rice's driveway. I figured he was a salesman or Realtor. They thinking of selling their house?"

"Not that I know of," I said. "When was this sighting?"

"Thursday afternoon," he said. "It was after lunch. Maybe one."

I nodded and put it into my puzzle. On Thursday, Mannie and Cassandra had lunch at The Mystic Garden at eleven. Matthew Rice was at work. After lunch, Mannie and Cassandra split company, but they evidently had a good enough time to meet up again at her place at one in the afternoon. My theory about an affair was starting to look better.

"Did you see the car leave?"

He shook his head.

"I wasn't paying attention."

"That's okay," I said. "Thank you."

127

Mr. Wall nodded and stood to see me and Roy off.

"Can I ask you what this is about?"

"A crime," I said. "Nothing you need to worry about, though. You're safe."

He nodded and looked across the street.

"The Rices are...interesting. The couple they bought that house from raised three boys. There were always kids doing something over there. Flying kites on the lawn, racing four-wheelers, having bonfires. The Johnsons walked their dog together every night. They were older than you, and they still held hands. Now...the place just looks abandoned. The Rices aren't even home together, as far as I can tell. What kind of couple doesn't want to see each other?"

I considered and shrugged.

"I don't know."

"Before my wife..." His voice trailed off. "I never liked being apart from my wife. I don't understand some people. If you've got a partner, you've got a partner. You don't run around on your partner and have boyfriends over in the middle of the afternoon."

I forced myself to smile.

"To be fair, we don't know why the driver of the red sedan visited," I said. "One of your other neighbors thought he might have been an HVAC repairman."

"Was he?" asked Mr. Wall.

"I can't say," I said. "You think the Rices had marital problems?"

He considered.

"I'd say they barely saw each other. That'd be a problem for me."

"Have you ever seen women visit Mr. Rice?"

"I try not to pay attention."

I smiled.

"You seem like the type to notice things even if you weren't paying close attention."

He considered me and then looked down.

"He has a guest as well. She comes on the weekends when his wife is at work. She's young."

I raised an eyebrow and lowered my chin.

"How young?"

"Your age," he said. "He's robbing that cradle blind."

I tried not to grimace, but it probably showed through anyway. Having an affair with a younger woman wasn't a crime, but it was a problem. If both Cassandra and Matthew had significant others, or if they had an open marriage, a new boyfriend wouldn't have been that big of a deal. At the very least, it blew a hole through my theory.

"Okay," I said. "Thank you for your time, Mr. Wall. I'm going to head back."

"Any time, miss," he said, nodding to me. He looked at Roy. "He ever go out duck hunting?"

I smiled and shook my head.

"Roy's an old dog in a young dog's body. He's not big on exercise, and retrieving waterfowl is hard exercise."

He smiled.

"Roy is a dog after my own heart," he said. "If I see that red car come back, I'll give you a call."

I almost told him the car wouldn't return but then thought better of it. I didn't want him deducing that Mannie was dead and thinking the worst of his neighbors.

"That would be much appreciated," I said. Roy and I left the porch and settled into my car. I drove off but then parked at a gas station about a mile away to think. Unfortunately, I couldn't come up with anything new. I still had more questions than answers, but the case was progressing. Now I just needed to keep things going. Whatever their relationship was like, Cassandra Rice had seen Mannie before he died. I needed to find her. Thankfully, I had a good idea of where to look.

Chapter 15

The courts said Ryan had two unsupervised weekend visits with Elijah per month. Julie was to drop him off at nine on Friday and pick him up at six on Sunday. It wasn't even five yet, but Julie didn't care.

She had gotten up that morning at eight, just as she did most mornings. Her mom wove baskets out of willow reeds and had a pretty good business. In years past, when St. Augustine still had a Spring Fair, she would rent a booth and sell a few dozen small baskets or garden statues. They were whimsical and fun. People loved them.

For the past two weeks, Lisa—Julie's mom—had been weaving three dozen identical vases that would hold tulips at a lavish wedding in Minneapolis. At the end of the festivities, the guests would take the flower arrangements—including the vases—home as party favors. Lisa and the bride's mom had bargained the price from a hundred dollars per vase down to seventy. It was an expensive gift, but rich people liked expensive, frivolous things.

Lisa's woven products sold well, but she had never received such a big order, and her stress was building. Julie couldn't weave the vases like her mom, but she packaged the orders and prepped the reeds. They had finished thirty-three so far. The money Lisa earned would return to the family. Lisa never complained about the weaving. She said it was her hobby. It may have even been at one point.

After a day's work, Lisa's hands hurt. She didn't complain or tell Julie, but Julie knew because she soaked them in paraffin wax. It eased her arthritis. Julie hated that her mom had to work. Lisa should have been able to treat her hobby as just a hobby.

Instead, she had turned her hobby into a business and paid for Elijah's preschool and health insurance. Julie worked full time, too, but it was hard to cover everything on her meager salary. One day, she hoped to go to college. She wanted to teach. With tuition costs rising faster than her salary, and her bills increasing every year, that dream felt further and further away every day. Still, it was a dream worth having. One day, she hoped she could help her mom out as much as her mom helped her. She'd help her dad, too. They had given up more for her than she'd ever know.

That job in the garage had been Julie's savior this weekend, but she couldn't wait any longer. Lisa and Julie were in the family's two-car garage, both surrounded by orange, five-gallon buckets from Home Depot. Big stacks of willow reeds sat on the workbench, soaking in the buckets and bundled along the back wall. The air smelled grassy and clean but held an undercurrent of gasoline from the lawn equipment.

"I'm going to get Elijah," said Julie.

Lisa glanced at her phone.

"It's a little early," she said. "Andrea won't be happy if you just show up."

"Andrea and Frank are in Florida on vacation," she said. "Ryan's been watching Elijah alone this weekend."

Lisa stopped weaving and looked at her daughter.

"That explains why you nearly bit my head off this morning," she said. "You've been nervous all weekend?"

"I've been fucking crazy all weekend," she said, her hands shaking. "Ryan's Elijah's daddy, but he's never cared before. Then I heard he's moving to St. Louis, and I tried to confront him about it, but he just yelled at me. I just want my baby safe. Is that too much to ask?"

"Ryan's moving?"

She shrugged and looked down.

"Maybe. There's supposed to be a girl involved. Ryan's got a job, and he wants to move out."

"I see," said Lisa, resuming her weaving. "You jealous?"

"Of Ryan's girlfriend?" Julie asked. Lisa nodded. "More like I pity her. I just want my son. If Ryan moves, we'll fight about custody again. It's too much. If Andrea and Frank were there, I wouldn't care. But Ryan by himself watching our kid? I wouldn't trust him with a goldfish."

"You trusted him enough to sleep with him. Why don't you trust him now?"

Julie lowered her voice.

"Mom, when I slept with Ryan, I was stupid. There's no getting around it. My trust in the past wasn't justified. I was a stupid, stupid girl who wasn't thinking with her brain."

Lisa rolled her eyes and shook her head.

"Then go get him," she said. "Everything's going to be fine. Just drive safely."

"Thanks, Mom," she said, already standing and running to the house. She hadn't needed her mom's permission but hearing her say she should get Elijah somehow lifted a cloud from her. She grabbed her keys from the bowl by the front door and headed out. With each mile she drove, she felt herself growing stronger.

This would be just fine.

The setting sun bathed Ryan's neighborhood in a panoply of oranges and reds. As she parked, a couple walking their dog looked at her from the corners of their eyes. The woman frowned, probably wondering why anyone in her shabby sweater and driving her ancient Toyota would park there. Her husband just stared. Julie didn't care. She had never fit into that neighborhood and hoped she never would.

Ryan opened the door at her knock but said nothing.

"I'm here for Elijah."

"You're early."

"Just get him. Don't tell me he's taking a nap."

"I'm supposed to have him until six."

Julie blinked and looked down.

"I'm an hour early. We've both got things to do. I'm sure you and your girlfriend have stuff to do in your new house. Give me Elijah, and you can get on with your day."

Ryan's back was straight, and he worked his fingers together. His throat moved as he swallowed.

"Come back at six. I'll have him ready."

His tone and posture were wrong. Yesterday, he had been so confident. He was smug, arrogant, and mean. Now, he was nervous. That made her nervous.

"What's your secret, Ryan?" she asked, a heavy feeling growing in her stomach. "When Elijah's home with me, he's always jumping off things, demanding chocolate milk, and screaming at the top of his lungs to watch Daniel Tiger. How do you keep him so quiet?"

His lips seemed to quiver before he spoke.

"He's taking a nap."

The heavy feeling in Julie's gut began solidifying.

"He was taking a nap yesterday, too. Why aren't you letting me see our son? What's going on?"

"Not now, Julie," he said. He stepped back and tried closing the door, but she stuck her foot in the crack before he could.

"Where's our son, Ryan?" she asked, enunciating each word. "You're not thinking of taking him to St. Louis, are you?"

"I don't even want your son."

"Good," said Julie, her voice high. "Give him to me, and I'll come over tomorrow with the paperwork severing your parental rights. I'll even do you one better. You sign my paper, I'll sign a paper saying you don't owe us anything. We'll cut you out. You won't even have to pay child support. You'll never hear from us again."

"How would you pay for stuff?"

"Don't worry about us," said Julie. "Just get my son, and I'll make it happen. He'll live a good life."

Ryan looked down.

"It's not six. I have him until six."

Julie crossed her arms, skin warming all over her body. She shook her head as a tremble began passing through.

"Tell me he's okay, Ryan."

He looked down but said nothing. Julie lowered her voice so that she was almost pleading.

"Please. Tell me you haven't hurt our son."

"I didn't hurt him."

Julie swallowed hard and nodded.

"Good. Go get him."

"I..." Ryan started to speak, but then stopped and cleared his throat. "I'm still looking for him."

Julie's back stiffened, and she drew in a breath. Her hands shook, so she balled them into tight fists.

"What do you mean, you're looking for him?"

"One moment he was there playing, and the next moment, he was gone. I turned my back for one second. That's it. I'm still looking for him."

A cold, hard spike passed through her as adrenaline began pouring into her system. It took every ounce of strength she had not to run into the house at that moment, shouting her baby's name.

"Where were you?" she asked, her voice wavering.

"Out back. In the woods."

Somehow, the world outside Ryan's front porch seemed to grow dim. Then it disappeared. Julie's heart pounded. It felt as if a giant had grabbed her ribcage and squeezed. Her breath had a ragged edge.

"No," she said. "No."

Ryan said something, but Julie ignored him and backed up. Then she sprinted across the lawn. The Powell family owned half a dozen acres, one of the largest plots on Pinehurst. Their contractor had tamed the forested landscape by ripping out the trees and installing tiers to level the rolling hillside. Julie jumped down the first tier, sprinted across the second, and jumped down again. Her feet hit mud, and she slipped, falling on her backside.

"Slow down," said Ryan, running across the grass toward her. Julie could barely hear him. She didn't care. She got up and ran. The ground was spongy. She skidded to a stop, her breath short.

"Elijah! It's Mommy! Where are you?"

Not a hundred feet away lay deep woods that grew ever darker with the setting sun. She turned to Ryan.

"Where were you when you last saw him?"

"Back there," he said, nodding. "There's a fort. My dad made it."

Julie looked for tracks on the ground.

"Elijah!"

She called again, running now toward a lean-to fort built just past the tree line on the edge of the lawn. Despite the trees, the ground was firm.

"Elijah! It's Mommy. If you hear me, shout, baby!"

"I tried that," said Ryan. "I don't know where he is."

"Baby!" shouted Julie. "It's Mommy. Please come on out."

Every time she spoke, her voice grew hoarser.

"Honey! Come on out. It's time!" she shouted.

Her legs felt rubbery, and her breath started becoming ragged. The world grew darker. Ryan stayed quiet.

"Elijah!"

"He can't hear you," said Ryan. "If he could, he'd be screaming. I tried this."

"Baby! Where are you?"

Julie didn't know her legs had given out until she felt the dampness on her knees.

"Please, honey. Just come on back."

She brought her hands to her mouth, unsure who she was even pleading with, but hoping someone would hear. Julie shouted until she couldn't shout any more. Then sobs started replacing intelligible words. Her shoulder hit the ground as strength left her core. She tried to keep calling for her son, but she couldn't get the words out. Then she just cried.

Chapter 16

I drove to St. John's Hospital. The last time I was there, Janelle Revis, the Assistant Operations Manager, asked me to leave. I understood why people refused to cooperate with my investigations. I had power and resources. Theoretically, the court system and laws held a detective's power in check, but even the most superficial dive into the recent history of the United States would find examples of egregious abuses of police authority. My colleagues and I tried to treat people fairly, but sometimes we made mistakes. Some officers didn't care about fairness or rightness at all. They were worse than many people we arrested.

Dr. Rice didn't need her boss's help or resources, though. She wasn't a suspect, but even if she was, she could afford her own attorney. She didn't need anyone's protection.

I parked and headed toward the ER. A nurse behind the front desk gave me a tight smile.

"What's your emergency?"

I unhooked the badge from my belt and held it toward her.

"My name is Detective Joe Court with the St. Augustine County Sheriff's Department. I'm looking for Dr. Cassandra Rice. Is she working today?"

The receptionist blinked and pushed back from the desk.

"Is this an emergency?"

I smiled.

"This is a criminal investigation. I'd like to know whether she's here. If she is, I'd like to speak to her when she's able."

The nurse peered around before leaning forward.

"Dr. Rice isn't available. Her husband isn't, either. I'm not supposed to talk to you. It's hospital policy."

I started to thank her but then stopped.

"Is the policy about me or the police?"

She frowned and looked away.

"I'm not supposed to say."

I smiled. It didn't matter. If the hospital didn't want its employees to talk to me, I couldn't make them.

"Thank you," I said. She nodded, and I stepped away from the counter. Cassandra wasn't at work or home. She'd come back, and I'd find her then. Roy and I drove back to my station, where I looked up both doctors. Matthew Rice had a criminal record. Twelve years ago, St. Louis metro officers had arrested him after they found him fighting with a fan from an opposing team at a Blues game. He had been drunk. They told him to go home and sober up. The prosecutors declined to file charges.

Gary Faulk, an officer with my department, arrested Matthew again three years ago for driving while intoxicated. He and Cassandra were together and coming home from a party. She was too drunk to drive, so a uniformed officer drove her home. Matthew spent the night in the drunk tank and was arraigned in the morning. After pleading guilty, a judge gave him probation for a year, ordered him to pay a five-thousand-dollar fine, and forced him to attend an alcohol awareness class. It was a pretty standard punishment for a first-time offender.

Matthew, evidently, had a temper, and he liked to drink, but that didn't make him a murderer. Cassandra didn't even have a parking ticket on file. I stared at the screen before pushing myself back. I had worked this case for two days, but I had next to nothing.

We had no witnesses, and we had no idea where Mannie died. We didn't know why someone wanted him dead, we didn't know why he had twenty-five thousand dollars cash, nor did we know why he came to St. Louis. We didn't even know what kind of gun his killer used. I rubbed my eyes and focused on the facts.

Mannie flew from Miami to St. Louis and checked into a hotel near Busch Stadium. For some reason, he brought cash and cell phones. Or maybe he withdrew the cash here and bought the cell phones. I didn't know. In his car, he had an iPhone and a burner. A passcode secured both, and I hadn't been able to get into either.

He came from St. Louis to St. Augustine, ate lunch with Dr. Cassandra Rice, and died a day later. I hadn't been able to get in touch with Cassandra, and her husband denied knowing Mannie. The neighbor saw a car that could have been Mannie's visit the Rice's home while Matthew was away. It could have been business or personal. I wouldn't know until I spoke to Cassandra.

If Mannie visited St. Louis to see Cassandra, I had no explanation for the cash in his room or the box of prepaid cell phones. Mannie's tailor said he loved and respected women. He was young and wealthy and lived in a city full of beautiful women. He could have picked up a dozen beautiful young doctors in Miami. Cassandra was lovely, but what made her special to him?

I had worked this case for two days, and I barely knew a thing. My department didn't have the money to send an officer to Miami to interview Mannie's friends and family, but maybe I could video chat with them. Somebody knew why he came to St. Louis. Mannie's boss had seemed to like him. Maybe she could give me a list of his friends at work. It'd be a start, at least.

I typed reports for a few minutes and then pushed back from my desk. Roy lifted his head.

"Want to go home and walk?"

He hopped to his feet and dove into a play bow. I smiled and rubbed his ears as he licked my hands.

"Okay, dude, let's go," I said, standing. My smile slipped as a screech filled the room. By design, the noise was jarring and incapable of being ignored. I grabbed my cell phone from my purse, already dreading what I'd see on the screen.

The message came from a dispatcher with the Missouri State Highway Patrol. A toddler was missing and presumed in extreme danger in St. Augustine. A trooper was already on-site, and he had called in every available unit—including those off duty. The address was in the Pinehurst development. The homes and yards were large. Woods, a lake, creeks, caves, and trails surrounded the entire place. That was part of the charm. It had plenty of outdoor amenities close by. With a toddler lost, those natural attractions became anything but benign.

I swore under my breath and dialed the highway patrol as I hooked a leash onto Roy's collar.

"This is Detective Joe Court with the St. Augustine County Sheriff's Department. Inform the first responder in St. Augustine that I'm incoming in civilian clothing. I'm ten minutes out, and I'll be driving a red Volvo station wagon. I have a cadaver dog with me."

"I will relay the message, Detective," said the dispatcher.

I thanked him and hung up. Then I looked to the dog.

"Let's get some exercise."

Chapter 17

Roy and I hurried to my car. It was fifty or fifty-five, but the temperature would drop by ten degrees at least overnight. An adult might be okay outside at forty-five, but a kid could die. This was serious.

I drove in silence and reached the Pinehurst development in about fifteen minutes. Then I kept driving until I found a highway patrol cruiser and several civilian vehicles parked on the road. Flashlights bobbed in the woods behind the house, and people scampered across the lawn. The search looked disorganized. If we had any chance of finding this kid, that needed to change fast.

I grabbed a flashlight from my glovebox and a rarely used police radio from a box in my trunk. Then I let Roy out. A uniformed officer came toward me from the home's front door. He flashed a light at me but lowered it when I shielded my face.

"You Detective Court?" he asked.

"I am," I said. "You the first responder?"

He nodded and introduced himself as Cory Sydow, and we walked toward the hood of my car.

"What's going on?" I asked.

"We received a 911 call at 5:35 PM from Ryan Powell. He's a twenty-year-old Caucasian male and lives at this address. His son is Elijah Smith. Elijah is a three-year-old Caucasian male with short brown hair and brown eyes. He was last seen wearing a light green sweatshirt and red pants. Ryan says he and Elijah were playing in a fort in the backyard. Ryan heard a noise and investigated. When he returned, Elijah was missing."

I grabbed a notepad from my purse and jotted down notes.

"He left his three-year-old in the unfenced yard alone?"

"For a moment. He went to the front yard."

It was lousy parenting, but we weren't here to judge anyone's parenting ability.

"When was this?"

"Approximately four in the afternoon."

I drew in a breath.

"He called us an hour and a half after he lost his son?"

"That's what I understand," he said. "Ryan Powell shares custody with Julie Smith, the little boy's mother. Ryan has Elijah every other weekend. Otherwise, he lives with Julie and her family. Julie came to pick Elijah up at 5:20 and learned the boy was missing. She called for Elijah, but he didn't come. Then, Ryan called the police."

If Ryan had called as soon as soon as he lost the kid, we would have brought in dozens of officers and search dogs in the daylight. Ryan's hesitancy to call the police had made a scary situation dangerous. It was too early to think of bringing charges, but, assuming we found Elijah safe and well, Ryan's days of unsupervised visits with his son were over. If nothing else, I'd see to that.

"What assets do we have?" I asked.

"We've got officers inbound, but the locals weren't on duty tonight. I don't understand that situation."

"It's a long story," I said. "My people will come. Who are these guys with flashlights?"

"Neighbors and Julie Smith's family."

"Round up the civilians and have them meet me here. We need to get organized, or we won't find anybody. Highway patrol sending us anybody else?"

"We've got eight or nine troopers inbound," he said. "They're coming from all over, though."

"That's fine. We'll use them," I said, glancing up as headlights flashed down the street. It was Officer Dave Skelton's truck, so I waved him over. He parked behind my Volvo, and I turned back to Sydow. "Tell them to meet me here. Where's Ryan Powell?"

"In the house."

"I'll talk to him," I said. "Thank you."

He agreed and started running a couple on the front lawn of the house next door. I focused on Skelton.

"Thanks for coming, Dave," I said. "How well do you know this area?"

"Well," he said. "I used to go hunting here before they built the development."

"Dangers for a three-year-old?"

He blinked, his eyes growing distant.

"Caves, sink holes, a lake, a creek, and the cold. There's a valley half a mile south of here that floods every time it rains. It comes up quick."

"I doubt our victim made it that far," I said. "We're looking for a little boy named Elijah Smith. He's three, and he was last seen wearing a green top and red pants. He's got to be here somewhere. Kids his age can't run that fast or far. We've got civilians out searching already. Officer Sydow's going to send them here to the driveway. I need you to organize them into teams. Coordinate communication as well. They've all got cell phones, so get everybody's phone number so we can contact them quickly. I want teams. Nobody's out here alone. Got it?"

"We have any maps?" he asked.

"Not yet," I said.

He nodded and waved a pair of civilians toward the driveway. I took out my phone and called Trisha Marshall, our dispatcher. She answered quickly.

"Trisha, hey," I said. "It's Joe Court."

"I'm in my car, and I'm on my way," she said. "You're at Pinehurst, right?"

"I am, but I need a communications coordinator, so I need you to go to the station. I also need maps of the area.

Anything you can get. We're going to need handheld radios, too, so charge everything we've got in storage. Once I have more manpower, I'll send somebody by to pick things up. And call the fire department. They've got infrared cameras to see people trapped in buildings. Ask if we can borrow some and see if they've got any volunteers who'll help us search. We'll need the crime lab's lights and tent, too, so call Kevius and see if he can bring them out."

"I'm on it," she said. "You're doing great. We're going to find the boy. Just don't forget to breathe."

I drew in a deep breath and nodded.

"Thanks, Trisha. I'll be in touch."

I hung up with her. Skelton had six civilians around him. Sydow and two additional civilians were walking toward us. I waved Sydow toward me while Dave Skelton started organizing the search.

"Officer Sydow, you were the first responder," I said. "Did you talk to Ryan Powell?"

"Just enough to learn his son was missing. Mom—Julie Smith—-was very upset. Ryan was more subdued. I searched and couldn't find the boy, so I called in help."

"You searched the house yet?"

He shook his head.

"They told me he was outside, so I stayed out here. I figured that was the priority. If Elijah's inside, he'll be okay. Out here, hypothermia is a concern. Then Julie's family started

149

arriving. I talked to them, but they were more interested in searching than talking to me."

He had the right priorities. I nodded.

"Good. Work with Officer Skelton. He knows this area better than anybody else on our staff, so I'm putting him in charge of the exterior search. He'll put your officers into teams. Officer Trisha Marshall in my station will act as our communications coordinator. I want everybody on the same radio channel. We'll be methodical. Nobody gets hurt, and nobody misses anything. I'd like to get the highway patrol's helicopter in the air, too."

"I'll call my boss, ma'am," he said, already turning toward his cruiser. He sat in the front seat and picked up his radio. I drew in a breath to slow my racing heart and give myself a moment to think. As I saw it, we had four scenarios to worry about. In scenario one, Ryan and Julie were telling the truth, and Elijah was lost in the woods. Ryan shouldn't have left Elijah unattended, but nobody had committed a crime. We'd search for Elijah and find him alive and well. In scenario two, Elijah got lost while playing. Likely, he hid in the woods, expecting his father to find him right away. Somehow, Elijah then became incapacitated—he might have even fallen asleep. We'd search for him and find him alive and well. Everybody would walk away a little wiser.

In scenario three, Julie and Ryan—or perhaps just one of them—murdered the kid. Our search would find a body, and Roy would get a workout. I hoped that wasn't the case.

THE MAN BY THE CREEK

In scenario four, Ryan abducted Elijah to keep him from Julie. That kind of thing happened often, unfortunately.

No matter which scenario we were in, the search outside would continue. Ryan had an expectation of privacy inside the home, though. Court precedent held that there was no murder-scene exception to the Fourth Amendment, despite popular belief. I didn't know what had happened to Elijah, but hell had a special place for child murderers. So did the prison system.

About a minute after my conversation with Trooper Sydow, Officer Katie Martelle from my department arrived. She wore a department-issued polo shirt and jacket. It was perfect.

"You're with me for a few minutes," I said. "Then Dave will assign you to a team."

Katie nodded and followed me toward the enormous home's front door. I filled her in on the situation and my thoughts. She blinked.

"What should I do?"

"We're going to take Roy through the house," I said. "We'll tell them Roy's a tracker. They don't need to know he's a cadaver dog. If they killed their kid and stashed him inside, we'll find him."

She looked uncertain.

"Do we need a warrant?"

"If we can't get permission," I said, knocking on the door. "If they refuse a search, we'll take the adults into custody and apply for a search warrant."

Katie swallowed and nodded.

"I hope it doesn't come to that."

"Me, too."

Chapter 18

Every moment mattered. Ryan Powell opened the door almost as soon as I knocked. He was tall and handsome and had broad shoulders that stretched his T-shirt taut. Like his son, he had brown hair and brown eyes. Julie Smith, Elijah's mother, stood back, maybe fifteen feet, in the two-story entryway. Marble covered the floors, while an oak staircase led to the second story. A chandelier lit the room, forcing me to squint after the gloom outside.

"I'm Detective Joe Court," I said. "With me is Officer Katie Martelle." I reached down and petted Roy. He wagged his tail but didn't pull away. "And this is Roy. He has extensive tracking training. If possible, I'd like to take my dog through the house to make sure Elijah isn't hiding somewhere inside."

Ryan looked at the dog and shook his head.

"My mom would kill me if I let a dog in the house."

"Shut up," said Julie. "Do whatever you need to do to find my baby."

I gave her a tight, hopefully reassuring smile before focusing on Ryan.

"I need your permission to come through," I said. "The chances of finding your son go up if you cooperate. If you're worried about mud, I can wipe his paws. Otherwise, Roy is an adult dog who lives inside with me. He's house-trained, and I'll be with him the entire time. He won't damage anything."

"Let her in, Ryan," said Julie, her voice low. Ryan licked his lips and nodded.

"Just to search for Elijah," he said. "He's not here, though."

"We need to be sure," I said. "If he's inside and hurt, we need to find him right away to get him the help he needs. I'll need a blanket or pillow or stuffed animal with Elijah's scent on it."

"You can have Mr. Stuffins," said Julie. "He's Elijah's bear. He sleeps with him every night."

I nodded and waited a moment.

"Great," I said. "Where's Mr. Stuffins?"

"Get him, Ryan," said Julie. "You know where Elijah's room is. I don't."

"Oh, yeah," said Ryan, already turning and bounding upstairs. I didn't know what kind of relationship Julie and Ryan had, but she was the dominant one. I appreciated that. She could help me out. Ryan returned with a limp, well-loved blue teddy bear a few moments later. I held it to Roy's nose.

"Find it, buddy. Find it."

The dog's nostrils flared, and he stuck his nose in the air, sniffing. He took a hesitant step forward and began pulling me down the front hallway to an enormous kitchen overlooking the backyard. Then he pulled me to a two-story, open concept living room. He sniffed an L-shaped sectional sofa and sat down beside it.

"That's where Elijah and I sat and watched cartoons," said Ryan. It was a good sign. Roy recognized the boy's scent. I pulled him out of the room, held the stuffed animal to his nose again, and implored him to keep working. We walked through the house and peered into cupboards, beneath beds, and in closets, but we couldn't find Elijah. Importantly, I didn't see drugs, guns, cash, blood, bloody clothing, or any signs of a physical fight, either.

Katie, Roy, and I walked to the front entryway about fifteen minutes after we arrived. Julie and Ryan had remained. Neither spoke to the other.

"You guys were right. I've not seen any sign that Elijah's still in here," I said. "We've got a lot of police officers coming. Hopefully, we'll have some firefighters as well. I've also requested the highway patrol's helicopter. Assuming they can find a pilot, they'll be able to cover a lot of ground. In the meantime, I want you guys to stay in here in separate rooms. Don't talk to each other, don't argue, and don't leave. If necessary, I can leave an officer with you, but I'd rather use everybody I've got outside. Can I trust you?"

Both Ryan and Julie nodded.

"We're going to do everything we can to find your son. Sit tight. I'll keep you updated."

They nodded again. I wished I could tell them something uplifting, or that they shouldn't worry. That'd be a lie, though. It'd be a soft lie, for sure, one designed to bring short-term comfort, but it would cause long-term pain. I didn't want to give them hope because I didn't know whether they should have any. It was dark, it was cold, and their three-year-old son had been outside for two hours. I had never met Elijah, but I felt sick for him. I couldn't give Julie and Ryan hope only to dash it later.

So I sucked it up and kept my mouth shut. Katie and I left the home and headed to the front. The crime lab's van was on the street. Somebody had erected a small pop-up tent in the driveway. Kevius and Darlene were carrying a white folding table beneath it. Both nodded to me when they saw me.

"Thanks for coming," I said. "Any news?"

"Not yet, ma'am, but we just arrived," said Kevius.

"We've got about a dozen firefighters," said Darlene. "Dave's ordering them to march in lines an arm's width apart."

It was a good way to search. The kid could have been anywhere. As dark as it was, a searcher could pass right beside Elijah without noticing him. By staying in tight groups and marching in a line, we'd have multiple eyes on every inch of the forest floor.

"Roy, Katie, and I went through the house," I said. "Elijah's not there. Or if he was, Roy couldn't smell him. He didn't smell blood or bloody clothes, either. If Ryan murdered his son, he didn't do it inside the house."

Katie drew in a sharp breath.

"I didn't realize that was a concern."

"It's always a concern," I said, glancing to my right as a flashlight bobbed across the lawn toward us. It was Dave Skelton, and he had mud on his shirt, cheek, elbows, and knees. "You hurt?"

"No," he said, his breaths deep as he recovered from a run through the woods. "I need a pencil and some paper."

I looked at Darlene.

"You guys got anything?"

"Yeah," said Kevius. "Give me a moment."

He ran to the van and returned a few minutes later with a binder full of graphing paper. He likely used it to map out crime scenes. Dave took the binder and drew a crude map.

"The landscape slopes downward to a creek about half a mile through the woods. There are houses to the north. You run about three miles to the west, you'll hit the highway, but the kid didn't run that far. You go to the east, you'll run into Waterford College. They own thousands of acres, and it's rough, virgin forest.

"I've got two teams of twelve combing the woods. They cover approximately seventy-two feet, and I'm having them walk straight to the creek and turning back. Every searcher has a flashlight, and each team has a pair of police radios. The state trooper has their cell numbers in case we can't reach them on the radio."

It sounded like a good search pattern.

"Could the child have crossed the creek?" asked Darlene.

Dave closed his eyes and drew in a breath before speaking.

"Probably. I ran along it for, maybe a mile. There's no standing water. If he got the gumption, he could have crossed it, but the mud was pretty thick. I fell twice, and I'm a grown man. If a little boy tried to cross it, he would have fallen and left tracks. I didn't find any."

"That's good work," I said, nodding. "Why don't you sit down and drink some water? You deserve a break."

Dave shook his head.

"I got my breath back," he said. "I know these woods. If Elijah's out there, I'm going to find him."

"You can't help anybody if you push yourself so hard you get hurt," I said. "Take a break. Go back out in fifteen minutes."

Dave's eyes flicked up and down my torso.

"All due respect, Joe, you're not my supervisor."

I straightened, surprised.

"Hey," said Darlene, her voice soft. "That's uncalled for. We're all stretched thin here, but we're all doing our jobs. If we argue with each other, nothing's going to get done."

Dave looked at me.

"I'm going to keep searching. Okay, ma'am?"

I considered letting him. Dave was older than me, but he could run half the night without tiring. Still, I shook my head.

"No good," I said. "You're the lead on this. Your knowledge is a force multiplier. So suck it up, buttercup. Get the radio, tell the teams where to search, and then join them later after you've had a drink. You'll be out all night. I can't have you burned out in the first half hour."

Dave's mouth moved, but no sounds came out. Then he nodded and blinked.

"Yes, ma'am."

"Good," I said. "We have any search dogs available?"

Nobody responded for a moment.

"The firefighters have two cadaver dogs," said Dave. "Scott Hall has Odin, but he's a drug dog."

"And Scott works in Farmington now," I said. "I think he took Odin with him."

Dave closed his eyes and rubbed his nose before nodding.

"You're right. Sometimes I forget who works where now."

I nodded and held Mr. Stuffins, Elijah's teddy bear, in front of Roy's nose.

"Find it, buddy."

Roy, once more, lifted nis nose and held his tail high. Then he pulled on my lead hard. He had something. I tossed the stuffed animal toward the table Darlene and Kevius had set up.

"Let's see what we've got."

Katie and I followed Roy down the side of the house. The route was circuitous and halting, but we were heading toward the woods, following the same path Elijah had followed with his father. At times, the ground was firm, but at other times, my feet sunk into the mud. It was dark and getting colder. I wished I had worn a heavier jacket.

"Find it, Roy," I said, my voice high and soft. "You can do it."

Roy couldn't understand my words, but he'd recognize the encouragement. Flashlights bobbed in the woods ahead of us as the teams searched. Somebody waved, but I focused on the dog. He pulled us across the grass toward a structure made from old sticks and logs. I ran my flashlight over the ground and found Matchbox cars in the dirt.

"He's been here," I said to Katie. She nodded and widened the beam on her light to better see the surrounding area.

"Find it, Roy," I said. "Come on, dude. Find the boy."

Roy had his nose in the area. He darted left, but then ran right along the edge of the woods, near the tree line. After a minute, he stopped and pulled me toward the grass. We walked a couple of feet. Then he yawned and looked at me. It wasn't a trained signal. It was a sign of confusion. I sighed.

"He had a scent, but he lost it," I said. "It might mean Elijah didn't go into the woods. He just stayed by the fort."

"If so, we should have found him."

THE MAN BY THE CREEK

"Yeah," I said. Before Katie could respond, my cell phone beeped with an incoming text message. I pulled my phone from my pocket. It was Dave Skelton.

Minor emergency. You out there?

I wrapped my hand around Roy's leash.

"Dave's got a problem," I said, already jogging up the lawn toward the home. Katie followed. Dave waved to us from the tent.

"Hey," he said. "We've got a fireman out there who may have broken a leg. Tripped on something and fell. I don't have a lot of details, but he's hurt. I've called in the paramedics. Ambulance is about five minutes out."

I grimaced. With a search party this large, injuries were inevitable. Still, a broken leg was more serious than I had expected.

"When the paramedics arrive, send them back. They'll have to carry him out on a stretcher. Hopefully, he's not too hurt."

Skelton nodded. Then he lowered his voice.

"Could Roy smell a fresh body?"

I blinked and squeezed my jaw before speaking.

"Bodies decompose almost immediately. Theoretically, a good cadaver dog could smell him fifteen or twenty minutes after death."

Katie exhaled a slow breath.

"So we think the kid's dead?"

I glanced at her.

161

"It's a possibility," I said.

"The kid's a fucking baby," said Skelton. "I don't accept that. He's out there. I won't give up."

"None of us are giving up," I said. "Are the parents still inside?"

Skelton looked toward the home.

"They haven't come out, if that's what you're asking."

"Good," I said. "Is Marcus Washington here yet?"

"He, Darlene, and Kevius are knocking on doors and asking the neighbors if they've seen Elijah."

"Good. Thank you," I said, taking out my phone to dial. Marcus answered on the first ring.

"Hey, Joe. I'm in the neighborhood. Nobody's seen the kid, but I've got new volunteers searching backyards, pool houses, and sheds."

"That's great. Thank you," I said. "I'm going to send Katie Martelle your way. She can work with Darlene and Kevius. Roy and I walked around. He smelled Elijah, but he couldn't follow the trail into the woods. I haven't found signs of foul play yet, but I need you to meet me at the house. We're going to hammer Mom and Dad hard and see if anybody breaks."

Marcus paused.

"You think that's the best approach?"

I grimaced and squeezed my eyebrows together.

"Best approach? Who knows? The longer we wait, the more likely Elijah will be hurt. If I have to step on toes to get information, I'll step on some toes."

"Then let's do it," said Marcus. "I'm on my way."

Chapter 19

Julie sat halfway to the second floor in the Powell's entryway, staring at the front door. Every time the floor creaked, she held her breath, dreaming and hoping it'd be Elijah bursting through the front door. That never happened. Her phone beeped every few minutes as somebody new texted her. She had tried responding, but her hands had trembled, and her voice had wavered. The phone couldn't understand her.

At first, Ryan had stayed near her and asked how she was doing. She told him that was the stupidest question he had ever asked. After that, he left to play a video game. Julie's knees bounced as she stared at the mahogany front door.

"Please. Please. Please."

She had started the evening by promising God elaborate sacrifices if He'd bring Elijah back. Over time, her prayers had grown simpler until they became a single word.

Then, somebody knocked on the door. Julie shot to her feet and ran down the stairs. The door opened, and the female detective entered. A tall man with curly black hair followed. Julie had seen him before at the high school. He gave presentations about the dangers of substance abuse. She had seen dozens over the years.

The woman looked at her. Julie held her gaze with pleading eyes.

"Where's your boyfriend?"

Julie's mouth opened, confused.

"I don't have a boyfriend," she said. "My baby's missing."

The woman's face faltered. Something soft and kind appeared. Then she became cold again.

"Ryan Powell," she said. "Where is he?"

"I'm in the kitchen," he called from another room. "I'm making a pizza."

Julie's head swiveled toward the hallway that led to the kitchen, smelling the sausage, cheese, and garlic for the first time. She furrowed her brow and sat down again. The two police officers focused on her.

"You okay, miss?" asked the man. She looked at him and nodded. "When did you last eat?"

Coherent thought broke through the cloud over her brain. She brought a hand to her face and rubbed her eyes.

"I'm fine," she said. "I'm just out of sorts. What's happened? Where's Elijah?"

The two detectives looked at one another. Then the woman looked at her.

"There somewhere we can sit and talk in this house?"

Julie blinked.

"Maybe in the kitchen. Ask Ryan. I'm just here for Elijah."

Again, the woman's face softened. She nodded and walked down the hall toward the kitchen. A moment later, she called out.

"There's a table in here."

The male detective walked to the foot of the stairs and held his hand toward her.

"Come on, miss. We'll talk around the table."

Julie stood and followed the officers down the hall and into the kitchen. Like the rest of the house, it was enormous and impressive. Andrea, Ryan's mom, had expensive tastes and had ordered marble countertops on everything and custom woodwork wherever she could put it. The kitchen's heart, though, was the oven. Andrea had ordered it from France. It was handbuilt and had cost almost two hundred thousand dollars. A professional chef would have loved it. Andrea rarely cooked, though, and its primary purpose now was to warm frozen pizza.

"You want pizza, Julie?" asked Ryan. She looked at him, her brow furrowed.

"Why would I want pizza?"

"To eat," he said, lowering his chin.

"How can you think about eating? Elijah's gone."

Though anger simmered just beneath the surface, it didn't enter Julie's voice. The question was genuine. She didn't understand how he could think about anything but their son.

"Get her a piece," said the male detective. He looked at Julie. "Miss, I'd like you to sit down at the table and tell me how you're feeling."

Julie's eyes flicked to him. Then she nodded, walked to the table, and pulled a chair out. Once she sat, he whispered something to the female detective. She nodded and looked at Julie, her eyes kind. She had a big brown dog at her side, and for some reason, she walked the dog to the table beside Julie. He sat beside her and panted, his tongue sticking out as he looked at her.

"He's friendly," said the woman. "His name's Roy. Try petting him."

Julie didn't know if she had a choice, so she reached out and patted the dog's cheek. He almost seemed to grin. Her heart slowed, and the world became clearer. The detective put the dog's leash on the table, but he didn't pull away. He just sat there with her. Julie closed her eyes and drew in a breath. The detective knelt beside her dog and lowered her voice.

"You're safe, Julie," she whispered. "Take some breaths. If you feel like you're going to pass out, tell me or my partner."

Julie nodded again. Then the detective stood.

"Okay, folks," she said. "I'm Detective Joe Court. My partner is Detective Marcus Washington. My dog is Roy. He farts a lot, but he's sweet. For my records, are your names Julie Smith and Ryan Powell?"

Both Julie and Ryan nodded. Detective Court looked at them both and drew in a breath.

"We've been searching for Elijah in the backyard and inside the home. My dog picked up Elijah's scent in the backyard, but he couldn't find it in the woods beyond the fort in the backyard.

"Ryan, your story was that you and Elijah were playing in the fort. Then you heard a noise, went to the front yard, and couldn't find Elijah upon your return. Julie, your story is that you showed up early to pick up your son and learned that he was missing. Ryan's custody paperwork says he gets Elijah until six. You came almost an hour early, Julie. Why?"

Julie tried to respond, but her voice faltered. Then she cleared her throat.

"I wanted my baby."

"That's understandable," said Detective Court, nodding, "but why did you come early? The paperwork says Ryan had Elijah until six. Ryan doesn't get to see his son very often. Why'd you come early? It's almost cruel, limiting a man's time with his son."

Julie blinked and shook her head, taken aback.

"Are you serious?" she asked.

"Answer the question," said the detective, her voice hard. Julie looked at Ryan.

"Because he doesn't care. He doesn't want Elijah," she said. "He told me so. I don't know why he even wanted Elijah this weekend. His mom and dad love him, but Ryan doesn't give two shits about Elijah."

"You don't get to say that," said Ryan, shaking his head. "That's not true. I loved Elijah."

For just a moment, a pained grimace passed over Detective Court's face. Then it was gone. Julie's chest felt tight, and she started having to fight her body to keep from trembling.

"What'd that look mean?" she asked. "What'd he say? Where's my son?"

"We're looking for him," said Detective Court. Detective Washington had crossed the kitchen to stand near Ryan. Julie shook her head, not understanding. Something had changed. The detectives were tense.

"What's going on?" she asked. Detective Court stood and focused on Ryan.

"Mr. Powell, you said Elijah disappeared in the backyard. You still feel good about that story?"

Ryan's eyes traveled from one detective to the other. Then he crossed his arms.

"It's not a story. It's the truth."

Julie brought her hands to her mouth, fresh tears coming to her cheeks.

"He murdered my baby, didn't he?" she asked, her voice warbling. "He never wanted him. When he found out I was pregnant, he told me to get an abortion."

"That's private, Julie," said Ryan. "Shut up."

"Tell them about your new apartment and new girl-friend," she said, her voice becoming stronger. "That's why you wanted him this weekend. You planned this."

Her voice trailed off. Ryan and the detectives stayed silent.

"You murdered our son," she said, feeling heat rise all over her body. "You murdered my fucking baby."

The dog barked as Julie vaulted across the room. She wanted to kill him, to break his bones, to see him bleed. Instead, she found an arm across her waist. Detective Court was holding her back. Julie clawed at her arms.

"Let me go!" she screamed. "Let me go!"

Even to her own ears, Julie sounded like an animal.

"Marcus, get him out of here," said the detective.

The big male detective put an arm around Ryan's shoulders and pulled him out of the kitchen. Julie tried to follow and twist out of Detective Court's grasp, but she was strong.

"Let me go!" she screamed again. "He killed my baby!"

"Calm down," said the detective. "You're safe. Breathe and calm down."

The front door slammed shut. Julie continued squirming and fighting, but then the strength left her. Her legs stopped working, and the detective lowered her to the ground. Julie drew her legs into her chest, the sudden heat leaving her body.

"He killed my baby," she said through sobs. "I want my baby."

"We'll find him," said Detective Court, her arms still on Julie's shoulders. There, on that cold, marble floor, Julie cried for the child she loved in the arms of a woman she didn't know, and she knew her world would never be right again.

Chapter 20

I stayed with Julie until she could breathe again. Then I called Dave Skelton and asked him to find her parents, who were out with one of our search teams. They sprinted into the house about ten minutes later and held her in the kitchen. She was hurt, and I couldn't blame her. Marcus and I had tried to keep our reactions subdued, but the moment Ryan started talking, we both knew.

Ryan had spoken about Elijah in the past tense.

Everyone viewed the world through the prism of their own understanding. Our experiences made us unique. When two different people saw a young couple fighting in a restaurant, they experienced the same event, but their minds interpreted those events differently. I watched for trembling lips, downcast eyes, stiff joints, rapid blinks... signs of fear. My job and experiences had taught me those things were important. When my dad saw that same young couple arguing in a restaurant, he might have seen an example of young but doomed love and thought nothing of it.

Our experiences of death were similar. We grieved and processed death in different ways because we processed the world in different ways. The key commonality, though, was the process. It took time. For the death of a child, it took a lifetime.

I had interviewed the families of murder victims years after they lost their relative, and many still hadn't accepted it. They held on to the hope that we had been wrong, that their loved one wasn't dead, and that we had identified the body incorrectly. Their hope was irrational—and some part of them likely knew it—but they clung to it because they weren't ready to accept that their loved one was gone.

Julie was in the very early stages of losing her son. She hadn't accepted anything. Nor should she have accepted her son's death. For all we knew, he was playing hide-and-seek with the neighbor's kid. Ryan, though, had accepted Elijah's death and continued on with his life. His stomach should have churned, his knees should have bounced, he should have felt sick. Instead, he had left the mother of his child alone in his entryway and made a pizza.

Ryan had *loved* his child. One word had changed my entire view of the case.

I left the home and joined Dave Skelton under the tent. He looked toward the house.

"Marcus said it got tense," he said. "You okay?"

I thought about lying, but I shook my head.

"No, but that's the job. You guys good out here?"

He looked at his hand-drawn map on the folding table.

"I think so," he said. "I'm marking quadrants off as we go. Once the searchers finish the map, I'll have them turn ninety degrees and go over the same areas again from a different direction."

"Did the ambulance ever get here?"

Skelton nodded.

"Yeah. The fireman who fell didn't break his leg, but he might have torn some ligaments. Paramedics took him to St. John's. I suggested calling the search off, but the teams want to keep going. They're good people."

"Glad to hear it. If I leave you here, are you okay staying in charge?"

"I'll stay until it's over."

I nodded and started toward my car, but then stopped myself.

"Are you okay, Dave?" I asked. "You were upset earlier."

His eyes went distant.

"I'm a father. That girl—Julie—lost her son. I don't know how I'd react if I were in her shoes." Dave looked down. When he spoke again, his voice was soft. "If we stay out here, we'll find a body. Makes me sick."

"We don't know anything yet. We can't assume things we don't have evidence for."

He shook his head.

"Tell yourself that all you want, but I know you don't believe it," he said. "It's cold enough that I can see your breath, and you crossed your arms to stay warm the moment you left the house. That little boy wasn't even wearing a jacket when he disappeared."

I wasn't ready to tell him he was right yet, so I shook my head.

"Just do your best," I said. "It's not over yet."

Skelton nodded but said nothing. Then Roy and I got in my Volvo. Marcus had taken Ryan to our station, but I wasn't ready to interrogate him. Instead, I drove to Sycamore Park and parked in the lot. The dog and I got out. He wanted me to take him for a walk—and I would—but first I walked him toward the picnic tables and sat down. He lay on the grass beside me. For a few minutes, I just sat and stared at the moon.

Elijah wasn't coming back. I had never met him, but I grieved for him all the same. My throat felt tight, and my chest ached, but—like Dave Skelton—I had a job to do. I looked at Roy. He lowered his belly to the ground and put his head between his paws. I slipped off the picnic table's seat and sat beside him, my arm over his back.

"You did great today, buddy," I whispered. "I wish it were enough."

Roy yawned and leaned against me. My dog was one of the few constants in my life. He was my friend. I hoped he knew how much he meant to me. Some days, he was the only reason I got out of bed. We stayed there for a few minutes. I didn't feel well when I stood up, but I had needed a break. We walked for another ten minutes before driving to my station.

CHRIS CULVER

Trisha sat behind the front desk, but she stood when she saw us.

"Marcus is upstairs with Ryan Powell. We've had a lot of phone calls about volunteers, but I've been turning them away and asking them to call again in the morning. Dave is still searching, but most of his volunteers have quit. He plans to stay until you make him come back. Julie Smith is at home with her parents. A lieutenant colonel from the highway patrol called and said their helicopter is unavailable for the evening. The FAA limits how many hours their pilots can fly per day, and they're maxed out."

I nodded.

"The helicopter would have been useful earlier, but I think we're past that stage," I said. "I appreciate your work. Can you stick around? When you need a break, I'll call in Doug Patricia. He's good with the phones."

She nodded, but before she could speak, the phone rang. I left her to it and took Roy to my office, where he lay on his bed and fell asleep. Then I went by Marcus's office down the hall. He had pictures of his spouse and kids on his desk and a bookshelf full of mementos from a lifetime spent in law enforcement. When he saw me, he pushed back from his desk but nodded toward his computer screen. On it, he had a live picture of Ryan in an interrogation room.

"I locked him in but left him his cell phone, hoping he'd be stupid enough to call a friend and confess."

"Any luck?"

He shook his head.

"Nope."

"You think he killed his kid?" I asked. Marcus considered and blinked.

"Given our search of his yard and home, his story doesn't make much sense. The jury's still out on whether he's a killer. I'm reserving judgment."

"You're much more fair-minded than I am," I said before pausing. "I want him first. If he hasn't broken in an hour, you'll get your shot."

"I'll be watching. If you need help, look at the camera. He thinks we took him from the house for his safety, so I didn't restrain him."

I nodded and slid my pistol from its holster on my belt.

"Hold on to this for me," I said, handing it to him. "If you need company, Roy's sleeping in my office."

"I'll let him sleep."

I nodded and hurried down the hall to the interrogation booths. Ryan waited and rubbed his hands together behind a metal table. His eyes were bloodshot. He looked jumpy. He was nervous. Good. He should have been. Everything I did in that room had a purpose. If I thought it'd help my interrogation, I'd yell and stomp my feet, or I'd pretend to flirt with him and become his friend. In this room, results mattered more than almost anywhere else in my station.

I pulled out a folding metal chair opposite Ryan and let the door shut behind me. Then I smiled and took a notepad from my pocket. I tossed it to the table.

"Hey, Ryan," I said. "As I told you earlier, I'm Detective Joe Court. A hidden camera is recording us both. Detective Washington is monitoring our conversation. This is an information-gathering interview. You're not under arrest, but your statements are admissible in court. If you tell me you've got two secret girlfriends, I won't care. I'll keep your secret. If you tell me you robbed a bank, I'll arrest you. Is that clear?"

"So I'm not under arrest?"

"Correct. We're here to discover what happened to Elijah. That's it. Are you going to help us out?"

He crossed his arms.

"What if I don't want to?"

"That's your right," I said. "In that case, I'll start getting warrants. We'll tear your house apart looking for evidence. We'll also search your vehicle, interview your friends, go through your finances, examine your parent's finances, search your phone and email, and talk to your employer and colleagues. It'd be intense. Because we'd be looking for blood evidence or other signs Elijah was hurt under your care, we could look anywhere. We could tear the walls in your house apart if we suspected you had stashed something behind the drywall. I don't want to do that, and I doubt you want to, either—especially if you haven't done anything wrong. Have you done anything wrong?"

He swallowed and shook his head.

"No."

"Good," I said, opening my notepad to a clean page. "Tell me about Elijah."

We spent twenty minutes talking about the boy. I didn't care what he said. Mostly, I wanted him to feel comfortable talking to me. Ideally, I'd feel like a confidant, someone who would listen without judgment. I wouldn't be a friend, but I'd be akin to one. He led me through his story twice. Then I scratched my forehead.

"Julie said you planned to move to St. Louis with a girl."

He rolled his eyes.

"That's none of her business."

"Are you moving?" I asked. He nodded.

"Yeah. With Maya. She's my friend."

"Does Maya like Elijah?"

He shrugged.

"They've never met."

I wrote it down but didn't mention how I odd I found it that he didn't introduce his son to a woman with whom he planned to live and with whom he'd care for that child at least two weekends per month.

"Moving out and getting your own place," I said, smiling. "Good for you. Is it nice?"

He leaned forward and put his elbows on the table.

"Yeah. The building's got a gym."

"That's great. You'll like having a place of your own. It makes things easier... especially with your friend Maya."

He nodded and leaned back.

"Julie seems a little intense," I said. "She ever hit you before?"

He made a face.

"She's all bark."

I tilted my head to the side.

"Still, she shouldn't have yelled at you. Being a dad's hard. You're paying child support, you're trying to be a nice guy, and you're working yourself to the bone all week. Then, when you finally get to see your son, she yells at you. It sucks."

He said nothing. I leaned forward.

"You won't get in trouble for agreeing with me," I said. "It sucks when half your paycheck goes to a woman who hates your guts. Believe me, I know. My paycheck goes to my ex-husband. I don't even see the kids, but I still pay for braces and doctor's appointments and books and clothes and everything else. It's hard when you only see them once or twice a month, and they barely know your name."

I didn't have an ex-husband or kids, but that didn't matter. In this room, lies were tools, a means to an end. After a moment, he nodded.

"That sucks."

"Do you miss Elijah when you don't have him?"

He nodded.

"Yeah."

"I believe that," I said. "And I'm here to help you. You may not believe that, but I don't like putting people in prison. I'd much rather help people. We're going to find your son. I can almost guarantee that. It'd be a lot better for you if you helped us now. Where is he?"

He looked at the table, his mouth shut.

"I won't lie to you, Ryan. It doesn't look good for you. Where is Elijah?"

His Adam's apple bobbed as he swallowed.

"I told you the truth. I lost him."

I stared at him before nodding and reaching into my purse.

"People lose car keys, cell phones, ChapStick, wallets," I said, throwing each item on the table as I named them. "You don't lose a child. Where's Elijah?"

He looked at the table.

"I don't know."

I gathered my things and put them back in my purse. Then I allowed my eyes to bore into him.

"You're under arrest for child neglect. Under Missouri law, that's a Class-D felony. If we find Elijah alive, you'll serve at least a full year in prison. You'll have a felony record your entire life, and it'll be on every job application you ever fill out.

"If we find Elijah and he's hurt, that felony jumps to a Class-B. You'll spend five years in prison without the chance of probation or parole. If Elijah is dead, that felony jumps to a Class-A. You'll get thirty years minimum. You'll be fifty by the time you're released. Nobody'll hire you because you'll have no job skills. Your family will have moved on. Nobody will remember you, and even if somebody does, it's because they hate you. You'll die alone. Statistically, there's a good chance you'll kill yourself. People will cheer your death."

I waited for him to say something. He didn't, so I continued.

"If I find out you killed Elijah so you could avoid paying child support, then it's a whole different ballgame. Then I'll take a personal interest in you. I don't like the death penalty. I don't believe in it. I don't want that power.

"I've threatened to send people to the death chamber to help them understand the gravity of the charges against them, but I've never fought for it. I've never wanted someone else to die. If you murdered your son and set this whole thing up to cover it up, I'll make an exception. I will fight with everything I have to send you to your death. You will die terrified and pissing yourself on a table with the loved ones of the little boy you murdered watching."

I stood and leaned forward so our faces were close enough that he could have headbutted me had he wanted to.

"I'll watch, too," I said, my voice soft. "I'll see your tears, I'll hear your pleas for mercy, and I will grieve for the little boy whose life you took, but I will never look away from you. I will watch the light leave your eyes and feel grateful for the opportunity. Think about it. You can live, or you can die strapped to a table. It's your choice. Frankly, my only concern right now is your son. I don't give a shit about you."

The room went quiet. I didn't move. He wouldn't look at me.

"I think I want a lawyer," he said.

"Fine," I said. I left and slammed the door shut behind me. In the hallway, I leaned against the wall, my eyes closed. Marcus joined me a minute later. He raised his eyebrows.

"You were a little intense in there."

"I may have overdone it," I said. "You mind booking him? I need to go for a walk."

Chapter 21

Julie stayed with her parents inside Ryan's house for almost twenty minutes. She didn't feel better, but she stopped crying. Mostly, she wanted out of there. The first time she saw the Powell's grand two-story entryway and their floor-to-ceiling windows, Julie had been awestruck. Her family had survived, but they never went to Disneyland or Europe, they rarely ate out, and they drove used cars with a hundred thousand miles or more on the odometer. Ryan came from a different, better world.

Julie had never fit into St. Augustine. The town attracted tourists, but it was a blue-collar area at heart. Julie liked art galleries and poetry readings. For years, she had carried a sketchbook with her wherever she went. The kids in school had thought she was weird. She didn't want to discuss boys or Jesus like the other girls. On the weekends, sometimes she and her friends had driven into St. Louis to visit the art museum or to see plays on college campuses. She would have had a lot of fun in a big city.

For their first date, Ryan had taken her to the St. Louis Art Museum. It was a special invite-only exhibit. Ryan's dad had given a lot of money, so he got an invitation, and he gave it to his son. Ryan didn't care about art, but for two hours, Julie had lived the life of her dreams. In every gallery, an expert art historian or museum curator stood ready to answer her questions. Waiters in tuxedos had served fancy hors d'oeuvres in the lobby. Ryan had worn a button-up shirt, and she had worn a simple black dress her mom had borrowed from one of her friends. She had felt beautiful.

Four weeks later, she took Ryan to Art Hill, just outside the museum, and told him she was pregnant. She had a romantic idea that he'd be happy—or at least supportive. Instead, he left her there, over an hour from home. She was too humiliated to call her parents, so she called Stacy to pick her up. Two weeks later, Ryan called and apologized and said he'd pay for an abortion. She refused, and he refused to talk to her for another two weeks. By then, his parents were involved, and she became a mistake to fix.

Scott, Julie's dad, parked in the driveway outside their home. The adults stayed still, taking their cues from their bereft daughter. Neither had cried, but they hurt, too. Elijah was their grandson. They loved him as much as she did. So she did what she should have done hours earlier.

"He's not dead," she said. "I'm his mom. I'd know if he had died."

Lisa, Julie's mom, looked out the window and drew in a slow breath. Scott shifted and looked in the backseat.

"We're a family. We'll get through this together."

Julie opened her door and stepped out.

"We're going to find him," she said, standing in the driveway. "My baby is just fine."

Lisa and Scott stepped from the car. Lisa put an arm around her daughter's shoulders and another on her elbow to lead her inside, but Julie didn't need it. The initial shock and fear at Elijah's disappearance had dissipated. Now she needed to focus on getting him back. The family went inside.

"You want something to eat, honey?" asked Lisa. Julie tried to say she was fine, but Lisa ignored her. "I'm going to make you some eggs and toast. You need to eat."

Lisa needed to keep herself busy to keep from worrying, so Julie nodded. While her mother and father took care of her, she sat at the table beside their kitchen. Scott and Lisa were good parents, and she appreciated everything they did. After Julie ate, her dad cleaned the dishes, while her mom changed the sheets on the beds. Until they found Elijah, Lisa would find all kinds of projects around the house. It was a fine way to deal with stress.

Finally, an hour and a half after they arrived home, Lisa and Scott sat at the table near their daughter. Lisa held her daughter's hands, while Scott sat beside her, silent. Then he cleared his throat.

"It's getting late," he said. "We should head to bed. We might have to get up early."

Julie agreed. Her parents suggested she stay in the guest room, but she told them she was fine. Had they gone to bed, she would have left immediately. Instead, she allowed them to escort her up. Then they went to their own room. She waited about half an hour before making her move.

The police thought Ryan was a murderer. They hadn't said it, but they didn't need to. The moment they made their minds up, their investigation changed. Now, they were focused on Ryan. They wanted to send him to prison, and she was okay with that. She wasn't okay with giving up on Elijah.

Julie had been sneaking out of her house since she was fourteen years old. Back then, she had just gone to Stacy or Madison's house. Now, she climbed out of her bedroom window, scampered across the roof, and lowered herself to the railing on the back deck. Within just a few minutes, she was in her car.

Ryan got a 1430 on his SATs. He wasn't a genius, but he could think. He was smart enough to know the police would investigate Elijah's disappearance—accident story or not. If Ryan had killed Elijah, they would have found the body. Then Ryan would never walk free again. Elijah was alive. He was Ryan's son. Not even Ryan would dump him with a stranger.

For years, Ryan's family had fought for more time with Elijah. Julie had thought the lawsuits were Andrea and Frank's idea, but they weren't. She knew better now. Ryan must have wanted a son. It was the only explanation.

And that made this easy. She knew where her son was: with Ryan's new girlfriend, in his new apartment. He wanted a family. Julie didn't plan to let him take hers.

*****

Marcus booked Ryan on child neglect charges. We'd arraign him in the morning. In years past, we would have kept him in our own cells, but we didn't have the staff to monitor them anymore. Instead, after fingerprinting him, Marcus loaded him into a cruiser and drove him to the St. Francois County Jail in Farmington. St. Augustine would pay for his incarceration, but at least we didn't have to keep an officer on duty twenty-four hours a day.

I wrote notes in my office and let Roy sleep for about an hour. For the past few days, I had worked Roy harder than he deserved. He needed a good night's sleep, but I needed his nose. The more time that passed, the more Elijah's body would decompose. The sooner we found him, the better.

After saving my report, I sat on the ground beside the dog and rubbed his side. He startled awake and then put his head down. I rubbed his side before he could go to sleep again.

"Come on, buddy," I whispered. "Just another hour. You can sleep later."

I stood, and he lumbered to his belly but didn't stand. I rummaged around in my desk for a package of beef jerky, his favorite treat. He licked his lips and followed the package with his eyes.

"Up and at 'em, buddy," I said, holding a small piece toward him. He shot to his feet, allowing me to hook his lead on his collar. He took his treat and shook himself awake. Two minutes later, we were in my car, driving to Pinehurst.

It was almost three in the morning. Few lights illuminated the neighborhood homes, but occasionally I saw a glimmer from a flashlight in the surrounding woods. Roy snored behind me. I glanced in the rearview mirror at him as I parked near Dave Skelton's pickup. Roy was healthy, but I wondered whether I was pushing him too hard. He slept eleven to twelve hours a day, but a lot of that came during naps. It was hard to keep track of everything. He hadn't been irritable or confused, though.

Even if we found Elijah's body tonight, little would change. The coroner wouldn't autopsy him until tomorrow, so we'd learn little new about his cause of death. Kevius and Darlene would investigate, but they wouldn't conclude anything about the forensic evidence until tomorrow. A toxicology screen would take days or weeks, depending on the substances being checked.

My dog was tired, I was tired, and I had little more to accomplish tonight. I should have driven home, but I couldn't.

Nights were hard for me. When I was a little girl, my biological mother sang to me when I had nightmares. She didn't do it every time, but she did it enough. She knew how to make me feel safe. Then I lost her, and for a long time, I stopped being safe. I lived in both wonderful and terrible foster homes. In one, I had a wonderful foster mother who read me stories at night and made me feel loved. In another, a foster father drugged and raped me in the living room. He had hurt other girls in his care, too.

Christopher went to prison, but the state released him before he finished his sentence. Then he came after me. I killed him and spit on his corpse and kicked his body until my leg hurt. Plenty of people dreamt of doing that to the person who attacked them. They thought it'd make them feel whole and strong again. For a time, I had felt good. Then the joy faded, and a familiar emptiness crept back in. I faced that feeling every night now. Some days, I drank until I passed out. Other days, I was stronger.

My adoptive family was wonderful. They loved me, and I loved them. It was hard to forget everything that had happened to me, though. For a long time, I pretended I felt nothing at all toward my biological mom because that hurt less than admitting how much I loved her. She ignored me when I needed her most, and yet, I'd give anything the world just to hug her again, to inhale that cheap, cherry perfume she wore, to smell the menthol of her cigarettes, to feel as if I were home.

Because that's what mothers were. They were home. Mothers were the first and sometimes only person we ever trusted with our hearts. Erin broke mine so thoroughly I still can't put all the pieces back together. Since then, I've grown up, and I've seen the world. Erin wasn't a bad person... she was an addict. She fought, she went to rehab, she tried to be a decent mom, but she failed every single time. I understood her, which is why I loved and hated her.

I created the Erin Court Home for Women as a place for those who needed help. More than that, I created it for their kids so they wouldn't experience the things I had. For the women and families the shelter housed, it had become a place of hope. For me, it was a monument to the monsters of my past. Every time I came home, I wondered if I had made a mistake.

Erin had left me and my biological half brother Ian a lot of money when she died. I should have taken the money and run. Erin hadn't left it to me so I could memorialize the past; she gave me to me so I could turn my back on it for good. Ian would go to college soon. He'd start a new life far from here. He'd move on. I wished I could. Peace is short-lived for those with long memories.

I put my hand on the gear selector when my cell phone beeped. It was Dave Skelton, texting me and asking to meet him in the driveway. When I glanced up, he waved at me from the tent. I cracked the windows and left Roy in the car.

"Morning," I said.

"Is it morning?" he asked. He didn't give me time to respond before he started speaking again. "Julie's in the house. She parked a couple of blocks away and followed the tree line behind the house. I get the feeling this wasn't her first time sneaking in. I planned to see what she was doing. You have some rapport with her, though."

I closed my eyes, felt my belly ache and my shoulders sag as if under a weight.

"I'll talk to her."

"If you need me, I'll stay for a while. Trisha and her husband are in the backyard with flashlights. Everybody else has gone home for the day."

"When you see them, send them home. You should go home, too. It's late," I said. "I'm going in."

He wished me well, and I walked toward the house. Ryan had locked the front door, so I walked to the back. There, I found an open window. It led to a first-floor powder room.

"Julie, it's Detective Court," I called. "I know you're in there."

She didn't respond, so I waited a moment and repeated myself. After another minute, I sighed.

"I'm coming in," I shouted, already pulling myself through the window. I stepped down onto the toilet. "Sheriff's Department. I know you're here, Julie."

She said something, but I couldn't hear her. I walked toward her voice and called out again. Once more, she spoke, but her voice sounded so strained, I couldn't understand her. I checked a couple of rooms before finding her in a small, yellow bedroom with a white toddler bed. Julie sat beside the bed, rocking, and clutching a stuffed orange monkey. I stayed in the doorway until she cleared her throat and looked at me.

"This is Robbie," she said. "He's an orangutan. We named him after an orangutan at the St. Louis Zoo. Elijah can't sleep without him. Robbie's his favorite. I need to bring it to him."

I knelt beside her and lowered my voice.

"Let's go outside and talk. Okay, hon? I'll call your mom and dad. Or a friend. I can call a friend, too."

She shook her head and clutched the stuffed animal.

"He's dead, isn't he?" she asked, her gaze absent, like she was staring at something I couldn't see. I swallowed the lump in my throat. "I didn't think so until now."

"We don't know anything yet."

She looked down again.

"He's got money in his sock drawer. It's in his room. I didn't count it."

I hesitated before standing.

"Which one is his room?"

"Go left in the hallway. It's on the end."

"Stay here," I said. "I'll be right back."

Her eyes went distant again, and I stepped into the hallway. Ryan's room had a vaulted ceiling, windows on three walls, and a king-sized bed. Six-panel doors led to an ensuite bathroom and walk-in closet bigger than my bedroom at home. I ignored most of that and walked to a chest of drawers. Julie had pulled the top drawer out, revealing banded stacks of cash. I almost swore under my breath. Stacks of cash in a young man's room rarely portended good things.

I checked on Julie before hurrying downstairs. Dave, Trisha, and Graham, Trisha's husband, stood in the driveway outside.

"Hey, Graham, you mind driving yourself home tonight? I'll make sure she makes it home as soon as possible. In the meantime, I need Dave and Trisha inside. We've got a problem."

Chapter 22

Dave and I counted and cataloged the money while Trisha sat with Julie in the home's entryway. This was tricky on a few levels. Julie had already lost her child, and we couldn't arrest her for trying to find him—no matter how misguided the attempt. Though she hadn't found Elijah, she had found twenty-five thousand dollars cash. That money changed the game. Twenty-five grand was too much cash to carry around. It made Ryan a target. Unfortunately, it made Elijah a target, too.

"Damn."

Skelton glanced at me. We were in Ryan's massive bedroom. Twenty-five stacks of ten hundred-dollar bills lay on the bed in front of us.

"Something wrong, Joe?"

"Yeah," I said, squeezing my jaw. "I thought I was dealing with a twenty-year-old father who killed his kid and covered it up. The money opens a lot of doors."

"You find any drugs in the house?"

I scratched the back of my head.

"No, and that's another problem. We'll confiscate the cash because we can't leave it sitting in a vacant house, but I don't think we can use it. Julie and Ryan share a kid, but she doesn't have the authority to be in the house, let alone allow us to search it. Her search was illegal, and so were her findings. We can't even use the money on a search warrant affidavit."

Skelton straightened.

"What can we do with it?"

"Hold it in the vault. Otherwise, nothing. We'll pretend it doesn't exist."

Skelton drew in a breath through his nose and shook his head.

"So this kid'll go free," he said. "He murdered his son, and there's nothing we can do."

"No. We'll keep working the case. Ryan's not walking away from this. I can guarantee you that."

Skelton blinked but didn't look at me.

"I'm glad you're on this. Marcus is a good detective, but he's not mean like you are."

He meant it as a compliment, so I kept my mouth shut. I wasn't mean, but I understood the world. People who hurt others didn't deserve pity or mercy. If you forgave your abuser, they'd just hurt you again, and if they didn't hurt you, they'd hurt somebody else. Worse, children who grew up in violent households expected violence when they grew older. Violence was normal to them. The cycle would repeat until someone else stepped in and ended it. So that's what I did. If that made me mean, I could deal with it.

"Let's bag the cash. We'll have to wake up Bob Reitz so he can open the vault. You and Trisha can deliver it. We'll need two people with the money at all times so Ryan's lawyers can't claim we tried to steal anything. I'll take care of Julie."

Skelton hesitated and drew in a breath.

"You mind calling Bob?" he asked. "He's cranky this time of day."

"Sure," I said, smiling. "I'll call him from the car."

Skelton agreed, and we started packing things up. As he and Trisha delivered the money, I escorted Julie to my car and called Bob Reitz before calling her parents. They knew she had snuck out and had been searching for her. They came over right away. As Julie and her mom hugged, I talked to her dad and told him the truth—minus the bit about the money. Julie might tell him, but it was too damning to become common knowledge at this stage of our investigation. I impressed on him the importance of keeping her from our crime scene.

Once they left, I got Roy. His nap had energized him, so I hooked a leash to his collar and pet his side.

"You're a good boy," I said, already dreading what I had to say next. Then I closed my eyes, drew a breath through my nose, and exhaled slowly before speaking. "Find the body. Find it, buddy. Find him."

Roy was well trained and understood the command. He stuck his nose in the air and sniffed deeply, but he didn't move. I started walking him toward the house, but nothing there interested him, either. It had been over twelve hours since we received the call about Elijah. If he was dead, his body would have started breaking down. Roy would have smelled it from miles away.

He and I spent twenty minutes behind the home, but never once did he pull or indicate he smelled decomposition. Elijah wasn't here. I suspected Ryan could find him, but he wasn't talking, which meant it was time to put the screws to him.

I secured Roy in the car and headed back to the station. We'd come back for our tent tomorrow and set up a command post again. Downtown, I led Roy to my office and brewed a pot of coffee in the break room. It wasn't great coffee, but it was black and would help me stay awake for a while. Trisha, Bob, and Dave had already left. Hopefully, they were at home sleeping.

Julie thought Ryan had an apartment in St. Louis with another woman. Ryan refused to talk about that, but that didn't matter. Landlords didn't get into business to lose money. They investigated their tenants and verified income, credit scores, and called references. Someone should know about Ryan's new apartment.

I sat at my desk and called up his credit report. Six months ago, he had applied for his first credit card. His mom cosigned, and he was given a five-hundred-dollar limit. Every month, he ran up a couple hundred dollars in charges and paid it off. Aside from the bank that issued his card, he had no hard or soft pulls on the report, which meant no landlord had looked him up. His new apartment must have been in his girlfriend's name. That would make things tough.

I pushed back from my desk and drank my coffee, thinking. If we could read Ryan's text messages and emails, we'd find his girlfriend's name within moments. Without leverage, though, that wouldn't happen. Ryan had already asserted his right to counsel and cut off communication. Normally, that didn't bother me. Police officers were human, and, like all humans, we made mistakes. Sometimes we arrested the wrong person; other times, we sent the wrong person to prison. Lawyers kept us in check. They forced us to follow the rules and protected the entire system. I liked lawyers. Part of me even admired them.

In a case like this, though, we needed communication. Ryan, a supposedly loving father who had lost his son, should have been screaming at the top of his lungs at us. He should have offered to walk us around the backyard, to show us everywhere Elijah liked to play, and to demonstrate exactly what he had been doing when Elijah went missing. He should have been frantic. Instead, he had made a frozen pizza. He didn't even call the police when the kid went missing. He waited until Julie arrived, well over an hour later.

Elijah was probably dead, but if he wasn't, I needed Ryan's cooperation. If he didn't want to help voluntarily, I'd change the incentives. Ryan was going to prison for child neglect, but if we could get Elijah declared dead, we'd enhance the charges against him. His year in prison would turn into life without the possibility of parole. If we put the screws to him hard enough, he ought to sing—and if he didn't, he'd never step foot outside prison again.

Though I doubted she had anything to do with Elijah's disappearance, I looked up Julie next. Her background check was easy, mostly because she had no criminal record. Her Facebook profile had over five hundred friends, but she never posted—not unexpected given her age—while her Instagram profile had hundreds of pictures of Elijah from the time of his birth to today. They looked happy. She also had videos of them playing together and of him running around the park.

The pictures were cute and sanitized. There was no drama or excitement. It was boring, almost. It made me wonder whether she kept this feed for her family and whether she had another secret feed for friends. I sipped my coffee and watched a few videos, but then jumped when my cell phone rang. It was after four in the morning. I didn't know the number calling me, but I answered anyway.

"Hey," I said. "This is Detective Joe Court with the St. Augustine County Sheriff's Department. Who is this?"

"Cassandra Rice. My husband said you came by the house this afternoon."

It took a moment to place the name, but then I nodded.

"Dr. Rice, thanks for calling," I said. "You're an early riser. It's ten after four in the morning."

"I just finished work."

I rubbed my eyes and yawned.

"That's fine," I said, struggling to remember what restaurants were still open. Able's Diner used to be open well before the sun rose, but with the local economy in the slump, they had started closing at night. "Normally, I'd ask if you wanted to get coffee, but nothing's open at four in the morning. You think you could come by my station for a conversation? It'll be the best terrible coffee of your life."

"I'm not comfortable with that," she said. "Sorry. I'd prefer to talk on the phone."

"And I'd prefer to talk in person," I said, forcing myself to smile. "You may be the last person to have seen Mannie Gutierrez alive. It's important that we talk. If you refuse, you might get swept up in an investigation. I don't want that. Your life is your own business, but if you make me, I will find out things about you that you haven't even told your husband. I'm working a murder. Everything's on the table. If you come to me, you control the narrative. If I have to dig, everything comes up. So what do you want to do?"

She went silent for a few moments.

"Fine. I'll be waiting for you on my front porch. We can talk here."

I looked down at my dog. He was snoring and seemed content on his bed.

"I'll be there as soon as I can. Thank you."

I hung up, slipped my phone into my purse, and then knelt beside the dog.

"Hey, dude," I said. "I'm taking you home. Mom's got an appointment with a doctor."

Chapter 23

I drove Roy home. Normally, I didn't like leaving him alone for long periods of time, but he needed the sleep more than he needed companionship. I had cleaned recently, so he couldn't get into trouble.

Roy was sweet, kind, and loyal, but he loved food, and he didn't care where it came from. The last time I had left him alone, he ate an entire baguette I had left beside the stove in the kitchen. I didn't think he could reach it, but he pushed a chair over and then climbed up. I left for five minutes, but when I returned, he was on the counter, ripping the wrapping paper to shreds and licking crumbs off the counter. As soon as he saw me, he jumped down and dove into a play bow—as if I wouldn't notice the crumbs stuck to his nose. My best friend was a butt.

I led the dog inside and walked to the bedroom where I changed into fresh clothes and brushed my teeth while he jumped onto the bed. He put his face between his paws and looked ready to spring up and follow me out, but I told him to stay instead. He whined a little, but he didn't follow me out.

Elijah Smith's disappearance had sapped most of my energy, but I still had a murder to work. As I drove to the Rice's home, I reminded myself of the case. Mannie Gutierrez flew to St. Louis from Miami with a box of prepaid cell phones and a significant amount of cash. He stayed in St. Louis, but he met Cassandra Rice for lunch in St. Augustine and visited her place afterward, presumably for a romantic rendezvous. Later, he was shot with a large-caliber weapon and likely died instantly. His shooter then dumped his body in a remote location in the woods in St. Augustine County.

Unfortunately, I had more questions than answers. Mannie's rental car had no usable fingerprints; no one had seen the murder; we had no clue what kind of gun had killed him; we didn't know where he had died; we didn't know how he had been dumped at the dump sight; we didn't know why he had brought that much cash; we didn't know who he planned to give his multiple cell phones to; we didn't know the extent of his relationship with Cassandra; we didn't know whether he knew Matthew Rice... we didn't know a damn thing.

About thirty percent of all criminal investigations were easy. An officer saw the crime, a criminal confessed immediately and without prodding, or a surveillance camera caught the crime. We closed those cases as soon as we picked them up. The remaining seventy percent of cases required us to put in some legwork, and every crime scene and social milieu had unique challenges.

Detectives in bigger cities investigated victims they had never met, some of whom came from cultures and backgrounds different from those of the detective. Depending on the victim, the witnesses might speak Serbian, Spanish, Persian, Vietnamese, French, or Pashto. The city would have translators available for all those languages, but the language barrier made it difficult to establish rapport. The victims themselves posed problems as well. Some had no stable address or even identity, making it impossible to conduct a background investigation.

On top of that, they had to deal with ambitious prosecutors who might be more interested in her next career stop than in doing her job. I didn't envy them.

In St. Augustine, we had different challenges. Our prosecutor meant well, but he didn't always have the money to bring every case to trial, forcing him to plead out a lot. Our crime lab had talented people, but we didn't have the technical resources to crack a victim's cell phone or search a victim's internet history for hidden information. And we didn't have the manpower to monitor the county's known trouble spots.

Our small population, though, carried a few benefits. When we had a murder, somebody on my staff usually knew the victim. In St. Augustine, kindly old ladies were very rarely shot for their social security checks. Here, if we found an old lady shot in her home, we'd find a meth lab in her kitchen or cocaine hidden in her toilet tank. We identified our troublemakers. We knew where they lived, who their friends were, and we knew the languages they spoke.

In this case, with a victim from Miami and no forensic evidence, our inbuilt advantages were nullified. That was frustrating.

I reached the Rice's home at a quarter to five. The sun wouldn't rise for almost two hours, leaving the sky black to the horizon. My headlights swept across the porch, and a woman stepped through the front door. She wore a white shirt, blue jeans, and a salmon-colored cardigan. A tie held her hair back from her face. Even after an exhausting shift in a busy emergency room, she was pretty. I could see why Mannie liked her.

Before getting out, I grabbed a notepad from my glove box. Then I hurried up the drive.

"Morning," I said. "Thanks for talking to me. I'm Detective Joe Court."

Dr. Rice flicked her eyes up and down me.

"My husband said you came by to ask about break ins. There haven't been any. My neighbors and I talk. What do you really want?"

"Tell me about Mannie Gutierrez."

She considered. Then she raised her eyebrows and looked away.

"I met him at The Mystic Garden on Thursday, invited him to my place, and fucked him in the guest room. After he left, I showered. I haven't seen him since."

She was forthright, at least. I jotted down notes.

"Did you kill him?"

Her gaze snapped to mine.

"He's dead?"

"That's why I'm here," I said, nodding to a pair of wooden patio chairs. "Can we sit?"

She hesitated before raising her eyebrows.

"Fine, but I barely knew Mannie. I don't think I can help you."

"I understand," I said, nodding and waiting for her to sit. I sat on the chair nearest hers. "As Dr. Rice told you, I'm working a murder. Before we get into those questions, let's start with some quick background."

She confirmed her name and address and that she was married to Dr. Matthew Rice. She also declared that she felt safe, and that she was answering my questions without inducement or compulsion of any kind. Finally, I smiled.

"Tell me about your husband," I said.

She blinked and tilted her head to the side.

"I thought this was about Mannie."

"It is," I said. "Tell me about Matthew."

She straightened and considered before shrugging.

"He's a doctor. He's a good man."

"That's good to hear," I said. "He stitched me up once in the ER. I'm glad he's here."

"Why are you asking about him?"

"Does he know you slept with Mannie Gutierrez?"

She looked toward the lawn.

"My husband and I are busy professionals. We love one another, but we rarely have time to meet each other's needs, so we each allow the other to have discrete liaisons outside the marriage."

"Did your spouse know about Mannie Gutierrez?"

"I told him after you visited."

I put my notepad on my lap and leaned back, my arms crossed.

"What'd he say?"

"He asked if I were happy. I said yes. We didn't know Mannie was dead."

I lowered my chin.

"That's it?" I asked. She didn't respond, so I smiled. "I talked to your husband. He was intelligent, confident, sure of himself...he knows his place in the world. If you had picked up a twenty-five-year-old personal trainer from your gym, I doubt he would have cared. A twenty-five-year-old kid wouldn't be a threat to him. You'd never leave a doctor for your trainer. You'd get bored. Mannie, though? Handsome, wealthy, smart, worldly... he's everything your husband once was. I'd be jealous. Maybe I'd even kill for that."

She shook her head, her expression neutral.

"My husband didn't kill Mannie, and I wouldn't leave my husband for anyone. We have a good life together. I wouldn't ruin that for a fling. He wouldn't, either. And if you think he's intelligent, confident, and all that, talk to him. You're his type."

"Thank you, but no," I said, picking up my notepad again. "How'd you meet Mannie?"

She sighed and rolled her eyes.

"As I said, I met him at the restaurant," she said. "We arrived at the same time. He said hello, I smiled, and he asked if I wanted to have lunch."

"You hadn't seen him beforehand?"

"No."

If true, that was a problem. I considered.

"What'd you guys talk about at lunch?'

She straightened.

"First date stuff," she said. "He asked about my work, and I asked why he was in St. Augustine."

I leaned forward, truly interested now.

"What'd he say?"

"Business. He was a lawyer, and he was visiting a client. And before you ask, he didn't get into specifics, and I didn't press. His work wasn't my interest."

"He worked in admiralty law," I said. "It deals with navigation and shipping. Did he talk about that at all?"

"No. Sorry."

I nodded and considered.

"What was your impression of him?"

She raised an eyebrow and lowered her chin.

"He was handsome, charming, and worldly."

"He stayed in a hotel in St. Louis. Did you meet him there?"

"No. I had lunch with him and spent two hours in bed with him afterward. He was charming, but it wasn't a long-term thing."

"It was just a one-night stand," I said, nodding.

She shrugged.

"Afternoon stand, I guess."

"I searched his hotel room and found a significant amount of cash and cell phones," I said. "He mention anything about drugs?"

Her eyes widened. Before she could respond, I reached into my purse for my cell phone and snapped her picture.

"Did you go to his hotel?" I asked.

She swallowed and shook her head, the movement almost imperceptible.

"Are you sure?" I asked. "Something's spooked you. I can't read minds, but I'm pretty good with body language. You are desperately seeking to come across as controlled and strong, but you're gripping the arms of your chair so tightly your knuckles are white. You're scared. When people get nervous, their autonomic nervous system goes a little haywire. As a doctor, you understand that. Your skin feels itchy or tingly, your muscles tighten, your heart rate increases. When I mentioned drugs, you pursed your lips and opened your eyes wide. I've got a picture if you'd like to see. This conversation makes you very uncomfortable. Why?"

She sputtered an answer, but it wasn't intelligible. Then she shook her head and closed her eyes.

"Mannie and I slept together, and now he's dead. You're telling me he's some kind of drug dealer? I'm nervous because I don't want his clients or suppliers or friends coming after me."

"Why would anyone come after you?"

"I don't know," she said, standing.

"If you'd like, I can walk through your house. I can point out ways you can help secure yourselves."

"No, thank you."

I stood.

"If Mannie was just a fling, I doubt you have anything to worry about. His killer came after him specifically, destroyed the forensic evidence, and dumped his body deep in the woods. It's a professional job. They won't risk coming after you unless they have reason. Do they?"

She shook her head.

"No," she said, her voice soft.

"Good," I said, smiling. "If you change your mind and decide you know more than you've told me, you've got my card. Call me day or night."

She said she would, and I walked to my car. The conversation had been frustrating. If Dr. Rice had been honest, her relationship didn't mean a thing. It was a coincidence that Mannie had died after their bedroom romp. I didn't know if

CHRIS CULVER

I believed that, but I also didn't have anything to contradict it.

I felt like I was wasting my time. Be nice if I had time to waste.

Chapter 24

I left the Rice's house, drove about a mile, and pulled into
the empty parking lot of a dentist's office to write a few
notes. My only theory about Mannie Gutierrez's death was
now so shot full of holes I'd have to throw it out. Matthew
Rice may have felt jealous of his spouse's new lover, or he
may have felt happy that she had met somebody. Either
way, he had agreed to their lifestyle. He wouldn't have killed
Mannie for sleeping with his wife.

So I was back to the beginning. I had little evidence, no
motive, and no witnesses to Mannie's death. He traveled to
St. Augustine, but he wasn't a local and didn't appear to
have any ties to the local community. Ideally, I'd fly down to
Miami and interview his neighbors, friends, and coworkers.
I'd learn why he flew to Missouri, why he brought so many
cell phones, and who wanted him dead. Then I'd trace those
enemies to Missouri, investigate them, and make some ar-
rests.

Since I didn't live in an ideal world, I'd have to call the
police department in Miami and convince their homicide
unit to do my job for me. That probably wouldn't happen,

but maybe I'd get lucky. Those were concerns for another day, though. It was five in the morning. I needed to sleep.

I drove home, went inside, and found Roy asleep on my bed with his paws in the air and his head on my pillow. He rolled over as soon as he heard me but didn't otherwise move. I didn't care. I lay down beside him and fell asleep almost immediately.

As tired as I was, I could have slept all day. Unfortunately, my dog was an asshole. He woke me up at 7:30, probably after hearing kids outside.

"Don't do this to me, Roy," I whispered. "Just let me sleep."

He nudged me with his nose and dove into a play bow.

"I let you sleep in my office."

He seemed to grin as he put his paws on the bed and tried to lick my face.

"I hate you," I said, pushing him away and sitting upright. He ran to the door, and I dressed and grabbed a leash. We went out and said hello. Though I hadn't gotten drunk in days, I looked hung over. It didn't matter. The kids petted Roy and got on the bus. As they left, I smiled at their moms and started to go home. Then I stopped when I saw two young women pushing baby strollers toward us. One waved to me. I waved back and glanced at one of the moms.

"These two ladies live in the shelter?"

She looked up the sidewalk. Her smile left, and she stood straighter.

"No."

I didn't know both ladies, but I suspected they lived in the same compound. One was Sophie Marie Hitler. Before he died—presumably of old age—Sophie had been engaged to the Church of the White Steeple's founder. It was a gross relationship, one for which her community had groomed her for years. The moms shuffled off as Sophie and her friend approached.

"Hey, Joe!"

I smiled at her. Part of me wanted to rescue Sophie from the church and its hateful ideology, but another part of me saw a happy, healthy young woman who lived within a community of like-minded people. Her clothes were clean, her stroller looked new, and her baby looked cute and well fed. She was an adult and could make her own choices—even if her choices created a haven for white supremacists.

"Hey, Sophie," I said. "You're up early this morning."

She looked down at the baby.

"Auggie's an early riser," she said. "I don't get much sleep these days."

"I can imagine," I said, smiling and glancing at the other woman. She was twenty-five or thirty and had straight auburn hair down to her shoulders and pale skin. Like Sophie, her clothes were clean, her baby looked healthy and happy, and she looked well. As a police officer, I didn't care how people lived their lives or what they believed, but I cared about kids. As abhorrent as Sophie's church was, they kept their members healthy. "I don't think we've met. I'm Detective Joe Court. Sophie's an old friend."

"And Eleanore's a new friend," said Sophie. "She and her husband just moved in with us from Idaho."

"My husband's teaching Sophie and her people how to farm their land," she said. "We're going to make the whole place self-sufficient."

"It'll help us all survive the race war," said Sophie. I nodded and pretended that made sense.

"It's nice to see you both. I'm going back to bed. I've had a late night."

Roy and I turned, but Sophie reached out and touched my arm. I stopped and smiled.

"Thank you for this place," she said. "I think it's great what you've done here. You don't agree with us, but we try to do something similar at our church. If a woman comes to us, we'll give her a home. No man will ever hit her. We treat them like queens. Two of our girls went to college this year. They came to us when they were teenagers, and now they're going to become teachers. That's the future. You shape enough young minds, you can shape the world."

I almost grimaced, but held it back.

"That's great," I said. "Teachers can change the world. You guys have a good day."

I started toward my apartment again, but Sophie cleared her throat.

"Joe, I heard you're on the County Charter Commission."

I squeezed my jaw tight before shaking my head.

"I'm the law enforcement rep, but I can't vote."

Sophie stepped toward me. Roy sat at my side, his tongue hanging out.

"That's an important job. My church put forward our own amendment for the new Charter. We even got five hundred signatures for it."

I had heard of their proposal, of course. They wanted to turn St. Augustine County into an official haven for white Anglo-Saxon Protestants. They wouldn't kick residents out right away. Instead, they'd give those with whom they disagreed five years to leave. Then, the county would begin eminent domain proceedings.

"I believe the amendment was voted down," I said. "Sorry."

"The Reverend told us," she said. "I'm not worried. Our voice is too strong to ignore. I hope you know you'll always have a place with us."

I nodded. The irony of Sophie's racism was that she meant so well. She legitimately believed that a segregated world was a better one. I felt sorry for her. Her whole life, she had been used. She had grown up in the church and became engaged to its elderly founder when she was barely out of her teens. Before he died, he got her pregnant.

Since then, the church had sent her with signs and a baby to protests, knowing she'd attract attention. Young men might look at her and pay attention, but she wasn't there to recruit new members or share the church's beliefs. She, Eleanore, and the others left the compound to stir up hatred. When they left the church, people yelled at them, spat on them, chased them, and made them feel ashamed of themselves—all for spouting the slogans they had heard their entire lives.

When they returned to the compound, their community welcomed them as returning heroes and reassured them that there was nothing wrong with them. The trips to town reinforced the divide between them and the outside world. The hostile reactions taught them they belonged at the church and only at the church. They had no place outside the church's gates, but inside those gates, they felt love and acceptance. Cults and other fringe organizations frequently used the same tactics.

Sophie wasn't evil... she was naive, programmed from childhood to be the person she had become. I didn't hate her, but I hated the world that made her.

I looked toward the home. Then I looked at Sophie and softened my voice.

"Thank you," I said. "If you or Eleanore ever leave the church, call me. I'll find a place where you'll be safe."

"You are so sweet, honey," said Sophie, her voice bubbly. "But the church is my home. My people will always keep us safe."

"I hope you're right," I said. She smiled and said she and Eleanore would see me later. Then she pushed her baby down the sidewalk. I watched her go. Every time I saw her, I worried about the day her church leaders realized she outgrew her usefulness and handed her a gun instead of a poster. That was for the future, though.

At the shelter, two ladies were already outside, pulling weeds from the flower beds. It was a huge house, and every resident worked to keep it up. Some pulled weeds, while others swept and vacuumed and made dinner for the community. The shelter was designed to help the residents live independently and sustainably. Sometimes, new arrivals were so hurt they needed time to themselves just to decompress. They were given it. Then, when they got their feet back under them, when they realized they were safe, they took on responsibility around the home.

Once they were ready, a social worker helped them get full-time jobs outside the house. With a steady income and insurance, Linda Armus, the director, helped them find affordable housing in the community. The building I purchased protected the women from the elements, but the community the residents created made it a safe, nurturing home. I had even purchased a second home. Linda called it The Annex. It had been a bed-and-breakfast, but now it was home to six ladies and their kids. I wished my mom and I had a similar place when I was a kid.

Roy and I started to climb the steps to my apartment when Linda Armus emerged from the shelter's back door. Linda

CHRIS CULVER

was about my age, and she wore dark blue jeans and a lime green top. I stopped climbing and waved.

"Hey, stranger," I said. "Haven't seen you lately."

"Morning, Joe," she said, smiling. "You got a minute? I was hoping I could talk to you."

I sighed inside but kept the smile on my face.

"If there's coffee involved, you can have several minutes."

"Come on down. We can talk in the backyard. I'll get you a cup."

Linda walked into the old mansion, while Roy and I descended the staircase to the lawn. When I purchased the building, the backyard had grass and a rickety fence but little else. Since then, we removed the old fence and installed a tall privacy fence so the kids could play outside without others watching. A former resident with a green thumb had planted azaleas, hostas, and hydrangeas along the foundation in the shade cast by the house. It was pretty.

I sat on a wrought iron chair on the patio. Linda emerged a few minutes later with two mugs of coffee. We chatted for a few minutes, but then our conversation quieted.

"So what's going on?" I asked. "The last time we had coffee, you said we needed more space. I don't have enough money to buy anything else. Sorry."

Linda smiled and put her mug down.

"I haven't announced it yet, but we received an anonymous donation last week that'll provide funding for the next two years or more."

I leaned forward.

"Are you serious?"

She nodded.

"Almost two and a half million dollars. I couldn't believe it."

"Who's it from?"

She smiled and looked at her mug.

"I don't know. It was funneled through a law firm. The person who made the donation wanted it kept quiet."

"That's amazing," I said. "I'm really glad."

"Me, too."

I smiled and felt my shoulders relax. When I founded the Erin Court Home, I worried the shelter would run out of money quickly, so I structured the deal to shoulder as many challenges as I could. I owned the building and rented it to the charity at a low rate so they wouldn't be saddled with extra expenses. With a hundred-year-old house, a lot could go wrong. The old cast iron plumbing could crack, the roof could leak, the siding could leak... they could be stuck with a fifty-thousand-dollar bill with no way to pay it. By owning the building, I owned the liabilities. Linda ran the charity, and I kept things afloat. When something broke, I called in contractors. The charity's rent covered the expenses but didn't make me rich. It was a good deal, I thought.

Linda blinked.

"We have fourteen families in the main house and annex and eight in the community," said Linda. "We need more staff. The residents and I have talked. After Emily, they'd like a staff member able to stay overnight."

Emily was a former resident. Like many women who arrived at the shelter, she had married a violent man. She thought he'd get better as he grew older. Instead, he nearly killed her. She came to us after her husband beat her with a broomstick until welts covered her back and legs. She contacted Linda, and some volunteers helped her escape. I didn't know the complete story, but, after a week in the shelter, she tried to hang herself in her room. Thankfully, other residents found her and cut her down before she died. She was in a psychiatric center now.

"That's a good idea," I said, nodding. "With that donation, you've got the funding, too. I say go for it."

Linda smiled, but looked uneasy.

"We've got everything we need except a place for her to stay," she said. "It's a big ask, I know, but you can't be happy living in that garage apartment."

My mouth popped open. Then I closed it. A pained look crossed Linda's face.

"You okay?" she asked.

I took a moment to think and mask my actual feelings.

"Yeah, I'm fine," I said. "I just didn't consider that you might need the space. It's fine, though. Put together a job listing. I'll contact a realtor. I'll find something."

"We'll adjust the rent," said Linda, quickly. "To cover the apartment."

"We'll work that out," I said, forcing myself to smile as I stood up. "This is great. You're turning this old house into something important. Thank you for all your work. I need to get to work, though. Roy and I are working a murder. It's rough."

Linda stood.

"This place wouldn't exist without you," she said. "You will always be part of it. I hope you know that."

I nodded but said nothing. Then I excused myself and walked Roy to our apartment. I sat on the couch in the living room. My back hurt, and my legs and arms felt heavy. I was tired, but this feeling went beyond exhaustion.

This shelter gave families hope when they had none. I loved this place. At work, I hunted bad people. I searched through broken lives, investigated broken people, and told broken families their loved ones would never come home. Here, I helped people pick up those broken pieces and rebuild.

When Emily hurt herself, I was the first responder. I checked her neck for a pulse and gave her chest compressions. When another resident's husband showed up screaming that he was going to kill her, I arrested him for violating a restraining order. When the kids lined up for the bus, Roy and I visited and wished them well. I liked the role we played here.

Becoming attached had been a mistake. This apartment was a temporary stop, as was the big house for the shelter's clients. I had moved into my apartment after the old county council stole my house in sham eminent domain hearings. I'd miss it, but Linda was right. It was time to move on. The shelter needed a caretaker. I already had a job.

I started getting ready for the day, but as I brushed my teeth and picked out clothes, the conversation lingered. I thought I had mattered here. Roy and I made people feel safer. At work, I mattered because I signed the overtime slips and doled out investigative assignments. To the Charter Commission, I mattered because I had to be present for every meeting. Everywhere I went, I mattered because of what I could do and what I could give people. Nowhere did I matter for who I was.

Maybe that was life, but it hurt.

Chapter 25

Some people processed their emotions outwardly. When Audrey, my sister, had a bad day, she'd call me, and we'd talk about her day and what had bothered her. Afterward, she'd feel better. I loved that I could do that for her. Other people—me, for instance—processed things inwardly. I thought about my experiences and put them into context. I wanted to understand my feelings instead of merely letting them out. Sometimes, though, even I just needed a hug—or at least a kind word. So I called my mom.

Her phone rang twice but then went to voicemail. A few seconds later, my phone buzzed with an incoming text message.

Can't talk. Touring houses in Chicago.

I furrowed my brow and texted back to ask whether she and dad were moving. She responded right away.

Will talk later. Don't tell Dylan.

A heavy feeling grew in my gut as I put my phone down. Intellectually, it made perfect sense. Audrey and PJ would need help with a baby. Moreover, Mom and Dad were retired. They had no real reason to stay in St. Louis except me and Dylan. Once Dylan finished college, he'd probably move to Chicago, too. The city would be full of young women he hadn't slept with yet. It was unconquered territory. He'd view it as a challenge.

I swallowed hard. My parents' house in Kirkwood was the first real home I ever had. It was the one place I knew would always be there and always be welcoming. Most of my best memories took place in that house. Then again, it wasn't really *my* home. It was always theirs. They bought it before I knew them and could do with it whatever they wanted. My throat felt tight, and my eyes felt watery.

My phone rang. It was my dad. I thought about answering, but I didn't know what to say, so I sent the call to voicemail. Then he texted and asked if we could talk. I texted him back and said I was working a child abduction and didn't have time. Then I turned my phone off.

In the grand scheme of things, my personal life didn't matter. The world would go on. A new family would move into Mom and Dad's house and live happily, and they'd move to Chicago. Still, this hurt. They didn't need my permission to move, but we were a family. My half brother Ian was so busy with school that I hadn't seen him in months. I rarely saw Dylan, either. Audrey and I talked once a week, but with her budding career—and now pregnancy and engagement—those conversations had grown shorter. Mom and Dad were the only real family I had left.

A therapist once told me I needed to put down roots of my own. I had taken the advice and tried my best. I bought a house, made friends, connected with loved ones. I got a dog. My world had grown bigger. But then those roots were pulled out one by one. The former county government took my house in eminent domain proceedings, my friends moved or died, my world shifted. My family was the one thing I had counted on. Now they were leaving, too.

I looked at Roy. He tilted his head to the side, confused. Then he stuck out his tongue and panted. I petted his cheek.

"I'm going to go to bed, sweetie," I said. "Thanks for staying."

He obviously couldn't understand, but he followed me to the bedroom and then hopped up beside me and lay down at my feet. With moments, he started snoring. I closed my eyes and let myself drift for a few hours.

If I had let him, Roy would have slept all day. I wished I could, too, but we had too much to do. I woke up at eleven, dressed, put a leash on Roy, and walked around the block. Afterward, I made a peanut butter and jelly sandwich and headed into work. Trisha was behind the front desk when I arrived. She looked tired, but she smiled and shuffled papers on her desk.

"Hey," she said. "I've got news. Ryan Powell was arraigned this morning. He's already out on bail, and his lawyer's called. He wanted to express his outrage at our treatment of his client and to assert that his client is an innocent father who misses his son. Mostly, I think he was calling for Ryan's benefit. He didn't seem enthusiastic."

I shrugged and closed my eyes.

"His client likely murdered a toddler, so it'd be hard to muster enthusiasm on his behalf."

Trisha's smile slipped, and she drew in a slow breath.

"You think the boy's dead?"

I looked toward the front door and nodded.

"We searched every inch of those woods and couldn't find him. I think he killed his son and dumped the body. Ryan may not be a murderer, but his story's horseshit."

"You might be right," said Trisha, her voice low. She sighed and cleared her throat. "The search continues unabated. The fire department has taken over. A drone enthusiast's club from St. Louis has come down. They've got some pretty fancy equipment with infrared cameras. They're searching all over the place."

"That's good," I said. "Maybe we'll get lucky and find out Dad's not a complete dirtbag."

"Maybe," said Trisha. She pulled a post-it note from her desk. "Shaun Deveraux wants you to call him when you have a minute."

Deveraux was the prosecutor. Until we had a new sheriff, he was also technically my boss, so I couldn't ignore him. I blew a raspberry and nodded.

"Okay. Thanks, Trisha," I said. "If you need me, I'll be in my office."

Trisha nodded, so Roy and I headed upstairs, where I poured myself a mug of coffee in the break room. The floor was empty. Marcus was out on a call. Once we reached my office, Roy yawned and lay down on his bed. Within moments, he started snoring. I sipped my coffee and called the prosecutor's assistant. She patched me through to her boss, who picked up the phone after a few rings.

"Detective," he said. "Morning. Thanks for calling me back. I know you had a late night and early morning."

"I hear you keep busy, too. Trisha said you arraigned Ryan Powell this morning."

"For endangering the welfare of a child," he said. "Given the circumstances of the case, we requested that Ryan be held pending trial or until we could file additional charges, but the judge wasn't interested. Ryan has no criminal record, and he has extensive ties to the community. Given the evidence, we couldn't even charge him as a felon. We'd have to prove that Ryan knowingly acted in a way that endangered his son, but we've not met that burden yet. At worst, he's a crappy parent who turned his back on his toddler when he shouldn't have."

My mouth popped open.

"He probably let his kid die, and you charged him with misdemeanor neglect. You're fucking kidding me, right?"

Deveraux went quiet.

"You don't have kids, do you, Detective?"

I blinked and shook my head.

CHRIS CULVER

"What does that mean?"

"No parent is perfect. When my youngest was three, he pushed a chair to a window in his nursery, opened it, and climbed out onto the roof of our house. I thought he was asleep until my neighbor pounded on my front door. Things happen. Kids, especially little boys, do crazy things you don't expect. Until you give me concrete evidence that Ryan hurt his kid intentionally, I have a hard time filing additional charges—even if the little boy ends up dead. Sometimes, tragedies just happen. Good people make mistakes. It's awful, but it's life. Losing a child would be punishment enough."

I squeezed my jaw tight and counted to five before speaking.

"Did you read my reports?"

"I did," said Deveraux. "You've done good work, and you're under a lot of stress. I know you don't trust Ryan, but I'm here to tell you—as a parent—sometimes awful shit happens, and you can't prevent it. Ryan may be a victim, too."

I squeezed my hand into a fist.

"Last night, Julie Smith broke into the Powell's house. I apprehended her at the scene and took her into custody. While in the Powell's home, Julie found twenty-five thousand dollars cash hidden in Ryan's bedroom."

Deveraux drew in a sharp breath.

"Where's the money now?"

"Our vault," I said. "Once I learned about the money, I called in Officers Dave Skelton and Trisha Marshall. Trisha took Julie into her custody, while Officer Skelton and I cataloged, counted, and bagged the money."

Deveraux went quiet for almost half a minute.

"You still there, Mr. Deveraux?"

"I am," he said, his voice soft. "I'm thinking. What does Ryan say about the money?"

"I haven't had the chance to ask him."

"Did Julie have any legal right to be inside the Powell's home?"

I sighed and scratched my head.

"No."

Deveraux swore before pausing.

"Would Ryan have any legitimate reason to possess that kind of cash?"

"Best I can tell, no," I said. "Julie heard from friends that he was moving to St. Louis. She was afraid he'd take the baby and disappear."

"And she heard this prior to breaking into his house?"

"Correct," I said, nodding. "It's in a report somewhere."

He grunted.

"A parental kidnapping might be our best-case scenario," he said. "Elijah would be okay."

"You might be right," I said, nodding and raising my eyebrows. "I haven't seen a lot to make me optimistic, though. Ryan was a disinterested father at best. Maybe he loved his kid on some level, I don't know. When I interviewed them last night, Julie was shaking and could barely sit. Ryan made a pizza like nothing was wrong. I'm nervous about this one."

Deveraux went quiet for another ten seconds.

"I can't use the money unless we can prove you would have found it anyway during an investigation. It's poisoned. What other leads do you have?"

"None. We've focused on finding Elijah, not finding culpability for his disappearance."

"Where would he have stashed his son?"

I squeezed my jaw tight and breathed through my nose.

"I don't know yet," I said. "Like I said, we've focused on Elijah so far. I checked out Ryan's credit, but I can't find an apartment in his name anywhere."

"Dead or alive, we need to find Elijah."

I counted to five before speaking so I wouldn't snap and tell him I understood my job.

"That's the plan. Since his apartment wasn't in Ryan's name, I'm going to look up his parents, aunts, uncles, anybody I can think of who might have given him a place to live. Then I'll take Roy out to the property and see what he smells."

"And Roy's your cadaver dog?" he asked. I said yes. Deveraux sighed and cleared his throat. "You can't do that. You've got reasonable suspicion that Ryan's hidden a body somewhere, but you don't have probable cause. If you were to stop Ryan for speeding, you'd be within your rights to detain him and have Roy smell his car for decomposition. If a licensed cadaver dog indicated he smelled human remains, you'd have probable cause for a search warrant. A homeowner enjoys a much stronger expectation of privacy in his home than in his car, though. Even knocking on Ryan's door with Roy would be an unreasonable search."

I nodded and considered.

"What if we visited a neighboring property—with permission—and Roy smelled something coming from the Powell's place?"

"Then you would have probable cause. You'd stop and get a warrant. Ryan's family has money. We have to follow procedure," he said. "Let me ask you one thing: if Ryan moved a body in his car, could Roy still smell it after he got rid of the remains?"

"Possibly," I said. "Depends on heat, the degree of decomposition, and a few other factors."

"If Ryan killed his son, he took the body somewhere. Are we agreed on that?"

"That's probably true," I said. "Even if he had buried Elijah, Roy would have smelled him."

"If he moved his son's body, he moved it in a car. Eventually, somebody will drive that car off the Powell's property. If you find it in a public location, Roy can smell it to his heart's content. Then, if he smells a body, we'll get a warrant. I can almost guarantee you that there'll be blood, hair, or fibers.

We'll use that to get a warrant for every location Ryan could have dumped the body. If we're patient, we'll get him."

It seemed reasonable.

"Agreed," I said. "Elijah's safety is my priority, but if he's dead, we'll do everything we can to send his killer to prison."

"We're on the same page, Detective."

I thanked him and hung up. The conversation rankled me. Deveraux could prosecute a case, but he hadn't sat across from Ryan, he hadn't looked in his eyes, he hadn't held Julie as she cried, he hadn't even gone out to the scene. Investigating a homicide forced me to become more than a detective. I had to become a friend, a counselor, a scientist, an archaeologist, a therapist, a babysitter, a psychologist, sometimes even a psychic. I had to combine evidence with feelings and intuition. Deveraux meant well, but we needed a real sheriff to head our department sooner rather than later.

I dove into my case but stopped a few minutes later when Sergeant Bob Reitz knocked on my door. He carried two paper cups from the break room.

"Hey, Joe," he said. "I heard you were in. I brought coffee."

"I am," I said, smiling. "Come on in. Pull up a chair."

He handed me a cup of coffee and sat down.

"You missed the briefing this morning, but I read some of your reports. How are you holding up?"

I nodded and sipped the coffee he brought. It was hot and awful, just as I had expected from our break room.

"Tired, but I'm good," I said.

"How's Mannie Gutierrez?" he asked.

"Still dead. He hooked up with a very attractive surgeon from St. John's before he died, so at least he lived it up before he kicked the bucket. His case isn't going anywhere, so I've pushed him to back while I look for Elijah Smith."

Bob grimaced.

"That's tough. Pam and I went out last night. We didn't find anything, though. It was a good idea to let Dave Skelton take lead. He's good outdoors."

I nodded.

"We're still looking for Elijah, but I'm not optimistic. I think Julie's in the clear. Ryan's going to prison."

"Anything I can do?"

"You got a time machine?" I asked.

"Fresh out."

"Barring that, I'll keep my head down and keep working. Once I find Elijah, we'll break into the petty cash and buy pizza for everybody to celebrate."

Bob stood.

"It sounds like you've got things under control. If you need a break, take it. We'll hold things down when you're unavailable. Good luck."

"Thanks," I said. "I need every ounce of luck I can get."

Chapter 26

My head throbbed, which happened when I was tired. I dug through my desk for a forlorn, nearly empty bottle of ibuprofen, dry swallowed two capsules, and focused on the job in front of me. Elijah Smith could be alive or dead. If he were alive and we were dealing with a parental kidnapping, I needed to look at people Ryan trusted. If he killed his son and stashed the body, Ryan did it somewhere private and secure, likely somewhere he knew—maybe even on property owned by a family member.

I flipped through my notepad until I found a page with interview notes and contact information. Within a couple of minutes, I had Julie Smith's mom and dad on speakerphone.

"Hey," I said. "This is Detective Joe Court. I have a brief update on the case and a few questions. You have a minute?"

"Have you found him?" asked Lisa, her voice breathless. I grimaced and felt my shoulders drop.

"I'm sorry, no," I said. "My update has to do with Ryan Powell. He was arraigned this morning, which means he was formally charged. He pleaded not guilty and was given bail. Our prosecutor requested he be held until trial, but the judge thought that was unduly harsh given the charges and Ryan's lack of a criminal record."

"He murdered my grandson," said Scott. "How could a judge release him?"

"We don't know what happened yet," I said, attempting to maintain a calm tone. "We're still working the case. If Ryan killed Elijah, we will do everything we can to send him to prison for the rest of his life. We're not there yet, though."

"Why did you call us?" he asked. I smiled, hoping it would come through my voice.

"I need information—specifically, I need a list of Ryan's friends and family."

Scott muttered something, but then the line went quiet.

"We've only met his parents once," said Lisa. "It didn't go well. They weren't very nice."

"They treated us like we were stupid," said Scott. "Aside from Frank and Her Highness, Andrea, we don't know Ryan's family."

"Would Julie?"

The two went quiet. Lisa sighed.

"She might. I'll get her."

She came back with Julie a minute later. Julie didn't know many details, but she gave me a list of Ryan's aunts and uncles. She and Ryan went to high school together, so she also knew his friends very well.

"What about work?" I asked. "Ryan ever talk about that?"

"Not really," she said, her voice soft. "He worked for a contractor building houses. He started as a general laborer who cleaned up the worksite, but now they're training him to be a carpenter. It's not a formal apprenticeship, but it's a good job. I don't know why he does it, really. His mom and dad pay for everything. His great-grandfather left him a trust fund."

I was glad we were only speaking over the phone. As soon as she mentioned a construction job, I slumped in my seat. Even entry-level construction jobs paid well and could lead to higher-paid work in the future. It probably was a good job. Unfortunately, construction sites were excellent places to bury bodies. The ground was already torn up, heavy machinery was on-site, and nobody would have noticed a laborer carrying a bag or box.

I thanked her, hung up, and focused on the task in front of me. Julie said Ryan had an Uncle Steven, an Aunt Mary, and an Aunt Sarah. She didn't know last names, so I looked up Ryan's Facebook page. He posted rarely, but Steven and Sarah Chambers almost always responded to his pictures of Elijah. They must have been on his mom's side of the family. Mary Powell commented that Elijah looked cute often, too.

I looked up the Chambers family and Mary Powell. Steven and Sarah lived in the town of St. Augustine, while Mary lived further in the county. Google Maps had satellite and roadside imagery of Mary Powell's property, and it looked like the perfect place to dump a body. Her ranch-style home was set back from the road with trees all around. Ryan could have hidden a grave there easily.

I pushed back from my desk and stood. Roy lifted his head.

"You ready to go out, bud?"

He lumbered to his feet and shook his body out as if he were trying to throw off water. Then he dove into a play bow, his tongue hanging out as he panted. Evidently, he liked the idea of going out. I hooked a leash to his collar, and we walked to my car. Our first stop was the home of Steven and Sarah Chambers. They owned a two-story, brick Italianate home. Elaborate dentil molding along the eaves and its bright yellow door made it stand out from the more sedate architecture of the surrounding homes.

I didn't expect to find anything, but I had a T-shirt owned and worn by Elijah. Roy and I got out of my car half a block away from the house, and I held the shirt in front of the dog's nose. He smelled it and looked at me.

"Find it," I said. "Find the boy."

He sniffed the air and stepped forward, but then stopped and looked at me.

"Find it, Roy," I said. "Find it."

Again, he smelled the air but didn't go anywhere. That was what I figured. I started walking toward the Chambers's home and tried again with the T-shirt. Once more, Roy found nothing. The Chambers had a tiny front yard surrounded by a low brick fence. The grass and flower beds looked undisturbed. Elijah wasn't there. Roy and I were about to turn back to our car when the Chambers's front door opened. A man in blue jeans and a dark purple sweater stepped out.

"Can I help you?"

"No, but thank you. Sorry if we disturbed you."

Roy and I started walking.

"I know who you are," he said. "You won't find anything. We don't know where Elijah is."

I stopped walking.

"You talked to your nephew lately, Mr. Chambers?"

"Get off my property."

I smiled.

"My dog and I are on the sidewalk."

"You're harassing my family. We've been hurt enough. If I see you here again, I'll call a lawyer."

"This is a public sidewalk. Call your lawyer. It's your money to waste," I said. "Have a nice day."

He may have said something rude, but Roy and I ignored him. We reached my car and headed to Mary Powell's rural home next. This time, I parked near a neighbor's home and knocked on the door. The woman who answered seemed a little unsure about me, but she gave me permission to walk Roy up and down the property line she shared with Mary. As before, he didn't smell anything. So I had now struck out twice.

I walked to my car and sat in the front seat. Julie said Ryan worked with a residential construction firm. I flipped through my notepad, but I didn't have the name of the company, so I looked him up on Facebook again on my phone. That didn't lead me anywhere, but then I found his Instagram feed, on which he had posted pictures of jobs he had completed. In one house, he helped install a subfloor. In another, he and a more experienced carpenter framed a bay window. I zoomed in on the bay window picture to read the sign in front of the house.

Bartholomew Brothers Homes.

I got the company's phone number from their website. Then I called. The phone rang twice before a woman answered.

"Hey," I said. "My name is Detective Joe Court, and I work for the St. Augustine County Sheriff's Department. I'm calling about one of your employes. Ryan Powell."

The woman inhaled a deep breath.

"We thought you might call," she said. "My boss gave me a statement. It says Ryan is a good worker. He shows up on time, he works hard until it's time to quit, and he learns quickly. We think he's got a bright future. Personally, I've met him a couple of times, and I can't imagine that he'd hurt anybody, especially his son."

Already, her response indicated how I needed to approach this. If it looked like I was trying to railroad him, she'd likely shut down and hang up. She liked him and wanted to help. I could use that.

"That's good," I said, nodding. "I get mixed messages from people. Ryan's friends tell me one thing, Julie and her friends and family tell me another. You guys are a neutral source. I appreciate your thoughts. I'm looking for background information at this point. As you know, the situation's a tragedy. My job isn't to jam Ryan up; it's to discover the facts and come to a conclusion. Do you want to help?"

"Of course," she said. "Like I said, he's a good kid. We always try to look out for our young guys. They're the future of our company. A guy like him, with the right mentorship, he can go anywhere."

"Good," I said, nodding. "If you want to help him, I need access to his jobsites. I've got a cadaver dog. He and I can walk the sites, he'll sniff the ground, and we'll clear Ryan. Unless you're hiding bodies for the mob, we should be good."

She laughed.

"No, we're not hiding any bodies," she said. "We have seven active jobsites right now, all in the same neighborhood in Jefferson County. It's a subdivision we're developing. Ryan has been working with a framing crew."

She gave me the address and its approximate location northwest of me. It looked like I had my whole afternoon set. I thanked her and hung up. Then I looked in my rearview mirror at the dog. He perked up when he saw my eyes.

"You hungry?"

He panted and licked his nose. Of course he was hungry. He was part Labrador. I put my keys in the ignition and headed back to town. Normally, I would have gone by Able's Diner for a late lunch. The diner was still open, but in recent months, they had cut their menu drastically. They served eggs and pancakes all day, but they had far fewer sandwiches and lunch items. With Waterford College nearby, they had a good niche serving drunk kids greasy food late at night, but the decreased tourist trade made the days tough.

Instead, I drove to the grocery store, bought a sandwich, and headed back to my desk at work. Five minutes after I sat down, my desk phone rang. It was Trisha.

"Hey," I said. "I've got half a giant ham and cheese sandwich, half of which has your name on it. Come on up."

"Raincheck, hon," she said. "Andrea and Frank Powell just arrived. They're Ryan Powell's parents, and they just returned from their vacation."

"Oh, boy," I said, sighing. "They here to yell or talk?"

"Talk," she said. "They're nervous about their grandson."

"They bring Ryan or a lawyer with them?"

"No."

I nodded and wiped my hands and face with a napkin.

"No lawyer, no Ryan," I said, nodding. "I like how this is starting. Now let's see how long they take to lie to my face."

243

Chapter 27

I took a few more bites of my sandwich before wrapping it up and taking it to the break room fridge. Roy didn't seem interested in getting up, so I left him in my office with a bowl of water. When the contractors renovated our station, they removed a lot of the internal walls and replaced them with glass partitions and blinds. It allowed more natural light through the building, and it allowed me to see people in the hallway even as I sat at my desk. I liked it, and so did Roy.

I left the blinds open, so he could see anyone who passed. Then I went down to the lobby. Andrea and Frank Powell were in their late fifties or early sixties, and both had deep tans. Frank wore beige chinos and a white button-down shirt. His wife wore a flowy green top and black pants. It was a cute outfit, but my eyes went to her thousand-dollar Jimmy Choo pumps. With those shoes, she could afford an attorney. I wondered why they didn't bring one.

"Afternoon, everybody," I said, walking toward Trisha and the couple. "I'm Detective Joe Court. Sorry we're meeting under these circumstances.

Nobody made a move to shake my hand. Both Andrea and Frank looked at me with confident, almost bored expressions. Already, I could see why Julie's parents hadn't liked them. I smiled.

"You here for a building tour, or..."

I allowed my voice to trail off. Andrea looked away. Frank closed his eyes and smirked.

"Do you have somewhere private we can speak? We'd prefer to talk to your supervisor, as well."

I considered before blowing a raspberry.

"A spot to talk is easy," I said. "A supervisor is tough, though, because I don't have one. If you have a complaint, you can take it up with Shaun Deveraux."

The two Powells looked at one another. Andrea's eyes flicked up and down me.

"Isn't Deveraux the prosecutor?"

"Yep," I said, nodding.

She rolled her eyes and shook her head.

"He's part of the problem," she said before sighing. "Who's in charge here?"

I raised my eyebrows and looked around the room.

"You're kind of looking at her. Sergeant Reitz supervises the uniformed officers, but I'm the most senior detective."

Andrea brought her fingertips to her face and exhaled loud enough that Trisha looked up from her computer.

"This is a nightmare," she said. "It's like we've stepped into a fucking Kafka novel."

I lowered my voice.

"Has someone you know been transformed into a giant insect? Is that what you're telling me?"

Both looked at me with furrowed brows.

"What the hell are you talking about?" asked Frank.

"*The Metamorphosis* by Franz Kafka," I said. "It's about a salesman who's transformed into an insect. It's brilliant. I read it in high school. What are you talking about?"

"We're here to find out why you're harassing our family," said Frank.

"Let's talk in the conference room," I said. "We'll shelve our discussion of bohemian literature for another time."

They, again, looked at me as if I were crazy. Good. They came in here with a plan and a goal. The more off-balanced I kept them, the more likely they'd be to deviate from that plan and give me honest answers. We walked upstairs and sat in the conference room. Had I planned this, I would have turned on surveillance equipment to monitor the conversation. Since I hadn't, I held up my phone.

"Do you guys mind if I record this? It's helpful for my records."

The two looked at each other. Frank crossed his arms.

"That's fine," he said. "If we can get a copy."

I considered.

"It'll be part of my report," I said. "If your lawyer makes a request during a discovery proceeding, you'll get it. Otherwise, why would you need it?"

They didn't have an answer, so I pulled a notepad from my purse and looked at them.

"So we're here," I said. "Welcome back from your vacation. Sorry it's under these circumstances."

Since we hadn't spoken yet, I gave them a rundown of everything that had happened and our department's response. Their expressions softened.

"I don't understand why you arrested Ryan," said Andrea. "He didn't do anything wrong."

Frank crossed his arms.

"I'm not even convinced Ryan had Elijah," he said. "How do you know Julie didn't take him? This has her fingerprints all over it. She's been angling to take him from us from the start."

I grabbed my notepad.

"This is the kind of thing I was hoping to hear," I said, nodding. "Has Julie withheld Elijah from your family, or has she threatened to take him and run before?"

Frank looked almost surprised.

"Well, no, but she barely even lets us see him. Elijah's our grandchild. We have rights."

I nodded.

"Did she set the visitation schedule or did a judge?"

Frank blinked.

"A judge, of course. What are you getting at?"

"I'm just trying to get the lay of the land," I said.

Linda leaned forward.

"You don't trust us. You're on her side."

I glanced at her and shook my head. It was time to monologue.

"Ma'am, I'm not on anyone's side," I said. "I'm here to do a job and find your grandson. That's it. Sometimes, I have to play a role or act provocatively to get the information I need because I have to break through people's defense mechanisms. As a detective, I don't care about people's secrets. If you or your husband had an affair, I don't care. If you cheat on your taxes, that's between you and the IRS. If you grow marijuana in your basement, more power to you. Secrets rarely change my job, but they give me extra work if you keep them from me because I have to chase them down.

"So, do me a favor—be honest and open. If you tell me you murdered somebody, I'll have to arrest you. If you tell me you and your husband are swingers, though, I'll put it in a report and destroy the report as soon as the case is closed. Nobody'll find out."

The two stared straight ahead.

"We're not swingers," said Andrea.

"Where do you think your grandson is?"

Frank brought his hands to his face and rubbed his eyes.

"We don't know. That's why we're here."

"We know he's not at my brother Steven's house, though," said Andrea, pounding her index finger on the table. "Your behavior is shameful. How dare you harass my brother."

I pushed myself back from the table and straightened as I considered her. Then I crossed my arms.

"Just to clarify, how did I harass your brother?"

She sighed and rolled her eyes but looked away.

"Shouldn't you be searching for our grandson right now?" asked Frank. "If you ask me, that's what you should be doing."

"I appreciate your input," I said. For a moment, I considered them. Then I pulled myself toward the table and grabbed my pen and notepad. "Let's consider this: is it possible that someone took your grandson, and your son is unable to tell us?"

They, once more, looked at me as if I were an idiot.

"What does that even mean?" asked Andrea.

"How far can a toddler hike through deep woods on his own? Half a mile? A mile?"

"Maybe," said Andrea, shrugging. "It depends on the child."

"It does," I said, nodding. "Which is why we've searched well beyond that area. We've used dogs, helicopters, drones, and foot patrols. If your grandson were within two miles of your house, we would have found him. We haven't, which is a problem. It tells me that your son's story of losing his son is bullshit."

"And now you're blaming my son," said Andrea. "I should have known you'd side with Julie."

I looked at her and held her gaze.

249

"I'm not taking sides with anybody," I said, my voice low. "To be fair, though, Julie's not lied to me. Your son has lied to me consistently."

Frank closed his eyes and leaned forward.

"What's he lied about?"

"Is it possible your son is into something dangerous and can't get out?"

The two parents went quiet.

"Like what?" asked Andrea.

"I'm not sure," I said. "Ryan works for a construction firm. His company says he's a good employee. How much is he paid?"

Andrea rubbed her eyes and shrugged. Frank seemed to think.

"Eighteen or nineteen an hour," he said. "It goes up as he proves himself capable of more complex work."

"That's a good salary," I said. "Does he have other jobs? Does he drive an Uber?"

"No. Why?" asked Frank.

I looked at him.

"Your son had twenty-five thousand dollars cash in his sock drawer."

Andrea brought a hand to her mouth. Frank blinked but said nothing.

"You guys know who his girlfriend is?"

Andrea opened her mouth but said nothing. Then she cleared her throat.

"He doesn't have one. He would have told us."

"So you two have a close relationship," I said. She nodded. "Where's his new apartment?"

She tilted her head to the side and narrowed her eyes.

"He doesn't have a new apartment."

"I've heard he was moving out. His car was packed to the ceiling when I was there last."

She shrugged but said nothing. I nodded.

"Maybe I heard wrong," I said.

"Of course you did. I'd know if my son was moving out." She paused, closed her eyes, and shook her head. "We're not here for Ryan. As you've clearly demonstrated, you don't know the first thing about my grandson or my son. We're done cooperating with your investigation. If you need to get in touch with us, you can call our lawyer."

I had expected it, so I nodded.

"Thank you for coming by. Your grandson is my first and only priority. I'll do everything I can to find him."

Andrea rolled her eyes again. Frank said nothing. I escorted them to the lobby and started to return to my office when my cell phone rang. It was Brett Mayhew, the chair of the County Charter Commission. I answered as I walked upstairs.

"Mr. Mayhew, hey," I said. "What can I do for you?"

"I'm sorry to call you, Detective, but I'm sitting in the courthouse with a bunch of angry lawyers. We had a request for an unscheduled Charter Commission meeting. I've got a quorum here, but I need you to make it a legal meeting. The public's not here. It's just us."

Mayhew was a calculating, intelligent man. If he wanted this to be an official committee meeting, it meant he wanted something specific passed that would bind the committee in future meetings. From the start, Mayhew had known exactly what he was doing on that committee. He understood how to press his colleagues and how far to press the law without incurring a legal challenge. He usually got what he wanted. Given the county's history with corrupt politicians, that scared me.

"When's the meeting?"

"Right now. Like I said, I hate to ask. If you want, we could make your role strictly advisory. Your voice is important, but these bureaucratic meetings are a waste of your time. You're too valuable a public servant to use up on things like this."

I sighed. Now he was buttering me up. He really did want something.

"Thank you for your concern," I said, "but it's not necessary. I'm happy to help. I'll be there in about ten minutes."

He thanked me and hung up. I groaned and hurried to my office. Roy stood and stretched from his bed. I grabbed his leash.

"Come on, dude," I said. "It's time for us to go swim with some sharks."

Chapter 28

It was barely spring, and already the temperature was in the eighties. Julie didn't know how long she had been out there, but her throat hurt from screaming Elijah's name, and her arms and legs itched where brambles and thorns had brushed her skin. Drones occasionally buzzed overhead. Half a dozen strangers walked through the surrounding woods, but nobody spoke to her. They may not have even known who she was. She appreciated that. Elijah didn't need their tearful sympathy; he needed their legs, their hands, their voices. He needed help.

Elijah wasn't dead. No matter what anyone else said, Julie refused to believe it until she saw his body. This was a mistake. He probably got lost and got picked up by a neighbor. It hadn't been that long, really. He was probably eating ice cream and chomping down on Oreos while his rescuer tried to find him. The woods were full of hunting cabins and deer blinds, too. He could have found one. People kept them stocked with snacks sometimes. He was just fine. Wherever he was.

As she walked, her cell phone rang. It was her dad. She groaned and answered.

"Hey, Daddy," she said. "I'm in the middle of a search. I don't know how long I can talk. Reception isn't so good.'

"That's okay, hon," he said. "You've been out for hours. Do you have any water with you?"

She slipped her backpack off her shoulder and sighed. At one time, she had carried three big bottles of water. Now, she had three empty water bottles and half a box of unopened protein bars.

"I've got plenty of water," she said. "I've been eating, too. If you're wondering."

"It's time to come in, sweetheart," he said, his voice almost a whisper. "You need a break."

"It's fine. You need a break, maybe, because you're so old, but I'm young and healthy," she said, her voice trailing lower the more she spoke. "You remember what that's like, don't you? Maybe you don't at your age. Memory fades early, right after your eyesight."

Scott said nothing. Normally, he laughed and called her a smartass when she said things like that. Julie swallowed.

"I'm going to find him," she said. "He's out here somewhere. He needs his momma. I should be the one to find him, shouldn't I? If a stranger sees him, he'll be scared. He might run away."

"You're working yourself too hard. Where are you? I'm in my truck. I'll pick you up and take you home. We'll get you

something to eat and drink. You can take a nap, too. Uncle
Mickey and I will keep searching. Elijah knows us. Mickey'll
do that Donald Duck voice Elijah likes so much. Elijah'll
come running. He won't be able to resist."

She shook her head.

"I'm fine, Daddy," she said. He didn't respond. She
counted almost to thirty and leaned against a tree. The moment her back touched the bark, her exhaustion hit her. Her
left arm dropped, and she put her head back against the
rough surface. Even her cheeks seemed to drop.

"You still there, hon?"

"I am," she said, her voice soft. She wiped her forehead but
found little sweat. "I'm tired."

"I'm on Pinehurst in my truck. Are you in the woods?"

She drew in a slow breath and nodded.

"Yeah. I'll walk to you. I'll see you in a few minutes."

He told her to be careful, and she hung up and headed east
toward the road. With every passing step, her legs seemed to
grow heavier. By the time she reached the road, she didn't
want to move. Her dad's truck was a couple hundred yards
away, so she sat on the grass while he drove to her. He helped
her stand and get inside. As he drove her home, she drank an
entire bottle of water and fell asleep.

Julie woke again an hour later. She was on the living room
couch. Her dad must have carried her in. She stared at the
popcorn ceiling and wondered why anyone had ever thought
it looked attractive. Then she turned her focus inward. Her

muscles hurt, her eyes felt watery, and her feet tingled. She felt like a guitar string under tension. Everything felt wrong. Her doctor had given her anti-anxiety drugs a couple of months ago, but she didn't want to take them. The drugs didn't make her feel better; they just made it so she didn't feel the same. She wanted to feel this, though. She should feel angry and sad and frustrated and everything else. Her baby was missing.

She sat up and looked around. Her parents had a late night. They were probably napping, too. She rubbed her face. It had been hours since she last ate, so she fried eggs and toasted day-old bread. Her mom heard her and joined her in the kitchen.

"Let me finish that, sweetie," she said. "You sit down."

Lisa took the spatula from her daughter's hands and turned the eggs over. Julie sat at the counter.

"I made three eggs," Julie said. "You should have one. If you're hungry."

"I'll take care of me. You focus on you," her mom said, getting a plate. "You were out there a lot today."

"I didn't find anything." She swallowed. "He's not out there. We're searching a grid four miles from Ryan's house now. We should have found him. Even if he were..."

Lisa turned the stove off, slid the eggs onto a plate and carried it to her daughter.

"Don't talk like that," she said. "We're going to find him. It's going to be okay."

"No, it's not," she said. "Ryan knows more than he's telling us. He's a liar."

Lisa hesitated before nodding.

"Let the police worry about that. Your job is to stay healthy for your son."

Julie didn't agree, but she stood, grabbed her toast, and returned to her seat as her mother plated her own eggs. They ate in silence for a few minutes.

"Where's Dad?" asked Julie, eventually.

"He, Mickey, and Pete are out searching," she said. "I've been manning the phones. Reporters from every TV station in St. Louis have called. We even had a producer from MSNBC call. They wanted to do a story."

"That's great," she said. "That's real good. The more news, the better, right? With more search teams, we'll have a better chance of finding him."

"That's right," said Lisa, nodding.

They were just going through the motions. TV camera wouldn't solve anything, and they both knew it. So they ate in silence. Then Julie pushed back from the counter.

"I'm going back to bed. Why don't you go out with Dad? I'll hold things down here."

Lisa straightened.

"You sure?"

"I'm sure, Mom. I want to be alone."

Lisa brought a hand to Julie's cheek. Then she brushed a lock of hair behind her ear.

"It's going to be okay."

"I know, Mom."

They stayed together, but then Lisa went to her bedroom to change clothes. Five minutes later, she was gone. Julie took a few deep breaths. The police weren't getting anywhere. It was time she got to work. She went to her mom and dad's room. Julie had grown up in rural Missouri, and firearms had been part of her life since she was a child. Her father had first taken her to the gun range when she was eight years old. She didn't fire a gun, but she learned about gun safety. In St. Augustine, with firearms everywhere, that was important.

A year later, she fired a .22-caliber rifle for the first time. It was bright pink, and it was all hers. Her dad told her how to hold it, how to clean it, and how to load it. It was fun. After that, he took her to a rifle range every other month. Eventually, she graduated to a Winchester Model 70. It was a beautiful rifle. She didn't plan to hunt deer today, though. Instead, she pulled open the drawer of her dad's end table and removed the black Glock 19 he kept inside.

The weapon was bigger than she preferred, but it'd be just fine today. She grabbed it and slipped it into her purse in the front entryway. Then she left the house. Julie had been near Ryan's house all morning, so she knew the police had pulled back. When she got to his street, though, she found six matching black SUVs out front.

She parked near them and got out, unsure what was going on. The moment she started walking toward the house, the front door opened, and a man in a black polo shirt and jeans stepped out. He wore a pistol on his hip.

"Julie Smith?" he asked. She hesitated before nodding.

"Yeah. Who are you?"

"Wait here, miss," he said, stepping back. He closed the front door. Julie furrowed her brow and hurried forward. She pounded on the wood until Andrea opened it. The two women stared at each other. Then Andrea reached forward and pulled Julie close. It was the first hug Andrea had ever given her. Julie didn't know how to respond, so she squeezed tight and hoped Andrea wouldn't bump into her purse and notice the firearm inside. After a moment, Andrea released her grip and stepped back, wiping her eyes.

"Come in, honey," she whispered. "We're getting Elijah back today."

"We are?" she asked.

"Yeah," said Andrea, looking around outside. "Come in."

Julie stepped inside. Someone had set up folding tables in the entryway. They held phones and laptops and coffee cups. Men and women in matching black polo shirts whispered to one another and glanced in her direction. Andrea ushered Julie to the kitchen. There, too, she found more strangers. They left.

"What's going on?" she asked. "Who are these people?"

"They're a security firm," said Andrea. "We called them this morning. Elijah was abducted. We're going to get him back."

Julie closed her eyes and exhaled. All over her body, it felt like something had lifted from her. Her legs were weak, so she grabbed onto the nearest counter.

"He's alive," she said.

"Yeah, honey," she said. "He's alive. We're going to get him."

Julie felt tears come to her eyes. Andrea hugged her again. Then Julie stepped back.

"I just need a moment," she said. "Excuse me. I need the powder room."

"Of course," said Andrea. Julie walked to the small bathroom. At first, she just stood there. Then she closed her eyes, drew in a breath through her nose, and took her cell phone from her purse. Before typing, she turned the volume low so no one would hear. Then opened the messenger app and texted Detective Court.

Help at Ryan's house. Be discrete.

She waited a moment until she saw the message was sent. Then she flushed the toilet, washed her hands, and rejoined Andrea in the kitchen. The Powells may have been content with their private security team, but Julie wasn't. Something was going on here. Ryan gave a bullshit story to the police, he had twenty-five thousand dollars cash in his bedroom, and now the family claimed Elijah was kidnapped all along.

Julie was tired of the bullshit. It was time to get some answers.

Chapter 29

R oy and I hurried to the courthouse. Unlike our last
visit, no protesters stood outside. Before going up the
steps, I checked to ensure my badge was visible on my hip
and wrapped Roy's leash around my hand, so he'd be close to
my side. I should have left my pistol at my desk, but the security team checked it into a locker for safekeeping and waved
us through the metal detectors. We reached the courtroom
a few minutes later. Four of the seven commission members
sat behind the judge's bench, while a man and woman sat
behind the plaintiff's desk, waiting for their turn to speak.

I smiled at everyone as Roy and I walked to the council
members. Brett Mayhew brightened and excused himself
from the group when he saw us. He was about fifty and
had a thin face, thinning gray hair, and a cropped black and
gray beard. Though I wouldn't call him handsome, his smile
came easily. He held out a hand for me to shake. His grip was
firm but not tight.

"Thank you for coming on such short notice," he said.
"I know you've got important work going on, so we'll keep
the meeting as brief as we can. We've got two representatives

from Columbia Holdings. They're an investment group based here in Missouri, and they've got some pretty exciting ideas for St. Augustine. They're going to help us solve a lot of problems."

I glanced at the two strangers. Then I looked at Mayhew.

"In my experience, if you ask other people to solve your problems, they create new ones."

"Sometimes, that's how it goes," he said, nodding. "Other times, though, they're what you need. How about you have a seat? We'll get started."

I nodded and sat beside the commission members. Mayhew walked to the chief judge's seat and remained standing. A young man stood in the gallery.

"Are we recording, Cliff?"

The young man nodded and gave his boss a thumbs-up. Mayhew thanked him and focused on a camera hanging on the wall above the main door.

"Okay, folks, thanks for coming. For the record, this is an official meeting of the St. Augustine County Charter Commission, and we're here to see a presentation from Loraine Fisk and Don Simpson of Columbia Holdings. With me today is Helen Krause, Debora Masterson, and Fred Ogletree. I'm Brett Mayhew. I'd like to extend a special thanks to Detective Mary Joe Court from the sheriff's department. She came here on short notice. With these four members and Detective Court, we've got a quorum."

Fred Ogletree pulled his microphone toward him.

"We all came on short notice, Brett. For the record, I request we postpone this meeting until the rest of our committee can make it. Jerry and Patrick are both teaching. You know they can't make it during the day. Gina's watching her kids and can't leave them without a babysitter. If you had given us more than a half-hour's notice, we could have a full debate. Instead, we're here with you and your friends."

Mayhew nodded and smiled.

"I appreciate your concern, Fred, but this is too important to postpone—especially considering we've got the required number of members present to vote. If our other members can't make it, I'm afraid that's their decision. We all prioritize our lives differently. If this commission isn't a priority to them, I can't make it one. Nor can I ask Loraine and Don to wait. They've driven all the way from Columbia for this meeting."

Fred leaned back and crossed his arms.

"And you had no advanced warning of their arrival?" he asked. "They showed up, called you, and said they could solve all our problems?"

Mayhew smiled but said nothing.

"You know Jerry and Patrick teach," continued Fred. "They can't leave their classrooms without prior notice. It makes me think you scheduled this so they couldn't make it."

Mayhew continued smiling.

"If I had scheduled this to snub anyone, don't you think I would have scheduled it during a time you couldn't make it?"

"I own my company, so I can leave when needed," said Fred. "It's hard to scheme when your opponent has a flexible schedule."

Mayhew drew in a slow breath and shook his head.

"That was supposed to be a joke. Lighten up, bud," he said. "This is important county business, and I didn't think it could wait. That's it. There's no conspiracy here. Sorry if you're upset."

"If it's important, we can give it the importance it deserves with a full debate in front of the entire county. We can invite spectators and roll it on public access TV."

Mayhew sighed and rolled his eyes.

"Transparency and debate? How many millions of dollars did Darren Rogers embezzle with your endorsement?"

"None," said Fred, lowering his chin. "I'm the president of the Chamber of Commerce. I don't endorse anybody, and I don't have investigative powers."

"You could have looked," said Mayhew. "Instead, you and your members grew wealthy while the county council sucked this place dry. It takes a lot of gall for you to talk about good governance now."

Fred started to say something, but Helen Krause spoke over him.

"Both of you hush," she said. "Children have better manners than you. We need to move on. I came to see a presentation. Let's start the meeting and see it."

"Helen's right," said Debora. "We haven't even seen the presentation yet, so we can't judge it. And Brett emailed us about this meeting days ago. It's been on the calendar."

The room went quiet. Frank focused on Mayhew.

"You didn't email me," he said. "You didn't email Jerry, Gina, or Patrick, either, or they would have planned to be here. We take this job seriously."

"Maybe you should check your spam folders," said Helen.

Frank looked at me.

"Did you get an email, Detective?"

I hadn't, but I held up my hands.

"This isn't my fight. Sorry."

Mayhew waved his finger at me and nodded.

"Detective Court brings up another issue. It's important that we have a law enforcement rep on the commission, but I'm not sure it's fair to the sheriff's department that we're required to have a rep at every meeting. It's a huge ask for a woman without a vote."

Frank gave an exasperated sigh and shook his head.

"Now isn't the time to change the makeup of our committee. We're down three members."

Debora gave him a sardonic smile.

"We've got a quorum," she said. "We can pass whatever we need to pass."

That started a fresh round of bickering. I cleared my throat after a few minutes and spoke over the argument.

"Hey, folks," I said. They stopped arguing and looked at me. "This is an emergency meeting. You called it. Let's stop arguing and get to it." I looked at the two representatives from Columbia Holdings. "Give your presentation. We're listening."

They looked at Mayhew. Nobody objected, so he nodded, and they started talking.

"First of all, I'm Loraine Fisk. I'm a project manager with Columbia Holdings. With me is Don Simpson. He's the managing director of our firm. We're smaller than many property development firms, but we love Missouri, and we love St. Augustine. My parents took me to the Spring Fair when I was little, and I've taken my kids to the Spring Fair half a dozen times. We look forward to it every year, so we were heartbroken when we heard about the county's difficulties."

I leaned back in my chair and crossed my arms, wondering why Mayhew had wasted my time with a pitch for a new strip mall—or whatever she was proposing. Fisk smiled.

"By your body language, some of you aren't excited to see me. Maybe this will change your mind: my proposal will bring in hundreds of jobs, millions of dollars in tax revenue, and revitalize St. Augustine. How does that sound?"

It sounded like she was peddling horseshit, so I said nothing.

"Please tell me you're proposing a monorail," said Frank, his voice flat.

Fisk shook her head and furrowed her brow.

"I don't understand..."

"Please continue," said Mayhew. "The peanut gallery will keep their comments to themselves from here on out."

Simpson, Fisk's partner, stood.

"We're proposing a major investment along St. Augustine's waterfront. Recent events notwithstanding, St. Augustine's long been known as a tourist town. Its restaurants, shops, and small hotels are excellent, but it also has areas of outstanding natural beauty. The area appeals to a wide demographic. We plan to expand that appeal by building a convention center, hotel, villas, restaurants, and a small casino.

"Our venture will directly employ nearly a thousand people and provide millions in tax revenue. We will revitalize this town and secure its future for the next fifty years."

Frank snickered and shook his head.

"Did you copy the plans directly from Darren Rogers, or did you make up entirely new plans of your own?"

Fisk looked uncertain.

"We're familiar with Mr. Rogers, of course, but I don't believe he ever proposed a casino."

"Just a hotel and convention center along the waterfront," said Frank. "You're more ambitious than he was. Good for you. Have at it." He leaned forward and looked to his left at Mayhew. "Can we go now?"

"Hear them out," said Mayhew, his eyes closed.

"Thank you, Mr. Mayhew," said Fisk. "As you can imagine, a development of this size requires a partnership. We're here to open lines of communication and to talk about how we can best develop this community to its utmost."

"I think this is just what St. Augustine needs," said Debora. "It's a real kick in the pants."

"I agree," said Helen. "I don't believe in gambling myself, but it would bring in revenue this county needs."

Debora, Mayhew, and Helen nodded along with each other. Frank crossed his arms.

"Okay," he said, nodding. "I'll play along. You'll bring St. Augustine millions of dollars in revenue and tons of jobs. That's great. What does this cost us? Tax breaks? Direct investment?"

Simpson held up a hand, closed his eyes, and nodded.

"We'll need some help financing the project, but that's for discussion down the line. We'll work with the future county council to hammer out the details. In our mind, it'd be better if we worked with the elected officials instead of appointed commission members."

It made sense, so I nodded.

"Then why are you here?" I asked.

Simpson looked at me.

"That is a good question. We need the ability to purchase property downtown for the development. We'd like the county charter to reflect that. Ideally, we'd also have a provision within the county charter specifically allowing for the creation of gambling enterprises in accordance with state and federal law. We'll do it by the book."

Frank snickered again.

"You're writing the book."

Neither Simpson nor Fisk responded. I leaned forward and spoke again.

"You want the county charter to allow you to run a casino? That's fine. You also want it to have provisions about the purchase of property. I guess I'm a little confused. What provisions do you want? If your company wants property, why can't you just make an offer to purchase it? I've bought and sold houses in St. Augustine before. Nobody stopped me. Why would they stop you?"

Simpson smiled.

"We're talking about a considerable amount of property. Sometimes, people fight progress for the sake of being obstinate. I believe that St. Augustine County should be able to determine how the property within its borders is used—in accordance with the law. The city should be able to say whether a certain area is commercial or residential, and it should be able to include or exclude certain businesses. Nobody wants a strip club next to a school. We're asking for the county charter to reflect the county's values."

I considered before speaking.

"Nobody's proposing putting a strip club next to a school," I said. "You came here because you want something. What?"

"With all due respect, Detective," said Helen, "you're not a member of this commission. You're a non-voting adviser. Do you think it's appropriate for you to be asking questions?"

She smiled patronizingly. I wanted to roll my eyes at her. Instead, I smiled in response. Before I could speak, though, Frank leaned forward.

"Detective Court asked a good question. I am a voting member of this commission. What do you want?"

Simpson looked to Mayhew. Mayhew smiled and looked to his fellow commission members.

"Columbia Holdings has requested that we include a provision within the charter outlining the steps required for the taking of real property. They've also requested a ninety-nine-year lease on county property and certain tax breaks, all of which we can put in the charter. It's all in accordance with the law. Our lawyers have already looked over things and approved them. I thought we could vote on it today."

Frank rubbed his eyes and sighed.

"Now it makes sense," he said. "If you called a real meeting, we'd outvote you. With this sham in the middle of the day with your flunkies, you've got the votes you need to turn St. Augustine into a corporate town run by a casino company."

"I don't appreciate your tone," said Mayhew. "We have a quorum. We can hold a binding vote right now to include Columbia Holdings's proposal in the charter."

Frank stood and shook his head.

"You can't do this. This isn't how it's supposed to work."

"It's how it works in St. Augustine," said Mayhew. "I'm going to call for a vote on the proposal. Any objections?"

"You haven't even given me a copy of the proposed amendment," said Frank. "This is horseshit."

Mayhew looked at Fisk and Simpson. Ms. Fisk stood and carried a thick sheath of papers to the judge's desk. Frank flipped through it and shook his head.

"This is fifty or sixty pages of legalese," he said. "I can't review this in two minutes. Nobody else can, either. For all I know, you're giving away the store for nothing."

"I trust Brett and Columbia Holdings," said Debora. "We're going to build this town up again. It's going to be great."

"This will fund the schools," said Helen. "We've got to do it."

"How do you know?" asked Frank. He threw up his hands "You haven't read the proposal. You don't know what it says. How can you vote on something complex if you haven't read it?"

"I trust Brett," said Helen. "That's all that matters."

"Please sit down, Frank," said Mayhew. "The chair has heard your objection to a vote. I'm overruling it. The commission will vote on the proposed amendment. All in favor..."

Hands shot in the air. Mayhew played me for a fool. I didn't like that. I liked politicians who rammed through major proposals without giving anyone a chance to object even less. Maybe this casino project was what the county needed, but I doubted it. If history was a guide, Mayhew and his friends would grow rich at everyone else's expense. That was how the government worked in St. Augustine. That cycle needed to end. I stood up and whistled before Mayhew could continue the vote. He furrowed his brow.

"Sorry to interrupt, but I've got to go," I said. "I've got an emergency call."

I stepped around the desk and headed toward the exit.

"We're almost done, Detective," shouted Mayhew. "Just a minute."

I ignored him and hurried toward the door.

"Detective Court? Joe?" he called.

I stopped at the door.

"I'm using my prerogative as the law enforcement rep to adjourn the meeting. Sorry. Duty calls. We'll have to hold the vote next time."

Frank chuckled and smiled.

"I guess that's that," he said, standing. "No vote."

"Don't do this, Detective," said Mayhew, shaking his head.

"Sorry. Gotta go," I said. "Call me if you need me."

I ran out of the courthouse before Mayhew could call a bailiff to stop me. I had made an enemy for life. Hopefully, it was worth it.

Chapter 30

As Roy and I walked back to the station, my phone beeped with an incoming text message from Julie Smith. She had asked for help at Ryan Powell's house and requested my discretion. I walked for half a block before sitting on a bench in front of a jewelry store and calling Julie's phone. It rang five times before going to voicemail.

"Julie, hey," I said. "This is Detective Joe Court. Call me when you can."

I waited about five minutes, but she didn't return my call, so I texted her the same message. Then I waited another two minutes, but she still didn't respond. I considered calling my station to have uniformed officers meet me at Ryan's house, but that wouldn't have been discrete. Roy started to lie down, but I gave his leash a gentle tug so he'd stand.

"We're going for a drive," I said. He didn't understand me, but he seemed agreeable. We walked another few minutes to my Volvo and climbed inside. The drive to Pinehurst didn't take long, but I slowed long before reaching the Powell's home. They had visitors—a lot of them, judging by the black SUVs in the driveway.

I parked two blocks away and drummed my fingers on my steering wheel, considering. Then I called Marcus.

"Dude," I said. "This is Joe. You anywhere near Pinehurst?"

"No, sorry," he said. "I'm working a traffic accident near Dyer. Just a fender bender." He paused. "You haven't found the kid, have you?"

"No. Julie Smith texted me, asking for help at the Powell's house. When I got here, I found six black SUVs waiting for me. They've got Illinois plates. The family might have brought in some extra help."

Marcus grunted.

"The Powells are rich. Makes sense."

I sighed.

"I suspect I'm about to have an uncomfortable conversation," I said. "You want to join me?"

Marcus chuckled.

"As it turns out, I think my traffic accident may be more serious than I implied earlier. Good luck with your uncomfortable conversation, though. You've got this."

"Thanks. As always, I appreciate your support."

I hung up and got the dog out. As soon as Roy and I reached the Powell's lawn, the front door opened. A man wearing jeans and a black polo-style shirt stepped out. He had a pistol on his hip, and he walked on the balls of his feet. He could have lost ten or fifteen pounds, but he knew how to move. As we approached, he shifted his hip so the bulk of his body blocked my view of his firearm.

I reached to my belt for my badge and held it up. He nodded. Roy sat and panted.

"Can I help you?"

"Yeah, I'm Detective Joe Court with the St. Augustine County Sheriff's Department. Who are you?"

His appraised me with his eyes. Then he went inside without saying a word.

Asshole.

Thirty seconds later, the door opened again. A second man wearing jeans and a black polo shirt stepped out. This guy was thirty-five to forty and had curly black hair, olive-colored skin, and thick, curly hair on his forearms. When he smiled, he revealed even rows of teeth, stained tan by smoke or coffee.

"Afternoon, Detective," he said, looking at Roy. "He friendly?"

"Overly so," I said. He smiled at the dog before holding a hand toward me.

"Chris Katrakis. I'm a project manager for Sentinel Security and Protective Services. I'm here because the Powells have hired my company. Sorry for my associate earlier. Gus isn't a talker."

I shook his hand.

"So I gathered. I'm Joe Court. I'm here because I'm required by law. So...." I raised my eyebrows. "What's going on?"

Katrakis's smile slipped as he looked over his shoulder to the house. Then it returned when he looked at me.

"Let's go for a walk. Ms. Powell doesn't like dogs inside."

I raised my eyebrows.

"You asking me for a walk because you don't want the Powells overhearing our conversation, or because you want to manipulate me and make me think you're taking me into your confidence?"

His smile broadened, and he looked down.

"You're sharper than Ms. Powell gives you credit for," he said. "It's a bit of both, if you want honesty."

I crossed my arms.

"Is Julie Smith inside?"

He considered for a moment before nodding.

"She is. She's worried about her son."

"And you're including her in your search?"

He shrugged.

"She's an information source."

It was a good answer. I nodded.

"Let's walk."

We headed down the street toward my car. Then we passed it.

"Your dog a Chessie?"

"Yep," I said. We walked another few feet. "What's going on?"

He looked around and grimaced as we walked.

"You couldn't find Elijah because he's been kidnapped. Frank Powell received a text message this morning from the kidnappers. My team will turn over everything we have to your prosecutor, but for the moment, we're keeping things quiet. If the press gets wind of this, our kidnappers might get jumpy. They wanted a hundred thousand dollars cash in small bills delivered in a black duffel bag."

I squeezed my jaw tight and inhaled through my nose.

"Were you planning to inform law enforcement, or did you plan to let us continue wasting our time and limited resources?"

"The illusion of a search is important for the press," he said. "We don't know who our kidnappers are, but they're not professionals. They're skittish. I don't want to spook them more than necessary."

"How many abductions have you worked?"

He glanced at me and smirked.

"A hundred, maybe?" he said. "Most of my team has worked for the United States government in various capacities."

"Anything about this feel off to you?"

He shrugged.

"All of it feels off," he said. "We work in Mexico and South America. When we negotiate with the cartels, I know who

I'm talking to, and they know me. We trust each other—or at least we trust the other to do what's in his rational self-interest. This one feels like a crime of opportunity. My guess is that somebody spotted an unaccompanied child in front of a rich man's house and saw the chance for a big score. This wasn't planned."

It explained why we hadn't found Elijah, but we had seen surveillance footage of the roads around the Powell's home. Every other house had a doorbell camera or a camera on their garage to catch thieves looking to steal packages. No cars had driven by when Elijah disappeared. Unless Elijah's kidnappers carried him kicking and screaming through the woods—which would have left evidence and which Ryan would have heard—the story was fake. Something else was going on here.

"They give you a proof of life?"

He hesitated before answering.

"Something I should know?" I asked.

"They made him scream," he said. "His grandma said it was Elijah's voice."

I squeezed my jaw tight. Hopefully, they hadn't told Julie that.

"So what's the plan?"

"The plan is that you go home, and I handle this," he said. "We'll get Elijah back, and we'll give you the evidence you need to arrest his kidnappers. I get paid, and you get the credit."

We walked for another few minutes. The woods beside the road were thick with trees and brush. I swatted a mosquito from my neck.

"Can you get Elijah back?"

He tilted his head.

"There's a good chance," he said. "We know what we're doing. Have you ever worked a high-profile abduction?"

"Yeah. We saved the baby, but people got hurt."

"Then let my team handle this one. We have resources and experience you don't."

"Is Julie Smith okay with this?"

"She is," he said, nodding.

"I don't like this."

He shrugged.

"If you did, I'd question your sanity."

"Then get the kid," I said. "I want to hear from you the moment he's safe."

Katrakis agreed, and we walked back to my Volvo where we exchanged business cards.

"You're making the right choice, Detective," he said. "This is a sound strategy."

"I hope so," I said, opening the rear passenger door for Roy. He jumped into his hammock, and I climbed into the driver's seat, turned on my car, and left the neighborhood. As I drove, I called Marcus. He answered on the second ring.

"Marcus, I've got a favor to ask," I said. "Your wife's got a new minivan, right?"

He didn't hesitate.

"She does. You need to move something?"

"No, I need a surveillance vehicle. My target knows my Volvo, and our station's SUVs stand out."

He paused and sighed, his voice crestfallen.

"I'll see what I can do. Where are you now?"

"On my way downtown."

"I'll call you back then."

I hung up and drove. Once Roy and I parked, I took him for a walk around the block. When we returned, Marcus and Trisha were talking in the lobby. He held up his hand, exposing a key ring.

"She gave me the van, but on a couple of conditions: I drive, and if we scratch it, the department pays for it. And we have to drape a towel over the seat for Roy."

"Deal," I said.

"Okay. When do we need to go?"

"Now. I'll update you on the way."

He nodded, and I jogged to get towels from the locker room. Within five minutes, Marcus, Roy, and I were driving to Pinehurst. I told him about the situation. He asked questions, but I had little information to give. We parked two blocks from the Powell's home in the shadow cast by some pine trees near the roadside.

Then we waited.

And waited.

Roy fell asleep, but Marcus and I continued watching the house.

"If I had known it'd take this long, I would have brought food," I said.

"Not in this car," said Marcus. "No food until it loses the new-car smell."

"Strict," I said, nodding.

"You have no idea," said Marcus. We waited another ten minutes, but then I saw taillights fire into life. By that point, it was almost eight and dark.

"They're moving," I said. "Get down."

Marcus and I slouched so the car would appear empty. A minute later, six black SUVs and the Powell's BMW drove past us. Once they turned, Marcus turned the minivan on and followed them.

"We know where they're going?" he asked.

"Nope," I said, taking out my cell phone. I texted Julie to ask if she could call. After five minutes and several miles of road, she hadn't.

"They're heading to the interstate," said Marcus. "We're going to leave the county soon. You want to keep going?"

"Yeah," I said, nodding. "Let's see where this goes."

Marcus agreed, and we kept driving. For almost two hours, we headed south on the interstate. Then something weird happened. The Powell's vehicle pulled into a rest area while the black SUVs continued.

"Where do we go?" asked Marcus.

"Rest area," I said. "We'll try to stay out of sight. The Powells are the targets."

Marcus flicked on his turn signal. The landscape was flat for miles. Fields surrounded us. We didn't have anywhere to hide. Marcus slowed and wound his way around the rest area's expansive lot. The Powells had parked near the entrance. Marcus kept driving toward the exit. It was darker there. Then he, too, parked.

Neither of us spoke, but Marcus shifted a few times. He looked uncomfortable.

"At times like this, I think about babbling brooks and waterfalls," I said. "Water rushing down a hill. When I lived in North Carolina, I saw people travel down the rivers on canoes and inner tubes. I never went myself, but it looked fun."

"You're not funny," said Marcus. "I drank a giant protein shake after working out this afternoon."

I waited a few minutes before glancing at him.

"They've not seen you," I said. "The Powells, I mean. Go to the bathroom. No one will notice you."

He barely waited before I finished speaking to step out of the car. He jogged toward the restroom facility but came out a few minutes later carrying a bag of pretzels.

"Breaking the food prohibition already," I said. "You rebel."

He nodded and pulled open his bag.

"You hungry?"

"A little," I said.

"Good."

I smiled and leaned back in the seat. We settled into an easy silence that stretched to an hour. Nobody emerged from the Powell's car, nobody knocked on it, nobody approached it or parked near it, nobody did anything. Eventually, I sighed.

"You think they're onto us?"

Marcus looked around the lot and shook his head.

"We're not the only car parked here," he said. "The guy beside us is asleep. A whole family is asleep in an SUV a few spots down. We shouldn't be suspicious."

We waited another hour in depressing silence before Katrakis's black SUVs pulled into the rest area. One parked right beside the Powell's car, while the others parked in nearby open spots. Frank and Andrea Powell stepped out and spoke with Katrakis near the hood of the vehicle. They looked angry. Then they returned to the car and drove away while Katrakis's men started walking.

"I think it's time for us to head out," I said, nodding toward a black-shirted man walking toward us. Then somebody knocked on the back window. A moment later, Katrakis walked to Marcus's window and glared at us both. Marcus opened the door and stepped out. I did likewise.

"I thought you planned to let us handle this," said Katrakis.

"I implied it, but I didn't mean it," I said. "This is my job."

Katrakis's smile slipped as he shook his head.

"Well, congratulations, Detective Court. You may have just gotten a little boy killed. I'll see you at your station. Call your lawyers."

Chapter 31

Katrakis left, and Marcus rolled up his window. The security team went back to their SUVs and left the area. Marcus scratched the back of his head and squinted at me.

"You sure this wasn't a real kidnapping?"

"Not positive, but pretty sure," I said. "Katrakis thinks they were amateurs who stumbled on a child in front of a rich man's house. It's reasonable, but there's no surveillance video of them entering or leaving the neighborhood, no footprints, no witnesses, nothing. Their proof of life was a scream that Grandma supposedly recognized. Screams are screams, though. Andrea couldn't recognize a toddler's scream. It was wishful thinking. They should have asked for video."

Marcus nodded and considered.

"Katrakis seemed to believe the evidence."

"Or he needed a story to justify the retainer the Powells paid his company," I said. "He brought a dozen people, six cars, laptops, surveillance gear, firearms, and who knows what else. They're probably billing half a million dollars for this. He's trying to give the Powells their money's worth. If he had called us as soon as he arrived, I would have worked with him and walked through the evidence. But my voice would have spoiled his story."

Marcus drummed his fingers on the steering wheel.

"And now he's got us to blame for the failure," he said.

"It's worse than that," I said, shaking my head. "Ryan killed his kid and hid the body. It's the only story that makes sense. But if we find Elijah's body now and arrest Ryan for his murder, his defense team will claim the kidnappers killed the kid, and we screwed up the hand off. It makes us look stupid and gives him reasonable doubt."

Marcus paused.

"You think this was a setup?"

"No. Probably not, at least," I said, shaking my head. "Andrea and Frank Powell probably thought they were getting their grandson back. Ryan's playing along because he doesn't know what else to do. Julie's caught in the middle. Then again, maybe I'm wrong. Maybe they're working together, and we're the marks."

Marcus nodded and turned on his van.

"It's late, and we're two hours from home," he said. "We should go."

I agreed, and we headed north. I tried to stay awake, but I dozed off. Roy slept behind us. When we reached St. Augustine, Marcus parked in the fire lane in front of our station. Katrakis, the Powells, and two men in suits met us near the front door. They looked pissed, and they started yelling the moment they saw us. I squeezed my jaw tight. Marcus whistled to get their attention.

"That's enough," he said. "You speak one at a time, or you don't speak at all. We'll go inside, and I will lead you to a conference room. There, you will speak to Detective Court cordially. She and I will explain the case to you, and you will listen. If you refuse to listen, you will sit outside. Clear?"

"Who's in charge of your department?" asked one of the men in suits. Marcus grunted and looked to me.

"Our prosecutor," I said. "I'll call him."

"Good. We want to talk to him. You've done enough tonight, miss."

I ignored them, unlocked the front door, and disengaged the alarm while Marcus led them upstairs to a conference room. Shaun Deveraux, the prosecutor, didn't appreciate hearing from me this late, but he agreed to come out. I brewed coffee in the break room and walked Roy around the block. After our short jaunt outside, I sat on the steps in front of the building and put my hand on my dog's side. He scooted forward to put his head on my lap and raised his eyebrows at me.

"Thanks for not yelling at me," I said. "It's nice somebody doesn't."

For fifteen minutes, Roy and I sat. The cool night air felt good, but we had unpleasant work ahead of us. My stomach felt tight. Shaun Deveraux arrived twenty minutes after my call. He wore a light blue oxford shirt and khaki pants. I filled him in on our evening and my thoughts on the matter. He rubbed his eyes.

"I've been keeping up with your reports," he said, nodding. "To clarify, do you have any physical evidence implicating Ryan Powell in the murder of his son?"

"No, but I can't clear him, either. Until we find the body or the kill room, we're lost."

"Assuming a body or kill room exists," he said. He paused. "I need you to consider this and answer honestly: do we have the resources to solve this case?"

I paused and thought about the initial call and everything my team had done since then. Then I looked down.

"It's not about resources," I said. "Some cases you just can't solve. We have an eighty to ninety percent closure rate on homicides in St. Augustine. Some cases will slip through. This might be one of those. It just happens to involve a child."

Deveraux softened his voice.

"The public won't accept that," he said. "If Elijah's dead, somebody'll take the fall. If it's not Ryan, it might be you."

I glanced at him and furrowed my brow.

"Are you threatening me?"

He shook his head.

"No, but my office is fielding calls from newspapers and TV channels across the country. Ryan Powell is wealthy, handsome, and young. Julie is pretty, young, and lower middle-class. We've got storylines that'll make true crime writers drool. It's getting ugly. I don't know how much longer we can contain this."

I squeezed my jaw tight and drew in a breath through my nose.

"Solve it or find a new job," I said. "Got it."

"I don't make the rules, Detective."

I forced myself to smile even as I seethed inside.

"Well, let's get to work, then."

Roy and I stood and walked to the building. Deveraux followed. The Powells, Marcus, and two lawyers waited for us in the conference room. As soon as they saw me, they started shouting. Just as he had outside, Marcus whistled for their attention. They went quiet.

"I'm Shaun Deveraux, and I'm here to answer questions and ask a few of my own. Mr. Katrakis, you're first. Introduce yourself, tell me why you're in my station, and what your complaint is."

"Sure, fine," he said, sitting straighter in a black leather conference chair. "I'm Chris Katrakis, and I represent Sentinel Security and Protective Services. We're a private security firm from Chicago. With me are corporate counsels John McCabe and Dean Stepan. You already know Andrea and Frank Powell.

"We're here to bring a formal complaint against Detective Joe Court and Detective Marcus Washington for recklessly interfering with a private business transaction that would have saved Elijah Smith's life. If they had stayed away, Elijah would be safe, and I'd be on my way to Chicago. If Elijah is dead, it's on Detective Court and this station, and I intend to make sure everyone in the goddamn country knows it."

Deveraux glanced at me. Then he looked at Katrakis.

"Let's back up. Detective Court told me you received a ransom demand and proof of life from the kidnappers. We'd really like access to those."

Katrakis started to speak, but I leaned forward and spoke over him.

"And I'd like access to Julie Smith. Where is she? She texted me from your house, but she hasn't responded. Is she okay?"

Andrea shook her head.

"I should have known she instigated this," she said. "Stupid, spoiled brat. If she just trusted us, she'd be a lot better off."

"To be fair," I said, forcing myself to smile, "she did trust you. She brought her son to you, and you lost him. That boy is gone because of you and your family. Where is Julie now?"

Andrea narrowed her eyes at me, but Katrakis spoke before she could lash out.

"She's at the Powell's home with Ryan and two of my associates. We confiscated her cell phone. She carried a gun, by the way."

"The gun is her right under Missouri law," said Deveraux. "Is she free to leave your custody?"

Katrakis glanced at him.

"She's not asked."

"How would you know?" I asked. "She is surrounded by people who, presumably, disarmed her and stole her cell phone. She's probably scared out of her mind. I'm tempted to send officers to arrest everyone in your employ on false imprisonment charges."

"She's fine, Detective," said Andrea. "Quite frankly, I would think you'd be more worried about your own criminal behavior."

I ignored Andrea and focused on Katrakis.

"Let her go immediately," I said. Katrakis started holding up a hand and opened his mouth to speak, but I interrupted him. "Make the fucking call, or I'll put you in a cell right now."

Katrakis looked to his attorneys. Both men nodded, so he took out his phone and tapped a message. Moments later, he looked up.

"Done," he said. "Your turn. Tell me why you and Detective Washington drove a hundred and twenty miles south to a rest area in the middle of nowhere. Bear in mind that there are witnesses."

I crossed my arms.

"Because that's my job. This is a murder investigation. If Elijah were alive, we would have found him. My primary suspect is Ryan Powell. I followed you and your team to that rest area because I needed to see what you were doing."

"Elijah is alive," said Andrea, her voice hoarse. "He was abducted. They sent us a ransom video. I heard him. He screamed for me."

"I'd like to see this video," said Deveraux. "Do you have it?"

"I've got a copy," said Katrakis, turning to one of the lawyers. The lawyer pulled a tablet from his briefcase and handed it over. "Our technical team in Chicago is already combing through it for identifying marks."

We waited a minute while Katrakis called up the video. On it, a shirtless man stood in a dark room. The walls looked like stacked stone with mortar. Modern foundations would have used poured concrete or cement blocks. This was older than that, obviously. The man wore a black mask over the top part of his face, obscuring his features. His chin was exposed. He had a goatee and tattoos on his neck, chest, and arms. He looked scary. Knives lined a table in front of him.

"I've got your kid," he said. "I want a hundred thousand dollars cash, or I'll cut his little balls off and feed them to my Doberman."

Then he looked over his shoulder.

"Make him scream for the cameras."

A high-pitched voice wailed. I shifted uncomfortably. Andrea brought a hand to her mouth. Frank's face went red, and he clenched his jaw tight. His nostrils flared as he reached for his wife.

"That animal has Elijah," said Andrea. "If you hadn't showed up, my baby would be safe, Detective. You're a murderer."

Deveraux looked at Katrakis, an annoyed expression on his face.

"Call your technical team and tell them this was filmed by students at Miami University in Oxford, Ohio. That's The Blademaster. He's a recurring character in a serialized horror movie published on YouTube. My teenagers think it's awesome and watch it every Friday when a new installment comes out. That video came out three or four weeks ago."

Katrakis made an incredulous noise.

"Excuse me?"

"Look it up," said Deveraux. "You've been played. Who sent this to you?"

Andrea and Frank looked to Katrakis, confused. Then Frank cleared his throat and looked at Deveraux.

"It was texted to me from a number I didn't recognize."

"Next time something like this happens, call the police," said Deveraux. "We have the resources to determine whether it's a serious threat or a cruel prank. Mr. and Mrs. Powell, my officers can assist you with anything you need. Mr. Katrakis, you and your attorneys can leave now. I'm going home."

Deveraux left the moment he finished speaking. The Powells looked stunned. Then they looked at Katrakis.

"He doesn't know what he's talking about," said Katrakis. "My team and I investigated..."

"I want my retainer back," said Frank.

"That's not possible," said one of the lawyers, leaning forward. "The contract you signed clearly specifies the circumstances under which you are entitled to a refund. This isn't one."

They started arguing, so Marcus and I left. In the hallway, Marcus raised his eyebrows.

"Wow," he said. "That was something."

"It was a waste of time. Let's herd everybody out. I'm going to find Julie Smith and make sure she's safe. Then I'm going to go home and sleep."

Marcus looked at the door.

"No matter what anybody else says, you're doing a good job on this case."

I squeezed my jaw tight and nodded.

"Thank you, but a good job isn't enough. We've got to find that child."

Chapter 32

Marcus and I kicked the Powells and Katrakis out of the station and locked the doors. Then I tracked down Julie. She was on her way home. Katrakis and his team hadn't held her hostage, but they had come close. We should have arrested the lot of them for hindering prosecution.

Roy and I drove home and arrived at two AM. Part of me wanted to stay up and pound shots of vodka until I felt better, but I would have paid for my temporary relief tomorrow morning. Instead, I crashed on the bed and fell into a nightmare-filled sleep.

As per his custom, Roy whined the next morning when he heard the kids outside. I had gotten about five hours of sleep, so I felt okay. On any other morning, I might have taken him outside to say hello. Today, though, I slipped out of bed, brewed coffee, and checked my emails on my phone. Roy sat beside me, his tail thumping on the floor. When he saw I wasn't moving, he whined and put his paw on my foot.

"They're lining up for the bus," I said. "They don't want to see us. We're just the people who live next door. Remember?"

Roy whined again. I scratched his ears but focused on my phone again. It didn't look like anything important had happened since I went to bed, so I poured myself a cup of coffee and told my Alexa speaker to play the news. She—or it, I guess—complied. The school bus arrived a few minutes later. Roy ran to the door. Then he barked. I looked at him and lowered my voice.

"No."

He lay on the ground, his face between his two front paws. As the bus rumbled away, Roy seemed to relax. He enjoyed seeing the kids, but he'd get over it. For ten minutes, I drank my coffee and ate toast and listened to the news. It was relaxing. Unfortunately, we couldn't hide from the world forever. I needed a new home, so I browsed a realtor's website. Nothing looked appealing, but I'd find something. As Linda had said, the shelter needed the space.

After lounging, I dressed, walked Roy a few blocks, and headed into work. Trisha sat at the front desk but had little to report. After our late evening, Marcus had taken the morning off. He'd be in at noon. While the events were still fresh, I wrote reports about the night prior. It had been a waste.

From the moment Julie Smith had called 911, we had been searching for a missing toddler. Elijah hadn't been abducted, though, and he hadn't gotten lost in the woods. We had mountain lions in Missouri, but they left remains. If a car had hit Elijah, we would have seen evidence. We needed to face the facts: Elijah was dead. This was a homicide investigation.

Motive, means, and opportunity. Ryan had all three. He slept with Julie to get his rocks off, not have a kid. By his own admission, he was alone with Elijah the day Elijah disappeared. He was my only possible suspect. Ryan may have claimed it was an accident, but I doubted it. Accidents left evidence. We had nothing.

Ryan had disposed of Elijah's body somewhere, and my mind kept going back to a conversation I had with a woman who worked for Bartholomew Brothers Homes, Ryan's employer. They had seven housing sites. All were excellent spots to dump a body, and Ryan had access to each. Once the company built a house on them, they'd become inaccessible, too. Ryan would have known that.

I called the company's office and told them I planned to visit their worksites. The woman to whom I spoke said she'd alert her colleagues. Then Roy and I headed out.

High Ridge, Missouri, was sixty miles northwest of St. Augustine. It had a lot of rolling hills and big trees. Spring Creek, the subdivision Ryan's company was developing, was a muddy field with a few skeletal future houses. One day, it'd be a beautiful spot. For now, it looked like a mess. I parked on the roadside behind a red pickup and got Roy out. A man wearing jeans, a white hardhat, and a Bartholomew Brothers T-shirt appeared from a jobsite with a partially finished home.

He waved to me. Nail guns thwacked, saws cut, and hammers smacked into nails as crews erected the frames of what would eventually be pretty good-sized homes.

"Detective Court?" he asked. I nodded, and he held out his hand. "Thad Bartholomew. Vanessa said I should expect you. You're from St. Augustine. Got any leads on the treasure your old boss hid?"

I forced myself to smile.

"There is no treasure, and my old boss was a bastard who cheated everyone he could," I said. "You've got a great spot for a subdivision here. How big are your lots?"

His smile faltered but then returned.

"Lots are about an acre each. Gives the residents room to stretch out and garden. You're not in the market for a house, are you?"

"This is a little far from home."

"If you change your mind, we'd love to give you a tour and tell you about the community," he said. "Vanessa tells me you're investigating Ryan Powell for murder."

"Unfortunately," I said, nodding. "You work with him?"

"I've supervised him," he said, nodding. "He worked hard and kept his nose clean. We don't know what we're going to get with young guys. They can be good workers, eager to learn, or they can be buttheads. Ryan was the former."

I grabbed a pen and paper from my purse.

"I'm glad to hear it," I said. "He have a temper?"

Thad smiled.

THE MAN BY THE CREEK

"This is a construction site. Everybody's got a temper," he said. "We try to be professional, but if you screw up somebody else's work, you're going to get an earful. That's how you learn."

"He ever get into a fight?"

Tad considered before shaking his head.

"Never physical. He had words with Rodney a few times, but Rodney's a jerk. I'd fire him if he weren't such a good framer."

"He ever mention his kid?"

"Rarely," said Thad, nodding. "Most of my employees are moms and dads. Kids are a frequent topic of conversation."

I jotted down a few notes and shielded my eyes from the morning sun.

"He ever complain about Elijah or his ex?"

He lowered his chin.

"Everybody complains about their kids and their exes," he said. "That's part of being on a construction site." Thad paused. "Ryan rarely talked about Elijah, though. I got the feeling he wasn't part of his life."

I wrote that down and nodded.

"He wasn't," I said. "Julie wanted the kid full time. I think Ryan was amenable to the idea, but his mom wasn't."

"That makes sense," he said, nodding. "He was young to be a dad. I think he would have grown into it, but it takes time."

I looked toward the crews working on the houses. He probably had twenty people out there.

"Ryan have any friends he worked with?"

"Everybody gets along, but Ryan didn't make too many friends. The guys go to bars after work, but Ryan wasn't 21. It made things tough."

We spoke for another few minutes, but I learned little new. Then he offered to show us around the various projects on which Ryan had worked. So we walked, and he pitched his company if I ever wanted to build a house. Maybe I would one day.

We walked through five different homes of various stages of construction. In each, Roy kept his head down, his tail low, and his body relaxed. At the sixth construction site, though, his tail shot straight up in the air, and he began pulling on the leash. His head swiveled left and right, and he had his nose in the air. He smelled something.

"Ryan worked on this site?" I asked.

Thad nodded.

"He worked on every site."

We stood near the foundation of what would be a three-thousand square foot home, but the slab looked finished. I let the leash out, and he stepped forward.

"What would Ryan have done here?"

"We're training him to frame houses, but everybody cleans up the jobsite."

"He do any digging?" I asked. Thad went quiet, so I re-peated the question.

"Everybody digs," he said. "It's part of the job."

Roy pulled us toward the slab but stopped at the edge. He looked at me and panted.

"Can we walk on it?"

Thad nodded.

"Should be fine."

I let Roy pull me forward. He sniffed the air. Then he caught a whiff of something again and started pulling me toward a corner of the slab. Then he sat down and looked at me, his tongue hanging out as he panted. Thad smiled.

"Looks like he just wanted a spot to lie down," he said. "Had me worried there for a while."

I swore to myself and took my cell phone from my purse. Before calling Shaun Deveraux, I looked at Thad.

"That's how he indicates he smells a body. Somebody's buried down there. When was this slab poured?"

"Saturday afternoon. Our concrete supplier was jammed. That was the only delivery window he could give us. I had to bring in guys for the job specifically."

"What time was this?"

"About two," he said. "Our crew was here until almost eight. It was a long afternoon."

"Before then, was anybody here?"

He thought and then shook his head.

"We shut down at three on Friday. I got here at 1:30 on Saturday. I was the only person here."

Julie had dropped Elijah off at nine on Friday. He could have killed him, dug a hole, and buried him almost any time before the concrete truck arrived. No one would have seen a thing.

"When you poured the slab, was the soil disturbed?"

He shook his head.

"We don't pour directly on soil. Beneath the concrete, we have a vapor barrier, insulation, and six inches of crushed stone."

"Did that look disturbed?"

He shook his head.

"We wouldn't have poured concrete if it had."

I nodded and considered.

"Does Ryan know how you prepare the site for a concrete pour?"

Thad sighed and looked down.

"He does, but he's a good kid. I don't mean any offense to your dog, but are you even sure it's a human body down there? Until we bought it, cattle ranged all over this area. You could have a dead cow down there."

"He can differentiate human from animal remains," I said. "Sorry. I'm going to get a warrant. We may have just found Elijah."

Chapter 33

M y chest felt heavy as I called the locals. I could work anywhere within the state of Missouri, but it was common courtesy to alert the locals before doing anything major within their jurisdiction. A deputy from the Jefferson County Sheriff's Department came out immediately. I introduced myself and explained what I had found. She called her supervisor, Sergeant Mateo Gomez, who came out and listened to my spiel again. Gomez called a canine officer who brought a cadaver dog out. This dog, too, indicated remains beneath the slab, so we had a body.

With confirmation, I then called Shaun Deveraux's office. His assistant patched me through.

"Mr. Deveraux, thank for taking my call. This is Detective Joe Court. I'm in High Ridge in Jefferson County, following up on a location at which Ryan Powell worked. It's a construction site with lots of heavy equipment and disturbed earth. From Friday afternoon to Saturday afternoon, the site was unoccupied and unsecured. This time corresponds to a period during which Ryan had Elijah."

I let Deveraux catch up.

"Understood," he said. "What'd you find?"

"I brought Roy. With the permission of the company developing the homesite, Roy and I walked around and checked out five houses under construction. Ryan had worked on each house, but I didn't find anything suspicious. Near the sixth house, Roy indicated he smelled human remains.

"I then called the Jefferson County Sheriff's Department. They sent out officers, including their cadaver dog. Scout indicated a body was buried in the same area. There's something down there."

"Okay," said Deveraux, his voice low. "That should be enough to convince a judge that we've got probable cause. You're at a building site, you said?"

"Yep."

Deveraux took a couple of breaths. It sounded like he was typing. He asked for the address and continued typing.

"Is it possible Roy and this other dog are smelling animal remains?"

"They're trained to focus on the smell of human decomposition. Pigs can confuse some dogs, but we're not dealing with a pig. We might have dead cattle nearby, but Roy can differentiate cattle from human remains. Scout, the other cadaver dog, can, too. I can get you in touch with his handler if you need."

"I'll call the prosecutor in Jefferson County," he said. "I've known her for a few years. She's a good lawyer, and she runs a tight ship. Is the construction company cooperating?"

I looked toward Thad and his employees. They had stopped working and were staring at us.

"They are, but this will get dicey. The dogs smelled the bodies beneath a concrete slab. Ryan worked here, and he knew when and how the company poured their foundation slabs. I think he killed Elijah, drove the body here, dug a hole where they planned to put the house, and then replaced the gravel so the site looked undisturbed. They poured reinforced concrete on top of it. We'll have to jackhammer the entire thing. We'll rip up their insulation, their vapor barrier, and disturb their site preparations. They probably spent twenty thousand dollars pouring that slab. We're going to destroy it. Can the county pay for it?"

He barely paused before speaking.

"We don't need to. In order to press a damage claim against us, they'll have to sue and prove we acted unreasonably. It sounds like you're doing everything right. You've confirmed your dog's identification, you've brought in the locals, you'll have a search warrant before you do anything...even if they sue you personally, the county attorney's office will defend you. You're under our insurance, anyway."

I smiled, more to myself than to anyone else.

"That's not what I mean. These people are just doing their jobs. They hired a worker, and he might have snuck on the jobsite after hours and dumped a body. Now, to find evidence against Ryan, we'll ruin their hard work. The company didn't do anything wrong, but this will cost them twenty or thirty thousand dollars."

Deveraux paused.

"That's how the law works. If you want it to change, contact your legislature. And they may not have to sue us. Once we find Elijah, they can sue Ryan for putting him there. His family has money."

"Still feels crappy."

"Life's crappy sometimes," he said. "Do your job. I'll call the Jefferson County prosecutor and put together a warrant."

I rolled my eyes and hung up. Then I called Bob Reitz, Darlene McEvoy, and the coroner's office. They agreed to drive up. Then I walked to Thad and his crew.

"I just talked to my boss. He and the Jefferson County prosecutor will put together a search warrant. I've brought in two cadaver dogs, each of which has smelled a human body. You guys have researched the property a little, right?"

Thad drew in a slow breath and nodded.

"Just enough to know we had a clear title when we bought it."

"In your research, did you hear anything about a cemetery around here?"

He shook his head.

"Nope."

I looked toward the building site. Then I looked at Thad.

"My team's going to bring in a jackhammer. We'll break up the slab and dig. Sorry."

Thad crossed his arms and sighed again.

"You get a warrant, we're going to get an emergency injunction against you," he said. "I already called my brother, and he already called the attorney. This will cost us money and time, neither of which we can afford."

"I understand," I said, nodding. "You need to understand something, too, though. I didn't come here lightly. A young woman has lost her son. She didn't deserve that. This is a big case. You seen it on the news?"

He nodded, his lips thin.

"Yeah. And I want to help, but if you destroy our slab, it's going to put us back weeks. This house is already sold. That means the person buying it can't move in on time, they can't move out of their old house on time, they can't close when they expect to close, they might even lose their loan. You never know how a bank'll react. This'll hurt people. My company can take the hit, but I don't know about my buyer. I don't want to destroy that foundation."

"Can you think of another way to get a body out from beneath it?"

Thad said nothing, but one of his crew members nodded toward me.

"Where's the kid?"

"Under the slab," I said. "How deep, I don't know."

"No, I mean, is he in the middle, or is he near the edge?"

"Closer to the edge than the middle."

The laborer looked to his boss.

"The slab is structural. We could get the vacuum digger. Shouldn't have to worry about compromising the structure as long as we backfill."

Thad looked at me.

"If I dug you a big hole right next to your body, would that be okay?"

"Could you be careful?"

"Yes, ma'am," he said. "We use this same system to dig around fiber optic lines. If we break a fiber optic line with a backhoe, we're out twenty grand to fix it. Our vacuum excavator can dig around them without damaging them. I never thought I'd say this, but if there's a body down there, we'll give you access without damaging it. If you let us do this, everybody'll win. We'll save thousands, and you'll get what you need."

If they could deliver what they promised, it sounded like a good compromise, so I nodded.

"Then get your vacuum. I'll get you a search warrant."

We had a plan. Thad got on the phone, while the rest of his builders returned to their assignments. Bob Reitz, Darlene McEvoy, Kevius Reed, and two techs from our coroner's office started driving down, while Shaun Deveraux started putting together a search warrant. I had little else to do, so I walked Roy around. Then we sat in my car and napped with the windows open. It was a nice way to spend the afternoon.

My team arrived a little over an hour after I closed my eyes. Deveraux had yet to acquire a search warrant, but he and his counterpart in Jefferson County were working on it. They were each trying to track down a judge. Darlene, Bob, Kevius, and I walked the site. Darlene was skeptical of the plan to tunnel beneath the slab, but Thad and his crew deserved a chance before we ripped up their work.

Thad joined us about ten minutes later with two giant trucks, one of which had a water tank on the back. Two detectives arrived from Jefferson County next. Their prosecutor had gotten us a warrant. They, too, sounded skeptical of Thad's plan, but they agreed to go along with it for now. Then everybody got to work.

Their excavator worked by shooting water at high pressure. The water loosened the soil, allowing a vacuum to suck the dirt and water slurry into the truck. It created a clean hole faster than any machine could have dug it. Apparently, they used them to tunnel beneath the slabs of homes they renovated in order to change out pipes and to install interior French drains and various other projects. The machine was loud but effective.

It was almost mesmerizing to see the tunnel form. Within three hours, we had a space beneath the slab big enough for a person to crouch in. Roy didn't want to go in—and I couldn't blame him—but Scout, the other cadaver dog, sprinted forward. He got in and started digging himself. His handler pulled him out before he could get far, and we started with shovels.

Because the work was hard, we took turns as the sun set. When it became too dark to dig and see what we were doing, the Jefferson County team brought in lights and a portable generator. Thad stayed, but the rest of his team left. At nine, Kevius shouted for the coroner. He had found black felt. It looked like a bag. He carried a piece of felt to us while the coroner's technicians continued excavating.

Thad drew in a breath. We were standing about thirty feet from the hole. I glanced at him.

"You all right?"

"This is roofing felt," he said.

"Would Ryan have access to it?"

He squeezed his jaw tight. Then he shook his head.

"We don't use it anymore," he said. "We use Huber Zip systems sheathing and an adhesive membrane where required. My team hasn't used this for ten years. It doesn't provide an adequate air seal. This is degraded, too. It shouldn't feel this thin."

I straightened and squeezed my jaw.

"That's not Elijah down there."

"Not unless he was buried twenty years ago," said Thad, handing me the square of felt. He ran his hands along his scalp and shook his head. "I told you Ryan didn't bury his son here. He's a good kid."

"I hope you're right," I said. "But Elijah or not, we've got a body. That's a problem."

Chapter 34

Despite Thad's protestations that the roofing felt was twenty years old, we didn't know what we were dealing with beneath that slab. Our teams worked slowly and methodically. The problem was that our hole kept filling with water, which was why they had built a slab-on-grade foundation instead of a basement. The water table was too high.

Eventually, the teams arrived at the body itself. Normally, they would have documented the scene and kept the body in place while they cataloged the remains and sifted through the soil for trace evidence. Here, because nobody wanted to remain in a dark cave that slowly filled with water, they dug him out and placed him on the ground.

The roofing felt was torn and threadbare. It looked like a body bag. The coroner's team cut it open a few moments after putting it on the ground to expose the skeletal remains of an adult. Roy and Scout, our cadaver dogs, perked up, but nobody else seemed very excited.

"Hips tell me it's a male," said a coroner's tech. "Size indicates he's a late adolescent or adult. The skull is caved in. It's possible he was hit by a blunt object. It's also possible the soil pressed it down. We'll have to look closer once we get him on a table. The degree of decomposition tells me he's been here for years. Skin and clothes are mostly gone. Sorry, Detective. This isn't your victim."

I sighed and nodded. Two detectives from Jefferson County stood nearby. My team started walking toward me.

"Sorry, fellows," I said. "This one's yours. We're going to head home."

"You should stay," said a detective. "Could be exciting. You never know what you'll find. Could be a gangster from the mob wars in the eighties in St. Louis. Could be a drug runner. This is history."

I smiled.

"Thanks for the offer, but I've got enough bodies in St. Augustine County to worry about."

They thanked me for coming down. Then I joined my team near our cars.

"Thanks for coming out, guys," I said. "Sorry for making you dig. Head home, shower, and drink some coffee. You've earned it. See you at work."

Bob chuckled.

"Feel like I've earned more than coffee."

"I'll buy everybody beer when we find Elijah," I said. "In the meantime, enjoy the overtime."

They grunted, got into their cars, and drove off. Roy and I took our time, but we headed home, too. I got into the station at about eleven and fell into my chair. I deserved to sleep, but I had reports to write and leads to follow up on—including a faux kidnapping claim.

I flipped through notes and checked my email. Then I dove into my work. Someone had tried to extort a hundred thousand dollars out of Frank Powell by claiming they had his missing grandson. I didn't care if it was a prank or an actual attempt to steal money; it was cruel, and it was unnecessary. They gave a grieving family hope. Then they stole it.

Part of me even wondered whether Katrakis and his team had set everything up. We had worked our butts off to find Elijah Smith. The evening he disappeared, we had dozens of people searching the woods, we had drones in the air, we had cars on the streets, and we had officers knocking on doors. With that many people working, I'd be shocked if the total bill for this search hadn't hit two hundred thousand dollars.

We did everything we could to find a missing child. Until they received that threatening phone call, the Powells had no reason to call in Katrakis and his security team. Once they got that call, though, their entire world changed. Suddenly, they believed Elijah wasn't missing; he was dead unless they acted. They became the only people who could save him.

Frank and Andrea did what they thought was right and called in outside help. Katrakis came immediately, but he wouldn't have come for free. He came with a six-figure bill, at least. If he were a professional, he never would have fallen for this fake video. He would have contacted us, traced the phone call and text messages, and brought in the FBI. Only after exhausting his options and learning everything he could about these supposed kidnappers would he agree to send the Powells to meet them.

There were no kidnappers, though, and the Powells didn't rescue their grandson. Katrakis got paid, Elijah was still gone, and we had nothing. It made me sick.

So I did what he should have done and started investigating. The text message Frank Powell had received from a number he didn't recognize. I called it, but the number wasn't in service. Then I started the real work. Frank Powell had a cell phone from a major carrier. I called their law enforcement line and explained what had happened and why I was calling. It took about half an hour, but I twisted enough arms of enough supervisors for them to do their jobs.

The call came from a spoofed number. It was easy to do, cheap, and legal. The caller downloaded an app, which allowed him to place calls from a fake number, to change his voice, and even to add background noise to disguise his location. The app company claimed they provided a valuable service that allowed people to maintain their privacy and stay safe when calling strangers, but mostly it was used to place spam phone calls and harass people.

Frank Powell's carrier couldn't give me the actual number used to place the call, but they gave me the caller's cell carrier, allowing me to call their law enforcement line next.

The second company took more work. I had to write an actual letter, save it as a PDF on department letterhead, and send it to their legal department for their records. Only after an on-call attorney read through my letter explaining the request did they give me the information I needed. Had this been a lower-level felony, I suspected it would have taken even longer. A kidnapping and ransom threat, though, sped things up.

At a little after one in the morning, I had a phone number, name, and address in Des Peres, a wealthy suburb of St. Louis. The number was registered to Sebastian Craig. License Bureau records pegged him at forty-one years old, six feet tall, and a hundred and eighty pounds. He had brown hair, blue eyes, and a chiseled jawline that belonged on the hero in an action movie. Craig wasn't an actor, though; a Google search indicated that he was a pediatric urologist at a major children's hospital in the city. He didn't seem like the sort of person to prank a grieving family, but stranger things had happened.

I called the St. Louis County Police Department's liaison and asked if I could borrow a uniformed officer in about an hour. He agreed, and I grabbed Roy, got in my car, and headed north. With empty roads, the drive into town was easy. I reached the neighborhood and parked in front of a brick two-story home that had probably been built in the mid-nineties. It was bland and big. The homes around us looked similar. Very likely, they each cost somewhere in the million-dollar range.

I called the St. Louis County Police again. They dispatched a uniformed officer who met me about five minutes later. I shook his hand and introduced myself. The late shift was tough and boring. You might find a few drunks or kids doing stupid things, but mostly you sat around in your car waiting for something to happen. And if you were called to an assignment, it was usually horrific. This was easy.

We drove another block before parking in front of a colonial style home with white clapboard siding, a gray roof, and black trim. A brass gas lamp flickered from the front lawn. Running a gas line to the front lawn probably cost a fair bit, but it was a nice detail. We parked and walked to the door. I wrapped my hand around Roy's leash and made sure my badge was visible as I knocked. The uniformed officer stood behind me and to my right, his hand hovering over his firearm in case this went wrong.

Given the neighborhood, I doubted I'd need backup, but having a uniformed officer behind me and a marked patrol vehicle on the street gave the visit a different feel. I wanted Dr. Craig to understand the shit he had stepped into. I rang the bell twice and knocked hard. As expected, nothing happened. Then I rang the doorbell twice more and knocked.

"This is the police," I said. "I need to see you, Doctor."

The uniformed officer noticed something and stepped back.

"Light just came on," he said. I nodded and knocked hard again.

"Police officer," I said, my voice loud. "Come to the door."

About a minute later, the officer's radio crackled, and he dipped his head to the right to speak into the microphone on his shoulder.

"Homeowner just called the police to make sure it was a legitimate call."

I knocked hard again.

"Open the door, sir," I said. "I can get an arrest warrant if you'd like. Otherwise, I'm just here to talk."

More lights popped on. Two minutes later, the door opened. A man wearing a blue bathrobe and pajamas stood on the threshold. His eyes were wide, and his skin was red. He looked as handsome in person as he had on his license.

"What's going on?" he asked. "Who are you? I've got kids. They're scared."

"Dr. Sebastian Craig?" I asked. His eyes flicked up and down at me. He nodded.

"Who are you?"

"I'm Detective Joe Court with the St. Augustine County Sheriff's Department," I said, showing him my badge. "Are you armed?"

He narrowed his eyes, confused.

"What?"

"Do you have any firearms on you or within your reach?"

He shook his head.

"No. Of course not."

"Step out onto the porch, please."

He sputtered something but didn't move. I stepped to my left, allowing him to see the police cruiser on the curb and the officer behind me.

"Please step onto the porch where we can talk," I said. He hesitated before stepping forward. He wore brown leather slippers and wrapped his bathrobe around him tight. "Do I need to pat you down for weapons, or can I trust you?"

"I'm not armed," he said, his voice softer. "Tell me what this is about."

I couldn't see any bulges on his outfit that might have been a firearm, so I nodded and removed my notepad from my purse.

"I'm here to ask about a text message and video you sent to Frank Powell. Are you familiar with a character known as The Blademaster?"

He closed his eyes and shook his head.

"What are you talking about? Who's Frank Powell, and who's The Blademaster?"

I recited the cell phone number. Craig's lips moved as he recited it to himself. Then he straightened.

"That's my son's number."

"Get him out here," I said. Dr. Craig didn't move.

"What's this about?"

I considered him before drawing in a breath.

"How old is your son?"

"Twelve," he said. "He's in seventh grade."

I grimaced and closed my eyes tight.

"Fuck."

"Why are you here?" asked Craig. "What are you accusing my son of?"

I squeezed my jaw tight.

"Get your son out here," I said. "You refuse, I'll call in additional officers, and we'll drag him out."

Craig understood the importance of my visit because he paled and drew a hand to his mouth.

"Has James hurt somebody?"

I exhaled through my nose so I wouldn't snap at him.

"Just get him out here right now."

He agreed and stepped back inside. I glanced at the uniformed officer behind me.

"Thank you for coming," I said. "I've got this from here. We're not arresting anyone tonight."

"You sure you want me to go?"

I drew in a breath and nodded.

"Yeah. I've got this."

He returned to his cruiser and left as Dr. Craig and a boy entered the doorway. The kid wore a tie-dyed shirt, black shorts, and glasses.

"Hey," he said, his voice hesitant. I thumbed through pictures and videos on my phone until I came to the one Frank Powell had received. Then I played it for the Craigs. The kid's eyes opened wide. His dad drew in a sharp breath.

"That's terrible," said Dr. Craig. "What's going on?"

"I've never seen that before," said James.

"It's from a horror movie on YouTube," I said, glancing at Dr. Craig. "Your son sent it to Frank Powell. Mr. Powell's grandson is missing and presumed dead."

"You can't prove that," said James. "I didn't do anything wrong."

I ignored him and focused on Dr. Craig.

"James used an app to spoof his phone number. Your cell carrier gave me the information I needed to track him down. James made Mr. Powell believe he had a young boy hostage and would turn him over for a hundred thousand cash in a duffel bag. Mr. Powell hired a private security firm because he didn't know what else to do. This private firm specializes in hostage negotiation and rescue and works primarily in Mexico.

"Let me be clear so you understand the gravity of our situation. Mr. Powell hired a private military contractor that works with former soldiers to rescue hostages from drug cartels. Had they found you, dozens of men with automatic weapons would have kicked your door down in the middle of the night to rescue a child from a murderer. The men Mr. Powell hired are not investigators. They kill people for a living."

James started backing up, shaking his head. I looked at him.

"You terrified an innocent family. I want to scream at you, but I can't because you're a kid." I threw up my hands and laughed. "I don't know what else to tell you. You're lucky to be alive."

My throat hurt, and the worn edges of Roy's leash creaked in my hand. The dog whimpered, so I pet him to let him know I was okay. My eyes felt glassy as a tremble passed through me. Dr. Craig's face was white. His son cried. I didn't care. I drew in a breath to calm myself down. Pain, anger, frustration, every emotion I had suppressed since I learned about Elijah broke through my guards and entered my voice.

Elijah was gone. It tore me up, but I had nowhere to put that anger, that rage, that pain. James Craig was a stupid kid. So I sucked in a breath my nose and squeezed my jaw tight.

"How'd you get Mr. Powell's phone number?"

The kid's lips moved, but he didn't speak. I stared at him until his father put his hand on his back.

"Tell the detective what she needs to know."

James blinked. Then he looked down.

"Reddit," he said. "Somebody doxed him."

I squeezed my jaw tight before speaking. I hated people some nights.

"Thank you," I said. "Have a nice night."

"Sorry," said the kid. "I didn't mean anything."

I ignored him and walked to my car. As Roy and I drove, the Craigs stared at us, unmoving, from their doorway.

Maybe they thought they were getting off easy, but they weren't. I'd do what I could to keep the story quiet, but it'd get out. Once that happened, they'd be front-page news. Their punishment would be as cruel and as wrong as James's prank. Hopefully, they had somewhere to go. Once their story aired, self-righteous strangers would line up to scream at them—never once considering they were causing as much damage as James ever did.

Roy and I drove home. I grabbed a bottle of vodka from my freezer and poured a drink, but I didn't put it to my lips. Instead, I stared at it and sat on my couch and petted my dog and grieved for a little boy I had never met and never would.

Chapter 35

J ulie had nothing left inside her. When she woke up yesterday, she had had hope. She had known Elijah was
alive. It was like she could almost hear him. She had felt him
in her bones, but he had been just out of her reach. If she
had searched an hour longer, or if she had visited the right
neighbor, she would have found him, digging in a sandbox
or rolling around in leaves.

Now, she felt nothing. Elijah had become a hole in her
heart. It wasn't just an absence. It was deeper than that. The
space he had occupied was cold and mean. She had tried
looking for her son, and she had tried sleeping. She had even
gone to Ryan's house to look for him. The security team had
taken her in. They had told her they would get Elijah back.
They said they knew where he was. Someone had taken him.

The abduction had terrified her, but they had claimed it
was a good thing. It was a business deal, no different from
buying a house from an inexperienced seller. If they structured the deal right, they had claimed, everyone would win.
Elijah would return, the bad guys would go to jail, and life
would continue. It didn't matter that the security team had

taken her cell phone or refused to let her go. They had had to maintain operational security, whatever that meant.

For a few hours, she had felt that hope build inside her. It had felt like they were heading to the big drop on a roller coaster. Every moment had lifted her closer to that dip, and her gut tightened.

Then, she had reached the top. The security team had received a phone call. She had been in the Powell's kitchen, a mug full of cold, black coffee in front of her. She had poured it hours earlier and forgotten to drink it. A team member answered the phone and then walked outside. When he came back, he grabbed her arm and told her to leave. That was it. He returned her cell phone and her pistol and kicked her out. Her roller coaster had reached the top of the ride and stopped. She hadn't dropped. It was just a pointless windup.

She had driven home confused and had found her mom waiting for her. As Julie had pulled into the driveway, her mom opened the front door. The two ladies walked inside and sat on the couch.

"Anything?"

Julie shook her head.

"No," she said. "I thought we had him, but we didn't."

Then the drop—and the tears—came. She had curled her legs up and sobbed against her mom, just as she had when she was a little girl. Her mom put her arms around her tight. Then her dad heard them and joined in. As a little girl, those hugs had made her feel warm and safe. Julie's parents could have solved her problems then. Nothing would solve this, though. Her mom and dad, despite their caring intentions, despite all the love they could give, would never heal this wound. With Elijah gone, a part of Julie had gone, too. It was her favorite part, the best part of her. She'd never have it again.

At four in the morning, she went to bed. She had tried to sleep, but sleep wouldn't come. Instead, she had stared at the ceiling and waited for the world to change. It didn't, of course. The world had its own inertia. If she wanted it to move, she had to move it.

At five, she swung her legs off her bed. She hadn't bothered changing earlier, so she wore the same clothes she had worn the day before. Her footsteps were light. Thankfully, her mom and dad had left the living room. She scribbled a note and put it by the coffeemaker in the kitchen before leaving the house. She still had her father's pistol. Today, she'd put it to use.

Julie couldn't get to Ryan, but his best friend, Ethan Pettrica, was a prime target. Ryan and Ethan had known each other since they were in diapers. Julie knew Ethan pretty well, too. He liked her and had told her so often. He thought she'd sleep with anybody. Once, he even tried to drag her to a bedroom at a party. She declined his advances, but he didn't care. If a boy on the wrestling team hadn't overheard her, he would have raped her and then claimed it was consensual.

He deserved everything that would happen to him this morning.

Ethan lived in an old Victorian home in the woods. His grandparents had left it to him, and he'd been restoring it since he moved in after graduation. His parents lived in town. Julie didn't know what Ethan did for a living, but he had taken every industrial arts class offered during high school. He had strong hands back then. She wondered if he had installed a security system or gotten a dog. Hopefully, not. A dog would make this harder.

She drove toward the house. The stretch of road ran straight for two hundred yards and then cut right. When the county built the road, they had stayed as close to the property lines as possible, so the asphalt rarely ran straight. It created a lot of nooks and crannies in which to hide. She killed her headlights and parked in the darkness. The sun would rise in another hour. She'd be done by then.

Before getting out of her car, she checked her pistol to ensure it had a round in the chamber. It did.

Had Ethan possessed half an ounce of common sense, he could have done well for himself in life. Despite his aggressive tendencies, many girls loved him. He was the kind of guy they thought they could change. If they were firm or supple enough, he'd bend to their will and become the alpha provider they had always dreamt of.

Of course, he wouldn't do that. To change and grow, he'd have to care about something more than his present needs. That wouldn't happen anytime soon.

She stayed in the tree line and crept toward his home. It was two stories and beautiful and had a big swing on a wraparound front porch. She hurried to the unlocked, detached garage where he kept his spare key. He had told her about it when she was pregnant with Elijah. He had heard that pregnant women often became more amorous than normal, and he wanted to sleep with her while she still had her pregnancy boobs. Somehow, she had stayed away.

Julie found a key ring hanging from a nail on an old workbench. She used that to let herself into the house. As she walked into the kitchen, she took the pistol from her purse and listened. The room was silent.

Like many old houses, Ethan's home had a kitchen at the rear. Black-and-white tile in a checkerboard pattern covered the floor. The plain oak cabinets looked dated but nice. She ignored everything and walked deeper into the home.

Ethan lived in the first-floor master bedroom, just off the living room. His door was open, and he was alone. Julie crept inside and then stopped at the foot of his bed. She held her pistol in front of her and whistled. Ethan stirred, but didn't rouse.

"Hey, sugar," she said. "Wakey, wakey."

Ethan's eyes fluttered open. At first, they lacked focus. She wondered if he was drunk, so she whistled again for his attention. He looked at her and jumped and pulled his blanket up.

"Julie?" he asked.

"Hey," she said. "I'm here. Just like you asked."

He sat up and shook his head.

"You shouldn't be here. You want dick, go somewhere else."

"I'm not here for that," she said. "Keep your hands on top of the covers. I've got a gun pointed at your head right now."

"Why the hell are you pointing a gun at me?"

"So I can shoot you in the head," she said.

He rubbed his eyes and shook his head.

"Get out of my house," he said. "You're not going to shoot me."

Julie slid the weapon an inch to the right and squeezed the trigger. She had fired that gun—or one similar to it—hundreds of times at a range. It had made her feel alive. Shooting it at the wall beside Ethan's head and seeing the plaster break and splinter made her feel more than that. She felt dangerous and strong. It was about fucking time.

"Jesus," he said, bringing his hands to his face and pulling himself into a ball. "You could have killed me."

"That's the point, dear," she said. "Swing your legs off the bed. We're walking to the kitchen."

"Why?"

She sucked in a breath through her nose.

"Because you know what Ryan did to my baby," she said. "He doesn't do anything without you. You're the closest thing he's got to a conscience."

"I'm not going anywhere. You're not going to kill me. You don't have it in you."

Julie laughed.

"You motherfuckers took everything from me," she said. "Without him, I have nothing to live for. That's a real bad situation for you."

He pushed down his covers.

"I'm coming. Let me just get my pants."

"No pants. Even if you're naked, you don't have anything I haven't seen before."

He started kicking his legs off the side of the bed.

"I'm wearing underwear," he said.

"Great," said Julie, nodding. "Walk to the kitchen. If you reach for me or try to get a gun, I'll shoot you and burn the house down around you."

"I believe you," he said. "I don't know where Elijah is, though."

"That's okay," said Julie. "We're old friends. I'm sure we've got lots to discuss."

She led him to the kitchen and told him to sit at the table. He sat and put his hands flat. She stayed standing, just out of reach.

"First things first," she said. "You and Ryan are best friends. If you tell me the truth, I won't hurt you or him.

Where's my baby? And don't give me this bullshit story about getting lost in the woods. Elijah's three. He can barely cross a room without falling on his backside. What did Ryan do with him?"

Ethan swallowed and shook his head.

"Ryan didn't hurt him, if that's what you're asking."

"Okay," said Julie, nodding. "What did he do?"

"Why do you care?" he asked. "Elijah's a good kid, I guess, but he ruined your life. You can't go out with your friends, you can't go to college, you can't even get laid without him showing up. Isn't your life better without him?"

Julie licked her lips and slipped her finger to the trigger.

"I'm going to pretend you didn't say that. What did Ryan do?"

"He gave Elijah a better life than you could ever give him. He's gone."

Julie inhaled through her nose, counting to five so she wouldn't snap at him.

"What do you mean? I need details. What did Ryan do?"

"He sold him to a baby broker."

Julie furrowed her brow, surprised for the first time that morning.

"What the fuck is a baby broker?"

"A guy who buys and sells babies," he said. "Rich couple asks for a baby, but they can't adopt or have one themselves, so they contact this guy. They tell him they want a boy with blue eyes and blond hair, and the broker sets up a deal. It's legal. There's paperwork and everything."

Julie shook her head.

"That's not how adoption works, dumbass. Ryan doesn't even have custody."

"Sorry, Julie," said Ethan, leaning back and crossing his arms. "The world's complicated. Possession's nine-tenths of the law, you know. Elijah's with a new family now. They're rich, and they love him. He'll never want anything. They'll give him new clothes whenever he needs them, they'll buy him food and take him on vacation. He'll go to college. He'll do everything you should have done. Why would you want to keep a baby in this shithole town, anyway?"

"No," said Julie, shaking her head. "Elijah was mine. He's not a car. You can't just sell him and move on."

Ethan leaned forward and put his elbows on the table.

"It's done, Julie," he said. "It's all over now. Elijah's gone." Julie kept shaking her head. Ethan lowered his voice. "I'll tell you what. Since you're so upset, I'll call Ryan and set up a meeting. You can talk about money."

Julie closed her eyes and drew in a breath as she ordered her thoughts.

"So the plan was to sell my baby and pretend you lost him? That was it? How does Ryan know he didn't sell Elijah to some kind of pedophile ring? He's a baby."

"We've got insurance," said Ethan. "Trust me. We thought this through."

She shook her head again and lowered her pistol.

"What kind of insurance?"

"A video of the baby broker," he said, licking his lips. "I filmed the exchange. As long as we've got that video, the broker won't let your baby get hurt. We'd ruin him and send him to prison forever."

Julie counted to five before speaking.

"I want to see this video."

"It's on my phone," said Ethan. "It's in the bedroom. You going to shoot me if I get it?"

"No. Get your phone," she said, sighing. "If done is done, I guess that's it."

He lowered his chin.

"You're cool with this?"

She threw up her hands and shrugged.

"I guess," she said. "Being a mom sucks. I don't even sleep through the night anymore. I don't want Elijah hurt, though. And I deserve compensation. I put in a lot of work."

"Okay," he said, nodding. "You stay here. I'll get my phone."

Julie clenched her jaw tight and waited while Ethan got the phone. As he said, he had a video. On it, Ryan and Elijah stood beside the road, holding hands. A guy in a red car parked and talked to Ryan. Then Ryan handed the newcomer Elijah's hand and got a bag in exchange. Julie's heart pounded as Elijah cried. The video went blank after that.

It took everything she had not to raise her pistol and shoot Ethan right there.

"Can you send this to me?"

Ethan agreed and sent it to her as an email attachment. Once she received it and ensured that it was downloading, she looked at Ethan.

"It seems I owe you an apology," she said. "This has been a real help. I'm going to go visit Ryan now. Seems I'm owed some compensation."

"Get your money," said Ethan. "We'll celebrate afterward."

"I might do that," she said. "Don't call him. It'll hurt my negotiating posture."

"If you promise to come back here, I promise I won't call him."

"Deal," said Julie. "See you later."

She left through the front door and walked down the road to her car. Her entire body felt as if someone had strapped her to a rack and pulled. Overriding everything, though, was rage. Once she sat down in the front seat and turned her car on, she called her father's cell phone. He answered immediately.

"Daddy, it's Julie," she said. "Is Mom with you?"

"No. I'm driving over to Ryan's house," he said. "I'm out looking for you. We woke up, and you weren't there. We were afraid you had hurt yourself. Are you okay? Where are you? I'll pick you up."

"I'm fine. Go home and get some guns. Call Uncle Mickey. Ryan sold my baby. We're going to get him back."

Chapter 36

My phone rang at a little before six AM. Roy was snoring beside me in the living room. I was awake and had my back against the arm of the sofa, and my legs curled to my chin. The caller was Ryan Powell. I flicked my finger across the screen to hang up. Then he called again. I squeezed my mouth shut and drew in whatever strength I had. My chest felt heavy.

"It's early. What do you want, Mr. Powell?"

"It's Julie," he said, his voice panicky. "She's here with her dad and her uncle. They're fucking crazy. They're trying to break into the house. Julie's got a gun. She tried to kill Ethan. I don't know what the hell's going on, but I need help now before she kills me."

I shot to my feet and reached to the coffee table beside me for my weapon, badge, and keys.

"Call 911. I'm on my way."

Roy yawned and stood, his tail thumping. I made a fist in his direction.

"Stay. This is too dangerous."

I slammed the door shut and took the stairs so quickly I barely avoided falling. As I got into my car, I called my station. Nobody answered, so I called Bob Reitz. His spouse answered after three rings. I started my car, pressed my phone to my ear, and looked over my shoulder as I backed out.

"It's early, Detective. Bob's asleep. He had a late night."

"I know, and sorry," I said. "I've got reports of multiple armed intruders at Ryan Powell's home. I'm on my way. I need your husband to put a response together. If we wait for the highway patrol, people will die. Our assailant is Julie Smith and her family. Tell Bob we're rolling heavy on this. If he's got a vest, he needs to bring it. I'm on my way, and I'm going to try to de-escalate. I'm armed, but I'm going to be alone until we get help. We need to move."

I let her catch up.

"Okay," she said. "I understand."

"Good. Thank you," I said. I hung up with her and called Julie. She didn't answer, so I left a voicemail telling her to call. Then I waited a moment and opened my texting app. I used voice-to-text to demand she back off. I also warned her we had multiple officers inbound. Then I called her again as I drove. Once more, she didn't answer, so I tossed my phone to the seat beside me. The roads were empty.

I reached Pinehurst in under ten minutes and opened my windows. Nobody shot at me, but I didn't hear sirens, either. There were two pickup trucks in front of Ryan Powell's house. Both had doors open. The dome lights were on. I slammed on my brakes behind them and honked my horn. The neighbors wouldn't like me, but I didn't care. Then I got out of my car and unholstered my pistol.

"Julie!"

Nobody answered, so I grabbed my phone and called her. Then I reached inside my Volvo and honked my horn again. This time, she answered.

"What do you want?"

"Where are you?" I asked, already hurrying around the house. Julie stood on the back patio beside two men with rifles. She kicked a back door, but it didn't seem to budge. Then she glared at me. I tossed my phone to the grass, raised my pistol, and adjusted my stance, my heart hammering. None of them pointed weapons at me, but they were an obvious threat to the family inside the home.

"Put your weapons down and step away from the house," I said. "Nobody needs to get hurt."

"This isn't your business, Detective," said Julie. "I'm handling this."

"No, you're not," I said. "If you hurt somebody, there's no coming back for any of you. Even if you don't pull the trigger, I'll charge you with felony murder. You'll never see your families again. I guarantee it. Drop your weapons and step away from the house."

"They're in there," said Julie, her voice a snarl. "I'm not letting them get away with it."

She kicked the door again. Her father handed his rifle to the other man before touching Julie's shoulder. The second man put the rifles—barrels away from me—on the outdoor table. Then he backed up and put his hands in the air.

"Let me go, Daddy," she said. "He sold him. He fucking sold him. Uncle Mickey, help me. Make him let me go."

She kicked the door again. Then her dad stepped forward. He pulled her back. I thought she'd fight, but she didn't.

"Put the gun down, Julie," I said, my heart pounding. "Please. We can talk. Whatever Ryan did, I'll make sure he pays for it. You have my word."

Scott took the pistol from his daughter's hands. A car screeched to a stop in front of the house.

"Put the gun on the table." Scott nodded and complied. Then he put his hands in the air and backed onto the grass. Julie followed, her hands over her face as she cried. Officer Carrie Bowen came running around the side of the house. She wore black leggings and a white T-shirt. Her badge hung from a lanyard around her neck. I lowered my pistol, and she slowed.

"I think we're backing down now," I said. "Right, Julie?"

"Right," said Julie, her voice soft. Carrie took a deep breath and focused on me.

"I've got the people outside," I said. "Knock on the back door, show them your badge, and then tell the family inside that they're safe. They may not come out."

She agreed and knocked on the rear door. The Powells let her inside. Another vehicle screeched to a stop. Doug Patricia sprinted around the house. He slowed when he saw me.

"You okay?"

"I am. Everybody's dropped their guns," I said. "Carrie's inside the house with the Powell family. Go out front and call Bob. Tell him the situation has calmed down. Next officer who arrives, send him back here, because I need somebody to take custody of these firearms."

Doug agreed and went out front.

"We had good reason to come here," said Julie. "Ryan stole my baby and—"

"Stop talking," I said, interrupting Julie. "Now isn't the time for conversation. I will talk to you in time. For now, all of you, sit on the grass, and keep your hands on your heads."

"Why?" asked Julie.

"To show me you're no longer a threat," I said. "You showed up at a home with firearms and tried to break in. It's been a long night. I'm tired of dealing with other people's shit, and I'm tired of talking. Sit down and shut up."

Julie's father and Uncle Mickey seemed to be the sane ones, because they complied. Julie sat beside her father a moment later. I breathed easier. Alisa Maycock arrived next. She took the firearms and promised to return once she got the weapons somewhere safe. True to her word, she returned just a few minutes later, and we put Julie, her father, and uncle in zip ties.

Julie's dad and uncle looked ashamed of themselves. Julie, however, looked angry.

"He took my baby," she said. "The motherfucker sold him."

I didn't understand the latter part, but I understood the first.

"He did, and I'm sorry," I said. "That doesn't give you the right to kill him."

"We weren't going to kill anybody," she said. "We came for information. Talk to Ryan about the baby broker. Or talk to Ethan Pettricca. You're pretty, so he's dumb enough to talk to you. Pretend you're interested in him. He'll tell you everything."

I had no idea what she meant, but I nodded.

"Just calm down," I said. "It's going to be okay. We'll talk soon."

Alisa and I led the three Smith family members to the front of the house. Julie and I sat on the hood of my car, while we put her father and uncle on the grass with their backs to an oak tree. Sergeant Reitz arrived a few moments later. He parked and jogged toward me.

"What happened? Everybody okay?"

"Everybody's safe," I said. "Spooked, maybe, but safe."

I told him about Ryan's phone call and everything I had done since getting there. Bob sighed and looked down.

"I'm glad everybody's okay," he said. "How are we going to handle this?"

"Julie, her dad, and her uncle will go downtown. We'll charge them with attempted murder. Julie said something about Ryan selling Elijah. I'll sort that out. If she's not up for talking, we'll use the charges against her as leverage."

Bob blinked a few times.

"Julie lost her child, Joe. If you charge her for this, she'll be on the news the moment you release her."

"She, her father, and her uncle brought weapons to a home and attempted to break in. They came here to kill Ryan and his family. I don't know how I can avoid charging her."

Bob looked away.

"I can't take part in this. My officers won't, either. You plan to charge Julie with a major felony, one that will land her five to fifteen years in prison. Meanwhile, you've charged Ryan—who probably killed Julie's child—with child neglect. He'll get probation."

I squeezed my jaw tight.

"I've got to follow the evidence."

"She's grieving, and she backed down when you asked her to," he said. "Julie is acting out of grief. Somewhere in your head, you know that."

"It doesn't matter. She came here with guns. She scared the shit out of the Powells. If we don't charge Julie, what are we going to tell the Powells?"

THE MAN BY THE CREEK

"You tell them the truth: the Smiths didn't come to hurt anybody. They came for Elijah. Then you sent them home and told them not to come back. You have discretion. Use it. I will not help you send that poor girl to prison for trying to find her baby."

"If she goes to prison, it'll be for her decisions and actions, not mine. Don't put this on me."

Bob sighed and licked his lips.

"You're wrong on this, Joe. As your colleague and as someone who cares about you, trust me. Talk to Carrie, talk to Alisa, talk to anybody with kids, and they'll tell you the same thing: Julie and her family are in an impossible situation. They shouldn't have come here. That was a mistake. You want to charge them with trespassing, I'll be all for it. You want to charge them with attempted murder, that's a hard pass."

I considered him and nodded. When I spoke again, my voice was soft.

"I appreciate your view. Consider this, though: what would have happened if I hadn't arrived when I did?"

Bob raised his eyebrows and shook his head.

"I don't know."

"When I arrived, she, her father, and her uncle were trying to break down the back door. That's the situation. I don't want to arrest Julie. She doesn't deserve anything that's happened to her. If she had information, she should have called me. Instead, she came here to kill a family. Circumstances

345

matter, but so do actions. Maybe there is no right response, maybe we screwed up... I don't know. The situation sucks, but so did her response."

Bob went quiet. I exhaled and felt the morning air on my skin. It was calming.

"What should we do?" he asked, eventually.

"Drink and hope for the best."

Bob smiled.

"I'll buy the booze when the case is over, and we'll argue moral philosophy all night," he said. "Until then, what do you want to do?"

I looked at Julie, her uncle, and her father.

"Let's take them to the station," I said. Then I paused. "I hope they have a good reason for being here. If I have to send a grieving mother to prison, I might be done with this job."

"You and me both, Joe," said Bob. "Give me ten minutes. I'll get some marked cruisers out here for a prisoner transport."

Chapter 37

B ob called in the day shift and requested three patrol officers come by the house in marked cruisers. I hated to worry about the department's budget, but I did. We were robbing the future to pay for the present. Maybe our future revenue situation would look different, but in our current outlay, we'd run out of money soon.

In years past, the department generated a lot of revenue by issuing traffic citations. Nobody enjoyed giving tickets, but we had all seen the statistics: more tickets meant we had fewer fatal car accidents.

Fender benders happened. People backed up into moving traffic, they turned slower than the car behind them expected, or they switched lanes while another car was in their blind spot. Minor traffic accidents cost money, but people were rarely hurt. They were hard to stop because they were hard to predict.

Deadly accidents usually involved high speeds, and they oftentimes involved alcohol. By ticketing motorists and having sobriety checkpoints on Friday and Saturday nights, we reduced both. Fewer people died. As much as it sucked to get a ticket, they lowered the death rate on our streets.

Unfortunately, we no longer had the manpower to maintain those patrols. Already this year, two teenagers died in car accidents. One was on her phone when she lost control, and the other, a young man, lost control of his car over a hill. Both hit trees, both had been speeding, and both had alcohol in their systems.

More patrols might have given them pause before driving home from a party. We couldn't know. I wish we had done something, though. If that meant we had to give out tickets, we'd give out tickets. That tickets provided funding was a bonus.

I got in my car and headed downtown. The building was dark still, but it smelled like coffee, and I heard soft conversations and laughter deeper in the building. I walked to my office and typed notes so I wouldn't forget what had happened that morning and at what time.

Julie, her father, and her uncle arrived about twenty minutes later. We put them in separate interrogation rooms. The Powells arrived shortly after that. We put them in a conference room with a uniformed officer. We'd interview them individually so they couldn't confer on their story. I didn't think they'd lie to me, but I wanted the truth, not a story they concocted to make themselves look good. Since they were ostensibly my victims, I started with them and took them to my office for interviews.

Each gave me the same basic story. They were asleep in their rooms when they heard someone pound on the front door. Ryan went down first and saw Julie, her father, and her uncle outside. All of them were armed. He shouted and offered to talk to them if they put their guns in their car. Unfortunately, the Smiths refused. Someone started kicking the door. Ryan then ran upstairs to tell his parents. They three then barricaded themselves inside the panic room, and Ryan called me.

The entire time, they were safe. The panic room had thick, reinforced concrete walls and a steel door like a bank vault. Julie would need a plasma torch to break in. Maybe Bob was right. Maybe it wasn't an actual attempt to get inside. Scott and Mickey Smith both had shotguns. They could have shot the hinges and kicked the door down. Maybe they were more interested in soothing Julie's feelings than exacting revenge.

In a case like this, intent mattered. Did they go there to kill? I couldn't say. If they had, they weren't good at it. I thanked the Powells for their time and asked them to stick around. Then I went downstairs to the interrogation rooms and tried to speak to Mickey and Scott Smith. Both invoked their Fifth Amendment right against self-incrimination. That shut down those conversations before they even started.

Finally, I knocked on the door outside Julie's interrogation room. She glared at me.

"What do you want?"

"A conversation," I said. "I didn't expect to see you at the Powell's house this morning."

"I wouldn't have had to go there if you did your job."

"Fair enough," I said. "What should I have done there? Kicked the door down and dragged Ryan out at gunpoint? What was your plan? Were you going to shoot him on the front lawn? Think that'd make you feel better?"

Julie's lips formed a straight line as she narrowed her eyes.

"He knows where Elijah is."

"And where is that?" I asked.

"I don't know," said Julie, throwing up her hands. "He sold him. That's where his money came from. He sold my baby for money."

I blinked a few times as my mind processed the statement.

"Okay," I said, nodding. "Tell me about that. Who'd he sell Elijah to?"

"I don't know. I was going to talk to him. Elijah's my baby. Don't you understand that? He was my baby, and that motherfucker sold him like he was a used car or something."

I nodded again and considered.

"Let's back up. Why do you think Ryan sold Elijah for money?"

"Because his best friend told me," she said. "The idiots filmed it. Ethan called it their insurance. Like, if the baby broker turned out to be a pedophile, they could take the video to the police and have him arrested. They thought that would help. I just want my son back. That's all I want."

My heart started beating faster.

"You said they filmed the sale," I said. "Have you seen the film?"

"Yeah. Ethan sent it to me. It's on my phone, clear as day. Ryan drove out to the middle of nowhere beside the road, and his buddy Ethan hid in the woods. Then a red car parked, and a guy got out. He gave Ryan a bag of money, and Ryan handed him my baby. Elijah was crying, and Ryan just fucking drove off. He abandoned my baby."

Tears had streaked Julie's face.

"You have every right to be upset, Julie, but I need to see that video."

She covered her face and breathed.

"It's on my phone. Just give me my phone, and I'll send it to you."

I nodded, stood, and pounded on the interrogation room door. A moment later, Marcus opened it. I stepped into the hall and let the door close behind me.

"You watching?" I asked. Marcus nodded. "I need her phone. We collected it at the crime scene."

"Bob's already getting it," said Marcus. "Do we know who the best friend is?"

I shook my head and opened the door. Julie looked up.

"What's Ethan's last name?" I asked.

"Pettrica."

"Great. Thank you," I said. "We're going to pick him up."

I let the door close. Marcus turned and started jogging. He looked over his shoulder.

"I'll get him."

"Thanks," I said. Bob ran out of the stairwell with a cell phone in a plastic bag. I thanked him, tore open the bag, and went back into the interrogation room. Within thirty seconds, Julie had her phone open to a video app. The video she showed me was just as she described it. The cameraman was about twenty feet away, hiding behind a tree. Ryan stood on the side of the road, holding his son's hand. Then a red car arrived. I couldn't recognize the make. A man stepped out, gave Ryan a bag, and took Elijah's hand. The exchange took thirty seconds, but it left me cold inside.

"That's why I went to Ryan's house. I've got to find that baby broker. He's got my baby."

My throat felt tight, so I swallowed hard.

"We already found him," I said, my voice soft. "His name is Mannie Gutierrez. He's a lawyer from Miami, Florida, and he's in our morgue. We found his body Friday afternoon."

"Oh, no," said Julie, bringing her hands to her face as she cried.

Chapter 38

I left the interrogation room and met Bob outside. His face was pallid, his lips thin. His eyes stopped on Julie before focusing on me. I shut the door and leaned against the drywall. Every part of my body felt heavy. I had worked cases involving children before. No matter how you prepared yourself, they always hurt. This one tore at me.

I slid down the wall as my legs gave out. The carpet felt rough. I blinked and stared at the wall opposite me.

"He sold him," I said, my voice low. "Ryan sold his own child for twenty-five thousand dollars. Julie has the exchange on video."

Bob drew in a breath.

"I heard. I was watching."

Even if we sent Ryan to prison for the rest of his life, it wouldn't change the underlying facts. He had sold his kid. It was almost too awful to believe.

"How could he do that to somebody?" I asked. "He was a child. Even if Ryan didn't care about Julie, how could he sell his kid?"

Bob slid down the wall opposite me but said nothing. He was a dad. He didn't need to say anything. I let myself feel the frustration, despair, and anger for a few minutes, but then I choked it down. We still had work to do.

"We'll call the lawyers because I don't know how to charge him for this," I said. I closed my eyes and forced my heart to slow down. "Do we have Ethan Pettrica in custody yet?"

Bob shook his head.

"Not yet. Marcus is picking him up."

"When he gets back, I'll need his help. We'll jump back into the Mannie Gutierrez murder," I said. "Elijah's disappearance interrupted the case. Mannie would be dead no matter what we did, so I thought we could put his case to the side while we investigated Elijah's disappearance. Maybe that was a mistake. Marcus was busy with traffic accidents and burglaries. We didn't have the personnel for two major cases."

"You did the best you could with what you had," said Bob.

He may have been right, but it didn't make me feel better. Still, I nodded.

"You find any signs the cases were connected?" he asked.

"Not at the time," I said. "Before he died, Mannie had lunch with a doctor from St. Johns. Afterward, he allegedly went back to her place for sex. My initial thought was that the doctor's husband found out about the affair, got jealous, and killed Mannie to keep his wife from cheating on him. What if it was a home visit prior to an adoption?

"Matthew Rice was at work, but Cassandra could have shown Mannie around and explained how they planned to keep Elijah safe. She may have even paid him. I found twenty-five thousand dollars cash in Mannie's hotel room in St. Louis. He also had prepaid cell phones still in their packages.

"It all fits. Mannie would have needed to communicate with the Rices and with Ryan, so he bought phones that nobody could trace. If the Rices paid him fifty grand for a new son, Mannie could have pocketed twenty-five and given Ryan twenty-five. Then the Rices killed Mannie to keep their scheme secret."

Bob's eyes went distant as he considered.

"There's a problem," he said, speaking slowly. "We've only got one grocery store in town."

I thought he had misspoken, but he seemed serious.

"I don't follow."

"You ever been to Branson? It's a tourist town on a pretty lake, but it's known for country music. Lots of singers have theaters, and they perform for the tourists a couple of nights a week. You'll never see those singers on the streets because they're busy people. Everybody's got to eat, though, so everybody goes to the grocery store. That's where you'll have your celebrity sighting. St. Augustine only has one grocery store. Eventually, they'll take their son. They do that enough, somebody's going to recognize him. They can't hide Elijah here."

I considered and nodded.

355

"Maybe I'm wrong. They're doctors, right? They're both pretty young, and they had resources to take care of a kid. They seem like the kind of parents an adoption agency would love."

Bob waved away the concern.

"They might, but the process isn't up to the agency," he said. "My brother and his wife tried to adopt, and they would have made great parents, but it never happened. They got close twice, but the adoptions never came through. After a while, it was just so heartbreaking they stopped trying."

I shook my head.

"The foster care system's full of kids who need families."

Bob held up his hands defensively.

"I'm not here to argue about the system. I'm just sharing one experience. My brother would have adopted a toddler, but it never happened. Maybe these doctors had a similar experience. Maybe they tired of waiting and used their resources to purchase what they couldn't get legitimately."

I squeezed my jaw tight as I nodded.

"If we're right, we need to move. We're talking about middle-aged physicians who make four or five hundred thousand dollars a year each. They'd have enough money to disappear and start a new life overseas."

Bob pulled his phone from a pocket.

"It's almost eight. You think they're at work?"

"Maybe," I said. "They work odd hours, and St. John's hasn't been very cooperative with me lately. Send somebody to the hospital. We'll work with their security staff. I'll go to the house."

"Not alone, you won't," said Bob, shaking his head. "You had good reason to race over to the Powell's house alone this morning, but you can wait two minutes while I put a team together here. If the doctors killed Mannie Gutierrez, they'll kill you, too."

I blinked and drew in a breath.

"We should have made you sheriff."

He smiled and shook his head.

"Given the recent history of St. Augustine, I'm not sure the job has the same call it once did."

"Sadly true."

As I hurried to the lobby, Bob started jogging, looking for a team to send with me. Within moments, Katie Martelle and Dave Skelton came running from the break room. Both wore uniforms. Skelton tossed me a set of keys.

"We've got Delgado's SUV," he said. "Let's roll."

George Delgado had been our sheriff for a brief while, but then he lost an election. After that, he was murdered. George and I had never gotten along, but somewhere along the way, I think I had come to peace with his memory. We had seen the world differently, but he tried to do right. Even if I disagreed with him, I could still respect his motives.

We hurried to the lot and climbed into the vehicle. The Rice's home wasn't far, but we hit a little early-morning traffic on our way to their property, which slowed us down. It also gave us a moment to talk. Katie sat beside me in the front seat. Dave sat behind us. I glanced in the rearview mirror at him.

"We're looking for Cassandra and Matthew Rice and any signs of a child. The Rices are persons of interest in the death of Mannie Gutierrez. Before he was murdered, Gutierrez ran a sham adoption service that bought and sold children. We believe he gave twenty-five thousand dollars to Ryan Powell for Elijah Smith. My suspicion is that the Rices purchased Elijah because they couldn't have a child of their own. We don't have a warrant, but we need eyes on the Rices. If they purchased Elijah, they won't stick around St. Augustine. Unfortunately, being doctors, they've got the resources to skip town and disappear. We can't let that happen. Any questions?"

Katie looked thoughtful. Skelton crossed his arms.

"If we see them, what do we do? We can't arrest them on a suspicion."

"We just need eyes on them. Elijah is our priority. If they have him, we'll arrest them on sight. If they don't have him, we'll watch them and talk to the neighbors. Kids are loud, especially one who's been abducted from a loving home. Elijah would have been screaming. He might have even tried to escape. Maybe we'll get lucky, and somebody will have seen something."

"Let's get your dog," said Dave. "He's a cadaver dog, but I've seen him track people, too. We give him Elijah's T-shirt, and your dog will tell us if he's anywhere nearby."

I shook my head.

"I've already talked to the prosecutor about that," I said. "Even bringing Roy to the door without probable cause would constitute an illegal search. We'll watch them and do things by the book."

"Fuck that,' said Dave. "They stole a child. Fuck their rights and fuck the prosecutor."

I glanced at Dave, drew in a breath, and blinked.

"The situation sucks, but we're going to play by the rules here. That's the only way we'll send them to prison when we're done. They can't escape if we keep our eyes on them. We'll keep their house under open surveillance. If they have Elijah, we'll find him."

Dave shook his head but said nothing. I glanced at Katie.

"You okay with the plan, Officer Martelle?"

"Yeah," she said. "We'll watch them and track them. If they run, they won't get far."

At least I had one of them on my side. We drove for another five minutes before I pulled into the Rice's driveway. I glanced at Dave again.

"Once I park, I want Dave to run to the back of the house. Katie, you're going to stay in front in case somebody runs. I'm going to knock on the door and see if anybody's home. Clear?"

They nodded, and I stepped on the gas a little harder. Once I reached the front of the home, I braked harder than I normally would have. The heavy SUV skidded to a stop. Dave hopped out even before I could put the car in park. Katie followed. I hurried to the front door, my hand over my weapon. The house looked dark, but it was still early. If they worked late last night, they might still be in bed.

I pounded on the door and then rang the doorbell six or seven times. Then I listened in case a child started screaming. Nothing.

I pounded on the door again and rang the doorbell another half a dozen times. Then I peered into the window, hoping to see movement...or something. The front room was dark, as was the wall to the adjoining hallway. Nothing moved. I tried opening the door, but it was locked. Then I looked to Katie.

"Stay here. I'm going to take a walk."

She nodded, and I hurried to the left, peering in windows as I passed. A Land Rover had parked in the two-car garage. The second spot was empty. Dave waited in the rear yard, far from the house to observe every exit. He started coming toward me, but I waved him back as I peered in windows and stepped onto the rear patio. The house looked empty. I pounded on the back door.

"Sheriff's Department," I shouted. "Open up if you're in there."

Nobody responded, so I looked at Dave. Then I considered and took a pick set from my purse and started working on the back door's deadbolt. I didn't have probable cause or exigent circumstances, but I didn't care. The deadbolt slid open. I looked at Skelton again.

"Stay here," I said. "I'm going in."

He nodded, and I slipped inside. Thankfully, no alarm beeped. The air smelled stale. Cold coffee filled the pot. A piece of toast rested in the toaster. It, too, was cold.

"Dr. Rice?" I called. "Elijah? If you hear me, make some noise."

Nobody called, so I ran through the house, checking every room and listening for knocking or crying or any noise. In the master bedroom, someone had thrown clothes all over the bed. An overnight bag lay on the floor and a duffel bag rested beside the closet.

I checked the other bedrooms out next. No kids' clothes, no toys, no toddler bed, no stuffed animals... nothing to make me think a child had ever been inside the home.

As I walked out the back door, I called Bob Reitz. He answered right away.

"Joe, hey," he said. "I'm at St. John's right now. The doctors aren't here. Nobody knows where they are."

"They're not at home either," I said. "There are clothes on their bed and suitcases on the floor. We're too late. They're on the run."

Chapter 39

M arcus swore under his breath.

"If they're on the run, what are our options? Matthew Rice skipped work yesterday. They could be anywhere." He paused. "If we call in an Amber alert, we can put pressure on them. Even if they're not here, their friends and neighbors will see our alert. We'll get thousands of eyes looking for them."

I shook my head.

"An Amber alert is inappropriate. We don't even know whether they've abducted Elijah. And if they did, we'd have no reason to believe they'd hurt him. If they've adopted him—or at least think they have—they'll take care of him. It's not time to panic. It's time to gather information."

"What do you want to do, then?"

I looked around me. Dave Skelton started coming toward me.

"I've got Dave Skelton and Katie Martelle with me," I said. "We'll visit the neighbors and see if the Rices told them about their plans. The guy across the street seems nosy. I might talk to him, too. Kids need clothes, car seats, toys ... all that stuff. If they've been buying diapers in bulk or new toddler furniture, somebody may have seen something."

"They'll need a pediatrician, too," said Skelton. "Aren't many in town. You could call and ask if they're new clients."

"That's a good idea," I said, raising my eyebrow and taking my phone from my ear. I put it on speaker, and Dave stepped toward me. "You hear that, Marcus?"

"Yeah. I'll ask around at the hospital," he said. "What have we got tying the Rices to Mannie's murder?"

I sighed, wishing he hadn't asked for that.

"The same thing we've had this entire investigation: circumstance," I said. "The Rices had motive, means, and opportunity."

"Could anybody else have killed him?"

I shrugged.

"I don't know," I said. "Mannie bought Elijah from Ryan Powell, so they knew each other. Ryan might have had a motive to kill Mannie, but if he shot him, where's Elijah? Where's the gun? How did he get Mannie to the woods without getting blood all over his car? Where are his bloody clothes? If this was a hunting accident gone wrong, where's Elijah? The Rices are our best suspects—if only because I haven't been able to eliminate them."

Skelton rubbed his eyes. Marcus drew in a breath.

"Where do we go from here?"

"We find the doctors," I said. "They're wealthy. Wealthy people love their money. We'll follow that and find them. Marcus, you interview their friends and colleagues at the hospital. We want to find out whether they've got a favorite vacation spot, beach house, or cabin in the woods. Also find out if they've talked about having kids. Treat them like they're missing persons, not murder suspects. If their colleagues care about them, they'll help.

"Dave, you and Katie will knock on doors around here. See what the neighbors say. I'll work with Shaun Deveraux and see if we can get into their bank accounts. If they withdrew fifty-thousand cash, the bank'll have a record. Moreover, they might have written the serial numbers from the money. If we can match that to the cash found in Mannie's hotel room or in Ryan Powell's room, we'll have them."

"It's a plan," said Marcus. "I'll see what I can find at the hospital."

"And I'll work with Katie," said Dave. "We'll visit the neighbors."

I thanked them, hung up my phone, and walked with Dave to the front lawn. He and Katie Martelle conferred for a moment. They'd call Trisha for a ride once they finished. I got into the department's black SUV and headed downtown. In my office, I called the prosecutor. As soon as he came on, I updated him on the day's events—particularly the baby broker angle.

"Okay, wow," he said. He paused. "We'll have to research the proper charges against Ryan."

"I'm sure you'll come up with something appropriate," I said. "We need to find Elijah before he disappears. Can we get a warrant for the Rice's bank records?"

Deveraux paused.

"I don't know if you have probable cause," he said. "It seems like your only hard evidence against them is that Cassandra Rice had lunch with Mannie and she's now missing."

"Cassandra and Matthew have also missed multiple shifts at work."

He paused again.

"Conceivably, they've been missing for twenty-four hours if they've missed multiple shifts," he said. "Do you have any reason to think they're hurt? Has anybody made threats against them?"

I shrugged.

"I don't know. They didn't cooperate with us."

"A known associate of theirs is dead, and they're now missing. How does that make you feel?"

I raised my eyebrows, unsure what he was getting at.

"Curious?" I asked.

He chuckled.

"No, that's not what I mean," he said. "Is it reasonable to believe they will die unless you find them soon? It's possible that Mannie Gutierrez's murderer will kill them, too, right?"

I blinked and drew in a breath.

"I can't swear to that," I said. "Sorry."

He sighed.

"Our hands are tied, then. We need something tying them to Elijah or to Mannie's murder. A lunch date and romp at home won't cut it. Get into Mannie's phone. He's dead, so he has no expectation of privacy. Find his text messages and emails. We'll use those."

I scratched my forehead and nodded.

"Sure. Fine. Thanks."

I hung up and clenched my jaw tight.

"Damn," I said.

I pushed back from my desk and spun around to think. Unfortunately, Deveraux was right: we had nothing. Breaking into a stranger's phone may have been easy a decade ago, but not anymore. By now, the Rices could be in Amsterdam, Thailand, Russia, China, almost anywhere on earth. I rubbed my eyes and felt my chair slow. Then I texted Marcus.

Got anything?

Within moments, my phone rang.

"I'm in the hospital," said Marcus. "The Rice's coworkers are cagey. There's a clear hierarchy, and the doctors are at the top. The doctors choose their own staff, so the nurses don't want to speak ill of them. If you get labeled difficult, your career here is toast. The doctors I've spoken to don't seem to know anything. Or at least they won't talk to me."

"Okay," I said, nodding. "Anybody mention kids or vacations?"

"No," said Marcus. "The Rices kept their personal and professional lives separate."

I considered my options and then squeezed my jaw tight.

"Deveraux doesn't think we have enough to request a search warrant for their finances," I said. "I'm thinking of calling Cassandra. We can't track her without a warrant, but I've got her cell number. If they've got a toddler with them, maybe Elijah'll start crying. Scared toddlers are whiney, right? If I can prove they've inexplicably got a child, it might give us enough to get a warrant for their location."

Marcus grunted.

"Might tip them off that we're looking into them, too," he said. "If they get scared, they may get reckless and do something stupid."

"I don't know what choice we have anymore. We have to take some risks."

He paused.

"Do what you've got to do. I'm almost done here. I'll head in soon."

I told him to drive safely before hanging up. Then I got coffee from the break room before sitting in my office once more and calling Cassandra Rice's phone. It rang twice before someone answered and said hello. It wasn't Cassandra, though. It was a man, but it wasn't Matthew Rice, either. This voice had a gravelly quality. He was a smoker. I narrowed my eyes and leaned forward.

"Who is this?" I asked.

"Who's this?"

"I asked you first," I said.

He hung up, so I dialed again. This time, the phone rang twice before he answered.

"My name is Detective Joe Court with the St. Augustine County Sheriff's Department. I'm looking for Cassandra Rice. Who am I speaking to, please, and how do you have Dr. Rice's phone?"

"Where's St. Augustine County?"

I squeezed my jaw, growing tired of the questions.

"Missouri. Where are you, and who are you?"

"Chicago. I'm Special Agent Erik Glaser. I work for the DEA. Why are you looking for Cassandra Rice?"

I leaned back and blinked.

"She and Matthew Rice are persons of interest in a kidnapping and murder. We think they're involved in an adoption scam. Someone abducted a little boy from St. Augustine and sold him to an adoption broker. Do you have the doctors in custody?"

"We do," said Glaser. I waited for him to continue, but he stayed quiet.

"Did they have a child?"

"No," he said. Again, I waited for him to continue. He didn't.

"What's going on?"

Glaser paused and drew in a breath.

"You're from St. Augustine, Missouri," he said. "Who's your CO?"

I closed my eyes and shook my head.

"That's a very complicated question," I said. "If you need to verify my ID, call our front desk. You'll talk to a woman named Trisha Marshall. If that's not good enough, call our prosecutor, Shaun Deveraux. His assistant will tell you who I am."

"Thanks."

He hung up. I stared at my phone a moment before leaving my office and heading to the lobby. Trisha got a call a few moments later. She glanced at me and raised her eyebrows as she confirmed who I was. Then she hung up.

"Why was the DEA calling?" she asked.

"Long story," I said. My phone rang a moment later. The caller's number was blocked. "I'll tell you later."

Trisha nodded, and I ran my finger across my screen.

"Agent Glaser?"

"So you are a detective," he said. "We have Dr. Cassandra Rice and her husband, Dr. Matthew Rice, in custody on a twenty-four-hour hold, but we'll be charging them in federal court with several offenses—none of which are kidnapping or murder."

I started heading upstairs.

"You captured them in Chicago?"

"At O'Hare," he said. "They were trying to board a plane to Frankfort, Germany, with half a million dollars cash."

I sighed and walked to my office.

"And you're a DEA agent?"

"That's what my badge says."

I blinked a few times and sat behind my desk.

"Why is the DEA interested in two small-town doctors? Pill mill or selling drugs on the side?"

"You'd have to talk to my colleagues in the St. Louis field office," he said. "They called and asked me to pick the pair up, so I did. As I understand it, the St. Louis office has had them under surveillance for months. When they bought one-way tickets to Europe and tried to board a plane, we figured it was time to move."

I sighed and felt my shoulders drop.

"Okay. Thanks."

I hung up and called Marcus.

"Come on in," I said. "The Rices aren't our kidnappers. They're drug dealers...or something. The DEA had them under surveillance. Our investigation spooked them and sent them running. The DEA arrested them in Chicago."

Marcus swore.

"They were our only lead," he said.

"Yep."

"What do you want to do?"

I blinked, sighed, and shrugged.

"Go home and get drunk?"

"Once you sober up, what's the plan?"

I thought a moment.

"I don't know," I said, my voice low. "I'll visit Ryan and see if we can get another lead from him. Maybe Mannie slipped and told him something about the family set up to adopt Elijah."

"You think he'll help us?"

I shook my head.

"Probably not," I said. "Maybe we can make a deal. A parental kidnapping charge gets heavier the longer a kid is missing. If we wait a hundred and twenty days, it becomes a Class-B felony. That's five to fifteen years in prison. Maybe he'll help us to save his own skin."

"That's one possibility," said Marcus. "With his parents' money, he's got the resources to fight. Deveraux hasn't shown much spine lately in court. Trials cost money, and he doesn't want to spend it."

My entire body felt heavy.

"You think Ryan's lawyers will just try to wait us out? It's risky," I said. Then I sighed. "Given our track record lately, maybe it's not. We've got him on video selling a child, but what's it matter if the county can't afford to fight Ryan's legal team?" I lowered my head. "I hate this. We can't even do our jobs."

"We've got Mannie's phone," said Marcus. "If we can crack that, we'll have his texts, emails, social media accounts, and call history. If he sold a baby, there'll be a record."

"If we can crack it," I said. "That's a big if." I drew in a breath through my nose, thinking. "We might have another

371

option. Mannie was a lawyer. We can contact the US Attorney's office in Miami and turn everything we've got over to them. They can pressure his firm to release information to us. Mannie crossed state lines to purchase a child. That sounds like something the FBI and US Attorney's office would want to know about."

"You think the firm's involved in this?"

I threw up a hand.

"I don't know Marcus," I said. "At the moment, I'm throwing out suggestions and hoping something sticks. Maybe the adoption stuff is a side hustle. I don't know anymore." I paused. "We may have lost this one."

"We'll do our best," said Marcus. "That's all we can do."

"Yeah," I said. "Thank you."

I hung up and tossed my phone to my desk and rubbed my eyes, knowing that our best, this time, may not have been enough.

Chapter 40

I needed a break for a few minutes, so I drove to my apartment and picked up Roy. He seemed a little perturbed with me, but once I got his leash on and took him outside, his attitude perked up. We walked for about fifteen minutes, but the tight feeling in my throat never left. The Rices had been my only lead.

In years past, when I got stuck on a case, I'd call my mom. She had been a police officer her entire career. She couldn't always help, but she listened and understood. Now, I didn't even know where she was. Chicago? St. Louis? Somewhere in between? The last two times I had called her, she sent my call to voicemail. Between Audrey's pregnancy and wedding, Mom had a lot going on. I'd talk to her later. For now, I was on my own.

After our walk, Roy and I got in my car, and we headed back to work. The station felt quiet. Marcus was in his office writing a report, but he had little to add to our conversation earlier except that the US Attorney in St. Louis had called to discuss the Rices. I didn't know—or care—what they had done. They didn't have Elijah, so they weren't on my radar anymore. He offered to follow up, which was fine by me.

I didn't have any leads left, so I walked to my office, flipped through my notes, and started at the beginning. Mannie Gutierrez was murdered, shot from a distance with a big rifle. Aside from Cassandra Rice and Ryan Powell, nobody in St. Augustine seemed to know him. It was time to broaden my inquiry. I searched through my notes until I found the phone number of his firm's managing partner. Her assistant remembered me and put me through to the boss.

"Hey," I said. "This is Detective Joe Court with the St. Augustine County Sheriff's Department in Missouri. I'm working the murder of Mannie Gutierrez. We spoke earlier."

"I remember, Detective," she said. "You have any news?"

I grimaced.

"Unfortunately, no," I said. "None of my leads so far have panned out. Are adoption proceedings part of your firm's regular practice?"

"No," she said. "There are a lot of firms in Miami that practice family law, and we happily give referrals, but we're a corporate firm. Mannie advised salvage companies, fishermen, and occasionally members of the petroleum industry."

"Mannie wasn't involved in adoption at all?"

She paused.

"He never mentioned it to me."

"We've found evidence that he might have assisted a couple during an adoption proceeding in Missouri. Mannie never mentioned adoption work?"

She blew a raspberry.

"No, and he's not licensed to practice in Missouri," she said. "He didn't come to your area to work."

Not legitimate work, at least. I leaned back.

"So you can't help me at all," I said.

"No, sorry," she said. She paused. "His sister might know something, though. They were close. She was heartbroken about her brother's death."

I straightened.

"I spoke to Mannie's mother. She didn't mention he had a sister."

"Valentina was the black sheep of the family," she said. "She's divorced."

I waited for her to continue, but she didn't.

"So they broke off communication because she's divorced?"

"Mannie's mom is very Catholic."

"I see," I said, raising my eyebrows. "You have her contact information?"

She paused and then gave me a number. I thanked her and then hung up. Valentina answered her phone on the third ring. I introduced myself and explained that I was investigating Mannie's death. She interrupted before I could continue.

"Have you found his murderer?"

"No," I said softly. "I'm sorry. My partner and I are doing everything we can, but this is a tougher case than we expected. We've exhausted our local leads, so we're casting a wider net now. Do you know why Mannie flew to Missouri?"

"No," she said. "He told me he had to leave and asked me to watch his dog. I thought it was a vacation."

"Okay," I said, nodding. "Has he ever mentioned adoption to you?"

She paused.

"My brother and I were adopted from an orphanage in the Dominican Republic. Adoption work was important to him. He believed every child deserved a loving, safe home."

I jotted that down.

"That's admirable," I said. "Did he have a significant other?"

"Nobody long term," she said.

"He was seen with a woman in St. Augustine. Does that surprise you?"

"What was she like?"

I thought of Cassandra Rice and spoke honestly.

"She was smart, young, beautiful. She's a physician. Did he talk about coming to St. Augustine to meet somebody?"

"No, but he wouldn't have talked to me about his love life. He doesn't approve of mine, and I don't approve of his. I'm gay, and he never liked that. He's a good brother, but he sometimes has his head up his ass. Or at least he did. Did you check his phone?"

"I haven't been able to open it," I said. "It's password protected."

"Try 112398. It's November 23, 1998. He uses it for everything. That was our homecoming day. When we met our American parents."

I wrote it down. Valentina and I talked for another few moments, but my legs were itching to get to the evidence locker and find Mannie's phone. Finally, I thanked her for taking my call and ran downstairs. Within five minutes, I had Mannie's cheap, disposable phone and his iPhone in my office. Both had dead batteries, so I plugged them in and typed in the password. Valentine was right: he used it for everything. My heart started pounding as I read through his messages.

On the iPhone, Mannie and Cassandra exchanged a few text messages, but nothing interested me. The burner was more revealing. He used it to contact a single number and exchanged dozens of text messages, including messages that described paying fifty-thousand dollars for a bundle. Mannie and his contact were hoping to meet in Forest Park in St. Louis for an exchange once he acquired the item in question.

My hands trembled as I grabbed my desk phone and called Shaun Deveraux.

"Shaun, I've got the people who adopted Elijah Smith. I need a warrant to track their phone now."

"Details," he said.

I spent five minutes filling him in on my findings. He typed as we spoke and yelled at his assistant to contact a judge. Within fifteen minutes, we had a search warrant affidavit. Within thirty, we had an actual warrant. I faxed it to a cell carrier in Delaware. Because our request involved a child abduction, the company's general counsel's office worked quickly.

Our mystery phone was at The Ritz-Carlton Hotel in St. Louis. The cell carrier couldn't tell us where in the building it was, but they traced it there. I thanked her, hung up, and ran to Marcus's office. Roy loped along beside me.

"We've got them," I said. "Come on. They're in St. Louis. We've got to run. Bring your phone. I'll drive, and you'll call the county police."

He pushed back from his desk, grabbed his phone, badge, and weapon, and nodded.

"Let's go."

We ran to one of the station's SUVs. Roy settled on the rear seat, while Marcus and I sat in front. I headed toward the interstate. Marcus had questions, but I didn't have too many answers yet. Hopefully, we'd get some soon. As I drove, he called the St. Louis County Police Department's liaison office and told them what was going on. The Ritz-Carlton wasn't far from their headquarters, and they agreed to send six officers to wait in the lobby. Once they were in place, Marcus called our adopters on speakerphone. Before the phone could ring a single time, a tremulous voice answered.

"Mannie?"

"No, ma'am," said Marcus. "I'm Detective Marcus Washington with the St. Augustine County Sheriff's Department. To whom am I speaking?"

"I had hoped this was Mannie."

The voice belonged to a woman. The room around her was silent. My heart pounded.

"I'm afraid not, ma'am," I said. "I'm Detective Joe Court. Do you know Mannie Gutierrez?"

"Not well."

"Are you in The Ritz-Carlton Hotel in Clayton?" I asked.

"Are you calling about our son?" she asked.

I glanced at Marcus but focused on the road.

"Do you have a son?" asked Marcus.

"We hoped to," she said. "My husband and I. We're here to adopt a little boy, but Mannie stopped taking our calls. We've been trying to call him, but he doesn't answer."

I grimaced.

"Are you in the hotel right now?" I asked.

"I'm not sure if I should answer," she said. "Who are you again?"

I squeezed my jaw and the steering wheel tight.

"That's my partner," said Marcus. "As she said, she's a detective. I am as well. There are St. Louis County Police officers in the lobby right now. They're wearing uniforms. I'd like you to go downstairs and turn yourself in, please. You'll be safe."

The line went quiet.

"Tell us our son is safe," said a new, male voice. "His name is Elijah. He's three years old. We were supposed to take him home."

I stepped harder on the accelerator and flipped a switch on the dash to turn on my lights.

"Elijah was abducted from his mother. His whereabouts are currently unknown. Mannie Gutierrez, the adoption broker, purchased him with cash from the boy's father. It wasn't a legal adoption, and Mannie is dead now. Come to the lobby. We need to talk."

"I want an attorney," said the man.

I clenched my jaw tight before speaking.

"That's your choice, but if you call one, make sure you tell him you spent fifty-thousand dollars cash to purchase a child. You used disposable cellphones and spoke in code, which shows you knew you were doing something illegal. Now Elijah is missing, and Mannie Gutierrez is dead. If you refuse to help now, it may reflect poorly on you."

He paused again.

"We'll go downstairs now," he said.

"Good choice," I said, looking at Marcus. "Hang up on them."

He did as I asked. Then he went quiet.

"You okay, Joe?"

I squeezed my jaw tight before speaking.

"It doesn't matter. We've got a job to do."

Chapter 41

Marcus, Roy, and I arrived in Clayton about forty-five minutes later. St. Louis was a region divided. The city and county were separate entities, and the county was further broken into almost a hundred municipalities, many of which had their own police, fire, EMS departments, and school districts. The arrangement was top-heavy and expensive, but each municipality guarded its turf—ostensibly because only they could serve their residents. In actuality, city administrators didn't want to lose their jobs.

Clayton, though, was home of the St. Louis County government and had its own police department that operated out of a gorgeous, Georgian brick building overlooking Shaw Park. A block away, you'd find the St. Louis County Police Headquarters. Visitors to the city might be confused and wonder who'd answer a 911 call in an emergency, but the locals took it in stride, mostly. As someone who lived elsewhere but who knew a little about law enforcement, I found it batshit crazy.

Before she retired, my mom had been a captain in the St. Louis County Police Department and had supervised the sexual assault unit in the Bureau of Crimes Against Persons. I had once asked her where her jurisdiction began and ended, and, despite an hour-long discussion, I still had no idea. The system made little sense, but every attempt to unify the various municipalities had ended in dismal defeat. On paper, unification was easy. In practice, it required hard choices and sacrifice, two concepts that gave politicians hives. It was a shame. St. Louis and its citizens deserved better than the fractured mess they had.

I parked behind a St. Louis County Police cruiser across the street from The Ritz Carlton Hotel. Mid-rise developments and parking garages surrounded us. Marcus hurried out. I got Roy from the car, and we jogged toward the hotel. A bellhop held his hand out to me as the dog and I approached.

"I'm sorry, ma'am, but we're a pet-free establishment," he said. I pulled my badge from my belt and held it up.

"Service dog," I said. "Where are my officers?"

He looked toward the building.

"Inside," he said.

"Do they have our suspects?"

He shook his head but said nothing. I raised my eyebrows.

"I don't know," he said. "I'm just here to work."

Roy whined beside me, so I stroked his neck and looked toward Marcus.

"You mind going in and grabbing them? I think Roy might need a walk."

Marcus agreed and went inside. The area around the hotel was pretty but had limited greenspace, forcing Roy and me to walk on the boulevard between the two sides of the street. By the time we returned, Marcus, two uniformed officers, and an older couple stood beneath the awning in front of the hotel. I nodded to everybody but focused on the county officers.

"You guys can head out," I said, reaching into my purse for my wallet. I pulled a pair of my business cards and handed them over. "Thank you for your help. If your office needs me to fill anything out, let me know."

They said it was no problem, got into their cruisers, and headed away. Then I focused on the couple. They had tried to purchase a child. Maybe they didn't understand the extent of Mannie's duplicity, but the instant he gave them a throwaway cell phone and demanded cash, they should have known something was wrong. If not for their money, Elijah would be at home, safe with his mother. I couldn't get over that. The world needed moms and dads. The foster care system was always short of qualified parents. Obviously, that wasn't an adoption, but a lot of foster relationships turned into adoptive relationships. If they wanted kids, they could have fostered some. They could have used the system. Instead, they had stepped outside it—and everybody got hurt. I tried to keep my revulsion out of my voice.

"Hey, folks," I said. "I'm sure Detective Washington has introduced himself. I'm Detective Mary Joe Court with the

St. Augustine County Sheriff's Department. We're here to talk about Mannie Gutierrez and Elijah Smith. We can talk in my car, we can drive to a coffee shop, or we can go to Shaw Park. It's a couple of blocks west of here."

The male flicked his eyes up and down me.

"Are we under arrest?"

I held his gaze.

"Do you want to be?"

He blinked and looked down.

"We don't understand what's going on," he said. "We came here to adopt a child. Now, you're telling me our son is missing and Mannie's dead? I don't know what to think."

"Neither do I," I said. "You weren't very forthcoming on the phone. Let's start with your names. Who are you?"

The male blinked. If I had to guess, he was about fifty. He wore a light blue shirt, navy cardigan, and well-fitting jeans. His spouse was probably forty. She wore too much makeup, but she dressed very well in a white shirt and pink pants. They practically smelled like money. But for his age, a legitimate adoption agency would have likely looked at them as ideal candidates to raise a child.

"I'm Dr. Jay Drake. My wife is Amy Drake. We drove in from Columbus last week."

I wrote the names down on my notepad.

"Great, thank you," I said. "We need to talk about the situation. Would you like to do that in my car, a coffee shop, a park, a police station, the hotel lobby, or somewhere else?"

Jay looked at his wife. She put an arm around his waist.

"Coffee shop?" he asked. She nodded, and he looked at me.

"Coffee shop it is," I said. "It's just to the east on Carondelet Plaza. Get a table. My partner and I will meet you there in a few minutes. Detective Washington and I parked illegally, so we're going to drive over."

"We'll see you in a few minutes," said Jay. I nodded, and he and his wife started walking. Once they were out of earshot, Marcus looked toward our SUV.

"I'll run the background check while you drive?"

"That's the plan," I said. "Let's go."

We got in the car, and I headed around the block. Despite the multitude of parking garages around us, it was more difficult to find a parking spot than I had guessed. I ended up parking almost two blocks away on a side road. Marcus stayed in the car to finish up his search, but already, the Drakes looked like solid citizens. Neither had a criminal record nor pending civil actions against them. We wouldn't find too many skeletons with such a quick search, but it'd give us a starting point.

Roy and I walked to the coffee shop. The Drakes sat at a table by the front windows. I ordered Marcus a fancy drink with caramel and whipped cream, while I had a black coffee. The barista poured mine right away and promised to be by the table with Marcus's drink shortly. Then I sat down and handed the Drakes my business card.

"That card has my contact information on it. I'm available twenty-four hours a day at that cell number. If you email me, I try to respond within twenty-four hours, but sometimes my schedule gets backed up. You mentioned earlier that you were from Columbus. I'll need your full names, address, phone number, and the name of your employer if you have one."

They wrote down their contact information and handed it to me. I'd put it into my notebook later. Then I looked up and raised my eyebrows.

"So you came to St. Louis to adopt Elijah Smith," I said. "Tell me about that. How did you meet Mannie Gutierrez, when did you last see him, and when did you plan to see him next?"

The couple looked at one another. Then Jay brought his hands in front of him as if he were praying.

"Well, I guess we heard of Mannie about six months ago. He arranged an adoption for a couple we know. He really seemed to know his stuff, and he was a lawyer, so we trusted him. Everything we did was legal."

I jotted down some notes and nodded.

"Okay," I said. "I'll need your friend's name."

He looked at Amy. She gave me a name, which I wrote down. I might track the friend down, but more likely, I'd just turn the name over to the US Attorney. If the FBI deemed the adoption scheme a priority, they'd look into things.

"So you contacted Mannie about an adoption. How did he present this?"

Jay rubbed his hands together.

"We contacted him and said we were interested in adopting a child. We didn't care if he was Black or White or Hispanic or anything else. Gender didn't matter. Our only concern was health. We wanted a healthy child."

"We couldn't have children," said Amy. "We tried traditional adoption agencies at first, but it never worked out."

Interviews and interrogations were about finesse. To get the information I needed, the Drakes needed to trust me and think I was on their side. In this case, I understood. They had spent their lives wanting a child, but then they couldn't have one. That'd be hard. The Drakes may have screwed up. Maybe they broke the law—I couldn't say yet. Their motives, though, I had no reason to question. If they had adopted Elijah, I had little doubt they would have loved and cared for him.

"I'm sorry," I said.

"Mannie seemed like the perfect solution," said Amy. "He specialized in difficult cases. We contacted him, and two months later, he said he had a lead from a single father who could no longer care for his child. The little boy was healthy and well. The dad was a construction worker, and he was so young he could barely take care of himself. We thought we were helping."

The lie was partially true and even more believable because of it.

"Did Mannie ever mention Elijah's mother?"

"She wasn't in the picture," said Jay. "She had a healthy birth. She wasn't on drugs, and she didn't drink while pregnant. Elijah was perfect."

"Julie, his mom, thinks so, too," I said. Jay's eyes went cold. Amy looked as if I had slapped her.

"We didn't know about her," she said.

"You were cheated," I said. "For that, I'm sorry. Mannie's dead now, but if he was still alive, I'd be sending him to prison. He stole a child from his quite capable, loving mom. That's wrong no matter how you parse it."

The two nodded but wouldn't meet my gaze. Marcus entered the shop a moment later. I suggested he go to the counter for his drink. When he came back, I flipped through a new page in my notepad.

"Tell me about the deal," I said. "You paid Mannie money. Cash?"

Amy nodded.

"Fifty thousand," she said. "We wanted to do a wife transfer, but he said cash was easier. We met him in Forest Park and gave him the money. He said we'd meet him again in a few days with Elijah. We had the whole day planned. We were going to be good parents."

I nodded and focused on my paper. Marcus stayed quiet.

"You would have done well," I said. "When did you last speak to Mannie?"

"Thursday of last week," said Jay. "He planned to pick up Elijah on Friday morning. We were going to meet him at Forest Park Friday afternoon. He didn't show up. We've been waiting in the hotel, hoping he'd call. I thought he had ripped us off. I didn't realize..."

His voice trailed off. The story corroborated part of my timeline, so I nodded.

"Where were you Friday morning?" asked Marcus, leaning forward. Jay looked at him.

"In the hotel," he said. "We were nervous. I exercised in the fitness center in the morning. Then Amy and I got massages. After that, we went out for lunch."

"Where'd you go for lunch?" I asked.

"Tony's. It's just up the street," said Jay.

Very likely, we could verify every step they made with surveillance cameras. If they were honest, they had nothing to do with Mannie's death.

We talked for a little while longer, but nothing they said helped me, and the longer we spoke, the heavier my shoulders became. Their primary interest seemed to be Elijah's well-being. They thought he needed a family. They had no idea they were taking a boy from his mom.

Marcus and I left them in the coffee shop. It was a shame a legitimate adoption agency hadn't seen fit to place a child with them. They would have been good parents.

Our drive back to St. Augustine was quiet. As we reached the outskirts of town, I glanced at him.

"I'm going to visit Julie Smith. She deserves to know where we're at."

"And where are we?"

I started to speak, but I couldn't get the words out at first. Then I swallowed hard and squeezed the steering wheel and swallowed the lump in my throat. The road in front of me became a little glassy, so I blinked hard and licked my lips.

"She won't see her son again."

Marcus looked straight ahead and nodded.

"You're not doing that alone," he said. "I'll go with you."

I nodded and drove another quarter mile.

"Thank you," I said, my voice low. He said nothing, and I drove to the Smith's home. Julie answered the door. She looked at us with hopeful, pleading eyes.

"Did you find him?"

"We need to go inside," said Marcus. "Are your parents here?"

She nodded and stepped back. We walked into the home. Scott Smith emerged from the back room.

"Everything okay?" he asked.

"Let's get the family together," I said. "I'd like to update you on our investigation."

Scott grasped the subtext and nodded, his face grave.

"Julie, why don't escort the detectives to the kitchen table?" he asked. "I'll find your mom."

Julie agreed and led us deeper into the home. Marcus and I sat on the far side of an oak, oval-shaped table. Julie offered us coffee, but we both declined. A moment later, Scott and Lisa joined us. For half an hour, I gently and irrevocably broke their hearts. I explained every step Marcus and I had taken, every piece of evidence we had found, and every suspect we had investigated. Even before I finished speaking, they knew Elijah was gone.

I tried to keep my grief out of my voice, but beneath the table, my hands trembled, and my toes never stopped moving. My heart felt as if someone were squeezing it in a vise. I hated this.

"I'm sorry, Julie," I said, reaching across the table, finally. Her mom took my hand. "We tried."

The two ladies nodded, tears on their cheeks. Scott's eyes were distant and red. He looked as if he were holding back tears.

"Thank you for coming and being honest," he said. "I'll walk you out."

Marcus and I stood.

"We'll be adjusting the charges against Ryan," I said. "This is a more serious crime now. I'll tell him about the case, though. Nothing excuses what he did, but Elijah was his son. He deserves to know about the investigation."

Marcus and I started to turn away, but Julie covered her face with her hands and shook her head.

"Wait," she said. She drew in a couple of breaths. Her mom put her arm around her shoulders.

"It's okay, sweetie," she said. "Everything's okay."

"Just give me a minute, Mom," said Julie. She paused. Then she focused on me. "Ryan isn't Elijah's dad. He doesn't deserve anything."

Scott and Lisa straightened, surprised. I drew in a sharp breath.

"Okay," I said, feeling my heart pound. "This changes a few things. Who is Elijah's father?"

"Mr. Ridgeway at school."

I went quiet. Marcus gasped.

"Brandon Ridgeway?" he asked. Julie nodded to him, and he put a hand on my elbow. "We need a minute."

Few things surprised Marcus. I had never heard him gasp. Something was wrong. I wished the family well, and Marcus and I walked to the front porch. He exhaled through his nose and laced his fingers behind his head.

"Spill it," I said. "Who's Mr. Ridgeway?"

"Dave Skelton's oldest boy. Apparently, Dave's got a grandson."

Chapter 42

This was a problem on multiple levels. I closed my eyes and tried to put my thoughts in order.

"First things first," I said. "Find Skelton and bring him to the station. We need him in an interview room."

Marcus shook his head.

"Dave's a good man," he said. "There's an explanation for this, I'm sure."

"And we're going to find it," I said. "If we step on Skelton's toes, we'll step on his toes. He should have been honest with us from the start and told us our victim was his grandson."

"Maybe he didn't know," he said. "Julie's parents didn't."

I nodded.

"I hope you're right. Either way, we need to talk to him now. Take the SUV and track him down. I'll call Trisha for a ride."

Marcus agreed and jogged to the vehicle. I knocked on the Smith's door. Scott opened it. He drew in a breath, his eyes still wide.

CHRIS CULVER

"I don't know what to say," he said. I held up a hand in a stop motion.

"Don't say anything," I said. "Julie was sixteen when she got pregnant. Mr. Ridgeway was an adult. I need information, but neither you nor Julie are the problem here. You're both victims."

He nodded and walked with me to the kitchen. Julie and her mother were holding hands. I sat across from them at the table. For a moment, nobody spoke. Then I drew in a breath.

"We're going to start over," I said. "First, Julie, do you feel safe and comfortable talking to me here?"

She nodded.

"Yes."

"Good," I said. "You may not believe this, but I speak from experience. Nothing that happened between you and Mr. Ridgeway was your fault. You were sixteen when you got pregnant, right?"

She nodded.

"Yeah, but he didn't hurt me," she said. "You're talking to me like I'm a victim."

"You were sixteen," I said. "How old was Mr. Ridgeway?"

"Twenty-two," she said. "He had just graduated from college. We knew what we were doing."

"You weren't old enough to consent," said Scott. He looked at me. "That makes this a crime, right?"

"A felony," I said.

"It wasn't like that," she said. "I loved him. Okay? He loved me. I didn't even meet him at school. I met him at work. We worked at Green Leaves together. It's a plant nursery. We were friends for, like, six months. Then, I saw him after school, and one thing led to another."

I had bought shrubs at the nursery. They hired a lot of younger people to water the plants in the spring and summer.

"So your relationship was consensual," I said. "What happened? Why didn't you tell us the truth? Why'd you make Ryan think he was the father?"

She looked down.

"I didn't want Brandon to go to jail. I needed a father, and Ryan was there. He'd hook up with anybody, so I broke up with Brandon and slept with Ryan, so he'd think he got me pregnant. It wasn't my first choice, believe me."

"Was Brandon involved in Elijah's life?"

"He wanted to be," she said, her voice soft. "Elijah didn't know Brandon was his real daddy." Julie paused. "This is my fault. When I told Ryan I was pregnant, I said I'd take care of everything. He wouldn't have to play any role in Elijah's life. I just needed his name on a birth certificate. But then his mom got involved. Ryan had no business being a father. I screwed up, and now I'm being punished for it."

Now wasn't the time to assign blame, so I drew in a breath.

"The case isn't closed," I said. "I'm not giving up. I'll work weekends, nights, whatever it takes."

"Are you going to arrest Brandon?" asked Julie.

I held her gaze and tilted my head to the side and answered honestly.

"No," I said. "You were underage when he slept with you, but the statute of limitations has passed."

She leaned back and closed her eyes, looking almost relieved.

"Good."

I turned to leave, unsure how to feel. At sixteen, Julie had a lot of control over her own body, and her sex life was her business. Brandon was an adult and a teacher, though. He had crossed a line he ought not have even approached.

The family had issues to discuss, so I left and called Trisha. Doug Patricia arrived about five minutes later in a cruiser to pick me and Roy up. We drove to the station, and I went to Marcus's office. He was on the phone, so I took Roy around the block. Then I found him in the lobby waiting for me.

"What do you know about Brandon?" I asked.

Marcus sighed and started walking toward the stairwell. I followed.

"Not a lot," he said. "Dave keeps it quiet. Brandon's mom was one of Dave's high school girlfriends. He doesn't talk about her much."

"Does Dave talk to Brandon?"

Marcus considered before nodding.

"Some," he said. "Dave was a shitty father for most of Brandon's life. Jessica was sixteen when she had him. Dave took off for the Army and ignored his kid until he was in high school. When Dave came back, everybody was a different person. They all grew up. It's a tough relationship, but Dave tries."

We reached my office and went inside. I sat at my chair and considered.

"I've seen Dave's boys. They're happy."

"Now he's a good dad," said Marcus, nodding. "Then? He was a stupid kid. He needed a kick in the ass, and the Army gave it to him. Then they shipped him to Afghanistan and fucked him up for years."

"Do you know Brandon?" I asked.

"I've met him," said Marcus. "I don't really know him, though."

"Dave's a hunter, right?" I asked. Marcus nodded. "Does he take his boys hunting?"

"Yeah, sure," said Marcus. "They're always outdoors when the weather's nice. Hunting, fishing, camping, canoeing...that's why they live in St. Augustine."

"Does he take Brandon?"

Marcus looked away but said nothing.

"Dave's the best shot we've got in the department," I said. "Did he teach Brandon how to shoot?"

"I don't know," said Marcus, his voice low. "Probably, though. It sounds like something Dave would try. He'd think of it as a bonding exercise."

"Mannie was shot at a distance with a high-caliber round," I said.

Marcus shook his head.

"Let's not jump to conclusions. Dave's our colleague and my friend. I don't want to paint him as bad guy. He's lost a grandson. He's a victim."

"Maybe," I said, nodding, "but he didn't tell us Elijah was his grandson."

"It wasn't our business."

I raised my eyebrows.

"It became our business the moment Julie Smith called our station to say her son was missing. Dave knew it and kept the information from us. We could have kept it secret. We wouldn't have told anyone, but we needed to know. Brandon, Elijah's real father, is an obvious suspect."

Marcus nodded but said nothing.

"Did you call Dave?"

"His cell went to voicemail," said Marcus. "He's been working a lot of overtime lately, so he's probably at home sleeping."

"Find him," I said. "I'm going to track down Brandon."

Marcus nodded, turned, and stopped in my doorway.

"Dave's a good man. He wouldn't hurt anybody. If he had heard Mannie was in town to purchase a child, he would have arrested him. At the very least, he would have called us."

"I sincerely hope you're right."

Chapter 43

M arcus hesitated before leaving. I focused on my computer and looked up Brandon Ridgeway's address on the license bureau database. He lived about half a mile outside of town. I wrapped Roy's leash around my hand and checked my firearm. Then we headed out. St. Augustine had a couple of massive corporate farms, but we also had small farms and homesteads as well. Brandon lived on a small five- or six-acre plot with fruit trees, a fenced garden, and a big chicken coop. A paddock out front could have held horses, but I couldn't see any. The house was older, but clean. A nearby barn looked ready to fall down.

I parked on the gravel driveway, took Roy from the car, and started walking toward the house. The dog wouldn't move. He had his nose in the air. Then he pulled toward the barn.

"You smell something?" I asked.

His nostrils flared. So this was a problem. Roy had been with me in the office, so I had brought him. Now that he was here and smelled remains, I couldn't ignore it. Unfortunately, I couldn't use anything we found in court, either.

The prosecutor could secure a search warrant, but that'd take time. If Ridgeway knew we were interested in him, he could clean up.

Damned if I do, damned if I don't. I unsnapped the strap that held my firearm in the holster at my side and unwound Roy's leash from my hand, giving him room to move.

"Find it," I said. "Find the blood."

Roy's sniffing intensified, and he stuck his nose in the air. Then he started running, practically dragging me behind him toward the barn. The closer we got, the harder my heart beat. I hoped we weren't about to find a toddler's body inside.

The barn was old wood. Time had given the exterior a rich, gray patina but left gaping holes in the roof. Ridgeway couldn't have stored equipment or hay inside and expected it to stay dry and well, but a padlock held the sliding door shut. I led Roy around the building but couldn't see another entrance. As we walked to the front again, my cell rang. I wouldn't have answered except that it was Dave Skelton.

I wrapped Roy's leash around my hand and swiped my finger across the screen.

"Are you standing by the barn?" he asked.

My heart started pounding.

"I am," I said. "Where are you?"

"In a deer blind about eight-hundred yards away. Remove your weapon from your holster and toss it to the ground."

I shook my head.

"I can't do that, and you know it," I said. "Climb down from your deer blind, and we'll talk. Nobody needs to get hurt today."

"You're here for my son. I can't let you take him."

Dave had spent years in the Army. He knew how to shoot. I didn't stand a chance if I ran, and the barn gave me little to no protection.

"Where's Brandon?"

"In the house."

I swallowed hard.

"Is Elijah in the barn?"

Dave paused.

"No."

"Who is?"

Again, Dave paused.

"The barn's empty. Toss your gun down."

"What if I refuse?"

"My family is all that matters to me. Don't take them from me. I know you, Joe. You're why I kept Elijah a secret. You'd arrest Brandon for doing the same stupid thing I did when I was his age."

I shook my head.

"Whatever Brandon and Julie did, it doesn't matter. Julie says they were in love, and the statute of limitations has passed. I won't pursue anything. If I put my gun down, are you going to shoot me, or will you talk to me?"

"We'll talk," he said. "But I want Marcus and Bob with us."

I nodded.

"That's fine," I said, reaching for my pistol. "I'm putting my weapon down."

Dave said nothing, so I unholstered my weapon and put it on the gravel driveway. Then I stepped away. My phone clicked as he hung up. A few minutes later, a figure walked toward me, a rifle slung against his shoulder. As he grew closer, I recognized Dave's features. I put my phone in my pocket and held up my hands, palms toward him, to show him I wasn't a threat.

"I'm not armed," I said. As if in response, he pulled the magazine from his rifle and ejected a round from the chamber. I didn't think he would have shot me, but I appreciated the gesture.

"You mind if I call in reinforcements?" I asked.

"I already did," he said. "They're five minutes out."

"Can I record our conversation?"

"Do your job," he said. I turned on a recording app on my phone. Then I looked at him.

"We've worked together for a long time, Dave. What are you doing? We're colleagues. We trust each other."

He gave me a halfhearted smile and shook his head.

"I trust you more than I trust anybody in our department," he said. "You'll follow the evidence and do what you think is right, no matter how much it hurts you or anybody you care about."

I lowered my chin.

"And is that a bad thing?"

He smiled.

"It is when you don't understand the world," he said. "Elijah's inside with his real father. He's safe. He's been safe this whole time. You should tell Julie."

I gritted my teeth.

"How long have you known Elijah was here?"

"Long enough."

I squeezed my jaw tight.

"I'm glad Elijah's safe, but you can't walk away from this one."

"That's okay," said Dave. "My son will. I shot Mannie Gutierrez in the barn with this rifle. Consider this a confession. It's a spontaneous admission, so it should be admissible in court."

I shook my head.

"You didn't kill him," I said. "You were on duty at the time of his death."

"I left," he said. "Ask Marcus and Bob. They'll be here soon. I went AWOL and told them I planned to visit a woman. Everybody knows I loved half the women in this county. It's believable. Instead, I tracked down Mannie Gutierrez, tricked him into coming to the barn, and shot him. You've got all the evidence you need, Joe. I did it. I pulled the trigger. Just follow the evidence. You don't even have to think."

I considered him and then looked around.

"This is your son's house?" I asked. He nodded. "There somewhere we can talk like normal human beings?"

He nodded toward the porch. I walked toward my pistol and knelt beside it but didn't touch it.

"You mind?" I asked. "I won't shoot you."

"Go ahead," he said. I picked up the weapon, placed it in my holster, and walked toward the porch. Inside the house, I could hear a kid laughing. Outside, Dave and I sat on cheap, white plastic chairs on opposite sides of a cheap plastic table. I put my phone on the table to record our conversation.

"It's nice to hear your grandson laughing," I said. Dave got a faraway look in his eyes as he nodded. "Tell me about that rifle. Where'd you get it?"

He looked at his weapon.

"It's old. I bought it years ago. I don't remember."

"You've got a Barrett MRAD, don't you?" I said. He shrugged.

"At home."

"It's a five- or six-thousand-dollar rifle," I said. "It's pretty accurate, isn't it?"

He smiled.

"If I'm shooting, it's about .5 MOA at sixteen-hundred yards."

I did the math.

"With that weapon, you can hit eight-inch clusters at nearly a mile," I said.

"Not to brag," he said, winking.

I smiled.

"If that's true, why would you bring an old hunting rifle to rescue your grandson? You'd only get one shot, right? You lured Mannie to the farm to kill him, and you didn't bring your most reliable weapon to do that. It doesn't make sense, Dave."

He started to respond, but then he closed his eyes.

"Sometimes life is funny," he said, finally. "It doesn't always make sense. Sometimes you make bad decisions."

"Everybody makes mistakes, but you spent fifteen years in the Army. You were a ranger. Bringing that old rifle to a gunfight was a tactical error. You don't screw up like that. I don't buy it."

He wagged his finger.

"You're forgetting something, Joe. The Barrett is a beautiful weapon, but it's heavy. I wanted to move."

"If I examine your hunting rifle, whose fingerprints will I find on the rounds in the magazine?"

Dave went quiet, so I asked again.

"Probably Brandon's. I took the gun from his safe. The combination is his birthday."

"Is it your weapon or Brandon's weapon?" I asked. "You said you bought it years ago. Now, you say it was in his gun safe."

Dave considered.

"I bought it for his twenty-first birthday and taught him how to shoot," he said.

"Makes sense," I said. "How'd you know about Mannie and the kidnapping?"

Dave snorted.

"Because Ryan Powell is a dumbass," he said. "He told his best friend, Ethan. Ethan told some girl. She told lots of people."

"And, somehow, that rumor reached you, a man thirty years out of high school."

He shrugged.

"Like I said, life's funny."

"You heard a man was trying to sell your grandson. Why didn't you call the police?"

He looked at me, his eyes flinty.

"Because my son made a mistake. He loved somebody and had a baby with her. Technically, it was illegal. He shouldn't have slept with her. The law matters, but they loved each other. But to you, Brandon would be a rapist. That's all you'd see. Even if you couldn't prosecute him, you'd ruin him.

"And don't deny it, Joe. I've known you a long time. I respect you, and I know the terrible things that have happened to you, but the world isn't black and white. Brandon screwed up and has spent every day since then regretting it. He watched another man raise his baby. Then, when he learned that man planned to sell his baby, he told me. I took care of the problem because that's what fathers do."

I didn't know what to say, so I went quiet. Then I heard a voice from the side of the house.

"Joe? Dave?"

It sounded like Bob Reitz. I held my hand toward Dave.

"Give me the rifle and go inside. Visit your son and grandson while you still can."

He hesitated, but then handed me the rifle. I took it and my phone.

"Thank you," he said.

"Good luck," I said, standing and starting toward the side of the house. Both Bob and Marcus walked toward me from a pair of marked SUVs. I handed Bob the rifle.

"Dave Skelton claims he used this rifle to shoot Mannie Gutierrez in that barn. It's locked, so you'll have to get a key. I've got Dave's confession on my phone. Brandon Ridgeway, he says, had nothing to do with the shooting. Elijah Smith is alive and well inside the house with his father and grandfather. Looks like we closed this one."

Bob brought a hand to his mouth. Marcus rubbed his forehead and sighed. I walked past them toward my car.

"Hey, Joe," said Marcus, hurrying up the gravel driveway toward me. "You're doing the right thing."

"No, I'm not," I said. I started toward the car but paused. "Dave said he went AWOL while at work and told you and

Bob that he was visiting a woman. That's when he shot Gutierrez. Make sure you keep the story straight."

Marcus nodded.

"I'll remember that."

"Good, because it's going in my report," I said.

"Follow the evidence," said Marcus. "That's all you have to do."

I opened my back door and put Roy in his seat. He seemed to grin at me. I petted his cheek but couldn't smile back. Then I looked at Marcus.

"Dave told me to follow the evidence, too."

Marcus said nothing.

"How long have you known Elijah was here?" I asked.

Marcus looked down. His lips didn't move.

"Look at me, Marcus. We're on the same team," I said. "I'm following the evidence to Dave Skelton, just like you wanted."

I heard footsteps. Bob walked toward us and stopped by Marcus.

"Great, you're both here," I said. "You going to remind me to follow the evidence, too, Bob?"

Bob held up his hands.

"You're the best detective we've got on staff, Joe," he said. "You don't need the reminder."

"Apparently, I do, because Marcus and Dave have both told me to follow it," I said. Roy whined, so I petted his neck. "The evidence says Dave killed Mannie Gutierrez to save his grandson. Dave gets to be a hero. Maybe he even gets redemption for being a shitty father for the first fifteen years of Brandon's life.

"My gut, after years of homicide work, says Brandon killed Mannie because he was too scared to come to the police and admit he knocked up his sixteen-year-old student. He used his own rifle with his own rounds and then called his father for help. You two came along for the ride because you're two of Dave's best friends.

"I can't prove any of my conjecture, though, so we're going with the evidence and Dave's confession. Everybody walks away a winner today—except for Mannie Gutierrez. He's dead."

I closed Roy's door and walked around the front of my car. My skin felt hot, and every muscle in my body quivered.

"Are you okay, Joe?"

"No, Bob. What do you think? How could I be okay?" I asked. "Jesus, buddy. I thought you and Marcus were my friends, but you're not. Friends don't use each other."

They both looked away from me. At least they had the decency to feel ashamed.

"It's complicated," said Marcus.

"You're right about that, at least," I said, raising my eyebrows. "Now that you've got your story locked in, here's what's going to happen: my report will indicate that you two covered for Dave so he could sleep with a girlfriend while on duty. Instead of visiting that girlfriend, Dave murdered

Mannie Gutierrez. He used you. Because of your gross incompetence, a man was murdered. This department can no longer trust your piss-poor judgment. I want your resignations on my desk by five this evening. Unless you're lying to help a friend. Please tell me you're lying about Dave's absence. Please. I don't want to do this."

The two men said nothing. I wanted to scream at them, but it wouldn't have changed anything. Instead, I got in the driver's seat, slammed my door, and drove off.

I hated this. I hated the position they put me in, I hated the choice they forced on me, and I hated them. Everything felt wrong, but it didn't matter. I had a job to do, so I drove to my station and parked out front. Trisha said hello to me in the lobby. I nodded to her but didn't slow down. Once I reached my office, I called Julie Smith's cell phone. Her mom answered the phone.

"Yes?"

"Lisa, it's Joe Court," I said. "Detective Court, I guess. You sitting down?"

"Have you found him?" she asked, breathless.

"Yeah. He's alive and well at Brandon Ridgeway's house. We're not pressing charges against Brandon at this time. There are officers on-site."

She started crying. Then she called for her daughter and her husband. They cried as well. They thanked me over and over. I didn't have the heart to tell them the truth. Instead, I just told them I was doing my job. Then I hung up and sat beside my dog on the floor and tried not to think about everything that phone call had cost.

Chapter 44

I had spent my adult life trying to send the bad guys to jail. That became harder when you didn't know who the bad guys were. I typed my report and delivered it to the prosecutor. Then I told him about Dave's confession, about our ambiguous evidence, about Marcus and Bob, about Brandon and Julie. The story was tawdry and complicated and hard.

I asked for a day to keep working. First, I'd send Darlene to Brandon's house. She'd fingerprint the gun safe in Brandon's basement to see if Dave's prints were on it. Second, I'd dive into the GPS on Dave's cruiser and see whether he had driven it anywhere near Brandon's house the day of the murder. Third, I'd talk to Dave's wife to ask about his mystery girlfriend and ask whether she suspected anything. I had a dozen things to investigate, but I only needed to disprove one element of the crime to cast Dave's entire confession into doubt. I could do it easily.

With the confession discredited, I'd go after Brandon. It wouldn't be hard. I'd get him in an interrogation booth and hammer him about the sacrifices his father was trying to make. I'd frame it as if only he could protect Dave from himself. By the time I finished, Brandon might even believe he was justified to shoot Mannie. Then he'd break. He'd tell me what I needed to hear, and I'd send him to prison.

Deveraux listened to my presentation and asked me a few questions. Then he told me to move on. In his mind, we had an acceptable outcome. Elijah was safe, and we had a confession. Moreover, if I went after Brandon, I'd lose the department. We were already losing Marcus, Bob, and Dave. If the rank and file learned I was going after a decorated officer's son—despite that officer's confession—we'd have mass retirements and resignations. We'd cease to exist. So I swallowed that bitter pill and moved on.

A week after Dave Skelton's arrest and Bob and Marcus's resignations, I was still angry, but I understood their choices better. Mannie Gutierrez pushed Brandon Ridgeway beyond the limit he could stand, and he broke. I still think Brandon killed Mannie, but I couldn't prove it.

Everyone should have come clean. Brandon should have come to the police the moment he learned Ryan Powell planned to sell his child. We would have sent Mannie and Ryan to prison, we would have reunited a family, and we would have followed the law. The law wasn't perfect, but it was the system we had. The police weren't perfect either, but we tried.

Though his judgment was terrible, Dave Skelton was right about one thing: if Brandon had come to me and said he impregnated a sixteen-year-old girl, I would have hated him. I would have rescued Elijah, but once Elijah was safe, I would have investigated Brandon. I would have questioned his colleagues, his current and former students, his neighbors, his friends, his family, everyone who knew him. I would have ruined his life through implication if not accusation.

And it would have been wrong.

I was sixteen when my foster father raped me. There was a difference, though, between a sixteen-year-old girl who slept with a young man with whom she was in love and a sixteen-year-old girl drugged by her foster father and assaulted on the family sofa. If Brandon loved Julie, he should have waited for her to grow up. If she still loved him then, terrific. They'd live happily ever after. That he couldn't wait, that he slept with her despite her age, was a crime. It was wrong, but it didn't ruin Julie's life or give her nightmares. He hadn't groomed her, and he hadn't forced her to do anything... he had loved her, and she had loved him. Had he been a year younger, Missouri law wouldn't have even labeled it a crime. That should have counted for something.

Julie brought Elijah by the office a few days after we reunited them. Elijah was a bubbly, healthy, well-loved little boy. Mannie and Ryan had scared him, but he had his mom...and his father. Julie was recovering well. She wanted to go to college. With Brandon willing to watch Elijah and eventually share custody, she might even pull it off. She'd live her dream. She and Brandon wouldn't grow old together, but she could be happy. I was glad and told her so. I even gave her a hug.

Dave Skelton pled guilty to involuntary manslaughter. He'd spend four years in prison and a few on parole. His law enforcement career was over, but he'd be alive.

Bob and Marcus did as I asked and tendered their resignations. Losing them was hard. Every police department in the country needed more officers, so they'd each find jobs. St. Augustine would miss them, though. They had cast long shadows in our department. I'd miss them, too.

Ryan Powell plead guilty to parental kidnapping. He'd spend a year in prison. Hopefully, he'd learn something. Andrea and Frank Powell filed an emergency petition for full custody of Elijah and claimed Julie wasn't a fit mother. Since they no longer had any relation or claim to Elijah, a judge dismissed their petition. Even though he wasn't theirs biologically, they loved Elijah. Hopefully, they'd work something out with Julie.

Life went on. Roy and I walked every morning, afternoon, and evening, and we looked at houses when we could. I'd miss my apartment, and I'd miss the families at the shelter, but I had no right to be angry at anyone.

Because of the Erin Court Home, dozens of families felt safe and comforted. When Linda had asked me to move out, it had hurt. It had felt personal, but it was personal in the best sense: we had created something wonderful, something that gave people hope. Time and distance had shown me what I couldn't see on my own.

The Charter Commission continued its work. The members argued, but they were vigilant, too. I didn't trust Brett Mayhew, but the other members did their best. We had work ahead of us, but it was work worth doing. We wanted a world that let people thrive. That was worth fighting for.

Eventually, I got in touch with my mom, too. She and Dad hadn't planned to move to Chicago, but then they received an unsolicited offer on their house. It was too much money to turn down. They hadn't found anything in Chicago that they liked yet, so they planned to rent an apartment near Audrey for a year. I'd miss having them so close, but I could drive to Chicago. Change was part of life. I'd get used to it.

A week after Dave's arrest, I was sitting in my office, writing a report about a traffic accident that turned into a fistfight, when someone knocked on my door. Roy stood from the dog bed beside me and shook himself before sauntering toward my guest. I finished the sentence I was typing and then pushed myself back. Trisha stood in the doorframe beside a quite pretty young woman with straight brunette hair. She was in her early twenties, and she wore a pink top and high-waisted jeans.

The moment our eyes met, she exhaled, smiled, and shook her head knowingly.

"I should have known," she said. I furrowed my brow and glanced at Trisha. She shrugged.

"Detective Court, this is Erin Carlisle," she said. "Ms. Carlisle, this is Detective Joe Court."

I flicked my eyes up and down her and crossed my arms.

"What can I do for you, Ms. Carlisle?"

"Call me Erin," she said. "I came by the Erin Court Home for Woman and spoke to Linda Armus. She sent me here."

I looked at her closer. She had no visible bruising, but the worst scars were almost always internal. If Linda sent her here, someone had hurt her. I softened my voice.

"Have a seat, Erin," I said. "My dog's name is Roy. He's friendly. You can pet him if you'd like. Trisha, I've got this."

Trisha nodded. It wasn't the first time Linda had sent a client to me. It wouldn't be the last, either. Erin stepped inside and sat near Roy. He smelled her and then sat beside her, his tail wagging on the ground. She laughed and petted his neck.

"You are friendly, aren't you?"

Most women who came from the shelter were quiet and unassuming, but victims came in all sizes and from all socioeconomic classes. Trisha shut the door behind her.

"As Trisha said, I'm Detective Joe Court. I volunteer at the shelter, but I am a police officer. You have a privileged relationship with the counselors there. You can tell them anything, and they have to keep it quiet unless you threaten to hurt yourself or someone else. We don't have that same relationship. If you tell me about a crime, I might be obligated to act. That could mean arresting you or your spouse. Do you understand?"

She nodded.

"My father's a lawyer, and my brother's a detective. I know more about the law than I care to. And I didn't go to the shelter because I'm a client. I don't need that kind of help."

I crossed my arms.

"Then why are you here?"

"Have you ever heard the name Brian Carlisle?"

I thought for a moment before nodding.

"I contacted his firm a while ago because I needed a lawyer. He referred me to Alexa Swaine."

"Alexa's good," she said. "Dad's better, but he mostly manages other lawyers now. Why did you need a criminal defense attorney?"

I considered not answering, but we were developing a rapport. She came here for a reason. It'd be nice if I could suss it out.

"It's complicated. I was facing a murder charge. It was a professional misunderstanding. That's all cleared up now."

"My brother, Homer, gets into trouble at work, too. He's a detective in St. Louis. It's kind of complicated. Homer and I have different moms but the same dad. Brian can't keep it in his pants to save his life. Really, Dad's kind of pathetic." She paused. "Sorry. I ramble when I'm nervous."

"If you're nervous, pet the dog. People say it helps."

She smiled and petted Roy's cheek. He shuffled and put his head on the seat beside her. She smiled and looked at me.

"You and Homer have the same eyes. I should have seen that coming."

I arched my eyebrows.

"Excuse me?"

"My dad recently made a big donation to the Erin Court Home for Women. When he gives money, he wants everybody in the world to look at him. He bought two hundred dollars' worth of Girl Scout cookies from his assistant's daughter, and he practically wrote a press release. Then, a couple of weeks ago, he anonymously donated two point four million dollars to a woman's shelter in St. Augustine. It was out of character, so I wanted to check it out. Now it makes sense."

I straightened.

"Thank you for coming, but I don't work for the shelter," I said. "If you have questions, you can talk to Linda."

"My dad named me after Erin Court. Linda Armus said Erin was your mom."

I shut my mouth and shook my head.

"My mom is Julia Green. My dad is Doug Green."

She looked confused.

"Oh, sorry," she said. "I guess I misunderstood. Did you know Erin? Dad doesn't talk about her much, but he got drunk on the Fourth of July last year and mentioned her to me. Dad's usually pretty buttoned up. He doesn't like to talk about his feelings, but he said he missed her. I looked her up, but I couldn't find anything. Then I saw this donation, so I wanted to learn more."

"Erin died on the Fourth of July," I said, my voice low. "She was murdered. It was a long time ago."

My throat tightened, and the room shrank. I wanted to tell her to leave, but I couldn't. Eventually, Erin took the hint and stood.

"You seem busy," she said. "I shouldn't have come."

I nodded, and she started toward the door. Before she could close it behind her, I spoke.

"Be glad Erin was just your namesake."

Erin's expression grew soft as she nodded.

"I'm sorry," she said.

"For what?" I asked.

She furrowed her brow.

"For everything. I don't know," she said. "I shouldn't have come. I'm sorry I bothered you."

I pushed myself out of my office chair.

"This is a secured building, so I need to escort you out."

We walked to the lobby. Trisha sat behind the front desk, pointedly not looking at us. As I watched Erin cross the room, I thought about everything I had seen over the past few weeks.

I saw a father sacrifice himself to save his son, I saw two men sacrifice their careers for a friend, I saw a family and community come together to rally around a young mom.

They took risks for the people they loved. They did it because they were family—in practice, if not name. Because that's what family does. They protect each other. They take risks.

Erin Carlisle took a risk coming to St. Augustine. It wasn't as dramatic as some risks I had seen lately, but she made herself vulnerable in the chance that a stranger might care. As the station's door closed behind her, and as the last scintilla of daylight disappeared, Roy and I hurried. I pushed open the door and found Erin on the sidewalk out front, walking to the parking lot.

"Hey," I said. She stopped.

"Hey," she said. I walked toward her and drew in a breath. The building cast a shadow over us both.

"Erin Court was my biological mother. She lost me when I was a child, so I grew up in the foster care system. It was hard. Doug and Julia Green adopted me when I was a teenager. They're my parents, and I love them. I love Erin, too. She wasn't a bad person—just a bad mom.

"Linda Armus and I created the shelter so women like Erin would have a safe home for recovery. I don't know your father, but my mom—my biological mom—clearly did. If you want to know about her, I'll tell you what I can. And I may look like your brother, but we're not related. Sorry. My biological father's name was Joe. Mom named me after him, but I never met him."

Erin looked down and blinked, a half-smile on her lips.

"Dad's middle name is Joseph. In his early career, he went by Joe Carlisle because there was a well-known Catholic priest in St. Louis named Brian Carlisle. When Father Brian retired, Dad started going by his given name."

"Oh," I said, straightening.

"You told me about Erin Court," she said. "You want to hear about our dad?"

I focused on her face. Her jawline was familiar, as was the part of her hair, and the way the skin curled around her eyes as she smiled. I had seen those things before in a mirror.

Life hadn't been kind to me, but now I found a well of emotions growing inside me, feelings I hadn't experienced in a long time. Curiosity, surprise, and feelings much deeper and better. Delight, joy...even hope. I wanted to grab those feelings with both hands, so I swallowed and shook my head.

"No, I don't want to hear about him. Someday, he can tell me about himself," I said. "Let's walk. I want to hear about you."

***

I hope you liked the book! Joe's adventures will continue, but I don't have a release date for book 11 just yet. The best way to keep in touch with me is to join my mailing list. I've got a pretty good offer for you, too. All you've got to do is turn the page...

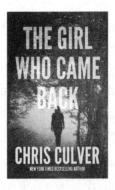

You know what the best part of being an author is? Goofing off while my spouse is at work and my kids are at school. You know what the second part is? Interacting with my readers.

About once a month, I write a newsletter about my books, writing process, research, and funny events from my life. I also include information about sales and discounts. I try to make it fun.

As if hearing from me on a regular basis wasn't enough, if you join, you get a FREE Joe Court novella. The story is a lot of fun, and it's available exclusively to readers on my mailing list. You won't get it anywhere else.

If you're interested, sign up here:

http://www.chrisculver.com/magnet.html

Stay in touch with Chris Culver

As much as I enjoy writing, I like hearing from readers even more. If you want to keep up with my world, there are a couple of ways you can do that.

First and easiest, I've got a mailing list. If you join, you'll receive an email whenever I have a new novel out or when I run sales. You can join that by going to this address:

http://www.indiecrime.com/mailinglist.html

If my mailing list doesn't appeal to you, you can also connect with me on Facebook here:

http://www.facebook.com/ChrisCulverbooks

And you can always email me at chris@indiecrime.com. I love receiving email!

About the Author

Chris Culver is the *New York Times* bestselling author of the Ash Rashid series and other novels. After graduate school, Chris taught courses in ethics and comparative religion at a small liberal arts university in southern Arkansas. While there and when he really should have been grading exams, he wrote *The Abbey*, which spent sixteen weeks on the *New York Times* bestsellers list and introduced the world to Detective Ash Rashid.

Chris has been a storyteller since he was a kid, but he decided to write crime fiction after picking up a dog-eared, coffee-stained paperback copy of Mickey Spillane's *I, the Jury* in a library book sale. Many years later, his wife, despite considerable effort, still can't stop him from bringing more orphan books home. He lives with his family near St. Louis.

Made in the USA
Coppell, TX
16 November 2024

40208430R20236